HAPPILY NEVER AFTER

LAUREN LANDISH

Edited by
VALORIE CLIFTON
Edited by
STACI ETHERIDGE

PROLOGUE

LANCE - ONE MONTH AGO

*M*y dress whites feel over the top, but I promised my father that I'd wear one of my dress uniforms for my homecoming, and since it's the last time I get to wear this high-necked, choker-collared thing, I might as well please him.

I chuckle as my taxi driver glances back at me for the fourth time since he picked me up from the airport in Portland. "Mind if I ask you something?"

"Go ahead," I reply, watching the highway roll by. We come over the bridge and around a curve, and there it is. Roseboro. My new home, apparently.

At least, temporarily.

"That's a SEAL trident on your chest, ain't it?" my driver asks, and I look down at my left chest, where the gold badge sits above my dual lines of other medals and pins I've picked up over the past ten years. "Were you in the Teams?"

"I was. I'm on terminal leave. My time with Uncle Sam is over." It doesn't sound real to say it, and the words sit hollowly in my heart.

"Oh. Mind if I ask which Team?" the driver asks.

I force a laugh. "You know the old line, don't you? I could tell you—"

"But then I'd have to kill you." My driver laughs, nodding. "Yeah, I'm old enough to remember that movie. I was a Marine myself. You boys were the only squiddies we really respected. If I can ask, why're you leaving? That's a Lieutenant Commander's board on your shoulder there. Most who get that high are lifers."

I clench my jaw, looking out the window unseeingly. "I . . . lot of memories. I've done my bit, and now I've got family matters to attend to," I reply honestly. "Guess it's time to handle the hard fight now."

He hums, likely hearing that there's a lot more to the story but respecting my privacy. I'm sure he had similar issues when he came home from his tours with the Marines. You can't just fall back into civilian life. There's an adjustment period where you lock up your reality in 'the sandbox' and acclimate to life stateside.

The rest of the drive goes quickly, and we barely skim the edge of Roseboro. I'm slightly disappointed. I wanted to see my new 'home town', but I'll have time for that now, I guess. *Home.* Doesn't sound right, doesn't feel right. But hopefully, it will. It's not too long before we're pulling up to a gated road.

"Whoa. Is this the right address?" At the driver's nod, I pick up my phone, telling him, "Okay, then. Let me get us buzzed in."

But the call isn't necessary because the gate swings open as soon as he starts to roll down his window. He glances back at me in the rearview and I offer a shrug. I don't know any more than he does at this point, having never been to this house.

The Jacobs manor on the outskirts of Seattle is big, of course, several acres overlooking a golf course and surrounded in the distance by tall trees and mountains.

I grew up surrounded by plenty of luxury, but this a whole

different level of flashy and fancy. One I'm not familiar with anymore, at least. I've spent the last decade living in whatever quarters the Navy afforded me, small bachelor officers' quarters or sharing claustrophobic quarters aboard ships. I doubt my last bunk would even qualify as a closet in this place.

"New family house, I guess. Things have changed while I've been gone," I lamely say, scanning the front of the house. "A lot."

The driver sounds sad, humming as he slowly makes his way up the driveway. "It always does, but whatever you missed, you'll catch up. The only easy day was yesterday, and besides, you can't quit. You ain't dead."

His reminders of the famous SEAL mottos are a kind admonishment to get my shit straight. No time for whining and wondering.

He parks in the big circle drive in front of the large mansion which gleams a mellow greyish-brown color in the fading sunlight. I get out, and the front double-doors both open, revealing a man in a black suit and a woman in a slim-fitting black dress and tights.

"Welcome home, sir," the butler says. If I remember correctly, his name is Hamilton. My childhood butler, Wilfred, retired when I went to college, and I haven't been home often enough to remember the new staff's names. "Your family is waiting for you in the great room. Mariella will show you the way."

Okay, the great room. Guess we're too fancy to call it a living room or a dining room these days. Fuck, how much has changed since I was last here? I try to remember my last trip home, but I'm coming up blank. Two years? Maybe more? I know my parents came to Virginia to see me about a year ago, and we'd talk on Skype when I had clearance to do so, but it's been a while since I've been home. Even then, it was Seattle, not *here*.

I turn to get my bags, but the driver already has them unloaded and Hamilton is directing him on where to leave them. The sea bag looks comfortable and familiar on his shoulder, as does the cocky grin he flashes me. "Welcome home, sir," he offers. "Oorah."

"Hooyah!" I respond, and I swear Mariella jumps a foot in the air at the sudden bark. I can't help but grin a bit too. Maybe this won't be so bad, I hope.

At the door, Mariella stops and stares at my shoes. I don't look down, knowing they're in pristine condition, having polished them myself this morning before dressing. "I'm not supposed to say, sir, but it seems prudent—"

"I know my parents," I reassure her, and she looks up through her lashes. I press a finger to my lips. "I'll pretend I'm surprised. How's this?"

I fake a look of shock, my brows lifting, eyes wide, mouth open in an O, and her shoulders bounce as she holds back the laugh. She's innocent and fresh, and as young as she is, probably new. She doesn't want to get in trouble, and I understand.

"Very good, sir," she agrees and then opens the door once again, leading me inside.

The great room is at least deserving of the name, large and high-ceilinged with fluffy couches and plush rugs. My parents jump out from behind the tall-backed chairs at the same time a remote-controlled banner unfurls to read WELCOME HOME, LANCE! I do my best to grin in shock, but I'm not sure my mom buys it.

"Hey, guys, it's good to see you too," I greet them, hugging them both at the same time and then shaking my dad's hand. "It's been awhile."

"I'm just glad to have my baby home," Mom says, pulling at the hair at the nape of my neck. "Dear Lord, Son, I thought they required military men to have their hair high and tight? What is this mess?"

I duck away from her touch but don't miss the look of loss on her face. But I'm not a kid anymore, and having my mommy pet my hair isn't quite my norm. "We've been through this. The Navy lets SEALs have more leeway, and I'm within regs . . . barely," I confess. "Starting tomorrow, I think I'm going to grow my beard back out too." I rub at my stubbly jaw, the day's growth barely a beginning to the scruff I wear in my rare off-times.

"A beard?" My mom gasps. "Bishop, say something—"

"Oh, hush, Miranda. He'd look fine with a beard. Like that Thor boy from the movies," my dad admonishes, and I'll admit I missed their banter. They're good together, an example I'd be proud to try to live up to, even if that's not remotely on the horizon for me right now. Primary target: the family company.

Speaking of family . . . "Where's Cody?"

Mom and Dad exchange glances, and I see a crack in their façade. My little brother, Cody, has always been the hellion of the family, and while neither of my parents were happy I enlisted, I get the feeling that Cody has more than once made them consider military school.

When we were kids, I tried my best to keep a handle on him, but with the age gap between us, I was caught up in my own life. Still, I tried my best, and when I left, I figured he'd grow out of it like most kids do.

But that was when he was younger, a teenager out to test every limit. He's a man now, already mid-twenties, and he should be well on his way to being an upstanding citizen, working at Jacobs Bio-Tech or striking out on his own and independently self-sufficient.

I get the feeling that's not at all the case. With as little free time as I've had since joining the Navy, I haven't been able to keep up. Too many rushed calls with that stupid ten-minute timer in the corner of the video screen, too many rushed emails filled with platitudes and little else. I've fallen out of touch with my little brother, slowly but surely losing what closeness we once had.

But I figure my being here will be good for us both, and I'm looking forward to rekindling the brotherly relationship we had when we were younger.

"He's taking care of some things at the new headquarters," Dad finally says, but I can tell he's hedging. "Maybe he can give you a tour?"

But it sounds like an empty offer, no real promise for follow-through. I let him off the hook, even as I make a mental note to do some serious follow-up on what the hell is going on with my brother. "Sounds good, Dad. If you don't mind, though, I want to get in civilian clothes and get the lay of the land first. Maybe clean up my sailor-worthy language before you put me in a corner office."

I grin and Dad looks relieved. "Deal. Of course, take all the time you need to settle in. Relax some. In fact, your mother—"

"Would love to introduce you around town," she takes over, finishing Dad's thought as she links her arm through my elbow. "I've met some nice people in Roseboro. It's feeling like home already for us, and I want it to feel that way for you, too. Some of my new friends even have daughters around your age."

She says it so casually, like there's not a myriad of innuendo and plans tied up in those words. I can virtually hear the wedding bells she's ringing for some unknown bride and me.

"Mom—" I start before shaking my head. How do I get through to my parents that I don't want a set-up life? It was part of the reason I left to begin with. And the Navy taught me discipline and duty, how to stand for myself, lead others, and complete missions according to protocol. I'm not coming home to be babied and led around by my nose like a good little boy.

I almost chuckle at the thought of my mom, who tops out at a solid five-five and maybe a buck twenty-five, trying to force me into anything. But it's not my height and weight that make it an unfair battle.

In fact, quite the opposite. *Though she be but little, she is fierce.* I don't want to disappoint her. So I'm better off making this clear from the start so she doesn't have any hurt feelings later.

"Mom, I'm not looking to date, not looking to get married right now. And when I do, it'll be a woman of my choosing, not because she's Joannie-from-the-club's daughter and quite lovely." I fasten a fierce look on my mother, silently ordering her to stand down.

Strong men have wilted under the weight of my hard stare, but my mother? She simply huffs and flips on her mega-watt smile, the one that matches my own. I swear she could stare down a pissed-off Admiral and have that same smile on her face as he crumpled at her feet. "We'll see, dear. I just want you to have friends. And you can't blame a proud mother for wanting to show you off a bit, now can you?"

Oh, I can. But we both know I'm gonna smile and wave like a damn pony from time to time, but I draw the line at dating at her behest. A man's gotta have limits.

Dad breaks the staredown, clearing his throat. "How about the nickel tour of the new house? We set you up on the east side since we figured you're used to being up with the sun."

Dad beams as we walk, talking about the house and the company interchangeably as I store every nugget of information away.

There's something going on. Dad virtually begged me to come home, which I would've ignored, but then Mom wrote me a letter telling me how stressed Dad has been.

Now that I'm here, they're all rainbows and unicorns. Except about Cody. They were obviously jumpy about that particular topic.

I'll get to the bottom of things, fix what I can, and go from there.

I'm a mission-oriented man, not Dad's business puppet, poised to take over whenever he deems me fit, not Mom's chip to bargain off as the matchmaker of the year, and not my brother's keeper.

Though that one may be up for negotiation if he needs me.

CHAPTER 1

CHARLOTTE

I'm doing it! I'm actually going to fucking pull this craziness off.

Looking around the grand opening melee of my new bakery, *Cake Culture*, is the biggest rush I've ever had. A dream actually coming to life before my very eyes with frosting, sprinkles, and cute pink awnings edged in chunky glitter to look like sugar.

A dream come true is something a girl like me doesn't get very damn often, and I'm going to enjoy the moment.

"Charlotte, move your ass!" my best friend, Mia Karakova, barks. Her blonde and blue ponytail flips as she whips her head around to give me a very pointed look. If I'm not careful, she's going to start cursing in Russian, which is how I know the shit's really hit the fan.

Apparently, I'll have to take a celebratory moment later. Instead, I do as she *requested* and haul out another tray of cookies. It's the least I can do since she's helping me out today. She didn't volunteer, more like I volun told her to be there to smile and wave at the masses.

I figured her presence would be a goldmine of publicity since she's all over the society pages now that she's engaged to

Thomas Goldstone. As in, *the* Thomas Goldstone of Goldstone Inc. and Goldstone Health, and basically the biggest poobah in all of Roseboro. Up to and including being a silent investor in the cakery of my dreams.

So if she wants to boss me around a bit, even though technically, I'm the boss, I'll jump to it. Because she's right, we are hopping like mad in here.

Helping the next customer, I tally their purchases, making sure to use the names I came up with. Branding. It's all about branding. "Okay, so one 'What Is That, Red Velvet?', one 'Crazy for Cocoa-Caramel Swirl', and a 'Peanut Butter Bomb Diggity'? That comes to nine dollars even." The customer hands over a ten, telling me to keep the change with a wink.

He's cute, but I'm on a no-men kick so I give him my customer service smile and offer, "Have a nice day!"

Trixie Reynolds, my new assistant who's been a lifesaver as we prepped to open, slithers up next to me. "Ooh, that one was a Mr. Hottie Tottie, girl! Why the Elsa freezing the world routine?"

I raise an eyebrow. Trixie knows I hate that damn movie. "You know the drill. I'm married to my cakes right now. It's all I have time for as a new business owner. Besides, I'm a redhead, not a blonde." I flip my slightly Elsa-ish braid over my shoulder, letting it fall down my back.

She tsks, stage whispering, "I think your cake is exactly what needs to get drilled. Maybe yank that cake pop stick outta your ass too." Ouch, harsh much? But she says it with a smirk and a twinkle in her eyes, and I feel the teasing giggle bubbling up. I can't help it today.

"No happily ever afters for this chick. I'm work, work, working my way to the top," I sing-song in my best Rihanna impersonation, which basically sucks because I'm an awful singer.

The fact of the matter is, I used to date. A lot. I kept searching for Mr. Right but settled for Mr. Right Now more times than I probably should've. Not in a skanky way—a girl's got standards, but also, a girl's got . . . needs. So a 'friends with benefits' here, a 'date who couldn't carry a conversation but was smoking hot and offering to lick me off' there, and even some serious relationships that didn't stand the test of time, all add together to make me disillusioned. Especially after some epically plot-twisting losses. As if I would seriously believe that he was separated from his wife, the one I didn't even know about? Yeah, guys can be asses.

And I'm not playing those games anymore.

Maybe never again.

Mia interrupts, loudly proclaiming over the crowd, "And you get a cookie, and you get a cookie." She's handing out my Grandma's Secret Recipe Chocolate Chip Cookies like Oprah, and people are literally screaming with outstretched hands to get one of my masterpieces.

It's almost enough to bring a tear to my eye as I scan the crowd.

But as I do, I see a table by the door that stops my happiness on a dime. Full stop. *Errrrrkkk.*

A single guy, sitting at a table alone, nursing a cup of coffee and the same muffin I gave him almost three hours ago. Steven.

My damn security guard. Well, you can't tell he's my security guard, not with the plain, unassuming polo shirt and jeans he's wearing. But his skills are just as deadly as his fashion is boring, and he's the only person in the shop not looking like they're having fun.

If people really knew what Steven and his compatriots were doing, I'm sure they'd have a simple question. *Why would I need security for the grand opening of my cake shop?* The answer's as simple as it is complicated. I need security because of a mental-gymnastics domino effect. I'm friends with Mia, and she's engaged to Thomas, and Thomas is the biggest rising star in the

Pacific Northwest and soon to be the richest man in Roseboro, a fact that pisses off my former boss to no end.

Blackwell. The name so chilling, so powerful, that like Madonna or Hitler, you only need one.

I worked as a receptionist and screener at Blackwell Tower for over two years. Hated every last soul-sucking minute of it, but it'd been a necessary evil to pay the bills even after I'd let go of the hopes of learning about running my own business.

Everything was fine enough, right up to the point Blackwell went batshit crazy and tried to take out Thomas, hitting him from every angle and playing dirty by sending a hitman after Izzy, the third musketeer to Mia and me.

Luckily, she's a fucking goddess and ended up sweeping her hitman off his feet. Yeah, Mia got the happily ever after with Thomas and Izzy got the happily ever after with Gabe. But now we're all on edge, wondering what's next, waiting for that big size-twelve shoe to drop, and jumping at shadows.

So Steven sits, one of my constant guards, my just-in-case insurance. He's so invisible in his blandness that the man's damn near a ninja, something I can relate to from my corporate days. But he thrives in his obscurity, whereas I just want to be seen, for a change. For something other than my red hair, which is what always gets attention first.

"Is it natural?"

"Yes, it is."

And that's where the often-repeated conversation divulges. Women have been as bold as to ask for a snip to take to their stylist to color-match their own tresses. A bit intrusive, but complimentary in a weird way. Men go straight south and ask if the carpets match the drapes, demanding to see my fire crotch. As if.

And again, why I'm on a no-men kick.

The double-doors to the back swing open, and Izzy steps through, already donning one of my polo shirts with the logo she created for me. It's pink and black striped to mimic the awnings out front with white bubble lettering that looks like frosting. Totally adorable, and her best graphic design work, if I do say so myself. She's got a tray of cherry pie tarts in hand, and the crowd oohs and ahhs at her timely entrance. I think I even hear stomachs growling in want.

"I've got five mini cherry pies, the perfect mix of Ranier and Black Tartarians so sweet and juicy that we don't even add sugar to the filling. Better get in line," she announces.

More than five people instantly stand in front of her, and Gabe points very clearly from beside her while declaring, "Not here. Over there."

He's indicating the line at the register, shooing people away from Izzy. Steven is my guard, but Gabe is Izzy's and he takes his job seriously. Like *deadly* seriously.

Izzy smiles at him like scaring my customers is the sweetest, most romantic thing he's ever done, and I force down the bile.

Okay, it's not disgusting. It's devoted, dedicated, and maybe I'm jealous. But I'm also really happy for my besties for finding guys who fit them so perfectly. Though who would've predicted the geek and the boss, that's Mia and Thomas. Or the innocent and the monster, that's Izzy and Gabe. Not sure where that leaves me, the cynic?

That's right. Busier than an air conditioner repairman in Hell with summertime coming on.

Izzy brings the tray up front, and Gabe goes to take a seat by the door with Steven. The two almost never talk when 'working', but they share a comfortable, if intimidating, silence. "They're gonna scare folks from even coming in the door," I lament to Izzy. "Seriously."

She grins, shaking her head. "Uh, not to brag, but have you seen

Gabe? He's like every woman's wet dream. You'll have people coming in just to stare at him. Maybe we should put him in a polo and have him hold samples outside?"

She tilts her head like she's considering that idea, or maybe fantasizing about it, so I tell her no way before she gets too invested. Gabe, who's got hearing like a dolphin or something, flashes me a dimpled smile from across the room, mouthing, "Thanks for the save."

I ring up the next customer, who buys all five pies for herself, drawing a groan from the masses. "More on the way!" I promise them and shoot Trixie a look. She salutes then tucks a lock of wavy blonde hair behind her ear like she means business.

"On it, Boss. I know there are two more trays just getting that last bit of browning in the oven. Y'all just hang tight, and we're gonna have you scooping up cherries and declaring them finger lickin' good."

I smile. She's a bit of a wild child and I never know what'll come out of her mouth, but Trixie's a great worker and doesn't mind if I pay her bonuses in product. Lord knows, I need every shiny dime that rolls in this place to keep it running since I'm at the investment stage, not the profit-turning stage.

Yeah, I've got Thomas backing me, but that doesn't mean I'm going to act a damn fool over things. I plan on paying him back every dime, with interest.

But today is going better than I'd possibly hoped, and I'd hoped so big it scared me. That's what goals are supposed to do, scare the bejesus out of you so you work for them. And now, as long as these customers keep coming back, maybe this venture will be bigger and better than my wildest imaginings. I cross my fingers and knock on the wooden counter by the register for luck.

I'm not superstitious, but it couldn't hurt.

We work for hours, Mia, Izzy, and Trixie each having my back and stepping in to help almost before I even know where to turn next. It's awesome and amazing and a solid step in the direction I want my life to go. Customers are happy, deliriously sugar-high and groaning their delight as they head out the door, until finally, it's closing time.

Trixie heads to the back to start prep work for tomorrow's hope-fully just as big rush, and Izzy and Gabe head out so she can get some studying done. I don't know how she does it. I'm ready to collapse, but she was rambling on about a test she has in two days and how she has her study time allocated by chapter between now and then. Gabe watched her like she was discussing the cure for cancer, not graphic design.

As Mia and I wipe down tables, she says, "Today was great! How do you feel?"

"I feel like I'm fizzy on the inside, like my skin is too small and I just need to jump out of it for a minute and shake off the energy like a dog." I grin huge and wide, probably looking more than a bit crazed, but I think she gets it.

She always gets me.

"So, I have an idea I want to run by you." She drops into her fake Russian accent, which sounds vaguely threatening even when she says nice things. Her father, who is actually Russian, suffers the same affliction except his is pretty permanent. Even when he says, 'I love you', it almost sounds like that's something to fear even though he's the sweetest man you could ever meet. "And you can say no, but I strongly urge you to say yes."

"Hit me," I say, fearing nothing right now because I'm on top of the fucking world.

"You know how Thomas has the gala next weekend?" she says casually, like a big gala is just par for the everyday course.

"Yeah, the charity one, right? To see if that bio-tech company can help with the pro-bono stuff Thomas is doing at the hospital?" I say, not sure where she's going with this.

Mia had wanted Izzy and me to attend as her friends, but Thomas had squashed that as a needless security risk. Too many out-of-towners, too many unknown 'plus ones', he'd said. Mia had argued that Steven could go as my date and Gabe as Izzy's, and we'd be just as safe as any other time, but I'd taken Thomas's side, not wanting to hobnob with the rich and fancy, anyway.

I've had more than my fair share of that mess, and I'm not looking for a repeat performance if I can get out of it.

"That's the one! I need you to make a cupcake tower!" she squeals, like it's the best idea in the history of ever, even clapping and jumping up and down a little bit. Her eyes are big and round, like one of her favorite anime characters, silently begging me to see the brilliance of her idea.

"What?" I ask, not catching on at all. "You want a cupcake tower?"

She settles, clicking into business mode like she wasn't just a giggly fangirl. Albeit, a fangirl of my cupcakes, so I'll give her some leeway. "It's a perfect opportunity to highlight a new business in Roseboro to people who can use you for corporate functions, weddings, their kids' ten-thousand-dollar birthday parties, and more. Your cupcakes in the hands of the people who move and shake things in the area. It's perfect."

"As long as they like them!" I say, shock and doubt worming their way through my veins. Moving and shaking is really close to making or breaking, and my confidence is waning a little in the post-work adrenaline crash.

Mia rolls her eyes like I've lost my damn mind. "Duh, of course they'll love them. Have you tried your spice cake?" She grabs a mini-cupcake off a tray and shoves it in my fish-gaping mouth.

True. It is a good cake. I'd worked that recipe over for almost two weeks straight, batch after batch, to get the perfect balance of spice and sweet. Around the delicious mouthful, I argue, "The gala's in eight days! You already have caterers that were booked weeks ago. I can't just waltz in there like that."

She scoffs, waving off my worries. "Uh, yeah, you can. It's my party and I'll have cupcakes if I wanna." She feigns being a petulant, entitled brat rather well, considering I know how down to earth she truly is. "Look, I'm nervous. This is a big deal for Thomas, and I need a friendly face there. And it really will be good for *Cake Culture*. Say you'll do it."

I consider her proposal long and hard. It'll be long days and some even longer nights, and . . . oh, who am I kidding? I don't think at all. I already knew I was going to say yes as soon as Mia asked and am basically fist-pumping inside my brain while simultaneously trying to decide on which flavors to highlight.

"Okay, on one condition," I negotiate. "I'm not going as a guest. I'll go as the baker and stand by the tower to answer any questions, hopefully make good impressions with the cupcakes, and represent the business." I add a snooty lilt to my voice, tilting my nose into the air. "Not as a fancy-dressed Roseboro elite."

Mia pushes at my shoulder, grinning. "Hey, that's me you're talking about. I'm a designer-dress-wearing boss bitch, but I'm not snobby like that."

I grin evilly, shaking my head as I look her up and down like a finishing school director. "No, and that's why you'll never fully fit in with that crowd." Her jaw drops at the jab, but then I explain, "You're way too good for them, and that's why I love you, honey."

EIGHT DAYS LATER, MY FACE IS BASICALLY STUCK IN A SMILING expression. My mouth is pretty much stretched wide, teeth flashing, eyes watering with happy tears after the past week.

The grand opening wasn't a fluke, and I've started to notice regulars who are coming in for their morning coffee and muffin, then returning for their afternoon sugary pick-me-up treat.

I'm doing it! I'm actually succeeding with my bakery.

Trixie puffs, brushing a lock of hair from her face. She's just as meticulous as I am about keeping her hair pulled back when we're baking, but right now, the baking's done. Instead, she's helping me get dressed in my apartment on the second floor above the bakery.

The apartment's still a bit of a mess, boxes here and there because I've spent every waking minute of the last few months downstairs, getting the bakery ready for business. Priorities in order . . . check. Trixie didn't seem to agree as she sidestepped her way to my bedroom though.

"Is this everything?" she asks. I can see her cringe though she tries to hide it.

I look to Trixie, with her long, permed blonde hair, miniskirt, booties, and layered tank tops. I rarely see her out of uniform, but I'm sensing that her personal style is circa-1994 in a cool way that only the young can pull off. Actually, she's pretty close to my age, mid-twenties, but I could never pull off her bold style the way she does.

I glance to my closet behind her, where my wardrobe goes from business chic pencil skirts and button-up blouses to casual jeans and T-shirts. There's virtually nothing in between. I've never needed anything else, and my yoga pants are folded in my drawers.

Trixie hums, flipping through the hangers and examining clothes. "Okay, so no Office Barbie attire. Too uptight. No store logo shirt. Too casual. Definitely not jeans." She gets deeper into my closet, and I can't even see what she's looking at anymore.

"Aha!" she exclaims. "Found it!"

She pulls out a pale blue dress from somewhere in the pit on the

18

left side of the generous closet. I don't remember even buying the dress, but the tags are still dangling off the side. It's gorgeous, though, and I wonder what was going through my mind when I bought it.

"Put this on," she orders.

"Shouldn't I wear black? You know, to blend in like the caterers and wait staff?"

Her eyes narrow, her forehead crinkling in frustration. "Do you want to *blend* in? Or do you want to make sure *everyone* remembers the hot ginger who puts the spice in Roseboro's *Cake Culture*?"

Decision made, I grab the dress and run into the bathroom to pull it on. I can't see in the mirror, at least not the full effect, so I step back into my bedroom. Trixie gasps and does a little finger twirl in the air, and I follow her instructions, pirouetting in place.

"Yep, that's the one. Check you out, Miss Thang."

Standing in front of the mirror, my jaw drops. I don't know when or where I got this dress, but I'm reminded now why I bought it. It's perfect, like it was custom-made to fit me. The cap sleeves make my shoulders look dainty but strong, the waist sits at my narrowest part, and the bottom flares out in a circle to hit a few inches above mid-knee. It's demure and conservative but stunning on me with my red hair and blue eyes.

"Wow," I say breathlessly, not feeling the least bit of embarrassment at my own reaction to how amazing I look.

Trixie beams. "Put these on."

She bends down, lining up a nude wedge heel for me to step into. Once I do, she buckles the straps around my ankles. "Are these comfy enough that you can stand in them for hours on end?"

I nod, cocking my toe, and she grins wider. "Good. You're

wearing them either way, but I wondered if I needed to set you up with a foot soak for when you got home tonight."

I can't help but giggle at her craziness, but when I turn back to the mirror, the laugh catches in my throat. The heels are the *piece de resistance*. I look good. Young and carefree, but also pulled together, like someone who knows their stuff and is damn proud to show off.

I'm gonna be proud to show off my cupcakes, I think happily.

Trixie helps me load the huge plastic storage boxes of cupcakes into my newly purchased used minivan. No one ever wants to drive a minivan, but sometimes, they make the most sense. Like for cake deliveries and as a big, moving billboard for a fledgling company.

Once onsite, I look for Mia, but the caterer tells me that Mia has already come downstairs, issued directives, and disappeared back upstairs to get ready. She happily lends me a worker to unload the boxes, though, and then I get to work putting everything on the tower so that everything is perfect.

It's huge, five feet tall on top of a table, with five layers, each holding a different flavor.

The overall effect is eye-catching, and the smell of sugary goodness will hopefully draw them close enough to sample my wares.

Tonight, nothing can stop me. I'm ready to let the spotlight shine on *Cake Culture,* and maybe me too. But only as the baker. I still don't want to do any of the social *Hunger Games* that I know will be going on tonight.

After a couple of hours of people milling around and happily sampling the five flavors of cupcakes I brought, a dark shadow falls over the night in the form of my family.

I haven't had the best of relationships with them, and to be honest, I'm surprised they're here. Thankfully, I see them before they see me, but it's not like I can leave my post. These are cupcakes, not canapes.

"Oh, my gracious, these are just divine! What's your secret?" the lady in front of me implores, and I tick my eyes back to her, though they desperately want to look over her shoulder again and see if my dad, stepmother, and stepsister are making their way over.

"Grandma's love," I say quickly, repeating the semi-honest answer to the often-asked question. "And quality ingredients sourced from fair-trade suppliers. The vanilla is from Madagascar, the chocolate from Ghana."

"Well, wherever you're getting it from, it's what you do with the ingredients that truly make it special. Well done. May I take a card?" she asks, already deftly slipping one into her clutch purse.

"Of course. Thank you for the compliment. *Cake Culture* would be happy to help with any of your bakery needs, personal or professional." It's another growth opportunity, a network connection created, a baby step toward future success.

The bubble pops nearly instantly, though, as the woman steps away and another takes her place.

My stepmother. Or *stepmonster*, as I like to call her, but only in my head because to do so aloud would only enrage her and drive me further from my father, which I don't want.

I might be his little girl, but we both know that she holds his reins, and she'll happily snap them tight and try to take him away with nothing but an evil smile.

"Hello, Priscilla," I greet her. "Lovely to see you." Ice crystals form on the crisp ends of each word, but she can't fault me for manners, at least.

"And you as well, darling," she says, with saccharin twisting through her politeness. She's sweet-looking on the surface, as always, but I know the truth. She's as deadly as a coral snake, and her grin's just a front. Those pearly whites are ceramic-capped knives ready to slice a chunk off anyone who gets in her way.

Pity my father never sees that.

He only sees what she wants him to see–her still-stunning beauty, perfectly-dyed raven-black hair not hinting at the grey I know she has in streaks, cool grey eyes that miss nothing, designer clothing selected by her personal stylist, and a Botoxed mask of pleasantness she can pull on at will. She's not natural, but she's still a head turner.

But I've seen beneath her façade to the real person. She's manip-ulative, opportunistic, narcissistic, and spiteful of my existence as a sign of my father's former happiness with my mother.

"What brings you to Roseboro? I thought you were sticking to the upper echelon of Portland these days?"

At least that's what I'd been hoping since I rarely see them out this far from the urban culture centers that Priscilla likes to run in.

As if on cue, my stepsister, Sabrina, glides up next to her mother, eyeing me as if I'm a glob of gum ruining the bottom of her red-soled shoe. "Special circumstances, you see."

It sounds like a brag, but I'm not sure what she's boasting about. If anything, at this party in particular, I have a bigger in with the host than she does. I don't think my family's ever had business dealings with Thomas Goldstone, while I'm sort of second-level besties with the big man. I just don't care to use my friends that way, unlike some people.

"Would you like a cupcake? I've got red velvet, lemon custard, vanilla, chocolate, and spice cake. Something for everyone."

I don't bother giving them the cutesy names I agonized over for each flavor, like 'What Is That, Red Velvet?' as an honor to the famous line from *Coming to America*, or 'Tell Me What You Want

Spice' as an ode to the Spice Girls. For Priscilla and Sabrina, I stick to the bare-bones basics in the hopes that they'll shoo away faster.

Priscilla looks down her nose, sniffing a single time. "Well, it does smell nice. I'll give you that."

Sabrina looks at the tower longingly, and I can almost see her debating flavors in her mind, but one nudge from her mother and she pastes the smile back on her face.

"No. I've been following a strict juice detox plan for the last two months. I've never felt better, and my hair and nails are perfect now." She holds her hands out, inspecting them before she twirls a lock around her finger.

Priscilla clears her throat, and Sabrina pops back into position, hands at her side, no fidgeting, chin lifted, back straight, and shoulders down. It's the perfect mimicry of Priscilla's own practiced stance.

"Congratulations," I say, but the devil in me can't help but torment her a bit. It's warranted after living with her and Priscilla for my formative years and putting up with their constant barrage of insults and putdowns. "There is some lemon juice in the lemon custard, though, if you'd like to try that? Fluffy, melt on your tongue sweetness with a bright spot of custard that delights your taste buds and makes you want another bite. The frosting is thick and rich, decadent, and sinful. Would you like?"

As I describe the yummy cake, I swear Sabrina's eyes have glazed over like I'm whispering sweet nothings in her ear. The best part is that I know she won't eat one, but she'll be fantasizing about how good it would've been for days.

Evil, I know. But I feel justified. Sabrina was never the worst offender, though. That honor was all Priscilla. Sabrina's more a clueless socialite, always doing as she's told and never having to work for anything other than maintaining her beauty.

But that was enough for her to get in a fair share of barbs back in the day as she compared us, and not surprisingly, I always came out the loser in her estimation.

Priscilla steps in front of Sabrina, literally putting herself between her and the cupcakes as if she doesn't trust her to not stick her tongue out and lick one. "So, Charlotte, tell me about this bakery of yours and why you're here as the *help*. I don't understand why you would choose to leave a stable position with so much opportunity at Blackwell's. It's the best place in Roseboro to work, as I understand it."

I roll my eyes, knowing as soon as I do so that I might as well have waved a red flag in front of a bull. Rookie mistake, but I'm out of practice in dealing with her. Ten years ago, I could have smiled my way through a lie detector test because of her. "Working for Blackwell was fine until it wasn't. Now I'm chasing a dream and doing quite well with it."

Fine. That's an unlikely description. Blackwell Tower is run like a slave shop from the bottom up. The whole monolith is a twenty-first century feudal kingdom, with a king who's gone mad.

She sneers, obviously not impressed, and I'm not inclined to tell her what a monstrous villain Blackwell is. It's not like she'd believe me, anyway. Who would believe that he hired a hitman to kill Izzy and placed a spy inside Thomas's own company to try to maneuver him to a losing position? And she certainly wouldn't believe that the guy in the black suit leaning casually against the wall and holding a soda water is my guard because we don't know Blackwell's next move.

She wouldn't hear a bad word about a man like Blackwell, whom she practically worships because of the clout he's carried in the area for decades. It's power she's aspired for her entire life and never had. She wouldn't believe anyone could care about my existence, or lack thereof, enough to warrant protecting my life.

But there's one man who would. My father.

"Where is Dad? I saw him come in with you," I ask, focusing our attention on the one thing we have in common. Abraham Dunn.

We scan the crowd and see him at the same time. Priscilla smiles, and while I'd like to light up at the sight of my father like I once did, he doesn't look well and worry blooms in my belly.

He's lost weight, going from lean to almost bony. His suit hangs on him, though I know it was custom made for him. I wonder if nearly twenty years of Priscilla's money grubbing and social ass-kissing have finally worn away at him the way they did me. Once upon a time, we were two peas in a pod, kicking back with a Mr. Pibb and talking about our day.

But Priscilla put a stop to all that, and she's been driving the wedge between Dad and me deep.

And he doesn't even see it, sadly.

Suddenly, someone calls Priscilla's name, and we turn from my father to see a family approaching.

Priscilla steps away from the table, Sabrina following like a dutiful puppy, to greet the newcomers, a pleasant-looking man and his wife.

Suddenly, my heart stops in my chest because next to them, several inches taller than his father and looking like sex in a tuxedo, is the most handsome man I've ever seen.

A tiny part of my brain stores away the idea of calling a chocolate and vanilla cupcake 'Sex In A Tuxedo', but the bulk of my grey matter is chanting, 'hubba, hubba, hubba.'

He stands out, his white jacket pristine as newfallen snow in the sea of blacks and charcoal grays, a shining beacon of light . . . almost like a prince. "Holy shit," I whisper.

Steven is at my side in an instant, his voice low and insistent. "What's wrong?"

I don't look at him, don't bother scolding him for being intrusive, which is against our I-don't-see-you deal, instead asking, "Who is that?"

He follows my sightline and answers, "Lance Jacobs, eldest son of Bishop and Miranda Jacobs. Heir apparent to Jacobs Bio-Tech. Are you okay, Miss Dunn?"

I'm about to tell him I'm fine when I see the way Sabrina and Priscilla are eyeing Lance. Like a piece of meat. Like a goldmine. Like a stepping stone to a richer future. And my blood pressure goes up a few notches.

Fuck.

Really, Fate? The one guy who makes my heart race, my body pulse, and my mind think about *things*, some sweet and some not-so, and he's already in Sabrina's clutches?

Well played. Well fucking played.

CHAPTER 2

"*A* white jacket?" I ask Hamilton, who's holding up said item for my inspection. "I just spent a decade in the Navy and now I'm supposed to wear a *white* jacket for this fucking gala? Are you trying to screw with my head?"

"Mister Jacobs felt that it would be good for you to stand out at tonight's proceedings," Hamilton says, unperturbed. He's been with the family long enough that he's comfortable, although he and I have just started to get on the same page since he was hired after I enlisted. "If you wish, I can—"

"No . . . no, Hamilton, I know you're just doing your job." I sigh, adjusting my black bowtie before holding my arms out. "At least it doesn't have that high choker collar that my dress whites had."

"Of course, sir," Hamilton says, helping me with the fitted jacket. "And you'll get to wear black pants as well. Better for any potential messes or confusion with a groom cake topper."

I chuckle at his dry humor, glancing into the mirror to see his straight face. Honestly, it's hard to tell sometimes when he's being serious and when he's joking. In the month that I've been home, I'm just starting to get back to 'the block,' as we used to call it in service, and I know I've got a lot on my mind.

Mostly, it's the company. Dad's basically wanted me to shadow him from sunup to sundown, doling out tidbits like he's dying tomorrow and wants to download his brain into someone to keep the lights on. After making sure that wasn't the case, that his health problems are nothing more than bad gas and needing a week's vacation in Hawaii or something, I've been focusing on handling my own transition.

Beyond that, it's Cody. I rarely see him, though he supposedly lives in this same gigantic house. I've stopped by his office at work, but he's constantly *unavailable*. We've scheduled dinners for which he's no-showed, and other than a handful of empty promises when I happen to catch him in the kitchen, I've had zero chances to figure out what's going on with him.

I'm almost certain he's only using the house as a laundry station and occasional drive-thru meal option, mostly staying in town somewhere.

Ever the rebel and quintessential playboy, I imagine he's got a girlfriend in town where he stays, one whom maybe he isn't comfortable having around the family. But that's supposition, not solid intel.

But why he'd hide someone away, if there is, in fact, someone, is concerning.

And Cody's work ethic, or lack thereof, I'm beginning to suspect, is also worrying. Was he unavailable because he was head-down, working hard, or not even in the office? Both are equal possibilities.

But if he's working so diligently, why would our parents be so concerned? The scale tips away from Cody's favor.

"Sir?" Hamilton asks, interrupting my thoughts. "Your cufflinks?"

"Of course, thank you," I reply, taking them from him. They're one of my personal mementos of my time in the Navy, small gold shields with the Navy crest engraved on them.

On a personal level, it's probably the most annoying thing about living a life of luxury again. For a month, I've never had to wash a pair of socks or even pick them up off the floor. I know Mariella feels insecure because there's so little she can do in my room, and no matter how many times I explain to her that years of Navy life means I'm used to cleaning my own stuff, I think she's worried that I don't like her.

"Hamilton?"

"Yes, sir?" he asks, looking professionally interested.

"Tonight's event . . . what can you tell me about the movers and shakers in Roseboro?"

"The biggest of tonight's attendees will be the host, Thomas Goldstone," Hamilton says, his eyes tightening in approval at my question. "Your father is working with his company on some projects, and he is one of the richest men in the Pacific Northwest. You've seen the large gold tower in the middle of downtown?"

I nod, recalling what I've read both online and in internal reports about my father's dealings with Thomas Goldstone. "Who else?"

"Abraham Dunn, sir. He's more from the Portland area than Roseboro. I know very little else of him, other than that your mother is pleased to see his wife and daughter again."

Isn't that the truth? With Dad trying to info dump my brain, Mom has kept to her promise of trying to match me up despite my protests. She's being sneaky and subtle about it, or at least she thinks she is, but I'm on to her games. Especially when all she's talked about is the charming, beautiful Sabrina Cohen, daughter of Priscilla Dunn and stepdaughter of Abraham Dunn, who's an up and coming player in their society circle.

I swear, according to Mom, Sabrina is more beautiful than Miss Universe, farts rainbows, and has been known to help nurse baby birds with broken wings back to health while working on world peace. I believe exactly zero-point-three percent of her assessment.

I finish getting ready, dismissing Hamilton to do the final tweaks myself, and then head downstairs where I see Cody in the great room, his tie loose around his neck as he pours a three-finger scotch.

"Cody, would you pour me one too? I'm not sure I'm ready for this dog and pony show tonight. You?" It's an olive branch, a way to connect with the brother I fear I no longer know in the least.

What happened while I was gone?

He hands me a crystal tumbler, equally filled as his own, though I know I can't down that much. I'm not a lightweight by any means, but we're going out and it'll be a full night of champagne, tiny appetizer bites, and banal chatter. It's more dangerous than a firefight in Fallujah.

I need my wits about me.

Cody tosses half the liquid back in one shot, swallowing easily and sighing loudly.

"You okay, man? I've been trying to catch up with you, but I keep missing you," I say, eyeing him. He looks bright-eyed, red-faced, and I wonder if that's his first drink of the night, or perhaps his second or third?

"Been working my ass off, as always, not that anyone notices. I could use a bit of relaxation," he says, tossing back the other half.

"Maybe try something less liquid for relaxation? Running, meditation, massage, maybe sex?" I venture, feeling him out to see if he's got someone.

He scoffs, setting his tumbler down just a little too hard. "You don't have a damn clue, do you? You have no idea the stress I'm under."

I can't hide the incredulous look as it washes over my face. "I don't understand stress? Seriously?"

I really don't get it. I can't talk with him, or anyone, really, about the specifics of my missions, but he's being ridiculous. "I've been responsible for a team of men on dangerous missions, have literally held a man's head in my lap, promising he was going to be okay even though I could see his leg was blown off, and so much more. *That's* stress. A project at work is pissant shit."

It's not the way I hoped this conversation would go, but I can't stand by and let him wallow in the self-pity party he's obviously started. Maybe a reality check will do him some good.

But of course, it doesn't. Nobody wants to compare trauma and drama, least of all, me.

"Oh, fuck you, Mr. All-American Hero GI Joe," Cody snarls. "You left and Dad put all of it on me. I've been handling it all, but is that enough for the old guy? Of fucking course not, so here you come to save the day."

I can't help the teenage eyeroll that comes out of habit from my younger days, but I try to offer a more adult pragmatic commentary as well. "Cut the problem child bullshit, Cody. If you need help at work, let me help you. If you don't want help, then fix whatever's wrong. Because something's wrong."

I pour the scotch down the drain of the wet bar, a tight restraint the only way I manage to not pointedly shoulder bump him out of the way like we're stupid kids again. If I'm asking for more from him, I have to demonstrate it first. *Be a leader by example*, I remind myself. "A man controls his vices, not the other way around. Perhaps you should have a water before we go?"

Cody looks like he's about to smart off again, but Mom and Dad come in, dressed to the nines, of course, and Cody bites back whatever he was going to say. "You look lovely, Mom," I say, kissing her cheek. It's not a lie. Mom's always been beautiful to me.

Mom preens while Dad looks between Cody and me, but none of us says a word about the discussion we were just having. There are better ways to get him to pull his head out of his ass than calling him out in front of Dad.

The ride to the Goldstone building is quiet, Mom and Dad pointedly not saying anything about Cody's scotch breath while I try to focus on anything but the fact that I'm walking into a setup. Mom will be in her element at this thing, and I'm predicting she'll drag me around for introductions to everyone in the room.

The lobby of the building is modern and beautifully elegant, a large section of glass leading into an atrium of sorts where the gala has been set up. There's a DJ and dance floor area, a swath of tables where I'm sure business deals will be discussed tonight, and a pleasantly large spread of delicious foods. I'll hand it to Thomas Goldstone. He knows how to throw a party.

Everything is glitz and glam but not arrogantly so. I ask an hors d'oeuvres waiter what he's passing and he tells me it's PNW salmon on a round butter cracker. He laughs when I ask him if that's the same thing as a Ritz and affirms that not only are they Ritz, but generic Ritz at that. I pop one in my mouth and groan at how good it tastes. I learned in the Navy that it doesn't take brand names to make it good. In fact, the best chef I've ever met didn't graduate from Le Cordon Bleu but from Naval culinary school.

It makes me wonder about the man, and more than what I've seen on paper. He's a billionaire but doesn't seem to suffer the affliction of entitlement so many of his wealth do. I'm interested whether I'll get the opportunity to meet him tonight.

On the other hand, my first meeting with the Dunns goes about as I expected. Mom and Priscilla Dunn compliment each other's dresses, discussing the upcoming resort season. For real, as if it matters that you get your tan in Hawaii or Catalina.

My first impression of Abe Dunn seems more shark-like than presidential. I don't want to brand the man too quickly, but I get the feeling any business deal he's a part of is substantially slanted in his favor. But overall, they seem cut from the same cloth as my parents, just a bit lower on the totem pole and ambitious, which isn't necessarily a bad thing.

Ambition is what fuels hard work, and hard work is what gets you to new horizons.

Sabrina, though, is everything my mother said she was and everything she didn't say too. She's beautiful in a vapid, bland way that seems almost repetitive in the room of socialites. Same heavily highlighted hair, same black dress with a slit up the thigh, same pink glossed lips, same willowy frame. Just same, same, same.

I could turn around and see five women just like her, and odds are I'd find another named Sabrina too. Mildly, I wonder if they manufacture them in a factory somewhere.

Cody interrupts the discussion of the latest tax implications of trade embargos, and I could kiss him for it. "I'm going to get a drink. Anyone need anything?"

I raise a finger, eager for the interruption. "I'll come with you."

Not surprisingly, Sabrina volunteers too. But we're mere steps away when I feel Dad's hand on my shoulder. "Lance, could you stay? You'll want to hear this. I'm sure Cody can fetch you something."

I see a spark flash through Cody's eyes and feel the shot myself, though I'm not sure Dad intended it to be such a dismissive hit. Cody's your son, not a Cocker Spaniel.

"Sure," I tell him, apologizing to Cody with my eyes.

He walks away, and I doubt that I'll see him again tonight. Although I'm not one for self-pity, after that dismissal, I wouldn't be surprised if my brother channeled Achilles sulking in his tent . . . at least until someone catches his eye.

Sabrina returns to her mother's side awkwardly, and I to Dad's.

Before the conversation begins again, Thomas Goldstone takes the podium, tapping on the microphone. He's wearing a classically fitted tux, tailored but not clingy. Even in the formal attire, though, you can tell he's a fit man. I've learned how to assess people's skills within a few seconds of seeing them.

The DJ stops the remixed Korean pop song he's playing and Thomas speaks. "If I could have everyone's attention? Thank you for coming tonight."

His voice carries across the room and stops all conversation as eyes turn to him. Every glass lowers, every mouth closes as he looks out on the room, not as a tyrant, but with just the pure force of his charisma. He's commanding, I'll give him that.

Thomas holds out his hand, and a gorgeous woman with blonde hair joins him. She turns to look at him, stars shining obviously in her eyes, and I correct myself. She's blonde, but there are a few chunks of purple and black woven in stylish streaks throughout her hair. She's wearing a purple dress and some platform-style boots that look straight out of anime, or maybe anime porn. If I'd ever seen such a thing, which I most definitely would never admit to.

Thomas kisses the woman on the cheek and I realize this is the fiancée number-cruncher I'd heard so much about. The rumors are true. By looking, they don't match in the least. But anyone with eyes can see they're in love.

"First, how's the food?" Thomas asks, smiling. "If you haven't already, check out the cupcakes provided by the wonderful bakers at *Cake Culture*. Charlotte, they're delicious. My only complaint is that I'll be up all night on the bike to work off the half-dozen I've already eaten." He pats his flat belly and the crowd laughs, and then he points to a tall tower of cupcakes I hadn't noticed before. "Save me another chocolate one though!"

Everyone laughs again, and he goes on to thank the caterers, DJ, and event planner by name. Slick and impressive. He doesn't have to hand out credit, but in doing so, not only does he give a boost to the local businesses supporting him, but they're going to be more loyal to him in the future.

"Again, thank you all for coming to our Charity Gala. I'm sure you're thinking, *'Hey, Goldstone 'charity' is pretty vague. Why are we here?'* Let me explain. To me, charity is not simply writing a check and donating money. It is the seed that grows into hope, and every person has seeds they can sprinkle around their community, their city, their world. Those seeds can flourish, creating hope big enough to truly affect change. Now, some of us have more seeds than others."

He pauses to look around the room, making sure everyone gets his meaning. Obviously, the attendees tonight are all wealthy, pillars of the community, both old money and new money.

"I look around this room, and I see a lot of potential. By using those seeds in truly influential, intelligent ways, we can create an entire movement of hope. For Roseboro and beyond." He pauses dramatically, letting his words sink in.

He's a good speaker, with a voice and manner that make you feel like he's not talking to a crowd but instead talking to you individually. But my bullshit meter is going off because he still hasn't discussed any specifics yet. I hope he's got something more than a 'give because you can' card up his sleeve.

"After several long discussions with my wonderful fiancée, Mia, and then several more with my legal team, I've come to two conclusions. One, everyone has their cause that inflames their passion, that they feel is important to the world. The second is . . . I can't do it all. So I'm issuing a challenge. A challenge to each and every one of you to join in a new Hope Initiative. Gathered in this room are not just the business leaders of the Portland-Roseboro-Seattle corridor, but community leaders, activists, and more. As much as we've already done to make our communities great, we can do more. We need to work together, discuss, debate, coordinate, and make things even better."

The crowd looks around at one another, and I do the same.

Looking closely, I can start to spot the differences. Not everyone is at home at this event like Mom and Dad. I can see the starry-eyed looks from folks in rented formal clothes who definitely don't do galas like this on the regular. It makes me smile to see their excitement, remembering when I thought these things were a fun night of fanciness, not a dreary responsibility.

"Tonight, we begin a competition, though that word seems not truly in the spirit in which I hope to proceed. Let's call it a . . . show-off show. Over the next three months, every business, group, and team in the region is challenged to come up with an innovative, impactful way to reach a portion of our community that needs help. You will implement it, work it, and report on it. At the end of three months, the winning project will be funded for the remainder of the year and receive a three-year grant of one million dollars per year afterward."

The audience responds, a wave of people murmuring to their neighbor about Thomas's announcement before an excited buzz starts to fill the room.

Thomas thanks everyone once again and leaves the podium. Media pushes forward, trying to get to Thomas and Mia, who smile congenially and answer questions.

"Wow," Dad says.

"Impressive," I agree. "The man's putting his money where his mouth is."

Abe stands a bit taller, like he's trying to impress my dad. "It must be nice to do business with the Goldstones. You're part-nering Jacobs Bio-Tech with him, correct?"

But before Dad can reply, a redhead bumps his elbow, sending him jutting forward. Priscilla catches her husband as the redhead exclaims, "Oh, Dad, I'm so sorry! I just wanted to say hello and see if you'd like a cupcake?"

A cupcake? Ah, this must be the talented Charlotte that Thomas spoke of.

She turns to us, and my mouth goes dry. Forget the dime a dozen Stepford debutantes . . . this is a *woman*. "Forgive the interruption. So sorry."

She's blushing, pink turning her fair skin bright in blotches on her cheeks and chest. A chest that, I'm not afraid to admit, I'm drawn to admiring and exploring, wondering just how far that blush spreads over the lush mounds hidden beneath her dress.

"Charlotte, how clumsy can you be, girl?" Priscilla hisses, clearly not pleased.

Abe pats his wife's hand, clearing his throat. "I'm fine, dear. So good to see you, honey." He leans forward, kissing Charlotte on the cheek and introducing her. "Mr. Jacobs, my other daughter, Charlotte."

She extends her hand to my father for a real handshake, not the limp-wristed kiss-it shake most socialites offer. But when she steps out from behind Mr. Dunn to fully join our circle, I get my first chance to look her over from head to toe.

She's more than just a woman. She's absolutely stunning. Her deep red hair is in a braid, with loose ends escaping the plait over her shoulder, her blue eyes sparkle in the neon strobe lights the DJ turned on, and she's wearing a simple blue dress that doesn't remotely fit the dress code for a formal event.

She looks ready for a date, not a gala. But the dress is doing amazing things for her, highlighting every curve and valley, making my palms itch to trace them myself.

Sabrina speaks, though it honestly feels like she's murmuring from the far end of a hallway, as enraptured as I am with Charlotte. "Charlotte, seems your little cakes are popular. Well done."

I can't decide if she's being snarky or congratulatory. There's not enough to her tone to decipher. Or maybe not enough to her period to have an opinion one way or another.

"Thank you," Charlotte says, but there's no warmth to the sentiment. In fact, she sounds rather cool. I can definitely read her.

Charlotte's eyes move to my mother, whom she also offers a handshake and introduction. Then her eyes meet mine . . . and time stops. At least for me it does, and I think for her too.

In all my life, I've seen so much of the evil, ugly, dirty side of the world that I've only kept my sanity by being a firm believer in the existence of a balancing force. That for every evil, there is an equal good. And while I've never felt it before, looking into Charlotte's eyes, I swear that I can see the world brighten a little. She's . . . what the world is meant for. She's what I spent all those years fighting to protect—the few, the good, the innocent and beautiful.

A smile tugs at the corners of her mouth and her eyes lower, almost as if she's shy.

I extend my hand, wanting to touch her if only to prove that she's actually real and not some divine being walking among us mere mortals. "Lance Jacobs," I say, noting that my voice has gone a bit husky, so I swallow thickly. "A pleasure."

She smiles back. "Charlotte Dunn."

The moment our fingers touch, I swear a spark jumps between us, and Charlotte seems to feel it too, judging by the speed with which she yanks her hand back and the way her eyes suddenly widen.

"Very nice to meet you," I reply, my voice laced through with a sexual desire that is pure, animalistic, and absolutely authentic.

My dad clears his throat, and the prattle between my parents and the Dunns begins again. I ignore most of it, tossing in uninterested non sequiturs from time to time, but mostly watching Charlotte.

"You know, Lance, I finally realize who you remind me of," Sabrina says, putting her hand on my forearm. It feels like she's marking her territory, but I'm most definitely not hers in any way. "You look so much like Charlie Hunnam that it's eerie. With those movie-star looks, although I'm not sure about the beard—"

She reaches up to touch my face and I pull back, utterly done with Sabrina's attempts at seduction. "Excuse me . . . I should visit the men's room."

It's a pretty weak excuse, especially since I've been eye-fucking Charlotte for the past five minutes. I don't miss the twin scowls from Priscilla and her daughter, but I couldn't give a damn right now.

I give Charlotte a pointed look as I leave the circle and enjoy the way her eyes widen in surprise. But from across the room, I watch and moments later, she makes her excuses and moves away from our parents.

I'm feeling pretty good about our chances as she moves through the crowd toward me, and a wild hope builds in my gut. Maybe my mother was on to something, after all. She just had the wrong sister.

But Charlotte takes a jaunt to the left, skipping me over in favor of heading back to the cupcake tower. She begins talking to Mia, not even once looking for me, and I can't help but feel a twinge of disappointment.

I head to the bar, assessing my next move. And once I have a scotch and water in hand, I turn to find her again. Instead, a man to my right intercepts my attention. "Jacobs?"

I turn, surprised to see Jonathan Goldstone, an elite Air Force Pararescue Jumper who saved my ass in the hairiest shitstorm of my entire service. One of those situations that imprints itself on your soul . . . and now the man's standing beside me, a grin on his face.

"Goldstone? Wait, are you one of *these* Goldstones?" I ask, only now putting it together. It's not a common name, but not exactly uncommon either, so I'd never connected them.

He laughs, offering his hand, and we shake. "Yep, though our branches are a bit spread on the family tree. Second cousins, I think, or cousins once removed? Not sure how that works, but our dads are related somehow. What brings you here?"

"Jacobs Bio-Tech, my dad's company, is partnering with Goldstone Health. I'm back to help with the family empire, I guess."

Jonathan takes a sip of his drink, clear and smooth, so it could be water, vodka, or tequila, for all I know. "Thought you were a lifer for sure. Especially after that op, and you stayed in. I still remember the way you guys looked when we HELO'd in with med support. Like we were the second coming of Jesus, there to save your asses." He spreads his hands wide, chin lifted and eyes looking heavenward, his voice sounding like a choir. "Aaahhhh."

I smirk, never letting an Air Forcer get one up on me. "That's not exactly how I remember that going, but I'll let you keep your fairy tale. I'm out now. You? Figured you'd still be fighting the good fight."

He shakes his head and finishes his drink. "Nope, after that Kandahar op, I was rotated back to training cadre. The brass thought I needed a break after the dust settled. I found my heart wasn't in it, and going back to the Jumpers didn't quite fit either, so I got out. Work the private sector now, security, surveillance, and investigations mostly. I could hook you up if you need a second career opportunity?"

I take a sip of my scotch, wishing I could take him up on his offer. I know I'm back home for one reason only—my family company. But dealing with their drama seems so pointless and useless when there are such bigger issues in the world. It'd be nice to work with other people who've seen the impact on a broader scale too, not my brother whose biggest concern is an arbitrary deadline. *Deadline?* I think. *No, a real deadline is making pickup before the bad guys actually kill you.*

"That sounds intriguing, but I can't take you up on that now.

Family shit. You understand?" I say, and Jonathan nods. "But thanks for the offer. I'll keep it in mind, if that's okay?"

He hands me a business card and I'll admit to being impressed by the heavyweight, embossed white cardstock. The engraving is a discreet, professional black *Jonathan Goldstone — For Personal Matters* and lists a Seattle phone number. "Very spy of you," I tell him, slipping the card into my breast pocket as Jonathan tilts his head, not saying a word.

I wonder what exactly it is he does. I know a lot of guys go the mercenary route after getting out, and while Pararescue has the skills to do that successfully, Jonathan doesn't have the person-ality or vibe that screams soldier for hire. He's still sharp as a tack, but there's the same look in his eyes I saw years ago. He wants to save a life, not take one.

After shooting the shit a bit more, he excuses himself, and I make an immediate beeline for Charlotte. I didn't forget about her while I caught up with an old buddy and actually used the time with Jonathan to watch her more, seeing her light up as she talks about the cupcakes to people as they try to decide between the delicious-looking treats.

I approach the table like I'm being drawn to her by gravity, locking Charlotte in place with my gaze. I swear the crowd parts for me to get there faster, and as I get close, Charlotte's eyes turn to me, and she freezes, unable to look away. Part of her looks like she's scared, wanting to be saved, for someone to pull her away. From me.

But I'm the one interested in sweeping her away, and I certainly won't let someone else get in my way now that it's just the two of us.

Careful, man. Don't scare her.

"Hi again. I hear great things about your cupcakes. Which do you recommend?" I ask politely, giving her a moment to catch her breath. Because I can see that she's not breathing, her lips parted but nothing moving past the pink fullness.

My words unlock her, and she smiles, transformed into a sassy spitfire right before my very eyes. "They're all quite delicious. Just depends on what you're in the mood for."

I can't help the obvious punchline, looking at her hair as I ask, "Do you have any *red* velvet?"

A laugh bursts out hard and loud, and she slaps her hands over her mouth. "Oh, my God, does that kind of shit actually work on women?"

I smirk. "You'd be surprised. Though I'm a little rusty. I was a little busy over the past few years in the Navy."

Her left eyebrow jumps up. "First swing, cheesy. Second swing, guilt trip with the soldier gambit thrown in. You're about to strike out, Mr. Jacobs."

I like her. I like that she's calling me on my shit, though my 'guilt trip', as she called it, wasn't intended as such, but rather as an honest explanation for my lack of game. "Maybe I should just play it safe and ask you to dance then? Harder for my mouth to get me in trouble there."

I point back at the dance floor with my thumb, noting the crowd that's dancing to a 90s hit and getting low, low, low with their apple-bottom jeans. It's an odd disconnect for the upper-crust tuxedo and gown group, but somehow, it feels comfortable.

But Charlotte shakes her head, popping my bubble. "As much as I'd like that, I'm not here as a guest. I'm working." She gestures to the huge tower of cupcakes.

But like an angel sent from above, Mia shows up at Charlotte's side. "Hi, Mia Karakova, and you are?" I swear I hear her mutter under breath . . . *besides talking to my best friend*.

"Lance Jacobs. Nice to meet you. Thank you for inviting Jacobs Bio-Tech to tonight's gala. The Hope Initiative sounds like an innovative way to implement real change." See, with other people, I can pull some slick shit together. I've been by Dad's side and a military officer. I have a brain in my head that can carry a conversation. Except when all the blood is rushing south, like it does with Charlotte.

Mia's face brightens, and I realize just how threatening her previous scowl had been. Apparently, I passed a test. She talks a bit about the goals of changing Roseboro for the better, and I listen politely, though my eyes are basically burning holes in Charlotte's dress the whole time. Charlotte is blushing, and I swear almost twirling in the dress, giving me different angles from which to appreciate her.

"How do you know my girl, Charlotte?" Mia asks, breaking the mutual eye fuck Charlotte and I are participating in.

"We just met. Our parents seem to know each other," I reply. "I was asking her to dance as you came up, but she seems to think she's unable to leave her post."

Mia whirls on Charlotte, virtually shoving her my way. "Go, scoot, get your groove thang on, girl. I'll hand out cupcakes like I did the cookies."

Charlotte laughs, slightly nervous, but I can hear her desire. She *wants* to dance with me. "Should I warn Thomas that you're about to get on the table and start chunking cupcakes? One for youuu . . . and one for youuu . . ." She drawls out the words, feigning tossing a football. "Gonna have frosting everywhere."

Mia's response is a finger pointed at Charlotte and a shaking head. "Don't you dare warn him."

I sincerely hope she's kidding, but either way, I'm taking the opening. Taking Charlotte's hand, I lead her to the dance floor and we begin to move. It's a fast song, something I've never heard before, so I can't take her in my arms, but I do let one hand trace down to her hip as we sway in time with each other.

I feel like there are eyes on us from every corner of the room.

When I take Charlotte's hand and twirl her, I do chance a glance toward our parents, and while our dads are deep in conversation, our moms are diametrically different in their responses.

My mom looks like she's floating on air, hands clasped beneath her chin, and I can almost feel her hopefulness that maybe I'm not a lost cause for grandchildren. Priscilla, however, looks like she would kill me with her bare hands, painfully and slowly. Sabrina stands at her side, looking petulant, with her bottom lip actually poking out in a toddler-worthy pout.

But none of that matters when the music changes and I get to pull Charlotte in closer. "Tell me about you, Charlotte Dunn."

I don't know how much time we have, and I want to know every single thing she'll share.

She looks at me like I've lost my mind, her body still pressing against me. "Why? I'm just the redheaded stepchild. Pretty sure you're supposed to be fawning all over my stepsister, Sabrina."

I smirk, purposefully keeping my eyes locked on Charlotte's baby blues. "I think I'm right where I'm supposed to be." I twirl her, watching raptly as her dress flares out slightly. "Why cupcakes?" I ask when she's pressed against me once more.

"Why *not* cupcakes? They're delicious little bites of happiness." Her smile is genuine, and I mirror it, infected with her obvious excitement. "But I don't just make cupcakes. I also makes cakes, cookies, pies, and muffins. Basically, if it's baked, I make it. *Cake Culture*, that's my bakery, is still in the baby stages with the same type of long hours and singular focus as a newborn. But it's my everything. God, I do sound like a new mother. Wanna see pictures?" she jokes.

"Sounds like a labor of love. I admire the commitment and guts it takes to open a new business," I reply, impressed with her.

"You have no idea. I quit my job for this and put every single penny I have into it, plus some, to get it off the ground. Scary as fuck, but so far, so awesome." As she speaks about her bakery, I can feel her relaxing in my arms, the passion for her work palpable in every word.

"I'm in somewhat of a similar situation. For a long time, I figured I was a career Navy man, but plans change and here I am. Back home for the family."

We continue talking, but the words start to drift off as the DJ rolls into another slow, sexy, damn near pushing the line for a gala like this song. This one has a thick baseline, and when he changes the strobes to a deep red and blasts the fog machine, the whole dance floor's vibe changes to something hot and sultry.

I expect Charlotte to pull away from me at any moment, but she doesn't. Instead, she links her hands behind my neck and moves in even closer. I know she can feel my cock thickening in my slacks, but I'm not willing to pull away from her, even to be gentlemanly. It's been too long and she feels too good.

I slide my hands around her lower back, pressing her against me, pinning my cock between us, and Charlotte gasps, her eyes popping to mine. "Holy shit."

I can see the lust burning in her eyes, can feel the heat racing along her skin. "Won't say I'm sorry for being so affected by you. You're a siren, Charlotte, luring me in with every word, every curve, every . . . thing."

I see her soft smile, pleased that she's responding to me just as much. We move like that for an eternity, or maybe it's minutes. Either is just as likely because I'm living fully in every moment I'm touching her.

She spins in my arms, putting her back to my chest, and she guides my hands around her waist, placing her own over mine. From this vantage, I can see the rise and fall of her breasts, even in the conservatively scoop-necked dress. I wonder if her nipples are pebbled beneath it and go in for a closer look.

Pressing my lips to her neck, I breathe her in. Sugar. Vanilla. Sweetness but with something deeper, darker too. Whispering in her ear, though no one could hear anything I say over the music, "You are making it very hard to control myself. We're in a roomful of people, some of whom are likely well aware that your lush ass is cradling my hard cock right now and that I desperately want to slide my hands up a few inches to cup your breasts and tease your nipples."

I'm being aggressive, more so than I usually am, but something about Charlotte calls to a baser, primal level of me. And to be honest, she's not shying away from it. In fact, I can feel her arching, pressing her ass against me and lifting her chest like she wants me to feel them too.

I'm contemplating asking her to ditch this gala and find the nearest horizontal surface—or hell, a vertical surface, anywhere without an audience including our parents—when a man in a black suit interrupts.

"Sorry, Miss Dunn. Miss Karakova needs you immediately." Something about the man seems familiar. Not that I've seen him before, but in his stance, his speech. He's former military, I'd bet my trident on it.

I wonder if he's one of Jonathan's guys, which would make sense that Thomas would hire family for his security detail.

His words break the spell, and Charlotte-the-Siren disappears in favor of Charlotte-the-Cupcake Genius. Unfortunately for my aching groin, while she's just as beautiful, she's focused on something besides our bodies right now.

"What's wrong?"

The man's eyes flick toward the tower, and I see that Mia is indeed on the table, handing out cupcakes like a birthday party mother, forcing two and sometimes three to everyone within reach. Even from here, I can read her lips, "Sooooo goooood."

Charlotte lurches away, already having forgotten me. But she only gets a few steps away before I grab her hand, stopping her flight. "Charlotte?"

She smiles, but it's tinted with regret at the edges. She steps back to me, pressing her lips to mine. She's soft, sweet, and gone too soon. "It was really nice meeting you, Lance. I've gotta go, sorry!"

She disappears into the crowd, and I'm left wondering what to do. I struggle to see her red hair through the sea of black sequins and tuxedos, but I lose her. For a moment, I sag, looking down at the red carpet that only reminds me of her.

Something glints against the red, and I bend to pick it up. It's a small bracelet with a *C* engraved on a tiny circle, like a monogram. It's not fancy, more a simple gold micro link, but I know as soon as I pick it up that it's hers.

The lights flash, making the metal gleam, and I wrap my fingers around the memento, remembering how she felt pressed against me, how her eyes lit up when she spoke, and how her sassy mouth made me want to taste her teases.

Damn it. I'm going to have to tell my mother she's right, and she's never going to let me live this down.

I do want one of Abe Dunn's daughters.

Just not the one she expected.

I want Charlotte Dunn.

CHAPTER 3

*"Y*ou heard that right. Thomas Goldstone, the golden child of Roseboro, laid out a very daring challenge to the communi-ty,*"* the idiotic talking head blathers on the screen, grinning widely.

"And he backed his words up with substantial financial support. It'll be exciting to see what ideas will come of this over the next three months. We'll continue reporting as progress is made by the various teams that are already forming. Reporting from the Goldstone Building, this is Trevor Olliphant, Channel 5 News."

It's hard not to slam my fist down on my remote with disgust as I turn off the television, growling. Yet again, I've been upstaged by Thomas Goldstone. Not that I've made any large public moves lately. No, my chess game is better played in the shadows, strategic moves hidden by layers of players who only know a portion of my greater plan.

Unfortunately, my plan hasn't gone accordingly, as of late. My agent inside Goldstone was discovered, and while my name didn't come out of it, it was still a setback.

Then my idea to hit Goldstone's weakness, his bleeding heart, resulted in Isabella Turner seducing the hitman I hired. That hurt even more, because now Goldstone knows I'm coming for him.

And a prepared enemy is always more dangerous than a surprised one.

To some people, that would be more than enough to send them scurrying in defeat. But this isn't a game. This is war. And war is a long game, a culmination of many moves that result in a win on a broad scale.

The history of warfare is filled with stories of men who would hit, get beaten, retreat . . . and eventually emerge victorious. George Washington lost more battles than he won, yet he was the Father of the United States.

And my next plan will be my Yorktown, where I will destroy in one maneuver not just the Golden Boy, but his woman, her friends . . . and everyone who might doubt me in Roseboro.

There will be no doubt who the king of Roseboro is when I'm done. I built this city, and it will remain mine. *In aeternum.*

Still . . . the 'Hope Initiative'. What a joke. I've already heard about certain community groups and organizations who are planning and implementing a mere twenty-four hours after Goldstone's announcement. The sheep are practically tripping over themselves to try and get lined up to play Goldstone's little lottery.

I've also heard gossip questioning why Blackwell Industries wasn't at the gala. Not that I was invited, which makes me smile. Goldstone's finally realized what he's dealing with, and while he's not being foolish, he's not inviting the wolf into his hen house. It makes things tougher, but the thrill of having a worthy adversary is at least rejuvenating to my old bones.

My company won't be participating in his Pollyanna schtick either way. Simply put, I won't entertain such idiocy.

There's a knock on my office door, and my new secretary opens to reveal Chief Frank Harris of the Roseboro Police Department. "Mr. Blackwell, your—"

"Show the Chief in," I interrupt her, standing up and giving a rare, true smile. "Frank, it's good to see you again. What brings you by?"

He gives a polite nod as he comes in. "Custis, how are you doing?"

"Do you really want me to answer that, Frank?" I ask, coming around to offer a handshake. He's the only person to use my first name, or at least to do so and not suffer consequences. But he's earned it, and I do have a certain fondness for the man.

Harris and I have been acquaintances for nearly thirty years, when I identified a smart, capable, but not totally honest police sergeant who could be very advantageous to me.

Over the decades, I've carefully nurtured our relationship, making sure that Frank's been placed in the right opportunities. Never overtly, of course, I don't want his good reputation within the community to be tainted with the scent of scandal, but when subtle pressures could be applied or information slipped to the Sergeant, then Lieutenant, then Deputy Chief, that could prove helpful to him . . . well, they were.

Frank, of course, isn't totally innocent. He's looked the other way plenty of times over the past thirty years as my plans have gone down, but in his mind, the net benefit to Roseboro far outweighs my . . . methods.

"I'm not too worried about how you're doing, more like *what* you're doing. The whispers and the names that I've heard around town over the past few months have . . . concerned me," Frank says, sitting down, and I do the same. "But I heard something that might prove even more worrisome to you. Figured you'd want to know."

"Oh?" I ask, tenting my fingers.

"There's an investigator in town, a new one. And he's looking pretty hard at you." He delivers this news like it's near-catastrophic. He is obviously surprised when I don't react accordingly.

"So?" I ask instead, unperturbed. "I've had plenty of dogs come sniffing at my door. They get shooed away easily enough. That's your job, isn't it?"

"Not when they're hired by Thomas Goldstone," Frank replies. He's one of the very few who knows of my hatred for the Golden Boy, though he doesn't really understand why. Frank is a resource, and while I have a certain grudging respect for his skills, accomplishments, and contributions to me and to Rose-boro . . . that doesn't mean I'm going to share my thoughts on the matter.

"Then deal with it."

For the first time in a long time, Frank shakes his head in refusal to one of my requests. "As much as I'd like to run this guy out of town for you, Goldstone has everyone at City Hall swinging from his balls right now. Hell, he's reaching all the way to both state houses. I try and get in the way, I'm just going to get run over by the Goldstone freight train and they'll just bring in some Feds or Staties. No offense, Custis, but I'm not going to play Sancho Panza to your Don Quixote."

I purse my lips. "And do you at least know who this private investigator is?"

"The word I'm hearing is it's some relative of his. But I can't be sure, and the one name I've got . . . he's bad news, Custis. I'll put it bluntly. I've covered your shenanigans for thirty years, and you've done right by me for it. But if this investigator is able to connect you to some of the things that you've done—"

"I understand," I reply, leaning forward though I know it's a pressure move against someone I consider to be on my side. "If it helps you, Frank, I don't blame you for wanting to cover your own neck."

"It's not just my neck. It's this whole city's!" Frank protests, his hand half clenching before he remembers his place. "Dammit, Custis, I know you're a ruthless son of a bitch, but you've done a lot for Roseboro. I remember what this place was before you arrived, a two-bit suburb, not even worth stopping for gas in. Half the folks were commuting to Portland for work, the other half were on food stamps, drinkin' down at the Mellow Tiger every night, and . . . this town was nothing. You made it better."

"And yet it is Thomas Goldstone's ass that they kiss," I remind him subtly. "Frank, I want this problem taken care of. Remember, if I'm taken down, the fallout will not be simply confined to this tower."

Frank pales but nods. "I'll see what I can do. I'm the police chief, but there's a limit to how far I can stretch the law and keep the spotlight off both of us."

"I understand," I reply, nonplussed. "Keep me updated."

Frank gets up, reaching down to pick up a small brown bag that I noticed he brought in with him. "Here, Joan wanted you to have this."

"Thank you," I answer, knowing what's inside. For some reason, Frank's wife, a woman with a blinding smile and a sweet disposition, thinks I'm just an errant soul who needs a little more love and affection. Adopting me at arm's length, for thirty years, I've put up with her misplaced affection, even though I can barely stand her.

I open the bag, my stomach curling in disgust when I see it's a sugar cookie, carefully iced and decorated. I grit my teeth, not wanting to smash it under my fist until Frank is gone. The woman is always trying to get under my skin with some sugary message of friendship, a relationship that does not exist no matter how many times she invites me to dinner.

At the door, Frank turns. "I'll be in touch."

He leaves, and I carelessly toss the brown bag and cookie to the trash, my mind turning to each chess piece in play, each potential move I can make.

An investigator, funded by Goldstone himself and possibly related to him. Seems he's not content to passively see what happens now that we both know the game is underway. My head start is hard-earned, through blood, sweat, and tears. Not my own, of course. Like any Grandmaster, I've sacrificed pawns along the way.

Perhaps it's time to unleash another weapon. I have them in so many places already, sleeper spies ready to do my bidding here, instigate and interfere there. Machiavellian, of course, but by keeping the pulse on every corner of Roseboro, I can direct this town in any way I see fit. For its betterment, and my own.

The stroke of genius hits me, a cherry on top of my other plans, so to speak. With a smile, I pick up my phone, dialing a number I have only called once before.

The answering voice is filled with nerves. They obviously remember who this number belongs to. "Hello?"

"Proceed. When you have things in motion, call this number." I hang up, imagining the click and dead air in the other party's ear and their fortifying breath as they prepare to do as told.

"Soon, the world will see your true worth, Goldstone. And mine as well."

CHAPTER 4

CHARLOTTE

*T*here's something Zen-like about baking. Maybe it's the ratios, or the constant humming of the machines I use, or the repetitive nature of rolling and shaping pastries? But there are times, especially in the early mornings when I'm getting the fresh batters together for the morning rush, when I love just being alone and letting my mind wander.

This morning, my wanders to only one thing . . . my bed.

I'm beat after the late-night gala. Cleanup duty had been fast, mostly because I'd been hoping I'd see Lance again and we could pick up where we left off. But I didn't see him the rest of the night.

Except for in my dreams. And holy hell, were they hot.

I'd imagined we'd snuck out of the gala and into a private alcove in the hallway, where he'd shoved me up against the wall and kissed the very breath out of me. I'd dreamed he pulled the thick cock I felt out of his tuxedo pants and I'd held my dress up for him to get access to my slippery pussy.

I loved the thought of him pounding me so hard, right there where anyone could've caught us, that he'd had to cover my mouth with his hand to keep us from being discovered because of my orgasmic yells.

And I'd felt ridiculously satisfied when he'd pulled out and iced my cupcake.

Shit. Somehow, over the past few months, thoughts of baking filter into everything, even to my dirty thoughts and fantasies.

But I'd woken up this morning in a fog, one filled with lust, excitement, and okay, some exhaustion at the early hour. Baker's hours start well before sunrise, after all. I'm the one who wakes up the roosters for the farmers.

The back door of the bakery opens, pulling me out of my reverie, and I look over my shoulder to see Trixie coming in, her jacket wet. "Whoo! The heavens are getting ready for a circle jerk up there!"

"That looks like rain," I deadpan, wiping my hands on my apron. "It's been a while since my last hand job, but I remember some things."

She grins like she's storing that info away for later dissection and then flips into a 'television preacher voice' straight out of the 90s. "Ah, but you don't understand the heavenly seed!" Trixie teases, taking off her neon color-blocked windbreaker and rubbing at the dark spots of water on the sleeves. "When the seed falls upon the Earth-ah, the heavenly seed-ah, takes root! The Earth, having been made pregnant-ah, bears forth-ah, the fruits! Let's raise an offering!"

I can't help it. I laugh at her antics. She's such a weirdo. "Then why don't you have a pine tree growing out of your hair? You telling me you're not fertile soil?"

Okay, so I'm a weirdo too. It's why we fit together so well after such a short period of time. Yeah, it's a lot of intense, long-houred, early morning work, but for someone I met only months ago, Trixie and I are almost thick as thieves.

Trixie thinks for a second and must not come up with any witty reply because she sticks her tongue out at me. Like the mature woman I am, I do the same but add a set of crossed eyes to the insult.

And then we're both laughing way too loudly and crazily to do anything else.

"Well, you're in a good mood this morning. That must mean the gala went well?" Trixie asks as she washes her hands and puts on her own apron. She'd stayed back to close up the bakery and do the evening prep while I went last night. I don't know what I'd do without her.

"It went more than well!" I almost squeal, tossing a ball of dough to the floured table in front of me. As I start to roll it out to the thickness I want for sugar cookies, I tell her all about Thomas's declared love affair with *Cake Culture* and the Hope Initiative. Last but not least, I tell her about meeting Lance.

As I describe him, her eyes get bigger, her jaw drops open, and I swear I can see sprinkles shooting out of her ears as I describe him. "So, some former military family type who's hotter than cakes fresh outta the oven damn near makes you have an orgasm in the middle of the dance floor, and then you run off and don't find him again to make him finish what he started, when I know damn well how long it's been since you've had a male-facilitated big O? Damn, Cinderellie, you'd better get to brushing that mop on your head before Prince Charming comes hunting you down."

I laugh and then freeze, another silly thought going through my head. "Oh, shit, does that make Mia my Fairy Godmother? Do not tell her that or she'll probably buy a damn wand and go around bippity-boppity-booing everyone on the head in a Russian accent and end up with assault charges."

Trixie's smirk is prep for the zinger I know she's about to unleash. "Uhm, excuse me, but if you'll recall, I'm the one who got you all gussied up and took care of matters so you could shake your tailfeathers at the ball. *Pretty* sure that makes me your Fairy Godmother. What's that gig pay?"

I shrug and hold up a limp, unbaked sugar cookie. She flashes me a thumbs-up, grinning. "Deal. You drive a hard bargain, Cindy."

The oven timer dings, and she turns it off, grabbing hot pads to pull a tray of morning muffins out. She places each fluffy Blueberry Hill Delight on the tray for the bakery case and I remind her, "Hey, can you pull one for Steven? And get his coffee too?"

She nods, plating one of the huge muffins, but before she heads out front to deliver it, she turns to me. "What's the deal with him again? At first, I thought he was like a super-overbearing boyfriend, but then you said he was security. Uhm, something worrisome about the bakery business I don't know about?"

I sigh. I haven't told Trixie about all the mess with Blackwell. She just knows that I used to work there before opening *Cake Culture*. Since most of the story isn't mine to tell, I've been hesitant to share that even though we've told each other all kinds of other stories.

"Long story short, Thomas is protective of his investments, and of his friends, especially Mia's besties. Steven and the boys are just a safety precaution, for the business and for me. So be nice to him. Lord knows, he must be going stark-raving mad having to listen to us all day, every day."

Trixie gets a twinkle in her eye, and I swear I can see the hamster in her mind running faster with ideas on how to spice up Steven's days. But she smiles sweetly, too sweetly, and says, "Sure thing, Boss. Nice to Security Steven and his boys. One muffin and coffee coming right up."

She adjusts her boobs through her shirt, making me wonder if she means an actual muffin or something a little more suggestive. She even wiggles a bit as she goes through the double doors, and

I'd bet my favorite mixing bowl that she's out there flirting her ass off. Spicy and sweet, that one.

I finish the cookies, setting them in the oven and traying the chocolate chip muffins I made earlier. When I swoosh through the double doors myself, Trixie jumps like she was busted and I realize that she was taking a picture of Steven.

I smirk, figuring she's stashing one away for the spank bank or maybe sending the hottie shottie to a friend for some girlish oohs and ahhs. "You good?" I ask, though I suspect she's more bad girl than good girl.

All-business Steven could probably use a bit of shaking up, Trixie style.

"Yep," she says, popping the *P*. "Just checking Tinder one more time before the day gets underway. Swipe city, ya know?"

She says it just a little loudly, and I wonder if she's trying to communicate that she's single and ready to mingle. I chance a glance over my shoulder, but Steven is looking out the window, eyes scanning left and right up the empty sidewalk as he sips his coffee. Trixie sighs.

"Can you make sure everything's ready out here? I'm going to grab the rest of the goodies for the case." I head to the back, leaving Trixie at her post.

Busting through the double doors, I stop at the sight before me. Flour-covered stainless steel prep table, two huge wall ovens filled with treats I made, a stack of boxes with my logo on them, and a whiteboard with all this month's special orders written out. Honestly, it looks like a barely-controlled bomb's gone off, and it's barely seven in the morning.

I never would've thought this would be my life. Didn't think I had the courage to chuck away everything I knew.

My normal life before the bakery was nothing like this. But what's normal?

Normal's boring. Normal's stagnating. Normal's sitting on your ass in a cubicle in a job you hate just so you can say you've got health insurance and a 401(k).

Normal's dying . . . just doing it slowly.

"So fuck normal," I tell the empty room.

This is my new normal. Risky, adventurous, something I'm passionate about, and something I can give to the world to make their day a bit better. Because sugar definitely makes everything better.

I take a couple of trips back and forth and am just loading up the last tray when I hear a loud knocking on the front door. Trixie pops her head through the door. "Hey, Char, you definitely want to take this. It's your stepsister, I think? Expensive dye job with streaky highlights, looks like she smelled something rank? Steven's about to go Judge Dredd on her ass."

"Shit," I reply. "I'm coming. Can you take this last tray, and maybe serve as a witness in my defense at the trial?" I roll my eyes, but I'm half-serious because I already know this is going to get ugly.

Up front, Sabrina is raging, slapping a palm against my freshly-applied logo, and Steven is standing wide-spread with his arms crossed in front of the door.

"I got this, thanks," I tell him before hollering through the door. "Stop banging on my door so I can unlock the damn thing."

She waits, but I can see her foot tapping, which makes me go even slower.

As soon as she hears the lock click open, she jerks on the door, finger pointing in my face. "What the hell are you thinking, bitch?"

"Good morning to you too, Sabrina," I reply, and while I sound sweet, we both know I'm faking. "What brings you by this morning? Need a coffee and muffin?"

"You know why I'm here!" she hisses. "Lance is *my* man. Mother already set it all up, so you can just crawl back to whatever basement you came out of and leave him the fuck alone."

A hilarious joke about Mia being a basement dweller who got the hottest bachelor in the city almost works its way out, but Sabrina wouldn't understand the beautiful irony of it so I let it go and focus on the rest of her statement.

"Sabrina, last time I checked, you can't call dibs on someone. It's not like you can buy him at an auction. And if we're going by childhood rules . . . *I licked him, so he's mine.*"

I know, even as I say it, that I'm poking the bear, but it's so fun to finally be at a point where I can get a rise out of her and give it back. I shrank under her insults and superiority complex for way too long. So what if I didn't actually lick him?

Sabrina sputters, a quiet squeak of affront passing her perfectly painted lips. Yes, at seven in the morning, she's already fully coiffed. Unlike my messy hair, bare face, and polo and jeans uniform covered with a floury apron.

"Whatever Priscilla might have told you," I say, because I *never* call Priscilla anything resembling Mom or Mother, "Lance is a grown man and can flirt, dance, and date anyone he wants. I know you'd hoped it'd be you." I fake a *tsk* and shake my head sadly, looking her up and down. There's nothing out of place. She's the perfect socialite, but I make it seem like it's not remotely up to muster. "But Lance seems to have felt otherwise."

Sabrina seemingly gets over her initial flashy rage and reverts to her training, which has been drummed into her head since birth, I suspect. She sneers, every snotty stereotypical bitch come to life before my very eyes. "And you think he'd prefer someone like *you* instead?"

She returns my head to toe appraisal, and where I used to cower, hoping she wouldn't fixate on any one thing to torment me over, now I stand proud. I've grown over the years, stronger in many ways because of the hell Priscilla and Sabrina put me through. Even my comfort in my own skin was shaped by their constant criticism.

I still remember the last time Sabrina scanned me this way. I was sixteen, she was eighteen, and she'd had a glint in her eyes as she told her mother that the baby hairs around my hairline surely showed my lack of basic hygiene.

It'd brought on World War III, with any and all body hair as the evil enemy. I'd been so young, still so innocent, that when the waxer started ripping off the strips, I'd cried, not understanding what was wrong with peach fuzz on my arms. I'd been mortified at the full bikini wax, though, feeling intimately violated. It wasn't until years later, when I finally got waxed by my own choosing, that I realized the first waxer had been intentionally and insanely rough, likely at Priscilla's behest.

But none of that matters now, not in my new and improved self-image. I may still have insecurities—*who doesn't?*—but I can see that Priscilla and Sabrina used every trick in the book to keep me small for my whole childhood.

I don't think they're jealous of me. It's more just that they used me to make themselves feel bigger.

In some ways, I don't even fault Sabrina for it. She doesn't know any better, having been raised and shaped by Priscilla. But she's a full-grown woman now, and she needs to get a grip on how the real world works.

"Judging by how he ditched you and swept me away on the dance floor, I'd say yes, he'd prefer me. The bigger issue is that neither you, nor your mother, can control others the way you think you can," I explain patiently but evenly. "And stomping your foot or throwing money at problems doesn't work. Come on, Sabrina . . . *do better* than your mother."

It's wishful thinking that she'll hear the slight encouragement, but it's all I can give the person who made so much of my life hell.

"Seems she did pretty well with Daddy." She lifts her chin, haughty and snarky at the same time.

She knows I hate it when she calls my father *Daddy*. He's not her Daddy. Hell, he's barely even mine anymore. Once upon a time, he was on my side, a fun guy who helped me, loved me. That man was Daddy. But Priscilla ate away at our relationship too, under the guise of guiding me into womanhood, something my dad basically got super-nervous about. And now he's simply Dad and has been for a long time.

My face falls as her shot hits a bullseye on the button she loves to push, and she knows it, her eyes lighting up. She hair-flips, walking toward the door like the victor she is, but she tosses over shoulder, "Don't forget your place, Charlotte. Make your little cakes and cookies." She smirks as she looks around the bakery. "But leave Lance to me. He is *mine*."

The jingling bells sound like a death toll as she walks out, the silence heavy as Steven and Trixie stare at me, having seen the whole showdown.

"Miss Dunn?" Steven asks softly. "Would you like me to put her on the *persona-non-grata* list?"

Trixie interrupts, clucking her tongue. "Uh, no. I'd like you to put her on the shoot-on-sight list, capiche?" She hurries around the case, wrapping an arm around me as she hustles me to the back, muttering the whole way, "*Security Steven*? He just stood there and let that bitch rail you over. Useless."

Guess Sabrina ruined Trixie's crush, along with my crush on Lance. A morning well-spent in her books, probably.

CHAPTER 5

LANCE

I've never been a man to daydream much. I've seen too many things. Dark, horrible things. Things that scar a man's soul. Things that can give the most hardened badass nightmares for the rest of their existence.

So I don't daydream because those are the memories that take the opportunity of a wandering mind to force their way to the forefront.

"Sir?" he asks me, and I know he wants the truth I can't give him. Not now when hope is all he has to hang on to. I won't take that away.

"It's just a scratch," I tell the badly wounded man. "You're gonna be on your feet in no time."

"Bullshit, sir." His brown-smudged face is covered in the very dirt he's talking about through choked swallows. Sweat and tears run rivers through the filth, making mud on his cheeks as the beat of the chopper blades fills the air.

A sudden burst of adrenalin shoots through him, and he grips at my shirt with surprising strength. "Don't die out here like me, man. Go and live your life, not someone else's. I should've been home with her."

His eyes swirl, unfocused on the shades of brown around us - brown dirt, brown buildings, brown uniforms, only the bright blue sky a relief. His voice is getting weaker. "Do one thing for me?"

"You can tell her yourself," I reply, knowing he's thinking about his young wife and the baby daughter he hasn't even met yet. He could have taken leave. I would have put the paperwork through in record time and the Commander would have stamped it no problem, but he didn't want to leave his brothers holding the bag on this shitstorm. Now, he'll never meet the babe.

He smiles, taking my hand. "Just . . . tell her about me?"

"I will," I promise, knowing that I'm admitting the truth . . . but I think he deserves to hear it.

His smile is pain-filled. "It was an honor, sir."

Tears burn my eyes, and I clasp his hand tightly. "The honor is mine."

He tries to say something else, but before he can, his breath hitches twice, the last exhalation exiting his lips without the heroic battle cry of a movie or the dramatic swell of music you grow up expecting. Instead, it's like a sigh, a tired, exhausted man at the end of his labors, setting down his load for a final time, never to pick it up again.

"Hooyah." I fare the body well just as the chopper starts to descend. Thirty seconds later, we're on the deck, and I have to let him go. There are other men under my command, under my care. And right now, they need me.

But I take one split second to look to the sky, promising that I'll tell that little girl all about her father, the man who faced death with honor and died as a hero.

Back in my bed, I shake my head, fighting the memory down and locking it in the box with so many others. I breathe slowly and deeply, remembering where I am. It's weird to even think about this as a bed. I'm so used to a *rack*, or a *bunk*, that even the term 'bed' feels foreign. But there's no way anyone would ever call a king-size memory foam mattress like this a rack.

I flop onto my side, and a sparkle on the bedside table catches my eye, along with the alarm clock. I'd purposefully not set it, hoping for a little extra shut-eye after the late night at the gala. Seems instead of my usual six AM wakeup for PT, I've managed to sleep in until almost seven thirty. Not bad for a civvie.

But the gold bracelet is what changes my mood from the dour dredges of my dreams, transporting my mind to the happier memories of last night.

I pick it up, holding the dainty bracelet in my hand and remembering the redhaired spitfire who wore it and the way she set me spinning. She's taking the world by storm, making her own way, despite her family and the odds against her. That takes guts.

And sometimes, guts are enough. Whether kicking in a door when you know there are half a dozen men on the other side ready to fill your body with bullets, or standing up to everyone and everything else to open a simple bakery . . . guts are guts.

And Charlotte Dunn has them in spades. I remember her smile, her sass, the smell of her skin, and the surprising feel of her lips on mine. She's the kind of woman my buddies and I would dream about back in BUDs, a fantasy woman who would make all the hell we were going through worth something. A scarlet angel, strong and innocent and ready to soothe our souls and tell us everything would be okay, despite the violence and ugliness we'd wrought.

A voice in my head says to me, *she's no angel.*

But I can't help but think of the way she moved against me, her lush curves dimpling beneath my grip, her ass cradling my cock as she arched, asking for more. And now, like last night, I'm rock fucking hard again.

I stare at the bracelet, a link near the clasp broken, and imagine her wearing it once again as her soft hands wrap around my shaft, the light twinkling as she works me up and down. I can't help myself. I slip my hand beneath the sheet and palm my thickness. A few massage strokes later, I'm delving into my underwear, pulling my cock and balls out and kicking the sheet out of the way.

I hold the bracelet, eyeing it as I jack myself with long strokes, mentally replacing my hand with hers. I rub over the head, wishing it were her lips, and the thought of her sucking me has me damn near the edge. A filthy thought takes root, and I wrap the delicate bracelet around the crown of my cock, just below the ridge. I thrust into my hand, careful to not break the bracelet further, and watch the monogram charm dangle against my skin, faster and faster in time with my heartbeat. I can barely breathe as I come in spurts, white-hot jets covering me and the gold links as I spasm, growling her name through gritted teeth, "Char . . .lotte."

Spent, I carefully unwind the links from my cock and wipe them on my underwear, promising myself to clean it properly. I wait for my breathing to return to normal, thinking sweeter thoughts about Charlotte but wondering if she went home hot and bothered last night too.

I'd wanted to track her down, but family obligations had gotten in the way, and I'd had to help a tipsy Cody into the family limo.

But today is mine. And so is Charlotte.

I get out of bed, energized by the thought of tracking her down to continue our conversation from last night. I shower and dress in a Navy PT shirt and shorts, taking a minute to soap and water wash Charlotte's bracelet before placing it into my sock drawer for safekeeping while I work out.

I find Hamilton in the kitchen, a carafe of coffee in his hands. "Mister Lance, good morning."

"Hamilton, I don't suppose I could convince you to not call me Mister Lance, could I?" I ask, smiling and taking an offered mug. "I mean, I couldn't like, slip you a fifty once a week or something, or duct tape your shoes to the floor if you don't stop?"

"Hardly, sir. And duct tape would just damage my shoes. But I would enjoy the cat and mouse game. It would provide an entertaining diversion from my day to day duties. Beware, though. I would retaliate." He narrows his eyes, which would probably be threatening if he wasn't grey-haired and so thin a strong wind could knock him over.

I laugh, nodding. "I learned long ago to never, ever mess with someone who is involved with laundering your underwear. Not every threat is so easily seen. The most dangerous opponents aren't the bigwigs but the little guys because they've got nothing to lose."

Hamilton nods, like I'm saying something quite wise, even going so far as to rub his nails on his lapel, like he's buffing them proudly at what he's capable of. "A wise lesson, sir."

"So, what's Chef whipped up for breakfast?"

"I'm afraid it's her day off, but I'd be happy to, ahem, *whip* you up an omelet, if you'd like. I'm quite adept, making them for your father regularly."

"I think I'll just grab some toast. No worries. Where is dear old Dad this morning? Figured he'd still be in bed after the late night." I glance around, listening and not hearing evidence of anyone but Hamilton and me.

He moves closer, almost whispering, "I'm afraid Mister Jacobs had a rather late evening, filled with discussions with Mrs. Jacobs. You might do well to make a run for it, but if you'd rather chance it, he's on the back patio. Wanted breakfast by the pool today, sir."

I wonder what my parents could've been up to all night. Well, I don't *wonder*, because I don't want to think about my parents having sex. I'm still partially convinced that I was delivered via stork and Cody was a medical experiment gone wrong.

But the conversation part of the evening is interesting. They're probably celebrating my interest in Charlotte, my mom strutting around like a peacock that she was right and already planning a wedding and baby shower.

I make a quick slice of toast, adding a dab of peanut butter for some protein, and head out back. Dad is by the pool as Hamilton said, his plate empty and eyes staring sightlessly at the rippling water. His face is stormy enough that The Weather Channel could make a report about it, probably give it an old-school name, like Storm Bishop. I smirk, laughing at my own joke of Dad's unusual name.

"Good morning, Dad."

He doesn't even look to me, just points to the chair across from him and says sternly, "Sit down. I want to talk to you."

"Sure," I agree, surprised at the tone but not wanting to start the morning with a fight. Based on his mood, his late-night conversation with Mom must have been about my brother, not me, and I wonder what the hell Cody did now. He was fine when I laid him in bed, still in most of his tux because I was only taking off his shoes and jacket. "What's on your mind?"

Dad takes a sip of his coffee, not seeming to stall but more as a power play. Against his own son? What the hell is going on?

"Your behavior last night was . . . embarrassing. Honestly, something I'd expect from your brother, not you. The way you treated Sabrina Dunn . . ." He tapers off, tsking under his breath like I'm a disappointing wayward child.

I pick up my toast, taking a bite as I digest his words. I'm not going to be baited into backing down like I used to, because I'm not the little boy he once knew.

I realize with a start that he doesn't know me at all. I've been gone for years, only able to make quick trips home for holidays and the occasional leave. He hasn't been able to bear witness to my growth as an officer, as a man, as a human being with his own wants, needs, and plans. That's going to change.

"I made it abundantly clear to both Mom and you that I had zero interest in being fixed up. I turned down setup after setup as you two tried to get me to meet every debutante you thought met your standards, but you refused to listen. Instead, you kept setting me up and somehow expecting me to sit down like a good little boy and do as I'm told. That's not who I am. That's not who I've been for a very long time now. And I won't let you and Mom box me into something I don't want." I lean back, having said my piece.

"You didn't even give the girl a chance!" Dad complains, and I can hear my mother in his words. I thought she'd been happy watching us dance last night, probably feeling victorious this morning. But I guess not.

Apparently, my shunning a vapid bitch was way more worthy of late-night discussion than Cody's overindulgence. "She's a fine young woman from a good family. She's a good match for you."

"In other words, she's willing to lie back, take enough doses of jizz to get her knocked up two or three times, be arm candy otherwise, and spend money like it's water the rest of the time," I rumble.

I swear I think my father's heart just stopped beating, "You will not use such crude language. It does not befit a Jacobs."

Realizing I might've been a bit crass, even if what I said is true, I take a breath. "I'm not looking for that type of woman, or any woman." Even as I say it, Charlotte's face floats through my mind. "I came home to help our family. That's it. Anything else is on my own, not your concern, and not Mom's either."

"I can't accept that, Son," he argues, shaking his head. "I've spent my whole life taking care of this family, and to be honest, I can't keep doing it by myself. I need you to step up, lean in, and pull your weight so we can keep it going. This isn't the Navy, Son. There isn't a constant line of people who will kiss your ass. This is the real world, and it's a reality I think you've lost touch with."

LAUREN LANDISH

"Out of touch with reality?" I ask, my pride pricked and my anger rising a little. "Dad, I hate to tell you, but I've been learning more in the past ten years than you seem to realize. I was learning what true sacrifice is, what leadership should be. You think I was dicking around, playing cops and robbers or something?"

It's hard to talk about, and my words falter. I don't know if I'll ever be able to tell him how I was learning lessons he'll never understand, lessons engraved in blood, sand, and cordite. And those lessons tell me that his expectation that I'd come home, fall into line, marry the idiot of his choosing, and start popping out babies is not the way to success.

Dad sputters, seeming lost at my words. "I'm not trying to hold you back. I'm trying to help you move forward. I'm sure you did learn a lot in your service, but I know a thing or two myself. Things that I had to learn the hard way, because I found out almost too late that family is everything. I sacrificed too much to the office and missed too many days with you, your mother, and Cody. Lance, I want you to be happy. And everything in my experience, my heart, my gut, tells me you need a wife and kids to do that. Something to ground you when the going gets tough."

I sigh heavily, knowing he's not evil, just a man who's probably getting the first real sense of his own mortality. But I've understood mortality in ways he never has, both by taking lives and having men die in my arms when their lives had barely even started.

"Dad, I'm not saying I'll never get married. I'm just saying let me do it my way. I want someone . . ." I pause, not sure what I want because I've never had to put it into words because marriage always seemed like a far-off, nebulous idea.

"I want a wife who is smart, capable, a partner who is damn well ready to support me but can also pick up the reins and lead herself if something happens to my ass."

I see a handful of women's teary faces flash through my mind.

72

Not every guy I knew in the service was married, but I've been to enough funerals to see the power it takes to be a military wife, always wondering and worrying and one day, getting the call you prayed would never come. But those women, with black clothes and ramrod-straight backs, served their country just as well as their husbands, who made the ultimate sacrifice. I need someone that fierce and fiery.

Dad gets up, his words clipped. "Be that as it may, we have a family dinner with the Dunns next week. Abe, Priscilla, and Sabrina," he says, pointedly looking down his nose at me, well aware that he's leaving Charlotte off that list.

He hasn't said one word about her in this whole tirade, but I can tell just from that look what he thinks of her. "And you will attend, you will be polite, and you will smooth things over with them for your egregious behavior, especially the so-called *dancing* you engaged in with Charlotte."

Without giving me a chance to reply, he brushes past me and goes into the house, already yelling for Hamilton. I watch him go, my fists clenching at my sides.

What the hell just happened?

I told them both I wasn't interested in dating. Honestly, if Dad's so worried about me finding someone, why isn't he excited about me showing interest in Charlotte? I told Dad specifically that I wasn't interested in Sabrina, but he expects me to sit at some family dinner like some sort of an arranged marriage? Fuck that.

I take a step toward the door to chase Dad down and tell him in no uncertain terms that I'm not smoothing things over with anyone, least of all the shallow, gold-digging Priscilla Dunn or her brainless daughter.

But then I remember Charlotte.

And I realize that I don't have to go full-frontal attack on whatever this deal is my parents are planning. It's not like they can force me into liking someone.

Especially when my interest already lies elsewhere. I'm doing things my way, whether anyone else likes it or not.

I smile to myself, decision made. I yank my shirt over my head, kick off my shoes, and execute a perfect dive into the pool. I hold my breath, powering through lap after lap underwater, wanting to keep my skills fresh. But I finally emerge, taking in oxygen carefully as I recover.

To hell with it. I've got plans today. I'm going to track down Charlotte Dunn. And maybe eat a cupcake.

CHAPTER 6

CHARLOTTE

"*C*an I get another dozen of those cupcakes I saw on TV?"

It's a question I've heard time and time again this week, ever since the news showed footage of Thomas and Mia's gala, complete with the *Cake Culture* cupcake tower. As I box up what we're calling the 'Tower Pack' with each of the five flavors from the gala, I shiver as I think of what it all means.

Most bakeries work for years to get this type of promotional notoriety, struggling just to keep the lights on before they're well-established. And that's if you're good. Because no matter how Instagram famous you may be, nothing will make up for crumbly cupcakes and dry pie.

You've gotta have skills, and I'd like to think that I do.

But you've also got to have a bit of luck and good fortune on your side, because the truth is, *everyone* has that grandma or aunt or neighbor who makes the best cake, the most badass cookies, or a mouth-watering pie. And you've got to get them in the door to try yours instead.

So I'm counting my lucky stars that Thomas's bit of magic has proven beneficial, and my culinary skills are exceeding the expectations of the customers. *The new and repeat customers*, I think with a shimmy-shake of my ass in my increasingly tight jeans.

Okay, the saying, 'Never trust a skinny cook,' might end up being true if I don't stop experimenting and sampling my own creations.

The lady eyes the box of goodies as I hand them over, and Trixie whispers from beside me, "That's the third time this week that lady's been in. She's a realtor and is putting your cupcakes out at every open house. Pretty sure she's eating one or two for herself, too, because she told me her favorite was the 'Black As Your Soul' and that's not in the tower box she keeps buying."

I grin, thinking of the prim woman devouring one of my creations, her favorite being a dark chocolate cake with bitter-sweet chocolate frosting infused with coffee. It's rich, dark, and decadent, and one of my favorites too because the coffee, choco-late, and sugar give a pick-me-up like no other. It's practically a Red Bull in a wrapper.

Trixie eyes the woman and then cracks up. "If we keep this up, we'll need to open a Planet Fitness next door. For our customers and ourselves." She pats her own slim ass, with nary a pinch of cupcake-given fluff.

"Oh, hush. If anyone's going to need a few days on the treadmill, it's me," I huff, but I'm not really concerned. I eat healthfully and work hard, and around here, that's workout enough between the cardio I get running back and forth and the strength training I get picking up the heavy trays and pans. Just need to stop sampling the merchandise.

Trixie reads my mind, quipping, "We are working our asses off, and with all the batter we're stirring, our forearms are gonna be as jacked as a fifteen-year-old who just discovered *PornHub*." She flexes, turning her fist one way then the other and showing off her tiny biceps.

"You're such a goof," I tell her, laughing way too hard. Oh, God, I

76

think I just snorted a little. Trixie's eyes go wide with laughter, and I rush to change the subject before she can start calling me a piggy. She wouldn't do that, probably, but I've got trust issues from Priscilla and Sabrina, who would take full advantage of my doing something so uncouth.

"I've been thinking about the Hope Initiative," I say, hoping it's a big enough distraction. Or that another customer will walk in, but we're in the afternoon slump, barely thirty minutes till six o'clock closing time.

"Hate to tell ya, but I think everyone in town's been thinking about it. That's some serious dough, and I say that as an expert in dough and the lack thereof." She starts out silly but ends the statement a bit more seriously than her usual cheekiness as she wipes the counter down.

"You planning anything?" I ask cautiously, wondering if she's open to sharing. I've learned a lot about her in our time working to get the bakery open, but I can tell she holds some things back. I get the sense she's not exactly proud of where she comes from. "Maybe we could work on something together?"

"Kids, maybe? Or old people?" she says aimlessly as we both move to wipe down tables. "Or maybe kids and old people together?"

"Sugar Daddies are kinda gross, and not exactly a community service," I say, hoping to brighten her back up with a joke that sounds more like her than me.

She smiles, but it's weak. "No, like kids visiting nursing homes, talking to the people who don't have family to visit. Or maybe a subsidized preschool at a nursing home, and the old folks can play cars and do puzzles with the kids. Kind of a grandma-on-demand deal."

My brows go up. "Those are great ideas, Trix."

Her smirk is more in line with what I'd expect from her when she teases, "You thought I'd suggest massage parlors for PTSD sufferers, or something equally awful, didn't you? *A happy ending every time* could be the slogan." I bust out laughing, my belly hurting from how crazy she is, which only fuels her fire. "Or what about a scholarship for strippers? You know, they always say they're going to college. We could help them actually go."

"You have such a dirty mind," I say, and honestly, it's a compliment. I love how twisted her sense of humor is and that she gives zero fucks to the appropriateness of the shit that comes out of her mouth. We move to the back, laying pans and mixing bowls in the sink and starting our closing cleanup routine.

She shrugs. "I half-mean that one. Where I grew up, most of the girls I went to high school with ended up working on their backs. Whether that was as a stripper or because they married a guy with a halfway reliable salary, it was the same result either way. Hard to get out of the trailer park when you have no skills other than the ability to spread your legs."

I stop, looking at her. "That's awful."

Her look is sad. "Just the reality. I didn't grow up in Roseboro. I grew up in the panhandle of Oklahoma. Our only claim to fame is that our county touches four other states. We were so far out there that we had to take a forty-five-minute bus ride to Boise City to go to school because picking everyone up with miles between the few bus stops made it take forever. Made for long days, and most kids just dropped out. I mean, why get some fancy diploma when you're going to scrape by, anyway? Nobody who could afford to hire you out there required the piece of paper."

I take a long moment, trying to imagine the type of childhood she's describing. Mine was far from perfect, really far. But at least I always knew I'd have a roof over my head, food on the table, and an opportunity to learn. "I'm so sorry. How'd you end up getting out?"

Her laugh is ironic, and she shrugs. "Because school was my only outlet. It got me out of my house, and I would've ridden that bus

78

twenty-fucking-four-seven if it meant not being at home with my dad. He . . . did his best when I was little, but he was stuck too and took that out on my mom and me as I got older. My desperation actually meant I got good grades, high enough to be valedictorian, which isn't nearly as impressive as it sounds. Being number one in a graduating class of twenty isn't all it's glammed up to be. But it got me a scholarship for an associate's degree in business, and I worked my ass off and got an internship in Seattle. The whole town pitched in to buy my one-way plane ticket."

She smiles like that's a good memory, at least considering the rest of her life story. "That's how I ended up in Roseboro. After the internship ended, I couldn't afford to get back to Oklahoma, and why would I go back there? Seattle's too rich for my blood, so Roseboro it is."

She shrugs like it all makes perfect sense, and in a roundabout way, it kinda does. Maybe it's why we understand each other so well. We come from very different backgrounds, but both of us had to claw our way out of our youth for a better future. And now we both have one.

I make a mental note to give her a raise as soon as I possibly can, though she already carries the Assistant Manager title. Of course, there's just me and her right now, but she deserves the title for all she does.

She seems weary from the heavy share, so I try to give her an out back to our previous conversation. "Still not sure a stripper scholarship is the direction we should go for the Hope Initiative. But maybe something as impactful, education or vocational training to give marginalized people a better tomorrow?"

She nods, dipping her hands into the sinkful of sudsy water. "Let's think on it, maybe come up with a few different ways we could meet that objective."

I can hear the business education coming out, and where before, I'd written it off as no big deal because she sounds like most people I talk to, I can hear just how hard she worked to even the playing field when everyone else had a head start from her humble beginnings.

We get to work, Trixie washing dishes as I mix dough for tomorrow's breads. She's got music blaring, singing along like she's under the spotlight at karaoke night. "Oh, baby, baby . . . how was I supposed to know . . ."

A knock rattles the back door, and we look at each other. I almost go answer it out of habit, but then I remember the rules and pop my head out the front. "Hey, Steven, you expecting anyone? Someone's at the back door and all my deliveries already came."

He's up in a flash, opening the door a small crack with a hard look on his face. He questions whoever's out there but doesn't seem concerned, and then he opens the door wide and I almost drop the big wooden spoon I'm holding like a weapon rather than the mixing utensil it was intended to be.

Lance Jacobs.

He's standing in the back alley behind my bakery, looking good enough to eat. He looks different from before, but no less gorgeous in blue jeans and a white T-shirt, his hair mussed and his scruff glinting in the waning sunlight.

"Hi, the sign out front said you were closed, but I figured you'd still be here." He looks at Steven, a question in his eyes. "Is it okay if I come in?"

I'm still a bit stuck on how hot it suddenly got in here. I need to turn the air conditioner on if Lance is going to come around. My mouth opens and closes but no sound comes out, so Trixie answers for me.

"Hell yes, boy. You can make deliveries to Charlotte's back door anytime."

My eyes widen and my cheeks flush pink, and I know they're splotchy. I'm not one of those girls who blush prettily on the apples of their cheeks. Nope, I'm a ginger through and through, and my blush is more of the mottled feverish variety. But I suspect Trixie knows exactly what she said, and what it sounded like she meant, because she's grinning widely.

I shake my head, waving him in. "Please, come in. Of course."

Lance grins a smile that tells me he was expecting that answer. Cocky.

But that reminds me of his cock, and I blush anew. Lance looks at me like he's reading my mind and liking what he's seeing.

Trixie interrupts the stare fest Lance and I engage in, shoving Steven toward the door. "So, I guess we'll be going if that's all, Boss Lady? Although, these dishes still need to be done. If you want me to stay and wash them all, I can do that?"

She lets the question hang, and Lance picks up what she's putting down. "I can help with the dishes and mop floors, whatever you have on your agenda for the evening."

I shake my head, genuinely confused at why he would want to work with me tonight. I mean, it's not like doing the dishes is sexy or rolling out dough for cookies is fun for most people. Me and Trixie are the weirdos like that. "Why would you do that?"

His shrug communicates the duh even better than his sweet words. "Because then I get to hang out with you."

"Oh, okay, but, uh, no funny business in my kitchen. This is my livelihood." I don't know if I'm reminding myself or him.

"No baby batter in the muffin batter," Trixie sing-songs, and I swear Steven chokes on his own tongue.

"Miss Dunn, if you're in for the evening, I'll clock out and street patrol will remain in place overnight. Mr. Jacobs has already been cleared. Are we good?" Steven says, his voice low and controlled.

I nod, not bothering to look Steven's way so I see the questioning look on Lance's face at the automaton summary, but I'm too far gone, ready for Trixie and Steven to get the fuck out. But maybe that's a bad idea because I'm afraid I'll jump into Lance's arms point-oh-two seconds after the door locks. But still, I nod. "We're good, Steven. Thanks." Distantly, I hear them both leave.

And we're alone.

I half-expect Lance to rush me, pin me against the table, and pick up right where we left off, but he surprises me by coming over slowly. He pushes a wayward curl behind my ear and plants a soft kiss to my lips. He tastes like mint, and I like the idea that he primped a little for me, like his showing up here uninvited and unannounced was as big a deal for him as it is for me.

I don't have guys chase me down. At most, they swipe right, I swipe right, we show up for drinks, maybe dinner, and that's that. Occasionally, we scratch an itch, but it feels like Lance is putting forth effort. For me.

"I missed you," he whispers, the words vibrating against my lips.

I chuckle. "It's been three days and twenty-some-odd years before that. I don't think you can miss someone you only met once."

Shut up, Cynical Charlotte.

But Lance's mouth lifts on the right side like he can read my thoughts, and it makes him look so kissable I'm tempted to lean in for another peck. "Oh? So you're telling me you walked away and haven't given me another thought?"

I shrug noncommittally, inwardly smiling at the first step in this little dance. "Work's been busy. New business owner, you know." But we both hear the lie. I've been thinking of him and he damn well knows it. But I know he's been thinking of me too, so I turn it back around on him before he can call me out on it. "What took you so long to track me down?"

"This." He reaches in his pocket, pulling out something in his hand, and I almost make a joke about having a rocket in his pocket, but I'm glad I held it back because he opens his fist and reveals my bracelet. It's nothing too expensive, just a pretty trinket I bought at the mall years ago on a whim, but the way he's holding it, it could be as precious as a Cartier original.

"It took me a day to find someone to repair it since I don't know the city, and then it took the jeweler two days to fix it. I just picked it up an hour ago and got here as fast as I could."

"Thank you," I stammer, my breath gone at the kindness. He reaches down, lifting my hand in his strong but gentle touch, draping the bracelet over my wrist and attaching the delicate fastener. His touch is electric on my skin, paralyzing me. "Really, it's not that big of a deal, but thank you so much."

"I think it was a rather *big* deal," he says, and I can see the tease at the crinkly corners of his eyes. He's not talking about the bracelet anymore. Well, two can play that game.

"So were you thinking you'd roll in here with my bracelet and I'd be so thankful, I'd just hop on the nearest table and leave butt imprints in the flour?" I ask, aiming for sassy but failing because honestly, it doesn't sound like a half-bad idea. "The health inspector might have an issue with that."

Lance takes a step forward, and I mirror him, moving backward until my ass hits the sink counter. My breath is coming in pants, and I'm scared. Not of him, but maybe of what he could do to me, in a *good* way. A really good way.

"I just felt like we didn't get to finish our conversation, and I wanted to see you again. And now it seems" —he pauses, looking around, and I'm expecting a line about our being alone at last, but he goes another way— "you're in need of a dishwasher. Good thing the Navy taught me how to wash a dish or two."

His smile is charming and silly, the heat still there, but it's underneath the lightness. He reaches behind me, dipping his fingers into the suds Trixie left behind and then blowing the iridescent bubbles off his hand. My dirty mind chants, '*Blow me, blow me, blow me,*' and that's not even really a thing for women, but the need in my veins doesn't seem to give a single fuck because it's racing hot from my head to my toes.

"Well, I guess you could put those muscly arms to good use for something. I do have some dishes that need washing, a floor that needs cleaning, some inventory to put away, and about a dozen things to prep for tomorrow." I wish I were lying. Or that I could just let someone else do the work and disappear upstairs with Lance for some crazy, flour-dusted sex.

But *Cake Culture* is my baby. And I won't half-ass it, even for a piece of ass as hot as Lance Jacobs.

He steps back away from me, and I miss his warmth, even in the heated kitchen. He claps loudly, like the decision's made. "All right, dishes . . . on it. You . . . baking or whatever it is you were doing with that spoon when I came in."

And just like that, we're teammates, working toward a common goal.

The work passes by quickly, with each of us sharing a bit about our families since that's what started this whole thing last night.

He tells me how he's worried for his dad and about his brother but doesn't know what to do about it yet. I tell him how I miss my dad but gave up long ago ever figuring out what he sees in Priscilla. We bond over our mutual distaste for stuck-up, entitled brats like Sabrina. It's a bitchy move, but my assessment of him goes up by four degrees when he imitates Priscilla's 'smelled something bad' face and Sabrina's blank stare spot-on.

We even talk about his time in the military, with the standard 'I'd tell you but I'd have to kill you' punchline.

He doesn't get it when I tell him that he should tell my friend Izzy's guy that joke and see what happens. But I don't explain, just laugh and shrug it off like Gabe's a scary guy. I mean, he is. But only for things that threaten Izzy these days.

I think.

Before I know it, the kitchen is spotless and there's not a single thing I can do to keep him here. At least, not downstairs. I know plenty of things I could do with him upstairs, but I'm not sure that's a good idea.

As amazing as he seems, I have a lot on my plate and so does he. Add in the family shitstorm our dancing caused, and this seems like a recipe for disaster.

I snort at the joke in my own head and Lance tilts his head. "What?"

"I'm just a little punny in my head sometimes. Who knew baking had so many double-entendres and dad jokes tied up in it?" I chuckle, shaking my head.

"Like Trixie's baby batter?" he asks, laughing.

"Oh, God, that's nothing. You should hear her talk about her muffin, her cupcake, her loaves. And the frosting jokes? Enough to make me not want to eat a glazed donut or toaster strudel ever again. Or cream filling. Cream pies. Cherries. It goes on and on . . ." I trail off, lifting a shoulder. "It's a baker thing. You wouldn't understand."

We both bust up in laughter, and the unspoken pressure of 'what now' floats away like the soap bubbles down the drain. "I'd like to see you again," Lance says confidently.

I want to say yes. Every cell in my body, especially the red blood cells singing through my pussy right now, want to say yes. "I can't," I say, forcing my brain, and not my body, to do the talking. "I'm focused on work right now, and it sounds like you are too. But this was . . . nice."

Nice? What the hell, brain? Come up with something a little less blah next time, please?

My brain shoots back, *I'm working on low blood flow here. Give me a break.*

Lance bites his lip like he knows exactly what I mean by nice,

85

and it's not just merely pleasant, for damn sure. "It was nice."

How in the hell he makes the blandest word in the English language sound like sex talk, I'll never know, but I don't analyze it too long because he plants his lips on mine.

He cups my cheek, fingers diving into my hair, and the kiss ignites. Tongues tangle, breath mingles, eyes close. And holy fuck, Lance can kiss. I swear I feel him everywhere, but he's not touching me except for the kiss. I want him to touch me . . . everywhere.

But he pulls back, smacking satisfiedly like a cat who got the cream. *Fuck . . . cream . . . yes, please.*

"Nice," he says simply, and then he moves to the back door. "Lock this behind me, Charlotte. Okay?"

The slam of the heavy door sounds like a death knell. What did I just do? *Come back*, my body cries. *Stay strong*, my brain argues. The battle goes on long enough that I know it wouldn't do me any good to chase after him. He's gone.

I flip the lock and then the lights before heading upstairs. I trace my lips with my fingers, still feeling the lingering burn of his kiss.

CHAPTER 7

LANCE

J think she fully expected me to give up that easily.

Like hell.

I survived a training course that has a ninety-seven-percent attrition rate. I went through a week where I got five hours of sleep *total*. I ran three miles once on a sprained ankle because I had men's lives, and mine, on the line.

So Charlotte's getting a bit of cold feet, when the rest of her is so blatantly hot for me, doesn't scare me off in the least.

It makes it . . . interesting.

I want to see how far she'll push herself to hold back from me, hear more of her silly puns, and learn every single thing about her, from her thoughts on the future of the world to where she's most ticklish. A big spectrum, I know, and that's why I'm guessing it'll take a lifetime to get it all in.

Ha, get it all in. Fuck, she's already rubbing off on me.

I snort. *I wish she'd rub off on me.*

But her thinking she's an easy pass, and that I'd just get on with my life, must be why her eyes grow to dinner plates when she sees me bright and early the next morning.

"What are you doing here? I thought we agreed . . ." she stammers.

My smile is cocky as shit and I know it. "We did agree that things were nice. That's why I figured I would hang out a bit today. Enjoy a nice *muffin* now and a nice *cupcake* later, maybe one with *loads of cream filling*."

I let every filthy thought in my head coat the puns she tossed at me last night. Two can play this game, Charlotte Dunn.

She looks a bit pink, the splotches faint but rising. They're not classic blushing beauty marks, but that makes them even hotter to me. They're authentic. "But don't you have to work?"

"I am working. I don't exactly have a corner office, or any office, really. Been mostly working at a conference room table to get caught up on the business, and I'm thinking that table over there has a much better view," I say, pointing to a round table in the corner. "So, you think maybe I could sample your muffin now?"

Fire lights her eyes, and I await her devilment with hope. This is the sassy spitfire who draws me in even as she tries to burn me down.

She pauses dramatically to get my hopes up intentionally. "Today's special is a cinnamon apple pie combination. The cake is a bit spicy, a bit sweet, with a warm, gooey apple pie filling you want to lick out and savor. I'll let you in on a little secret, too —if you ask *just* right, we'll lay a drizzle of glaze on top or it's good with a big scoop of vanilla ice cream too, just melting into the cake, covering it in sweetness."

Fuuuuuck.

Her words have me rock-hard in my jeans, throbbing stiffer than I've been in days. And it has absolutely nothing to do with food and everything to do with the way her tongue curls and her lips purse as she seduces me, knowing damn well what she's doing and doing it expertly.

She's way better at this than I am.

I swallow, or maybe it's more of a gulp, but I step closer. "Sounds like something I'd love to eat every morning, just to start the day off right with that flavor on my tongue, lips, or running down my chin."

My voice is quiet, husky, and dark, and I can see Charlotte's breath catch. Smooth? No, but it works because it's passionately honest.

"Girl, if you don't run your ass upstairs with that chunk of man right this second, I'm liable to shove you to the ground and take him upstairs myself," Trixie says from way too close.

Shit. Neither of us had noticed that we have an audience now, but Trixie is smirking so much I think her face might crack. The same guy is sitting by the door, and I swear he's fighting a smile too.

For a split second, I can see Charlotte consider doing exactly what Trixie said, but responsibility reigns and with the slightest shake of her head, she steps back. I don't hide that I adjust myself, wanting her to know how much she gets to me and not giving a shit about the rest of the eyes that see.

"I'll just sit over here and work. Don't let me bother you, and I'll take a muffin whenever you've got it ready." It's a promise as much as a breakfast order. I'll wait for her, but I'm not going anywhere.

I sit, opening my laptop and getting to work. The bakery starts to get busy, and before I know it, Trixie and Charlotte are running around like mad.

At one point, Trixie delivers my cinnamon apple pie muffin, whispering that Charlotte didn't trust herself not to sit on my lap and ride me like a pony if she came any closer. My guess is that's Trixie's take on the situation, not Charlotte's actual words, but when I glance up, Charlotte is watching me closely from across the room.

I take full advantage of her attentions, picking up the muffin she made with her own hands and inhaling deeply, savoring the rich smell that I can imagine is the same as what she smells like in her most secret of places before taking a huge bite.

Trixie chuckles from beside me, but it's Charlotte's reaction I'm looking for. I see her shift behind the counter, pressing her thighs together as her mind goes to the exact places that I'm going, distracting her with the fantasy. I give her a wide grin, cheeks stuffed full like a chipmunk, and hold up the muffin in praise.

We all resume our dance, me working on my laptop, Charlotte and Trixie feeding the hordes of people coming through the door, and the security guy holding watch by the door. Steven, she called him, and it makes me wonder what he's doing here.

It's not unusual for people to have security or bodyguards in our level of social circle. Hell, my parents' driver is trained and could safely pull off a movie-worthy car chase scene in a Toyota Corolla. He's that good.

But the Dunns aren't exactly at a level where I'd expect possible threats warranting a full-scale guard worthy of a royal. Thomas Goldstone would warrant that type of treatment in Roseboro, but not many others.

But there sits Steven, discreet enough that he doesn't disrupt business, but it's in his subtle movements that I realize he's well-trained and situationally aware.

It causes me to look around a little more closely. The front windows to the street look a little thicker than I'd expect and with that slight difference in the diffraction of light that makes me suspect they're polycarbonate. If so, that means they're bulletproof, which worries me.

And Steven mentioned street patrol. Whatever other issues may surround the business, someone feels Charlotte deserves 24/7 security, and that worries me even more.

It's an intense amount of coverage for almost anyone, but certainly for a baker, even one as gorgeous as Charlotte. I'll have to ask her about it, make sure she's okay or if there's anything I can do to help if she's not. I've got some skills of my own, and they don't just extend to sucking the filling out of a muffin.

My attention is drawn back to the woman sitting across from me, who's been rambling non-stop since she sat down ten minutes ago. Kelly Washington, she'd said her name was. She's my third seatmate of the day because *Cake Culture* is frantically busy and there's not an empty seat in the house. Even Steven has a table-mate, although he looks like he'd rather share the table with a rabid Rottweiler.

"So, anyway, after I had a single bite of the cookies here, I knew this was my new favorite treat. I told our pastor that he needed to get these cookies for the post-service social every week because if people knew they were getting this kind of goodie, they'd come for the service. He's a great speaker, you see, and more folks need to hear the good word . . ." She continues babbling in one long run-on sentence, and I'm not sure if she's hitting on me or trying to recruit me to her church. I'm hoping the latter because she's probably a few years older than my mom, and I'm not into being anyone's cougar cub.

I let her ramble on, smiling politely but mostly watching Charlotte. She's slammed, or what's busier than that? I don't know the proper food industry slang, but it's what *Cake Culture* is. Charlotte and Trixie are bouncing around like rubber balls, rushing between serving the line and scurrying to get more from the assembly line they've got back there. Every time Charlotte comes out with a fresh tray, people cheer like she's bringing food to the starving, which maybe they are, I guess, because then they descend on her like it's Shark Week, begging to buy each and every morsel.

It's a miracle those two haven't buckled under the pressure, but they both have genuine smiles on their faces, not fake customer service ones, like they're enjoying the madness. And the well-oiled machine they're keeping in motion means that every customer walks away with a treat and a smile on their face.

It's impressive, but I can see the strain. They're running at full capacity, and all it's going to take is one pebble thrown in the works and they're going to have problems.

Charlotte disappears to the back to turn off the beeping alarm of the oven, and Trixie continues helping the swirling line of customers. Suddenly, I hear some grumbles near the front of the line.

"You're buying them *all*?" A man's voice shouts out grumpily. "That's not right, and I promised my kid."

"Too bad, so sad," a woman's voice taunts, not helping matters in the least.

Aaaaand . . . the pebble is tossed.

The glob of people moves a bit, almost the swirl of a mosh pit before things go bad, and I can see Trixie's eyes widen in surprise and a bit of panic. She's losing control, and a crack under pressure for a new business could be the kiss of death.

Not on my watch. I leap into action, standing up and letting out a shrill whistle that can and has stopped entire troops of men.

Everyone freezes, turning to look at me.

"I know these treats are the best thing this side of heaven, but *no one* is fighting over frosting. Understood? If everyone could line back up, you'll be served as quickly as possible. Everything here is delicious, and there's more on the way from the back."

I make my way over to the bakery cases, slipping behind to stand next to Trixie. She starts to protest and then seems to think better of it. "Okay, Commander Cookie, take your shot, but if Char kills you, I'll cover for her and you were *never* here. Wash your hands. You do the boxing and I'll do the register."

I nod, doing as she said and donning the white half-apron she tosses my way. "What can I get you?" I ask the next customer.

I'm on my sixth order in four minutes when the door opens and Charlotte sticks her head out, her eyes going wide when she sees me boxing up a six-pack of red velvet cupcakes along with a French silk pie. But she also notices that the line's now at the register where Trixie's being held up more by the credit card machine than anything else, and she seems agreeable, or at least not murderous.

"Chill yourself out. Go make magic back there," I assure her, giving her a thumbs-up. "We've got this."

The rush lasts another hour, and when Charlotte brings out her third big tray of cookies for the case, she jerks her head toward the back. Saying nothing out front, I follow Charlotte into the back, where she turns on me. "What are you doing?"

"Trixie was drowning, and you were being sucked down at the same time," I explain easily. "You can't say you weren't, and look at this kitchen. That sink's full, and you're going to be here until one in the morning cleaning up at this pace. Then what, up at four to start cranking the next set of cupcakes?"

Charlotte looks over at the mountain of stuff in the sink and sighs, nodding. "I can't have you out front though. You don't have a food handler's license or health certificate or any of that stuff. Health Department comes through here and my ass is grass."

I make a mental note to look into what it would take to get the paperwork she's talking about. It's not that I want to be a baker, or a bakery worker, but I want to spend time with Charlotte and this is where she is. So if being legal to throw some cakes in a box is what it takes, I'll get that piece of paper.

"Fine, for now. I'll just help out by cleaning up back here so you don't have to stay so late tonight," I retort, walking over to the sink. "Unless Roseboro has a dishwasher's certificate?"

She bites her lip like she's going to stop me or maybe like she's going to jump me. I'm okay with one of those options. But eventually, she just shakes her head, chuckling. "Have it your way. Thank you."

She disappears back to the front to help Trixie.

It's weird, but her letting me wash the dishes feels like a victory. I can tell she's not someone who asks for help often, so I feel like she's letting me see behind the curtain a little bit. *Progress*, I think.

For the next hour, I scrub, scour, and rinse plates, silverware, and big baking pans, sending them through the industrial machine just like Charlotte showed me last night. I didn't plan on ever using the teaching session again, but I'm glad to help her if this is what she needs.

Besides, it keeps me distracted from the shit with my family. The hours I spent working this morning helped me get a better handle on things, but I'm basically reviewing the last ten years of Jacobs Bio-Tech.

Before I left, I had no real idea what Dad did. He mostly seemed like a paper pusher and handshaker to me, which is why I wanted out of that gig. I didn't want to be some boardroom suck-up or pampered prince who gets handed the keys while his ass shines an office chair.

I'd wanted adventure, to see the world, to make a difference, and though the bio-technology that my family company creates makes life better for some, it didn't appeal to me. So when it came time for college, I bounced my way across the country.

Florida was where I ended up, and for two years, I was a party guy in a party school. But one day, I saw a Naval ROTC booth, and all that changed. I earned my commission, went straight to the SEALs, and I found a home for a long time.

But now I'm back and woefully out of touch with Jacobs Bio-Tech. I'm remedying that, getting in deep and engaging with everything a decade of Naval professionalism has taught me, but shit, it's so boring and dry. Not that dishes are exciting, but at least they're wet.

I smirk at the pun, thinking that Charlotte would like that one.

Every once in a while, Charlotte makes a trip back to start another round of baking. As I work, I can feel her eyes on me, and I watch her too, entranced by the way the sweat-darkened hair at the nape of her neck clings to her skin and the way her muscles flex as she lifts a heavy bowl of cake batter to pour it into the floured pan.

It feels like we're dancing again, but instead of being body to body with only the thin layers of fabric between us, we've got space and stainless steel. And instead of pulsing music, we've got humming machinery. It's a seductive tango, and I can see that she's as affected as I am.

It's almost closing time, and I'm betting Charlotte is ready for a repeat of last night, maybe an extended version where we head upstairs after all her prep work is complete. It's tempting, so very tempting.

But I don't want her to think I'm only helping to get in her pants. Oh, I want in her pants for sure, but I want more than that too.

So I take a look around and do as much as I can to get her set up for the work she needs to do tonight—a stack of mixing bowls ready on the prep table, a set of spoons and spatulas nearby, the ovens preheated, and I order dinner to be delivered for her, Trixie, and Steven in two hours.

I step back out front, pleased to see near-empty cases, tables full of happy cake eaters, and a smiling Charlotte. I step behind the counter, close enough to put my hand on her lower back where no one can see, but Trixie notices and suddenly becomes very invested in cleaning on the other side of the room.

"You are amazing," I tell her honestly, murmuring into her ear so I can smell the sweetness that surrounds her.

She smiles even bigger, and I love that as happy as she is about her fledgling business, she's happy to see me too. "You're pretty awesome yourself." She shoulder checks me, flirting.

"The kitchen is spotless, I've got you all set up for your work after you close, and dinner will be here shortly." I press a soft kiss to her temple, not quite goodbye, but she senses that I'm leaving.

"You're not going to stay and help me tonight?" she asks, and her cheeks get splotchy as she realizes that she's admitting she likes me being around. "I mean, not that I expected you to just suddenly become my helper, but last night . . ."

I lower my lips to her ear so that only she can hear, my words a silky caress of her ivory shell. "Last night was so nice I stayed up for almost an hour when I got home replaying every minute of it in my mind and jacking off to thoughts of you bent over your prep table."

I hear her intake of breath and I continue, "So tonight, do what you need to do as quickly as you can, and then . . ."

It takes every bit of restraint I've got to give her the order she needs, not the one I want. "And then go to bed because I'm hoping you were up a little extra-late last night too. You're running yourself ragged, and I won't be the cause of your burning out too soon. I've got a vested interest in making sure you keep baking."

Her eyebrows lift, and she glances over her shoulder. "To make me happy?"

Hope and romanticism are woven through the words, but I can't help but lob the ball she setup so perfectly. "To keep my belly happy. I'll be back in the morning for breakfast. I'll expect my table to be available and the muffin of the day to be hot and ready for me."

My voice is barely a rumble, a promise only she can hear.

Laughter flashes in her eyes, and she turns to face me squarely.

"You are smoother than buttercream frosting, aren't you? I think you could read the phone book and make it sound like the dirtiest of bedroom talk."

I lean down until my lips are a fraction of an inch from her ear again, whispering, "Aaron Abernathy, Allison Ackard, Amber Ada, uhm . . . that's all the *A* names I can think of. I'm much better when I get to the *O*s, though."

She doesn't laugh, instead sighing blissfully. "I think I just want you to say my name."

"Trust me, I did. Every time I've come since the gala, I've had your name on my lips. Sweet dreams, Charlotte."

I want to kiss her fully on the lips, not giving a single fuck about the room full of people or that this is her place of business. I want to publicly claim her even though we're still doing this dance around each other. Let every single person in here know that I'm the lucky fucker who gets to frost her cookie and fill her Twinkie.

But I don't. This is her place, and I want to show her that I respect her as not just a woman, but as the baker and businessperson I know she is. So I can't . . . not in front of her customers.

Fuck. I've got to get out of here or my attempt at being the good guy is going to fail miserably because I'm at the end of my rope, about to drag her upstairs to fuck her right now. I'm not a total shit. I'd feed and listen to her talk about anything she wants to talk about for hours after, but we'd definitely end up fucking all night. I can feel it in the sparks floating between us.

"I'll see you in the morning, beautiful."

Grabbing my laptop and bag, I make a beeline for the door. Steven gives me a smirk, recognizing the gait of a man trying to walk with a boner hanging thick between his legs. Fucker. He gets to stay, but at least he doesn't seem interested in Charlotte at all beyond his job. Again, I meant to ask her what that's all about.

Tomorrow, maybe?

CHAPTER 8

CHARLOTTE

"*How* do I look, Trix?" I ask, coming down the back stairs into the bakery.

"Dayum, girl, you look good enough to eat!" she says, biting at the air. "You sure you don't want me to make myself scarce today? I think you and Lance could handle everything just fine without me."

Today's technically my day off, or at least the one day *Cake Culture* is closed. With just me and Trixie working here, we need Wednesdays to bake all day and prep for the weekend's special orders. Today, we're making a huge multi-tiered cake for the Fredricks wedding, a monstrosity that could take more than a day to finish.

At least we don't have any custom birthday cakes on the schedule for the day too. I try not to worry about that because the wedding order is big enough to float my custom cakes budget for the month.

I shake my head, feeling my bouncy ponytail brush my shoulders. Reaching up, I adjust the white scarf tied around the elastic, which I maybe chose because I know it pops against my red hair, something I consider my best feature. "No, please. You have to stay. That's like a direct order. If you leave me here alone with him, nothing will get done but *me*."

I hate to say that, but it's the God's honest truth.

Lance has spent the last the three days coming in like clockwork. I swear, yesterday, Trix yelled out 'Lance' like he was Norm coming into his favorite bar. He works at the table in the corner, staring sexily at the computer screen and eating my muffins. Sadly, an actual muffin, not the one I'm getting desperate for him to dive into.

But when we get extra-busy, he'll pitch in and help. And he's got the back cleaned and set up for me every day. But before I can do much more than say thanks, he leaves, and it's driving me nuts.

I'm so horny I actually proposed a new cupcake called 'Nutz for Nutz' to Trixie, totally oblivious or maybe wanting the double-entendre of the almond cupcake with butter cream frosting covered in almond slivers. Thankfully, she'd advised that maybe I wait and see if I still think that's a good idea after I get laid.

Unfortunately, no laying has happened here. He kisses me when we're in the kitchen, hidden behind the big double doors, and I damn sure kiss him back, but that's as far as things have gone and I'm about ready to make a move myself. And today is going to be hard to hold myself back because he said he'd come and help me all day.

Seriously, there is nothing sexier than a man cooking, except maybe a man who cooks because he's doing it for you.

I turn around, looking at myself in the convex security mirror over the register. I check my lip gloss, and Trixie sighs.

"Not sure I understand why that's a bad thing. Girl, get you some while the getting's good."

"I know, but I've done the dreaming of Mr. Right and settling for Mr. Right Now. I feel like I need to be focusing on the bakery now, not out gallivanting around with some guy."

She rolls her eyes and turns back to me. "I don't know if you've caught on to this, but that boy is plum crazy for you. Hey, wait . . . write that down for a fall flavor. Plum Crazy. I'm thinking muffins, maybe streusel-topped or sugared? No, with ginger."

She taps her head, like she's a slightly demented genius or something. "What was I saying again? Oh, yeah. Lance is gone for you. He's just slow rolling because you're scared and he's respecting that. I don't know if that makes him your Prince Charming or some shit, but it'd definitely make for some good times away from the stress of the bakery. All work and no play makes Charlotte run out of batteries faster than an industrial mixer."

I laugh. She's gone too far with that one. "The mixer is plugged into the wall. Actually, so's my favorite friend."

Trixie's jaw drops so far she gets a double chin that she doesn't actually have. "Your vibe plugs into the wall? Hell, how much horsepower that thing get? Giddy fucking up and yeehaw!"

Thankfully, she doesn't say anything else because there's a knock at the back door. "Who is it?" I say, pointing a warning finger at Trixie, who blinks at me with a look of pure innocence on her face that's about as authentic as a Hostess cupcake.

"Lance Jacobs, reporting for duty, ma'am." I hear him report, military-style, through the thick metal door.

I won't say that his official, powerful-sounding voice has no effect on me because that'd be a bald-faced lie.

I open the door and Lance steps inside. He's got on a T-shirt and jeans, both of which hug his muscles deliciously. I'm not usually a biceps girl, but something about the way the sleeves are straining over his tan, toned bulges makes me want to bite them. And then he turns, setting a bag down on the table, and I change my mind. *Mmm, dat ass.* I want to bite the apple of his ass.

"Sorry I'm late," he says, and then he looks at me, totally catching me eyeing him. His eyes light up, one brow raised like he's saying *busted* without a word. But when I bite my lip, his eyes darken.

Trixie clears her throat, not ashamed at all. "Uhm, not to interrupt the eye sex you two are in the middle of, but that bag has a bow. Is it a present? I love presents, but it's probably for Charlotte, right? That's okay. I like to watch other people get presents too. Open it!"

His grin blooms like the sun popping out from behind a cloud on a summer day. "It is a present. One for everyone, actually."

Trixie jumps and down like a little kid, clapping, and I remember what she told me about her childhood and I'm guessing she probably didn't get many presents.

"Go ahead, Trixie. You can open it," I tell her, and she doesn't have to be told twice, grabbing the bag from the table and tossing the tissue paper into the air.

She pulls out an apron, then another, then a third. Each one has the *Cake Culture* logo on the front, each in a slightly different shade of pink.

She spreads them out and then hands me the darkest one, and I see it says, *Sweet Scarlet* on it below my name. She holds hers up to her chest, and I see the pink embroidery emblazoned says, *Not for Kids*. The joke is good, and very apt. Trix aren't for kids, and neither is Trixie.

The last one, she holds up and then laughs hard. It has Lance's name and below reads, *Commander Cookie*, making Trixie laugh. I look from her to Lance, missing something.

Trixie explains, "When he stepped up to help, I called him Commander Cookie and told him not to mess anything up."

He laughs too, taking the apron from Trixie but pointing out, "Actually, she said that if you killed me, she would be your alibi. It was appropriately, threateningly protective."

I slip the apron over my head, tying the strings around my waist.

"This is very sweet. Thank you." I press a friendly kiss to his cheek, but my face flames anyway. "Okay, we've got work to do, troops. We'd better get to it, or this wedding cake might be my first and last."

There's no argument, just a feeling of unity as Trixie and Lance tie their aprons on and we get to work, using the forty-quart industrial mixer to draw the batter together. The only hard part is that since the bride wants a white-white cake, we can't use any yolks at all, and just to be extra-sure, I'm using a very special type of butter as well that is almost white too.

I've tried using other methods, including one recipe that had me using coconut oil, or one that used lard, of all things, and while they did make a whiter cake . . . frankly, lard cake is something that *nobody* should eat.

"Okay, so the plan's for two hundred servings," I relay, "and the couple wants a really big bottom layer, so we're going to do two twelve-inch rounds on the bottom, then a ten, eight, and six. They've got their own porcelain topper, so we just need to have a smooth surface with ruffled edges up there to prep the top."

"Two hundred servings?" Trixie asks. "There's no way they've got two hundred guests coming to their wedding, right? I mean, that seems like a lot. I don't even know two hundred people!"

I spray down another one of our cake rounds. "I don't care if they have ten people show up. If they order a huge cake, they get a huge cake."

Lance looks into the mixer, watching the dry ingredients blend. "Biggest wedding I've been to was five hundred guests, give or take."

Trixie and I look at each other, whispering simultaneously, "Holy shit."

"Can you imagine how big that cake was?" I ask Trixie, who shakes her head. Hell, the payment on that would probably float me for months. Raising my voice, I look up at Lance. "Who was it?"

"Navy wedding. They met on board the *Reagan*, so they invited a ton of the crew. It was nothing like this cake though. Just a normal wedding cake and a ton of sheet cake."

The timer dings, and I go over to the mixer, shutting it off. I fill the cake pans with the white liquid, praying my hardest that Trixie doesn't make any cum jokes right now. But when I glance over, she's looking back and forth from Lance to me, missing the opportunity.

She fills two of the smaller rounds while I get the big twelve-incher, and then we get the spring forms into the preheated and waiting oven.

"Next, let me show you how to make buttercream because we do it in small batches," I explain to Lance once the timer's set. I take two pounds of butter and hand him the big chef's knife. "First, cut this into chunks about an inch wide. Don't worry if it's not perfect."

Across the room, Trixie hums tunelessly, a bit of an upgrade from her usual 90s hits redux, and then says, "Tell us about you, Lance."

It sounds like she's interviewing him for something, but I'm interested to hear his answer. He told me the basics already, but I'm hungry for more.

He keeps cutting butter but answers, "I was born in California. That's where my family's company used to be headquartered. It was Jacobs Pharmaceutical then. Went to Florida, graduated, went military, much to their absolute *not*-delight, worked my ass off and got my MBA degree while I served, and became a SEAL. Along the way, I got to travel, see the world, in both good and bad ways, and basically grew up. Now, I'm home, seeing if my next step in life is with Bio-Tech."

"Why'd they change names?" I ask, taking the butter cubes and putting them into the smaller mixer.

"When my dad realized that pharmaceuticals is a crapshoot and bio-tech is *the wave of the future,*" Lance says like he's heard the phrase from someone else, maybe his dad. His accompanying shrug tells me there's more the story, or to his feelings about the change. He doesn't say anything, though, as he finishes the last of the butter, handing me the cubed-up pieces on the cutting board. "Okay, now what?"

I drop them in slowly, watching it swirl for a moment. "Add three droppersful of this vanilla extract," I say, watching him do as I instruct. "Then we'll slowly add powdered sugar. For each batch, we're going to use about four cups, but it's more art than science so we go by texture. We're looking for fluffy peaks. Think Bob Ross, happy little clouds."

Lance watches, his eyes intensely taking in what I'm doing, and minutes later, I add my secret ingredient, organic cream for the richest, smoothest texture possible. A pinch of salt for balance and the first batch is done. "Okay, now we scrape all this into a big container for storage and repeat for the next batch, and the next, until we've got all we need. Got it?"

He nods and opens the refrigerator, grabbing more butter. I like that he's a fast learner, confident but willing to be taught.

"How about you two? What led to baked goods heaven?" he asks as he starts cutting again.

Trixie goes first as she pulls the first batch of smaller cakes out of the ovens for testing. "My high school was tiny, very few options for classes, especially back then. I could take keyboarding, which I already knew how to do, or home ec, where you got to eat what you made. It was pretty much a no-brainer, especially since cooking days usually meant I got more to eat in one meal than I usually got to eat in a day."

She pauses, checking off our progress on the job board on the wall, thankfully not seeing Lance and me lock eyes, the sad realization of just how fortunate our privileged upbringing was. I certainly never went hungry and I sincerely doubt Lance did either.

"Turned out I was pretty good at it, so when I was out here and my business internship ended, an assistant manager gig sounded pretty sweet. The business of baking, if you will." She looks back and smiles at me, and I feel warmth flow through my heart. I'm so glad we found each other.

"Your turn," she says, like she wants the focus off her.

"My grandmother," I tell Lance, then explain. "She's how I found baking. When my mom died, my Dad was lost a bit. I don't remember much. I was little. But I was excited when he married Priscilla. I didn't know her well, but I thought having a sister would be like a sleepover every night. But . . . well, you've met them."

Trixie and Lance both scowl, nodding. Lance gets the butter whipping, and I stand back, watching him work as I talk.

"So Dad would send me off to my grandmother's at least one or two weekends a month and quite a bit of time each summer. I always thought it was because he knew how awful they were to me, but looking back, I think he was just keeping my connection with my mom's family strong. And Grandma Winnie took full advantage of our time together. She taught me everything she knew, from gardening and canning to baking and sewing. Though the sewing didn't stick. I always bled all over everything because I couldn't get the hang of the needle." It wasn't that I couldn't push the needle, but I was the kind of person who always, somehow, would push it through into a waiting finger on the other side, no matter what I did.

I smile, remembering her patiently helping me, her wrinkly hands over my small ones so I could cut things safely in her kitchen that always smelled of pine cleaner and baking bread.

"I went to college here in Roseboro, worked at Blackwell for a while, but it was basically hell, so when Thomas offered to help me get started on my dream, I jumped at the chance. And here we are."

Highly edited, but I'm not sure if Lance is ready for the deeper story. Hell, even Trixie doesn't know much more than the surface. Meanwhile, Lance has his butter just right.

"Okay, ready for the powdered sugar," I say, looking into the mixing bowl of the second batch. "Nice fluffy peaks."

Trixie goes into the supply closet and then comes out with a look of horror, rambling fast. "Oh, no, sorry, Boss. We're out somehow. I'll tell you what . . . I'll run over to the mega warehouse store over by the highway and get a big bag or two, and grab the rest of the things on the shopping list. I'll be back before you know it." She pauses. "Or in about an hour."

She emphasizes the time and then is gone in a flash.

Lance and I look at each other, and then we both laugh. He wipes his eyes, turning off the mixer after he's done. "That was some awful acting on her part. She could've just said, 'Hey, I'll leave you two alone,' and then bounced."

I shake my head, knowing exactly what she pulled. "No, she couldn't, because I full-on Boss ordered her to stay today so she had to come up with an excuse. And I know it's an excuse because we order out supplies from a delivery service, and we just got restocked yesterday. Even the warehouses don't carry fifty-pound industrial bags of sugar." I point to the bottom shelf of the rack where we prepped all the things we'd need for today's work. "See?"

Lance sobers, his face looking a little guarded for once. "You didn't want to be alone with me? I can leave if you want." He wipes his hands on his apron, stepping away from me.

I blurt out unceremoniously, going by gut instinct, "I didn't want to be alone with you because I'm about to drag you upstairs and fuck you six ways 'till Sunday. And I'm doing everything I can to *not* do that. I purposefully didn't shave my legs, I have on my worst granny panties, and I was hoping for a chaperone. Because I have to finish this cake today. It's a big deal. A really big one. So I need you to man up here and *not* fuck me, okay?"

I slap my hands over my mouth, stopping the word confetti. I can feel the heat on my face, and I mostly want to sink into a big puddle on the floor.

Lance's guarded look turns cocky and then serious again. "You really know how to take a guy on a roller coaster, don't you? I literally just went from 'mayday, mayday' to 'fuck, yeah' to 'Responsibility Rick' in one monologue. I'm going to do my absolute best to focus on the last part of that and not the image of you in high-waisted cotton briefs because right now, that sounds damn near as sexy as a thong. Fuck, do you wear thongs?"

His eyes trace down my body, focusing tightly at the apex of my thighs, and he shakes his head. "Wait. Don't answer that. Do not answer that right now." He adjusts himself and takes a big breath, like he's shielding himself for battle. Against both our urges. "Tell me what's next. With the baking, with the cakes. Please, talk about cakes."

I remember how much he liked when I talked about the muffins, but I don't think either of us could stand the tease right now, so I keep it professional. Well, as professional as I can when I can feel my nipples pebbled up beneath the apron he gave me and my panties getting wetter with every step.

The first round of cakes is cooled, the frosting is ready, and oh, this is going to be bad. "The next step is dirty frosting," I say, the colloquial term sounding more sexual than it ever has before.

He groans, looking to the ceiling. "Are you shitting me, Char? Dirty frosting? Are you trying to drive me insane?"

His voice is a rumble that I can feel even from five feet away.

Shrugging apologetically, I shake my head. "That's really what it's called. Let me show you."

He moves closer, coming to stand next to me, but I can hear him muttering, "Yeah, show me your dirty frosting. Why the hell not?"

I can't help but grin a bit. "I swear, I'm not trying to poorly seduce you. I really do need to finish the cake. Dirty icing is a sort of glue that holds the cake layers together, and to get the right shape for the decorative work that I'll do later. We've got to get the bottom layers down, like the foundation of a building, and then the other layers will sit safely on top." The drier explanation helps tamp things down a half-notch, thankfully, and we get to work.

But even though a twelve-inch round is a giant piece of cake, it's not a lot of space to work, and Lance and I are forced tight together. Time after time, his arm brushes up against mine as we undo the latches on the springform pans and take the cakes out.

"Okay, now lift carefully. We don't want to crack the layers."

I feel a slight pressure against my left breast and realize that Lance's muscled forearm is touching it as he carefully rotates the ring of the pan like I showed him. It's side boob, but my nipple doesn't seem to mind because it perks right up, sending a thrill through me. His eyes are focused on the cake, but my attention is totally on what he's doing to my body.

"How's that?" Lance asks, his eyes cutting to me, and he realizes where his arm is. "I . . . I'm not going to apologize for that."

"I wouldn't want you to," I murmur, taking a shaky step back. "Okay, what we need to do next is get the bottom layer. It's going to be our base."

I get the flat cake knife, and we transfer the cake to the frosting turntable, aware every moment of Lance's eyes on me. Still, we work together well, and I have to grin as I grab the bowl of buttercream. "Okay, now the part that'll get you all hot and bothered . . ." I say, not sultry because we're already too close to the fire, but playful and teasing. "Playing with my cream—I mean, the buttercream."

He rolls his eyes, but I can see the dirty thoughts behind his baby blues that are darkening fast even as he tries to keep focused. "So, what's first?"

"First, let's get a big dollop in the middle, and we'll use this cake knife to spread it out. Don't manhandle it, but don't be too gentle, either."

"A little roughness is okay. Got it," he deadpans, but I swear it just got hotter in here.

My voice is a bit shaky, but I power on, flipping one cake as I attach the two layers. "Always try to keep a flat surface up, other than your bottom layer," I hint. "It makes decorating and frosting easier. The light domes in the cakes will be filled with the dirty frosting like a wall spackle."

I show Lance what to do, and after a quarter of the cake, he takes over, carefully using the turntable to get the sides smoothed out. "Well?"

"Not bad," I admit, stepping in and checking carefully. "I might just feel better about this afternoon now."

"What's this afternoon?" Lance asks. "More of this?"

"I wish. No, I'm gonna leave most of this in Trix's hands to get the first pass done. She'll get the fondant on the bottom layer as well. But I've got a meeting today . . . with my father. My presence has been requested."

Lance clucks his tongue, humming. "You don't sound happy about that."

"I'm not," I admit. "I've been basically summoned. I'm sure it's about the charity ball. I figure I'll get my ass chewed out for the way I behaved with you. I'd bet the entire fee for this cake that

Sabrina whined to Priscilla, who then whined to Dad, and now it's up to him to reinforce the threats."

"Threats?" Lance asks, instantly on guard, and I can see the warrior in him stiffen at the word. I half-wish I could take him with me tonight and let Dad try to bully me into leaving Lance to Sabrina with him standing right there.

I tell him about Sabrina stopping by the bakery, and he laughs. "So I'm just a slab of beef with a wallet, that about right?"

"And social standing, don't forget that," I add, knowing that climbing the social ladder is just as important a factor for my stepmother and stepsister.

"I get it," he says quietly, his hands reaching out and pulling me close. "Your stepmother is playing matchmaker and my mom is playing matchmaker. They think they've got it all figured out. But they forgot one important detail. The biggest one, actually. I make my own choices, and I'm already interested in a woman."

"And who might that be?" I ask coyly, the beatdown little girl inside me wanting to hear him say that he's picking me over Sabrina. It's stupid and a bit broken, but when it was between the two of us, there was never a question. Sabrina got everything, and I dealt with whatever scraps were tossed my way.

But Lance is not scraps, not by a mile.

He draws me in, his hand cupping my cheek and his lips so close to mine I can feel our bodies pressing together again. "Here's a hint . . . if I were going to choose Sabrina, I'd be wearing a suit and tie and be in an office at Jacobs Bio-Tech, not in the back of a bakery looking at the most charming streak of frosting on the tip of your nose and wondering what it would taste like to lick it off your skin."

Our lips are barely an inch apart, and I want him so badly, it's me who starts to close the distance when suddenly, I hear the sharp sound of a tailgate being dropped open and a second later, Trixie comes in the back door. "Whoo . . . sorry, should I come back later?"

"Crap!" I growl, slapping Lance's chest to hide my embarrassment, "You weren't supposed to frost my nose, you clumsy oaf!" My acting skills are even worse than Trixie's, though, and no one is fooled, least of all Trixie.

"Hmph, frosting her face already?" Trixie teases, her eyes twinkling, and I blush even deeper. "Kinky."

"A gentleman never tells," he quips, wiping my nose with a paper towel.

"Well, does a gentleman help a lady unload heavy bags of sugar we don't even need after she gave you a solid hour and a half of alone time?"

I knew she was making shit up to bail on me and leave us alone, but a glance at the clock sends a jolt through my system. She's right. It has been a while and I'm behind schedule now.

I can't let this cake get away from me or I'll be up all night decorating it. Lance presses a soft kiss to my cheek, but I'm already head-down in work mode.

CHAPTER 9

LANCE

I brush my hands off on my apron and follow Trixie out to her truck, parked in the side alley by the bakery. She grabs a cardboard box of supplies and motions for me to take another.

"Seriously, I left you alone with her for that long and you were *just now* making a move? What is this, amateur hour? I figured you military types would be all '*target acquired*' and dive right in. Charlotte needs a good fucking, for damn sure," Trixie says, needling me.

I grin at her bluntness and heft a bag onto my shoulder. "Me too, but I want more, and I respect that she's got other priorities right now. Besides, target acquired is some tanker shit, not SEAL."

Trixie's brows furrow, and she side-eyes me through slits so narrow you can't even see the color of her eyes. "You one of those romantic gentlemanly types?" I don't answer, not willing to open the curtain around my heart to just anyone, and she hums, like she's trying to decide. "Hell, maybe I need to up my estimation. I was just happy for her to get a little sumpthin'-sumpthin' and for a warm body to help with the busy times."

It's a friend evaluation if ever I've heard one. She might as well have asked me my intentions with Charlotte. But I'm a man of action, not words. At least not words with Trixie. I'll save whatever sweet talk I have for Charlotte herself. So I heft the bag a little higher and make a move toward the door, giving Trixie a wink instead of an answer. She smirks in return like she's got my number, loud and clear.

Back inside, Charlotte has turned into a drill sergeant. "Trix, honey, we've gotta get our asses in gear. I need these dirty-frosted, refrigerated, and ready for frosting ay-sap." Every word is sharp and crisp, and I have to smile. I know that tone.

"On it, Boss," Trixie replies, haphazardly saluting and clicking her heels together.

"I'll get the rest of the supplies while you two get to work."

It seems playtime is over for us all. Outside, I grab a bag of flour, slinging it over my shoulder and carrying it inside. Charlotte looks up, a grateful look on her face, and she jerks her chin toward the supply closet. I nod and put the big bag on top of the stack of three others. Charlotte was right. They had plenty of supplies.

I head back out for another load and the blistering sun glints off a window across the street, grabbing my attention. There's a big, black Suburban sitting at the curb, angled just right to keep watch on the bakery.

I remember that Steven's not here, so this must be the overnight or off-day guard. Questions I've been squashing down float back to the surface.

I walk across the street, holding my hands out at my side to show I'm no threat. Well, I'm still a threat, but I'm unarmed, at least. And I'd bet my right hand the guys in the SUV are packing, so I err on the side of caution, hoping I don't get shot in the street based on a misunderstanding.

The window rolls down with a smooth whir. "Good day, Commander Jacobs. Can I help you?"

The guy knows who I am. Not sure if I think that's invasive or thorough. But I can see that they're professionals, though they're in jeans and generic black polos.

"Who are you? Name, rank, serial number?" I deadpan, well aware that the Geneva Convention doesn't hold sway here.

"Need to know only, sir," the driver says, putting his forearm on the window sill purposefully, and I see the trident tattoo he's flashing me. "No offense."

"None taken," I reply, nodding my chin toward him. "What Team?" It's the question he wants me to ask, and an answer will at least give me something to go on.

"Four," he says with a smirk.

"Did you like San Diego?" I ask, and he laughs. It's an easy check for 'fake' SEALs. The even-numbered teams are in Virginia.

He shakes his head, his grin growing. "The East Coast is beautiful this time of year. You ever been?"

"Nah, Team Three. I fucking loved San Diego."

It's not a perfect check. There's enough information on the internet that people can fake being a SEAL halfway decently, but it's a start and lets me know what kind of guys I'm working with here.

"Can you give me anything? Charlotte doesn't quite seem the type to warrant the royal treatment." Well, at least not with security. I could give her a damn fine pampering like a princess.

The driver looks to the passenger, who shrugs. At least I know who the high rank is of the two now, and my hard look returns to the driver, who's clenching his teeth like he wants to say more, but he barely gives me a crumb.

"It's a security gig, sir. For Miss Dunn's protection. That's all I can say."

The look in his eyes says that's all I'm going to get. But I try once more, laying my cards on the table, so to speak.

"I'm here daily, along with Steven. And inside, when he's gone in the evenings sometimes, hopefully more often, if she'll have me." I glance over my shoulder at the pink and white awnings, the glass letting me see into the dining area of the bakery, but my eyes track to the covered windows upstairs, hoping that we'll eventually get to that point. "If there's anything going down, I can be a resource. I'll protect her. Even if you can't tell me what's going on, can you tell me if I should be armed?"

The driver presses his lips together. "If you'd like. Won't be needed though. We'll do our job."

I nod, offering him a handshake and then reaching across to shake the passenger's hand as well. I walk back across the street, feeling their eyes on my back as I grab the last bag and take it inside.

I've got no more answers than I had before. In fact, I might have even more questions.

CHAPTER 10

CHARLOTTE

W *hat in the hell am I doing?*

I ask myself the question repeatedly on the drive over. I wish the drive were longer so that I could put this off as long as possible, but on the other hand, it might be better to get it over with. Either way, the thirty-minute drive to Dad's house goes by before I know it.

I say 'Dad's house' but really, I mean Priscilla's house. She's the one who picked it out, who 'convinced' Dad that it was just the house to have even if it was too much money for our family, and who decorated every room.

Still, I grew up here for so many years, I even have a room on the far end of the hall on the second floor, overlooking the front yard. Not the gorgeous garden in the back yard, of course. Sabrina got that one because it had the view and the bigger closet.

But this house has never been home to me.

Once upon a time, I'd hoped that Dad would come to his senses and see what a bitch Priscilla is and how shitty Sabrina treats me.

But he was always so busy with his work, mostly to pay for Priscilla's lifestyle. So before too long, the pecking order was established. Priscilla was the queen of the household, Sabrina the pampered princess, and I ranked somewhere . . . lower.

I feel like in a lot of ways, Dad just didn't know what to do with a daughter. The little time we had, just the two of us, certainly was more tomboyish than anything else. So he left me to my own devices with Priscilla, hoping for and only seeing the best.

To her credit, Priscilla was good. I can see that now in hindsight. Her criticisms were always couched in way to make it seem like she was helping me . . .

"Oh, dear, your hair is so unfortunate. Those curls are just as unruly as you are, poor girl. Let me fix it."

And then she'd yank and pull, ripping my hair from the root and scraping my scalp with the cheap plastic brush she kept just for me, until it was smoothed into a bun so tight it gave me headaches. She'd spray it with hairspray, making sure to get it in my eyes so they burned and watered. I learned not to jump or cry out because then she'd slap her hand on my shoulder, her nails digging in as she ordered me, *"Sit still and quit squawking like a crybaby."*

Dad never seemed to notice, the few times he was around. If anything, he'd simply smile and tell me my hair looked nice when Priscilla prompted him, proving once again that she had him fooled. Or he'd say that he was glad I was growing up into a young lady, like jeans and T-shirts were somehow the devil's garments.

Over the years, Sabrina couldn't help but learn at her mother's side. Her snide remarks and blatant role as the favorite made me an unwanted guest in my own home.

I pull into the driveway, looking at the house. It's not the nice, comfortable family home I'd lived in when my mom was still alive so long ago, though I only remember it from looking at pictures so many times.

Then, Dad was a man who made a six-figure salary and lived a five-figure lifestyle. Now, he's worked his way to a seven-figure paycheck but lives like it's eight.

This monster of a house is one sign of that, pretty unless you grew up here. Six bedrooms and seven baths, a pool out back surrounded by flowers and statues. The brand-new BMW sitting out front is another sign of Dad's indulgences, this year's model because Priscilla gets a new one every year on her birthday. Black every time, just like her soul.

Sighing, I get out of my car, the very sensible eight-year-old Volkswagen that Dad got me as a high school graduation gift. It's been a damn good car, and I have zero need for anything newer, and Dad quit offering when I refused after college. With Priscilla taking advantage of his money, I refuse to do the same.

I ring the bell and a second later, it opens. Dad looks like he's just come home from work, which is likely the case. His suit and tie are still pristine, though I'm sure he's spent the day at the office. "Charlotte, come in."

Uh-oh, the Disappointed Dad routine has already begun.

I close the door behind me, following him into the living room and sitting down like he does. I look around at the latest décor. It's straight out of *ELLE Décor*, probably last month's issue, so it must be Priscilla's latest update.

The chair beneath me is uncomfortable, but even worse is the discomfort between me and the man I still hold out hope for. Hope that he'll hug me, apologize for the suffering I've been put through, and hand me a Mr. Pibb once again.

Instead, he draws out the moment until I start fidgeting. "Where are Priscilla and Sabrina?" It's a rookie question, and I know it'll only highlight the gaping distance between Dad and me, but the desire to know if I'm going to get taken out from behind is hard to resist.

"Out. I wanted this to be just us." Like the silly little girl I still am inside, that hope starts to blossom. But it's quickly squashed when he looks at me harshly. "How could you do that to your sister?"

"Sabrina isn't my sister, just like Priscilla isn't my mother. We've had this conversation," I say, disappointment making me roll my eyes. I'm sure to him I seem petulant and immature, but really, it's a conglomeration of frustration over the fact that he never sees the truth.

"We have. So let's have a different one." His tone is distant, professional, as if I'm an employee in his company, not his daughter. "Priscilla has worked very hard to cultivate a relationship with the Jacobses. And to present Sabrina as a good match for Lance Jacobs. I am embarrassed that you would interfere, slotting yourself into a position created for your sister. Your behavior at the gala was grossly unacceptable."

"My behavior?" I sputter. "You think *my* behavior was unacceptable? But Priscilla conspiring with Mrs. Jacobs to marry off their children, with zero regard for whether Lance is actually interested in Sabrina, is perfectly fine? Like we're in medieval times, marrying for land boundaries. If you'll remember, I was nothing but polite when I met them. Lance followed me, at the gala and at the bakery."

Shit. I didn't mean to say that. I don't want them to know that Lance is hanging around and helping me at the bakery. It feels like it's private, between me and him. Maybe Dad won't notice? I cross my fingers and toes, praying that he's too riled up at my hinting at the horror of an arranged marriage in this day and age.

"Speaking of the bakery, I still do not understand what prompted you to give up such a promising position for drudgery."

Well, one crisis averted in favor of another. "Dad, working at Blackwell was never going to be what I thought it was, or the lessons you said I'd learn at a big company. I wasn't learning anything, and it was . . ." I freeze, the word 'dangerous' on the tip of my tongue. But I can't tell him about Blackwell's attempts to hamstring Thomas, can't tell him about the SUV parked outside even right now because my security followed me here. "It was a dead end."

"Hmph."

I punt, changing directions. "I love baking. And *Cake Culture* has been a roaring success. I'm working hard, but I love it. I've learned so much, building something great from the ground up. I thought you'd be proud of me for that."

"I have always been proud of you, upset at your teen rebellion, occasionally, but proud of your work ethic. This step is too far, though, Charlotte. Working before dawn until late at night, requiring a singular focus. You do always pick the hard way, sometimes just to spite everyone around you." He sighs, like my bakery has anything to do with him, Priscilla, or Sabrina. "But why struggle when there is an easier path? You could've worked your way up at Blackwell, worked for me or one of a dozen companies . . ."

His voice trails off, and though I know the definition of insanity is to do the same thing and expect a different result, I explain what the bakery means to me again for the hundredth time. "I love it, Dad. It's my heart and soul, hard work, and creativity in each of those baked goods. I've taken the lessons Grandma Winnie taught me, the recipes she shared, and improved upon them. I'm succeeding. Yes, it's hard and takes more time than exists in a twenty-four-hour day, but I love it."

I beseech him to understand, pleading with my eyes.

His gaze locks on me, and that stupid hope tries to rise again. His answer is a mixed bag, though. "Fine. If you're so staunchly sure that this is the path you want to traverse, I'll support that. Not financially, of course. But you have my blessing." He pauses long enough for my brain to celebrate his support and scoff at his unneeded blessing to do whatever the hell I want.

"But if you want that, you need to step aside and let others, who choose differently, have a clear path. You will leave Lance to

Sabrina. She needs a good man, one who can take her in hand and deal with her high-strung personality. Priscilla has worked hard to make this happen, and you will not interfere."

"Dad," I say, my jaw dropping.

He shakes his head definitively. "We are hosting a family dinner with the Jacobses on Sunday. You will attend, you will obviously rebuff any advances from Lance, you will redirect positive attention to Sabrina, and you will be pleasant to Priscilla. She's been a good mother to you, and as your father, I need this from you."

His laundry list of to-dos is laughable, but the rest sticks in my craw. A good mother? Priscilla? She turned my family inside out, made my life a living hell, and took my Daddy away from me.

I shake my head, the mirror image of his earlier movement, and his lips quirk. "You are the spitting image of her, you know?"

My heart stops, and for a moment, I think he means Priscilla, which is the worst insult he could ever give me. But he continues and my heart cracks wide open.

"Your mother was a stunner, had me wrapped around her little finger." He doesn't often talk about Mom, but the idea that both women in his life have had him at their beck and call is an uncomfortable comparison between the woman I hold in the highest regard and the one I hate with a vehemence bordering on unhealthy.

"She is the reason I succeeded in those early days. I was young, foolish, and slacked off too much, but she would sit me down and make me study. Later, when I had all these pie-in-the-sky dreams, she'd force me to make a step-by-step plan to make them a reality. She taught me how to work hard and see a goal to fruition. My company, my everything" —he looks around the house that Priscilla designed— "it's all because she loved me and saw something in me. In you, I see both of us. Your mother's focus and my dreams. Hopefully, the very best of us both."

He smiles softly, and I see my Daddy for the first time in years.

"Thank you. That means a lot to me," I confess.

He stands up, arms open wide, and I stand up too, never too big for a hug from the man I miss desperately. He feels smaller in my arms than I remember, the giant of a man suddenly more human, more flawed, and I realize that he's doing the best he can. I might not like it in the least, but he's choosing his life every day the same way I am. He doesn't understand my bakery and I don't understand his wife, but we can still love each other in spite of the differences in opinion.

"Sunday, Charlotte." His tone broaches no argument.

I nod but push back slightly to meet his eyes. "I'll come, but Priscilla and Sabrina are wrong in this. Lance isn't a car they can buy. He's not a horse they can choose as a stud. He's a man, one with his own opinions. You'd do well to remember that."

He presses his lips together, nodding. "As would you. Sabrina is a beautiful young woman whom any man would be fortunate to call his wife. Don't interfere. Don't risk yourself when you say your focus is devoted solely on *Cake Culture*."

He presses a quick kiss to my forehead like he did when I was little, and I turn to go before the tears burning at the corners of my eyes can spill over.

That he knows the name of my bakery is a small feather in my cap, a sign that maybe he has been listening. But as I get into the car for the drive home, I know I'm going to this dinner, not because I'm doing it for him. And certainly not for Priscilla or Sabrina.

I'm going to dinner because Lance deserves to have someone sitting at that table who's on his side. I don't know what we're doing beyond the fact that he basically makes my ovaries twerk like they're backup dancers in a Nikki Minaj video, but I know that he shouldn't get ensnared in Sabrina's scheming web, even if it is gold-encrusted.

Sunday dinner, it is.

CHAPTER 11

*G*ood luck today, not that you need it.

I consider adding a tongue emoji to the cake one I include on the text to Charlotte.

Today's her big day with the wedding monstrosity we've been working on. Purely by necessity, I've been helping more in the shop because of it. In addition to helping with cleanup, I've been running things from the back up front and pulling trays out of the ovens while Charlotte does the finicky decorations needed on the four-foot-tall wedding cake. Still, I want her to know I'm thinking of her, so I click *Send*.

She says *~*Thank You~*~*. You should see the heart emojis popping out of her eyes right now. But for real, she's busy. Leave us alone. –Trixie

I appreciate that she took the moment to reply, even through Trixie, knowing that they're likely swamped. Charlotte told me that she'd spend a chunk of time getting the cake set up and that Trixie would be running the shop today, but they'd both denied my offer of help, saying they had it well in hand.

I feel surprisingly adrift without a plan to go to the bakery like I've been doing every day. It's just not as meaningful to me without Charlotte there. But I have been working on the information download for Jacobs Bio Tech, going through files and familiarizing myself with almost a decade of data.

Honestly, the company seems mostly to be headed in the right direction, which makes me question why I was needed home so desperately.

Research seems to be on the cutting edge, a ballsy risk, but one that makes sense for the industry. Payroll doesn't seem excessive, and while the marketing materials I've looked at seem a bit dry and boring, that's not my area of expertise.

All in all, I'm mostly impressed with what Dad's accomplished in his quest to make the family company thrive. I can see his blood, sweat, and tears in every facet.

Maybe that's what made him ask for help? The sheer volume of work he's been shouldering has to be wearing on him, even with Cody's help. And while he's in good shape, a man pushing sixty might not have the same energy as a younger man.

Of course, I can see Cody's touches here and there. He's done some project management on some new designs that look good. They're nothing groundbreaking, but they were completed on time and the financials on the results seem to be good, at least to me.

But the progression of his responsibilities does seem lacking. I wonder if that's his own preference or Dad holding him back.

Needing to clear my head, I throw on athletic shorts and tennis shoes and make my way to the home gym Dad installed when he built this place.

In some ways, I'm still adjusting to civilian life. Instead of clean, beautifully lubricated and maintained equipment, part of me still looks forward to a workout where there's sand in my shirt, rough metal digging into my hands, and saltwater stinging my eyes. Still, it feels good to move, to challenge my body and push myself.

No, desk life is not for me.

Finishing up with my favorite machine, the Jacob's Ladder, I swipe at the sweat running down my face, then toss the towel around my neck for my cooldown stretches. It's only because I'm changing positions that I see Cody pause in the doorway. He's dressed like he's here for a workout too, but as soon as he sees me, he turns to walk away down the hallway.

"Cody! Wait, come back," I call. In the hallway, I can see him look upward and sigh, like he's stuck between a rock and a hard place. But he does come back.

"Fine. But I'm not talking business with you. This is my escape from that shitshow, so don't even try it, Mr. All-American Hero, come to save the fucking day."

Bitterness drips from every word as he steps onto the treadmill, which surprises me.

Once upon a time, we were close. Well, as close as we could be with the years between us.

When I was off to the military, he was still in high school, so the years before that had us mostly interested in different things, but I'd always had a soft spot in my heart for my little brother. I hope that we can find some common ground again, now that we're both adults.

"We don't have to talk business if you don't want. Trust me, the SEALs were a lot simpler than that corporate jungle. Wasn't perfect, but I had sun, sand, and could wear a T-shirt for half my damn job. But when Dad and Mom said they needed help, here I am. Woof, woof," I say, letting Cody know that being caught up in Dad's games isn't sitting well with me either. I want Cody to drop whatever burr he's got up his ass about my being here.

He smirks, shaking his head. "You can stop the woe is me sacrifice act, Lance. At least you get to be a fucking Goldendoodle, coming back all decorated and welcomed and shit. I'm like the chihuahua that gets shoved off to the side, no matter how much I bark. Yip, yip, yip."

The joke is harsh, but he sounds funny, and I can imagine him bouncing around like a tiny dog that thinks he's the fiercest beast. I can't help but laugh, and after a minute, he does too. Cody's laugh is rough, though, like he hasn't done it in way too long, and I wonder just what the hell went wrong here for him.

"Fuck, that feels good," I say, wiping the salty combination of sweat and tears from my eyes. "I missed you, brother. I swear, I went away and you were this gangly kid with his head down in school work. Before I knew it, you were a man who was making your own way. I feel like I don't even know you now, like maybe you don't even like me anymore."

It's a big confession, one that might send him stomping out of here when I barely forged a crack in the wall between us, but I'm a gambling man. And if anything, I think it'll give Cody an opening to dump all his venom on me. I'll take it because then I'll know what I'm dealing with, at least.

"Like you give a single, solitary fuck about what I want or like?" Cody asks, snorting derisively. "First off, I'm not walking my own path. I'm walking the one Dad wanted you to follow. So when the prodigal son returns, you get set up for the good life, and once again, I'm reminded that I'm a poor substitute for you in every way."

"Substitute? You were never . . . Cody, you've always been an important part of this family. And from what I can tell, you've done a great job at Bio-Tech." He scoffs, but I soldier on. "I'm honestly not sure why I'm needed here. It seems like Dad's stressed to the max and you and he are damn near at each other's throats, but from what I can tell, the company is okay."

"You have no idea, do you?" he shakes his head, rolling his eyes. "You're so fucking clueless you don't even know what you don't know."

"Fine. Fill me in then, Cody. Tell me what the hell's going on!" My voice raises in frustration.

He snarls, years of anger bubbling to the surface and overflowing in a rage-filled rant as he starts pacing back and forth, letting it out maybe for the first time ever. "You want to know what happened? Fine! You happened! You ran off to go do your own shit and never cared what I had to do back here. You think I wasn't a substitute? They compared every single thing I did to what you would do and I came up lacking each and every time. So I tried to do better, be better, and fill in the gaps you left behind. You didn't want the family business, so I joined right up. You wanted to see the world, so I stayed right here at home. I've done all the things you weren't willing to, worked my ass off as a junior executive, paving the way to a life I thought I wanted as a VP. I figured eventually, he'd have to see that I'm just as good—" his lip curls, and he points a thick finger at my chest. "No, *better* than you. Because I'm willing to do what the family needs, not run off on a whim."

He turns to leave, but I can't let it end like that. He's said his piece, but I've got one of my own, so I yell back, stopping him in his tracks. "You think I ran off on a whim? My whole life has been plotted out for me, expectation on top of responsibility, with zero concern over what I wanted. So yeah, I got out. And you could've done the same, but you *chose* not to. Now, I get lured here under false pretenses, all because they've decided I should be ready to settle down. I'm not back for five minutes before they're pairing me off with a socialite who has more ass than brains, and her ass is *flatter than a fucking crepe!*"

I cringe, the food pun rolling off my tongue and not having near the thorny emphasis I'd intended. Cody looks angry, but then an incredulous grin washes over his face. "A crepe? What the hell kind of military slang is that for a piece of ass like Sabrina?"

"Sorry, I've got a bit of baking on the mind," I say, shaking my head.

The tense stalemate is broken by my unfortunate slip. "Ooh, I know what's got you thinking about cupcakes and popping cherries."

I shove at Cody, feeling good again as we laugh. "Leave Charlotte out of this."

He pushes back at me, and for a minute, I swear we're kids again. We're not really trying to hurt each other, but we end up bear hugging, mock-wrestling in the hallway. I'm better than him, trained in ways he's not, but I let him get in some pushes, rolling up and down the hall and banging off the walls.

We both need to burn some of this testosterone out because we don't need to fight for Alpha, not in our own family. Neither of us is out of shape, but between the pretty aggressive wrestling horseplay and mouthy taunts, we're out of breath quickly and both flop to the carpet, laughing. I'm spread-eagle, leaning back on my hands, and Cody is laid out on his back, staring at the ceiling.

"They'll never go for it, you know that, right?" he says and then turns a side eye to me. "Charlotte won't happen."

He sounds resigned, like he's used to Mom and Dad getting their way. And I guess with his way of dealing with them, they always have.

But I've always handled their intrusiveness a bit differently, and I have no problem saying, 'fuck it all,' and walking away. Even though neither of us, my parents nor me, truly wants that.

"We'll see. She's not why I'm here. I'm here for you, man. Dad too. Tell me what I need to know. I'm on your side. There's got to be more than what I'm seeing in the spreadsheets and quarterly reports."

I get that Dad probably wants me to take over, but Cody seems a reasonable, if not good, heir to that responsibility.

Which would leave me open to whatever life I wanted, maybe even a return to the Navy.

I imagine that life once again taking over my every moment, a simpler life in some ways, one of mission-oriented focus.

But that image blurs in a red haze, one that clears and focuses into a certain redhead with fair skin that blushes in splotches, blue eyes that enflame me, and a sense of humor that makes me feel lighter than I have in a long time. Another kind of mission . . . but one just as important.

Cody, not privy to my thoughts, gets up after a minute and goes into the gym again, and while I know Dad feels like Cody isn't pulling his weight, I can see the heavy weariness Cody wears. Whether real or imagined, the expectations are drowning him.

"Cody."

He stops at the door and turns back, his eyes cold and hard again.

"Look, Lance, I know you're not doing it on purpose. But just stay out of my way. This will be my company. I've worked for it. Fuck knows, Dad didn't give me a damn bit of it just because I share his name. I've earned this, and I won't let them hand it to you just because you're their favorite."

He closes the door, and while I'm tempted to go back into the gym and settle this, I know this isn't the time. Despite our playfulness, he's still angry deep down. That anger is going to bring things to a head between him and Dad sooner or later. I only hope we can all survive the fallout. We've been a mostly happy family, or at least Mom and Dad have always had our best interests at heart even if I didn't agree with their methods. But I'm afraid this meddling is going to cause irreparable damage to our family if we don't change course.

CHAPTER 12

CHARLOTTE

I have never been so not-hungry for dinner in my life. But I'm here all the same. I spent extra time on my hair and makeup and have on a lovely A-line floral dress I've worn a few times, but never in front of Priscilla.

That I'm even conscious of that irks me on a cellular level because I couldn't care less about who sees me wearing what, but I don't want to give them ammunition and start the night off at a loss.

The door opens after I ring the bell, and Sabrina appears, looking gorgeous. I'm not a troll by any stretch, but to myself, at least, I'll admit that Sabrina is a beautiful woman. On the outside.

Her freshly-highlighted hair sheens, falling in a smooth sheet down her back. Her blue eyes are played up, her full lips blood-red. Her designer-label white lace sheath dress looks nearly bridal, save the low V-neck that highlights a full cleavage. Her heels give her a height advantage of several inches, all the better to look down on me from upon high.

"Well, don't you look *pretty*," Sabrina says, her tone relaying the opposite. "So . . . ladylike."

Like she knows the first fucking thing about being a lady. But I remind myself for the tenth time since I left home that I'm going to be on my best behavior. For Dad and for Lance. "Thank you, Sabrina. You look lovely as well," I say civilly, my tone bland.

"You don't have to fake being nice. No one is here to see it yet, since *my* man isn't here yet." The smile on her face is venom-filled, like she's daring me to disagree with her decree.

Ooh, bitch, if I weren't . . .

Well, there goes my promise to Dad. It's hard for me to hold my tongue and not tell Sabrina that Lance has been hanging out at the bakery, working oh-so-close and oh-so-late with me, sneaking in kisses here and there. I imagine doing it and the look on her already Botoxed face.

But I'm not going to lay any traps for Lance. I'm here to help him through them. He'll have enough to traverse tonight without my laying it all out there before he even gets here.

I head into the living room, noting that there are already a few subtle changes to the décor. The artwork over the fireplace is a new, and likely expensive, abstract in swashes of pink and gold, and the pillows on the couch are woven through with metallic threads, giving everything a gilded appearance.

Priscilla doesn't acknowledge my entrance, but Dad gets up, kissing my cheek. Though it's more polite manners than affection, it renews my resolve to behave and keep my tongue in check.

Thankfully, it's only moments later that the doorbell rings again, announcing the Jacobses' arrival.

Mr. and Mrs. Jacobs come in, looking elegant. Mr. Jacobs wears a finely-tailored suit in a deep charcoal grey, and Mrs. Jacobs is in a knee-length pale grey dress with an architectural portrait collar that makes her collarbones look regal.

After handshakes and air kisses—yes, for real, and prompted by Priscilla, of course—Sabrina can wait no longer.

"Where's my Lance-y?" Her voice is practically an octave higher than usual, making her sound childish. In my gut, I feel something churn, and I know I'm going to be scarfing an extra cupcake tomorrow to make up for a very lightly eaten dinner tonight.

"Lance and Cody elected to drive over together. I believe Cody said something about showing off his latest modification? Something to do with speakers, I believe, but I'll admit to being a bit befuddled by his love of loud music. Must be a young man thing. It simply hurts my ears," Mrs. Jacobs says, laughing lightly at herself. "Likely just an excuse for some brother time. I'm sure you understand."

She looks from Sabrina to me, and I have to bite back my reply.

Oh, sure. Sabrina and I are the best of buds. A regular Obi-Wan and Anakin, we are.

I blame my geeky metaphors on Mia, the ultimate geek who's forced me to watch more Sci-Fi, both animated and live-action, over my lifetime than I'll ever admit.

A house staff member comes in, holding a tray of white wine, which we each take gratefully. I almost drink it as a shot, needing the fortification, but I manage to sip slowly and politely.

"So, what does Cody do?" Dad asks Mr. Jacobs. "I must admit, I've heard so much about Lance" —he looks to Sabrina— "but Cody's a bit of a mystery."

He looks at me, like he's giving me permission to go after Cody Jacobs as long as I leave Lance alone.

"As he likes it," Mrs. Jacobs says, gripping her glass a little tightly. "He's an executive VP for Jacobs Bio-Tech, began there while still in college, in fact, and has never worked anywhere but the family business. He's a homegrown exec, you see."

There's a bit of pride in her tone, but simultaneously, she makes it sound like Cody only holds his position because of his name.

It's a delicate balance I suspect she's perfected through many tellings.

It does make me wonder, if Cody is already here, working under Mr. Jacobs and being the good little silver-spoon boy, why they're so hellfire-bent on bringing Lance back and marrying him off. It seems any desire for grandkids and a legacy could be well fulfilled by the younger of the two Jacobs sons. Probably with a greater degree of ease and control than they seem to have over Lance, who is a man who does whatever the hell he wants.

He hasn't done you yet, and he definitely wants you. You want him too.

I don't get a chance to uselessly argue with myself because a fast tap-tap-tap sounds on the door. A moment later, Lance and Cody enter, and the temperature in the room jumps about ten degrees.

Cody, for his part, looks every bit the carefree playboy. His suit is expensive but not fresh-pressed, his jaw has at least a day's worth of stubble glinting along it, and if I'm not mistaken, his eyes look a little red as he flips his sunglasses up onto the top of his head.

"Sorry we're late," he says, not looking the least bit sorry.

Lance has the wherewithal to look sheepish, but he's the opposite of his brother in other ways too. His scruff is well-kept, trimmed neatly, his hair not compulsively styled but neat and tidy, and his navy suit is pristine, highlighting the blue of his eyes to perfection. "Yes, our apologies."

"That's okay, Lance-y, you're just in time for dinner," Sabrina says, and I fight to hold back the hip-thrusting victory dance when I see his eyebrows shoot up at the nickname.

Lance doesn't respond, just makes his way to my dad, shaking his hand, then Priscilla's, and then Sabrina, who looks disappointed he doesn't kiss the back of her hand. Suddenly, we're face to face, his eyes burning into mine.

"Charlotte." His voice is deep, the timber making all the hairs on my arms stand up.

I try to warn him off with my eyes but probably fail since his hand is still wrapped around mine long after is proper. "Nice to see you again, Lance."

My voice is purposefully neutral, not hinting that not that long ago, we were *this close* to making out over a wedding cake. Hell, not even letting on that we've seen each other since the gala.

Priscilla notices something, though, and claps, saying sharply, "Dinner." She plasters a fake smile on and gestures with her hand. "I mean, right this way, please."

She leads us to the dining room, and oh, my God, there are place cards noting who's to sit where. Seems Priscilla isn't leaving anything to chance. Dad and Priscilla take their natural places at the ends of the table, Mr. and Mrs. Jacobs sitting at Dad's right and left. Lance is sandwiched between his mother and Sabrina, I'm between Mr. Jacobs and Cody, who at least also looks like he doesn't want to be here.

Lance looks like he's preparing for the Spanish Inquisition and reaches for his water glass almost immediately. Meanwhile, Cody is looking across the table, blatantly staring at Sabrina's cleavage. Not that she notices, because as soon as she sits down, she's practically rubbing her tits against Lance's arm, damn near climbing into his lap right here at the table.

Dinner is served, something pretty on the plate and likely delicious, but I don't taste a thing. All my attention is on the conversations going on around the table, both verbal and nonverbal.

"So, Lance . . . what's it like being a real American hero SEAL?" Priscilla purrs.

Like she was prompted, Sabrina leans into Lance. "Yes, Lance-y. You're so brave, rushing into danger like that. So strong and powerful," she simpers, squeezing his biceps.

Okay, so she's not wrong, exactly. Lance is all those things, but the needy, worshipful way she compliments him rubs me wrong. To help, I glance over, where I'll give Cody credit, he seems to see through Sabrina's charade because he's rolling his eyes so hard they might get stuck that way.

Lance ignores Sabrina's manicured hand and looks at Priscilla instead. "If you want to know the truth, I spent most of my time in combat, scared out of my wits. 'Courage is not the absence of fear, but rather the assessment that something else is more important than the fear.' That's the mission."

Sabrina interrupts, "Ooh, you're so smart. That's brilliant."

"FDR seemed to think so," I say under my breath, and Lance looks at me, a smirk on his face that I caught the famous quote that Sabrina seems woefully unfamiliar with.

"Are you a presidential fan, Charlotte?" Lance asks, and four sets of parental eyes turn to me, plus Sabrina's glare.

"Oh, uh, not particularly. I just bake," I say, trying to avoid making myself sound small and unfortunately failing. I have more experience with that than I care to admit, and with Priscilla's narrowed eyes, I revert more easily than I'd like.

"How is the bakery coming, dear?" Mrs. Jacobs asks. "I heard your cupcakes caused quite the stir at the gala."

I dab at my mouth with my napkin, smiling a little as Priscilla scowls. "Thank you, Mrs. Jacobs. Thomas and Mia really helped me get the word out, and business has been going better than projected. I've got quite a few regulars already and a rather large wedding cake custom order going out this weekend."

"Way to work those connections, dear," Priscilla quips. "You certainly need them, considering you won't be getting any real recognition when people can buy a cake at Albertson's. Not like they give Michelin stars for baked goods, though yours are good, I suppose," she jokes, laughing lightly like she's teasing, but the only person who laughs with her is Sabrina.

I'm at my max, the threshold for bullshit about two feet ago, and now I'm swimming through it to wrangle my hands around Priscilla's neck, not literally, but figuratively, as I respond.

"I don't use my friends that way and don't choose them based on what they can do for me like a narcissistic user. Mia has a quote I think you'd be interested in. 'Don't beg for it . . . earn it. Do that, and you'll be rewarded.' And *that's* what I'm doing. Not trying to *suck up* to people to get my way up the social ladder."

My emphasized words, combined with my pointed look at Sabrina, sends a very clear message. It isn't missed as Dad slams his napkin on the table, the sound sharp before he barks. "That's enough, Charlotte. Once again, despite our conversation, you can't seem to understand proper decorum. Priscilla put on a lovely dinner so Sabrina and Lance could get to know one another, and all I asked is for you to not interfere. But you sit here and insult them. I'm disappointed in you. Apologize now, young lady."

I can see the twitch at the corners of Sabrina's lips, her delight that I'm getting reamed out. I guess this time, she didn't really do anything to me. It was Priscilla who insulted my bakery, but I threw them both under the bus as fast as I could. It's deserved time and time over, but I look like the bitch right now.

"My apologies," I offer the table, my head held high and my tone saying I'm anything but.

I hear Cody murmur beside me, "Best part of the whole night, hands down."

I'm encouraged by Cody's words, but it's the look in Lance's eye that pleases me the most. His hot gaze bores into me, making me rub my thighs together for relief because I can feel the dark promise in his eyes.

Conversation begins again, pointedly veering away from anything that I can contribute to.

Mrs. Jacobs and Priscilla discuss upcoming events on the social calendar for the season, including the value in going with a staunchly respected designer for gowns instead of gambling on a new uprising hotshot. Priscilla devours every word like they're gospel, and maybe to her, they are.

Mr. Jacobs and Dad then move to talk about Roseboro and the move of Jacobs Bio-Tech to town. "It's been an exciting change," he says, "though I may feel differently when the winter snow hits."

Dad agrees, sipping his drink. "It takes getting used to, but Roseboro is worth it. The town has changed a lot over the last twenty, thirty years. While we're not quite in Roseboro, I've of course kept my eye on things. It's quite exciting."

Their talk turns to Blackwell and the changes he's brought to town, and then to Thomas Goldstone and the changes he's bringing along with the partnership with the bio-tech company.

Sabrina interjects. "Mr. Blackwell has done such great things. It's a pity Charlotte couldn't keep her job there." I have intentionally kept my mouth shut, letting all the attention drift away from me, but Sabrina couldn't resist the opportunity to cut me.

Mr. Jacobs turns to me, lifting an eyebrow. "Oh? You used to work at Blackwell? Why'd you leave?"

I nod, looking at Dad. "I did. I decided to pursue a dream and left."

I'm leaving off *so* much to that decision, but I don't want to push it considering my earlier outburst.

Dad frowns, shaking his head as he explains to Mr. Jacobs, "You remember what it's like to be young, taking the more difficult path despite every advice to the contrary? I'm afraid she has the best and the worst of both her mother and me, and she refuses to see sense from a voice of reason and experience."

It's not the harshest thing he's ever said and mirrors the way we'd left things the other day, but this feels more patronizing. I can feel myself shrinking in my seat, and I bite my lip to keep from saying anything else.

Lance suffers no such need to keep quiet, standing and tossing his napkin to the table, similarly to how Dad did earlier. "Seriously? Do you hear yourself?" He looks at Dad as if he expects an answer, but Dad merely looks back in total shock. After a moment, Lance expounds. "Charlotte left a job to chase a dream, one that I've seen her work hard at and she's flourishing with. Yet you continue to downplay her success, all the while, playing up a daughter whose sole 'work experience' is sitting still for the amount of time it takes to have her extensions attached in the salon chair."

Sabrina lets out a weak sound of offense, but Priscilla's is loud. "Why, I never!"

Lance turns to Priscilla, a look of disdain on his face. "You're right. You never. But I do. *I see you.* Every snarky comment, every jealous look."

Priscilla has the gall to look offended, like she doesn't know exactly what he's talking about.

"Lance, please!" Mrs. Jacobs exclaims, but he whirls on her next.

"Mom, I understand that you think you have my best interests at heart, but back off. I'm a grown man, and I'm not marrying someone because you've deemed them an acceptable match or worked some backroom deal with Priscilla. What you think you're getting out of this, I don't know, nor do I care. I'm here and I'm home, but not for this circus."

He thrashes his hand around, gesturing at the table.

Lance pushes his chair further back, stepping away from the table and taking a few steps toward the doorway.

"Lance, I demand—" Mr. Jacobs starts, but Lance doesn't give him a chance to finish his sentence.

"You'll demand nothing of me, Dad. You're asking me to help

with the family company, and I've done so, in spite of my own career and despite there being a Jacobs son ready and willing, and from what I see, more than able to take over the company mantle."

The only people at the table not sputtering are me and Cody. We both have huge shit-eating grins on our faces, and I'm guessing similar wishes that we could've said all that ourselves.

I guess he's said everything he's had brewing up, because Lance moves to the doorway but pauses to glance back once more. His eyes meet mine again, challenge sparking in his baby blues. "You coming, Red?"

My smile falters, my jaw dropping as I look around the table. Shock, fury, and even Cody's still-growing smile greet me. I should do as I'm told, sit still and not make a fuss, like I've done so many times before.

Fuck that.

I get up, dropping my napkin to my chair. "Yep, let's go."

CHAPTER 13

LANCE

$\mathcal{O}$n the front porch, Charlotte sags, and we can hear Sabrina whining loudly inside. "Mommm, get him back! Charlotte can't have him!"

"Oh, my God, oh, my God. What the hell did I just do? What did you do?" she says, eyes as big as dinner plates meeting mine.

I can see the fear, and I hate it. She's strong, sassy, and badass, not this scared and quiet mouse they try to get her to be. "It's all right. I've got you. There's just one thing."

"There's more?" she says, starting to breathe again.

I nod, a grin spreading on my face as I take her hand. "I rode with Cody. Is your car here?"

She adds a couple of inches to the space between us and I can see the fire relighting in her eyes. "All that, a massive hair-flip out after telling everybody off, and now we're going to have to do a walk of shame out of here as we call for an Uber?"

I blanch. "I didn't think that far ahead. I just couldn't sit there and let them manipulate me like that and put you down that way. Of course, if I were solo, I'd just do that whole walking against the wind shit. Stalk off like a badass."

She smiles, breaking the tease. "My car's over there." She points to a black VW, pulling me that direction as she takes my hand. It feels casual, comfortable, like her hand has always belonged in mine.

We get in, and she pulls out of the driveway carefully, waving to the SUV across the street I hadn't noticed when we came in with Cody's music blaring louder than a firefight in the dead of night.

It's probably a good thing she's driving. I would've peeled out, tires squealing just to emphasize my points further with our families still inside.

The drive to the bakery is quiet, and though I don't want to assume, I'm hoping we continue this attempt at running away right up the stairs to Charlotte's apartment. She parks and reads my mind, waving at the SUV once more before opening the back door and leading me up the back stairs.

I get the vaguest impression of a small apartment before I make my move, pressing her up against the door she just closed. "What are you doing?" Charlotte asks, her chest heaving as she tries to catch her breath.

"This," I say before moving in to kiss her deeply. She resists at first, but her hands don't push me away, instead weaving into my hair to pull me in tighter. She opens her mouth, and I claim her, feeling like we're on the same page. I press closer, pinning her between the door and my body, and she arches her back, pushing against me, hungry for more.

I trace my hands down her side, brushing the sides of her breasts before gripping her hips and lifting her. Her hands lock behind my neck, her legs going around my waist, her pussy centered over my cock. I can feel her heat, and my control slips.

"Where?" I demand.

"Down the hall, on the left," she mutters between kisses.

I move across the living room and into her bedroom before

letting her slide down, never losing contact. I tug at her dress, finding the buttons on the back and fumbling with them. "Are you trying to torture me?"

She chuckles, her hands running down my chest to my belt. "I wasn't planning on needing it off in a hurry."

I pause, her words not dimming my passion but putting steel back in my self-control. "Do you want to slow down?" Even as I ask, I kiss her neck, praying she doesn't ask me to stop again.

She shakes her head, getting my belt undone and moving on to my slacks. "Fuck, no. If you can't get it, turn me around and push the skirt up."

Now I'm the one disagreeing, even as the image fills my mind. "I want to see you, all of you."

As if it's choreographed, we each reach for our own clothes, her getting the rest of the buttons undone and dropping her dress to puddle at her feet. I yank my button-down shirt over my head after only undoing a few buttons and then drop my slacks down, kicking my shoes off at the same time.

She's glorious, a scarlet-haired angel in a satiny cream-colored bra and panties that look almost golden against her pale skin. My cock, which is already rock-hard, twitches, and Charlotte hums as she gets a good look at the bulge in my boxers.

"Gorgeous. Come here," I growl, grabbing her hand and pulling her back to me, but she reacts quickly, keeping a hand between the two of us. She cups my cock, hesitantly at first but growing confident as she explores my length through the thin layer of cotton.

"This is . . . wow."

We tumble to the bed, our mouths never leaving one another. She cradles me between her bent knees, and I run my hands up her thighs, massaging the perfect twin globes of her ass. The sound of her moans drives me lower, and I start kissing down her body. She whines as I move away and she loses contact with my cock.

"I want you." She pouts.

I ooze precum, already on edge at the needy sounds coming from her lips. "You'll get me, I promise. I'm not going anywhere, but I need to taste you."

She arches as I lower myself, pressing my lips to the fullness of her breast escaping from her bra. She reaches behind her back, undoing the fastener quickly and taking her bra off completely.

Her tits are snowy white, and I cup and press them together before burying my head between them to kiss and suck on her skin, enjoying the way it pinks up beneath my lips and teeth. I lick and suckle at first one rosy nipple, then the other, as I run a finger up the inside of her leg to the flat of her panties over her slit.

Her lips cling to the damp satin, outlining the narrow valley between, and I stroke her with my fingertips, learning her body by her responses. Charlotte's moan when I find her engorged clit is held back as she bites her lip, but her hips lift up to my touch, begging for more. I focus my attentions there, rubbing her clit through the now-soaked fabric and sucking hard on her nipple, giving her occasional nips that make her arch anew.

Her fingernails scratch at my back, urging me on. "Fuck! Oh, *fuck*!" Her whole body quivers beneath me, muscles tightening and spasming. "I'm gonna . . ."

"That's it, Charlotte. Come for me. I've got you," I tell her supportively, my breath hot on her cleavage.

She rides the wave back down, her eyes peeking open to stare at me in wonder as a smile breaks on her reddened lips. "Holy shit, I never come that fast."

Part of me wants to preen and puff up like I did something awesome, but mostly, I just want to make her do it again and again. This time, I want to taste it, and the next, I want to see the convulsions of her pussy lips hungrily sucking my cock deeper inside her waiting body.

"I want more," I say. "I want it all."

She nods, agreeing, so I push her legs open and drop to my knees beside the bed. I tug her panties down, and she wiggles to help me get them off. She's fully nude before me, and I let my eyes drift up her body to see just how stunning she truly is.

Her hair is spread out like a burning halo, her wide blue eyes watching me in lusty anticipation, her body curvy and built for sin, all framing a pretty pink pussy that's already gleaming, messy with her cum. I can't help but lean in, inhaling her sexy scent and pressing a soft kiss to her bare mound.

My cock twitches, a fresh drop of precum releasing as her sweet taste hits my tongue. I could drink from her morning, noon, and night and still be thirsty for more, but she reaches for me. "Fuck me," she pleads, her eyes begging. "I need you."

"Yes ma'am," I say, teasing as I move up her body, lining my cock up with her entrance. I push slowly, giving her just the tip to let her feel me before I enter her, coating myself with her honey as I rub my thumb over her clit.

"*Yes*," Charlotte purrs. She tilts her hips, and I dip in deeper, feeling her tight walls fight the intrusion.

Our eyes lock, and I watch her every movement for any signs of pain or discomfort as I thrust in inch by inch, pausing to pull back and slip in again. With each stroke, I open her a little more, stretching her. "That's it, take me. Relax and let me in, Char."

She nods, biting her lip. "Feels . . . like . . . you're splitting me in half," she gasps out. But when I try to retreat so I don't hurt her, she locks her feet behind my back, keeping me in place. "More."

Carefully, I start thrusting faster, letting my thick girth fill her. I can't believe how tight she is, but maybe it's been that long for her or maybe she hasn't had someone my size before. Whatever the reason, it's enough to drive us both to the brink faster than I'd imagined.

Her breasts bounce as I start to pound harder, careful not to bottom out but still plunging deep into her pussy and deeper into her soul. Suddenly, she opens up, and I slide all the way in, our hips clapping together. We both freeze as she cries out, but the sharp gasp turns into a moan of delight. "Oh, my . . . fuck!"

I grin, kissing her hard and staying in place. "Good girl, Charlotte. You ready now?"

Her answering smile is pure joy with a hint of challenge as she unlocks her legs and grabs my ass, a cheek in each hand as she guides me. I let her lead for a moment, but she quickly becomes overwhelmed, letting me take over the pace. "Fuck, you feel good. That tight pussy squeezing my cock. I'm already ready to blow. I need you to come with me."

She cries out, bucking and fucking me back as we chase our orgasms with the same intensity we're chasing our futures, not giving a single thought to anyone or anything else. It's us, together in this moment, needing only each other.

My balls slap against her ass, and in the back of my mind, I can hear something telling me that this is my future, right here, buried in the heaven of her slick pussy. She cries out, and I lean over her, pressing our bodies against each other, wanting every point of contact I can get.

Her body contracts, curving beneath me, and she calls out my name before burying her tiny teeth in the muscle of my shoulder to silence herself. The sharp bite of pain sends me over, and I bellow, exploding to fill her with shot after heated shot of my sticky cream, claiming her deeply.

When the waves pass over us both, I hold her in my arms, staying inside her as she flops to the bed beneath me, spent and exhausted. Eventually, we both open our eyes, matching smiles on our faces. "You've got a mark on your shoulder," she says apologetically.

I shrug, not minding it. I could wear her mark happily. "You'll probably be walking funny tomorrow."

She wiggles a bit, and I can feel my cum leaking out around my cock, covering us both in the creamy mess. "I think I'm good."

I raise a brow, smiling a little. "Is that a challenge?"

She grins, clenching herself around me. "Didn't mean it to be, but feels like certain parts certainly took it as such."

I flex, pulsing my hardening cock inside her again, ready for round two.

Hell, we've already broken plenty of expectations today between both our blow-ups with our families. The least I can do is burst through every single one of her expectations about being with me and surpass each and every one, tonight, tomorrow, and for however long I can keep her here before she needs to disappear back downstairs for her early morning call to work.

I roll her over, seating her on top of me. "Ride me, Red."

CHAPTER 14

BLACKWELL

"*A*re you sure, sir?" my driver asks, holding the keys out to me despite his concerns. He's more than just a driver, of course, highly trained in many useful arts, although he spends the bulk of his days making my armored Cadillac Escalade perform like a vehicle one-third its size.

But tonight's work needs to be done . . . alone. It's a turning point, for me and for Roseboro. The game has been changing slowly, amping up in increments. But tonight begins the final moves. The plans that will ensure that my mark is indelible.

"Quite sure," I reply, removing my tie. In addition to leaving no witnesses, I will be sure to leave no trace evidence either. Not that anything pointing toward me would be a problem, not in a city where I own the police. "I assume it handles as a normal vehicle?"

The driver dips his chin once, acquiescing to my demands. "Yes, sir. It requires more time for braking and slowing down for sharp turns, but that's mostly due to its center of gravity, not the security modifications you require."

I get in, tossing my tie and jacket into the passenger seat before pulling out of the deserted lot. Despite my driver's warnings, the Cadillac handles like a fond memory of my youth, when cars were truly land ships and a Cadillac was the king of the asphalt seas.

Things have changed since then, some for the better and some perhaps not. But my reign at the top of the food chain is one of the best progressions from my younger days.

Approaching the house, I scan the road around me. Everything is quiet, all of suburbia sleeping soundly in their beds, not knowing that hell has come for them.

No, not them all. But one in particular.

I've let him live, thinking he might be useful in the future, and though he's kept his mouth shut as instructed after failing his previous mission as an insider at Goldstone, he's fallen too far into a black hole to be worth anything to me. Now, instead of a resource, he's a loose end.

I slip leather gloves on, smooth and soft as butter, as I get out and close the SUV door quietly. Two knocks at the door have shuffled movement sounding from inside the house.

"Patricia?" he slurs out in the false, desperate hope of a truly broken man. The door opens a heartbeat later, and the light in his eyes goes out when he sees me on his doorstep.

He knows why I'm here. I know why I'm here. But still, he tries to dance away.

"Mr. Blackwell, nice to see you." He lies horribly, the only truth the cheap whiskey on his breath.

I don't wait for an invitation, stepping inside and closing the door behind me. The house is a mess, a bachelor pad of the worst kind, and I suspect, based on the rank smell in the air, that the garbage hasn't been taken out in days.

"Is there anything you'd like to tell me?" I ask the open-ended question, interested in what he'll spill as his last words. Mere gibberish, or something useful, perhaps?

He shakes his head, his eyes losing focus at the fierce movement, but it must rattle a memory loose because he changes, nodding just as hard. "Yeah, yeah. There was a guy, a guy at work."

He stumbles, his steps deeper into the house, and I follow, maintaining my distance. Tonight's work will not be up close and personal. "A guy at work?"

Since his trial, a showcase that resulted in some pre-trial detention as a warning and a quick plea deal that resulted in a supremely generous probation, he's been working a blue-collar job, laying tar on roofs. I did it as an exercise to him, not only of the breadth of my reach but as a way to keep an eye on him when I thought he could be useful. Even his job was useful. He's tarred a few of my roofs recently.

A significant downgrade from his previous office life, but since he failed so spectacularly at that, the menial labor seems an appropriate prolonging of his punishment.

"At work, a temp guy chatted me up. Nothing too weird, just asking how I ended up pulling roof duty. Which wouldn't have been a big deal, but he knew my name. Most guys who know who I am, they stay far away, telling me rats get bats." He falls to the couch, unable to stand any longer with the alcohol in his blood, but he manages to mimic swinging a bat, as if to take off someone's head.

My lips quirk at the saying I haven't heard before, finding it amusing in its promise of violence. But the man seems lost in self-pity, as if his lack of friends at work is a sadness I could possibly empathize with.

"This man, what did he look like?" I say, feigning interest in his story. There is only one tidbit of information I truly want, whether he spilled anything incriminating.

He blinks, like he's trying to remember through the boozy haze of his wasted mind. "Big guy, dark hair, young . . . maybe thirty?"

"And you told him what, precisely?" My patience is wearing thin. It's time to get to the crux of the situation.

His eyes widen as he hears the warning in my voice. "Nothing, I swear it, Mr. Blackwell. Just told him that life takes you on bad trips sometimes, that I'd lost my job, my wife, my daughter in one fell swoop when I went on trial, but I was working my way back. That's it, that's all I said."

I give him a slight nod, like he's a good dog. "I believe you," I say, and he sags in relief, a feeling that doesn't last. "It's too bad you won't succeed."

Tension shoots through his body, the smell of fear scenting the air as he looks around the room, searching for a way out. But there is none, only one last choice to make.

I sit on the coffee table in front of him, pulling a gun from my waistband with my right hand and a rope from my back pocket with my left. I hold them out, like a magician who just did an amazing trick and expects applause. Ta-da.

The man offers no applause, only a slight widening of his eyes in horror as he sees the items.

"You have a choice to make. Option one, I will shoot you in the heart. You will die, but be certain that no investigation as to your murder will take place." I pause, letting him remember that I have significant sway over the police and everyone in this town.

He gulps, looking to the rope.

"Option two, you can hang yourself. Choose option two, and I'll make sure your wife gets a nice payday. It's doubtful your family will mourn you either way."

My every word is ice-cold, no sway either way. This is a game to me, one with a deadly result no matter his choice, but I find entertainment in the mental gymnastics he goes through, first looking for a way out and finding none, deciding which fate is the lesser of two evils.

I can feel my own heartbeat racing with excitement, anticipation of seeing the light leave his eyes. I'm not an innocent by any means, but I do not have the amount of blood on my hands as say, Gabriel Jackson. Witnessing the moment where life truly ends is like a fine wine, something to be cherished as the gift it is. I look forward to savoring it tonight.

His hands twitch, and I turn my right hand, pointing the gun at him. "Ah, so you have chosen."

Tears stream down his face as he nods. "If I choose the rope, can I write a note? I just . . . I want to say goodbye to them."

It's almost moving, his single final desire. I don't need to ask who 'them' is, his estranged wife and daughter. Not that I'm moved.

And the experiment continues as I agree, interested beyond measure at what his last words to his family will be. He's brought this upon himself, upon them, when he betrayed Goldstone in favor of me. He knew the devil he bargained with. I never hid it from him.

He reaches for the pen and pile of papers on the coffee table. They are, ironically, legal papers. It seems that Patricia, instead of wanting to come back to him in an attempt to rekindle their failed marriage, has served him with papers. Divorce.

How appropriate, then, that his final message to his family is written on them. His hand shakes, the writing nearly illegible except for its simplicity.

I'm sorry. I love you.

He pauses, like there's more to say or as if he wants to postpone the inevitable, but finally, his head falls, his elbows resting on his knees, and the cheap Bic falls to the dirty carpet.

Sobs rack his body, but he stands, his eyes meeting mine. Sad resignation shines from their depths, but also relief. He's thought of this himself, a way out from the catastrophe he created. Oh, I

155

helped, guiding him and feeding his hatred, but the first step was his. The last will be his as well.

He takes the rope, already tied, and slips it over his neck, ironically similar to the silk ties he used to wear so often.

Stepping to a chair, he loops the rope through the unique little cutouts in the walk-through arch between his living room and the kitchen. Looking at me one last time, he pleads.

"Take care of my family as you promised. Please."

I nod, wondering if he'll have the guts to actually do it the way it needs to be done for this. "I am a man of my word. The payment will be made as soon as the coroner deems your death a suicide."

I lick my lips, ready for the show and to move on with my plans.

His lips move, as if he's praying, and time stretches. He goes to step off the chair, but as the rope tightens, he chickens out, standing up again. He looks back over his shoulder, tears trickling again. "I can't. Help me."

I sigh, disappointed. Maybe he was strong . . . once. But not anymore, so I kick his feet out from underneath him. His weight jerks down, tightening the noose savagely.

He flails, jerking, and his hands go up to his neck reflexively, and I watch, fascinated. All he needs to do is pull his feet underneath him and step back to the chair. It's right there. But alcohol, panic, and the quickly diminishing oxygen in his brain have robbed him of any rational thoughts.

It's riveting. I can't look away, not that I would. I feel God-like and want to remember every moment as his life drains out, filling me with exaltation and renewed vigor.

When it's over, I shudder, euphoric at my dominance and ability to make a man perform such a feat. He was useful for a while, but in his death, his true disposability is what is most remarkable.

I do a thorough scan to insure there is no trace of my presence left behind. Though I was careful the entire time, it wouldn't do to leave accidental evidence. Not when I've gone through so much to set the scene.

Back in the car, I can't stop the smile that sweeps over my face. It feels foreign, an odd stretching of my lips and cheeks as I enjoy the pleasure of a mission accomplished. I will send his wife a payment, true to my word, through a shell company, of course.

But this was merely a cleaning up of one loose end.

I have so many agents in motion, so many plans in play, that Goldstone will never see what's coming next. Rough laughter rings through the SUV, my belly shaking with diabolical mirth at how I will bring the Golden Boy to his knees, fell his empire, and shake the very foundation of Roseboro. They will all remember me, the man who built this city, who will always rule even long after I've turned to ashes.

Roseboro is *my* legacy.

CHAPTER 15

CHARLOTTE

*I*t's amazing how things can return to some surreal sense of normalcy after such an earth-shaking event.

The morning after we fell into bed, Lance and I went downstairs together to start the morning baking and found Trixie already hard at work in the kitchen. Well, she'd been taking selfies in the kitchen, but she'd had the ovens pre-heated, at least, with a mixer of cupcake base mixing on the stand.

I couldn't even give her any shit for a photo break either when she'd been so shocked at seeing Lance and me obviously post-hookup that her screech had brought the security guards running.

But after some teasing questions that I dodged as much possible, we got to work in the kitchen, the guards went back outside with apology muffins, and Lance sat down at his table in the front.

And that's been our normal for three days. Bakery work for me and Trixie, laptop work for Lance, cleanup, and then back upstairs for some cupcake fun that has zero to do with flour and sugar.

But our phones have been blowing up, both our families texting us and calling like mad.

Lance got pretty lucky. His parents were aghast at his lack of manners but basically agreed to disagree on what would make him happy. It seems their desire to have him home and coming into the fold at Jacobs Bio-Tech is the main priority. His mom had just thought that a good woman would be another way to keep him here. But as long as he's giving daily reports on his assessments of that day's spreadsheets and making headway on analyzing current and proposed projects, they're mostly copacetic, or so he says.

I know Lance is worried about his brother. Not that Cody gives a shit about us or whatever we're doing here, but Lance shared that he thinks Cody isn't getting the recognition he deserves at work and that it's driving a huge-ass wedge in the whole family.

My family, on the other hand? Basically, I started World War III, with me on one side, Priscilla and Sabrina on the other, and Dad staying as neutral as Switzerland.

According to Priscilla, I've always been selfish but now my need to be the center of attention is physically harming Sabrina, who has taken to her bed in a state of depression over my betrayal of our sisterhood. It was hard keeping my eyes from rolling with that one. Sabrina and I are about as far from sisterly as we can be.

Sabrina's texts started out angry, blaming me for everything from her lost Barbie when she was ten to resigning her to a life of spinsterhood, but they've gotten more desperate, basically pleading with me to let her have Lance. I want to explain to her that her whole issue is treating Lance like some sort of toy when he's a man. He's not like her Barbie . . . which I will secretly admit I stole.

But I can't really hide Lance in the flowerbed like a Princess Diana Barbie, although the thought of getting a little dirty with him sounds like fun. I bet he'd look great with a few streaks of mud on his washboard abs to highlight just how deep those ridges are.

"Ooh, do tell what naughty thoughts are running through your head," Trixie teases, breaking me out of my thoughts. She would catch me the second they turn dirty, not in the previous thirty minutes I've been on auto-pilot thinking about how to make things up with Dad. I could care less about Priscilla and Sabrina, but I want him to understand.

"My family drama and trauma," I reply, and she winces like she sucked on a lemon. I did tell her that dinner was awful, and she's seen some of the texts coming in, calling me a bitch and worse. She's put two and two together.

"Ugh, leave their drama to your stepmama. I know the dreamy look and red cheeks didn't have a thing to do with that. I want to hear the sexy thoughts about Lance, or the dirty details from last night, if you're feeling generous." She clasps her hands beneath her chin, eyelashes blinking heavily.

"I told you that what happens between Lance and me stays between us," I remind her for the billionth time. She's been hounding me like crazy for anything I'll spill, which isn't much. It feels too personal and private, and honestly, as close as Trixie and I are, this feels beyond big, and the only people I'll share that type of thing with are Mia and Izzy.

"Come on, Char," she pleads with an exaggeratedly fake pout. "It's not like I can't tell that you're walking like you rode in the Kentucky Derby last night. How many times did you ride that stallion . . . two? Three? Did you even get any sleep at all? I'm living vicariously through you. Help me out or I'll be forced to imagine him licking icing off every inch of your skin, you sucking that Twinkie dry, and sweat glazing every bit of his skin." She looks over at Lance, who's typing away as per usual, and my eyes follow hers, hungry to look at him every chance I get. "He's hung like an eggplant, right? And a six-pack better than Miller Light too?"

I shake my head, even though she's right. "Is everything about food to you?"

"Food porn is a thing," she deadpans. "Have you seen that video where they make chicken cordon bleu? They butterfly the chicken breast so that it totally looks like a spread-open vajeen, stuff it full of ham, then pour white, creamy béchamel sauce over it. I damn near had an orgasm just from the chef slicing into all that creamy, meaty goodness. I couldn't decide if I was hungry or horny."

She pauses like she's thinking, but we finish her sentence together. "Both."

We giggle loud enough that Steven and Lance both look our way. Lance gives me an *I know what you're laughing about* wink and his cocky smirk promises to fulfill whatever dirty ideas Trixie and I are discussing.

I turn back to Trixie, calming down a little. "Everything's great there. But I'm just worried about my Dad. I just know that whatever Priscilla and Sabrina can't unleash on me, they're probably doing to him. He doesn't deserve being stuck like that."

Trixie places her hand on my shoulder. "He's not stuck, honey. He's choosing to be there. I know that hurts and sucks eggs, but it's the truth. Has he called or texted?"

I nod, biting my lip. "He did." I pull my phone out of my apron pocket, pulling up the text Dad sent the afternoon after Lance and I stomped out of dinner, and show it to Trixie.

It seems your focus was not as you'd led me to believe. I do hope that you can be successful, both with the bakery and Lance.

It almost sounds like a dismissal or a goodbye, which slices into my heart deeply. My apologetic response has gone unanswered so I'm not sure whether he's angry and giving us both some time to cool off or if he's written me off completely.

Trixie coughs. "Damn, that's . . . hard. Sorry, babe."

"I know. Can you, uhm . . . I need a minute," I blurt, making a dive for the kitchen and praying Trixie can handle things up front for a second.

God, everything is such a mess. Not with my pristine baking space, but with my life outside these walls. Here, I'm safe and I know what I'm doing, the recipe for success so easy to follow. Add ingredients, mix, bake, and voila . . . happiness in every delicious bite. But out there, in the rest of the world, I'm falling flat.

I've got a business I'm only just beginning that requires all the time a newborn baby does. A family who's angry at me. Friends who are in danger from a madman. Hell, it's possible that I could be in danger, a real enough risk to warrant guards.

The oven dings, and I pull out a tray of cupcakes, ironically dubbed 'Sinful Secrets' because of their decadently dark chocolate cake that surrounds a rich pocket of chocolate-flavored liqueur. The frosting is an ooey-gooey ganache.

Sinful Secrets.

As of late, it seems like I have more than my fair share. I've been hiding Lance from my family, hiding the reasons I need security from everyone, and hiding the fabulous details of Lance's lovemaking from my friends. That one can probably stay hidden, but the rest, I need to come clean about. As much as I can.

I take the tray of cupcakes out to the front, their presence mocking me every step of the way. "Hey, Trixie. Do you think you can handle closing duties tonight? I need to" —I look over at Lance, who is staring at me intently— "deal with some things."

Trixie doesn't tease like I expect her to, reading that I'm not taking Lance upstairs for more fun and games. "Go ahead, I've got this. Steven will hang out with me, right?" she flirts over at the quiet man by the door.

He lifts his chin in agreement, and Lance is already at my side, his laptop stowed away in his bag.

"What's wrong?" he asks, his eyes worried.

I shake my head, taking him by the arm. "Nothing, not really. I just need to check out for a bit. Can you stay?"

His smile warms the cold pit in my stomach and his voice is quietly reassuring. "Char, I'm not going anywhere."

Upstairs, I move into the kitchen to make spaghetti for dinner. It's one of the first things Grandma Winnie taught me to make as a little girl. It was fun because she would let me literally throw the cooked pasta against the wall to check for doneness, though I'm not sure that really works. But it was fun and I love the memory of us both flinging pasta and giggling when it would fall to the floor.

Lance sits at the counter, watching me move around the small space. "What's up?"

"The fallout's just gotten to me a bit. Trixie asked about my dad." His brows lift in question because he already knows what my dad's text said. "He hasn't responded."

"I'm sorry. I know you're close to him or want to be close to him. But I still wouldn't change what happened at dinner. They were talking about us like chess pieces to be used, but I'm not a player in anyone's game but my own. And you are so much better than anything that was being said about you that night. I just couldn't stand by any longer."

It's basically a repeat of the same conversation we'd had the morning after and several times since then. We've shared a lot about our families in the aftermath of that night, from his desire to make his own way in the world to my feeling like I didn't have a place in my own family. In a twisted way, both of us have made life choices for the same reason, in an attempt to make our fathers proud of us but also not to live under their thumbs.

"I know. I wouldn't change it either," I say softly.

Lance swears under his breath and starts pacing around the living room and fluffing the pillows on the overstuffed couch. He's a neat freak from his time in the military and can't help but set things right when he sees them out of place, even if they're barely mussed.

It's cute and lets me know that he's anxious too.

He strides to the window, peeking through the blinds. "What about them?" he says. I don't have to look myself to know what he's talking about. The bakery closes in thirty minutes so the overnight guard is likely getting into place and getting an update from Steven. "I thought you had guards because of your family. It's not unusual in a certain tax bracket, but your dad doesn't quite seem the type to pay for round-the-clock skilled coverage for you. No offense."

I stir the pasta, coating the strands with the sauce I jarred myself. He doesn't know it, but what he's asking is a test, a barometer of how deep I'm in with him.

The cynical side of me, the one that wants to focus on the bakery and not on another relationship that will likely burst into flames like every one before it, says to dodge and redirect.

The tiniest seed of hope in my center, the one that still hopes Dad will come around, wants to confide in Lance, wants him to know and accept the craziness my life truly is.

He's taken my resolution to focus on the bakery in stride, backing off when I needed to work but being right there, ready to catch me when I couldn't help but fall for him.

He's handled the outrageous behavior of my family, and his own, in a way I'd only dreamed of doing, my knight in camo armor who threw down the gauntlet when I was ready to retreat. Lance won't let me hide behind that reflex. He wants me to shine like a diamond.

But can I tell him this? It's not only my secret. That's the biggest risk of all. Not that I'm putting my life into his hands, but my friends' as well.

I take a steadying breath, praying to the gods of pasta as I sprinkle parmesan on top of the spaghetti that this is the right thing to do. "Thomas pays for them, the security."

Lance lets go of the blinds, looking back at me. "Your best friend's soon-to-be husband pays for you to have that type of security? Why?"

He's already standing taller, recognizing that if this isn't some familial show of wealth through guards, there must be an actual threat being monitored.

I set the plates on the table. "Sit down and I'll explain."

He does, his eyes steady as he looks into my soul. "Tell me what's going on, Charlotte. I'm here, and I'm not going anywhere."

As we eat, I tell him everything. About Mia finding a saboteur implanted in Thomas's company and how they sent him to prison. About Izzy helping catch the spy, which resulted in a hitman contract on her head. But Izzy being Izzy, she made the hitman fall in love with her instead.

"You know Gabe? Who sits with Steven sometimes?" I say, trying to help him place everyone in the huge web of a story I'm weaving.

"The scary dark-haired guy?" Lance says, thinking.

"Well, he is scary, really scary, in fact, but usually people think he's more boy-next-door charming," I say with a shrug.

Lance leans close. "I'm a soldier, Char. I can see the wolf in sheep's clothing. That guy might have a panty-melting grin, but he's stone-cold."

I wipe at my mouth. "Never melted my panties, that's for sure."

"Good. So does Thomas think you're the next target?" Lance asks, his mind making the important jump.

He looks ready to go to battle for me, and I can't explain, even to myself, how secure that makes me feel. I've never been one to depend on a guy, but something tells me Lance is someone I can count on.

"It's precautionary," I explain. "We just don't know what Black-well is going to do, but now that we know he's got some big grudge against Thomas and went as far as going after Izzy, Thomas wanted me to be safe. And the bakery, too, since he's a silent investor. Mia's got guards, Thomas has guards, Izzy has Gabe, Gabe has himself, and five days a week, I've got Steven and Larry and Curly."

Lance laughs at my list, lifting an eyebrow. "Larry and Curly?"

For the first time in a long hour, I laugh too. "That's what Trixie calls them. She used to call Steven 'Moe' but that ended about the time she started thinking he was hotter than a fresh-baked apple pie."

"I feel sorry for him," Lance says after a moment. "I don't think he'd know what to do with her in full-on Trixie mode."

"I don't know . . . he might be good for her. The calm waters to her craziness."

Lance nods, and I can see the thoughts swirling in his head. Have I given him too much?

CHAPTER 16

LANCE

I feel like Charlotte just dumped a lot on my plate, and I'm not talking about the spaghetti we've barely picked at. It's delicious—everything she makes is—but the information is too heavy to leave room for anything else.

Charlotte lifts her glass, taking a long sip of the iced tea she poured for us before she began her tale. "What do you think?" she asks, like she's already sure I'm about to bolt for the door.

I say nothing at first, just processing the twists and turns her explanation took. It's definitely far beyond what I'd expected when I asked about the security guards.

My fists clench in anger that someone would want to hurt her or her friends.

No, her family. More than the people who share her name, these people are her family.

"Sometimes, the people we choose are more important than the ones chosen for us," I say, and her brows knit together in confusion. I'm not sure where I'm going with this, but I try to tease out the words from the knot in my stomach. "Your family, your Dad, let you down by not being there for you. So you went out and made your own family with Mia and Izzy."

I look around the room, pointing at the framed pictures Charlotte has, all of them containing her with her two friends. "The family you chose is growing with Thomas and Gabe. And you're a fierce believer in family, Charlotte, with expectations of what that word truly means. Your own family might not have lived up to that, but you damn sure will yourself. I think you're doing exactly what a family does, circling the wagons, watching each other's backs, and preparing for war."

Tears glisten in her eyes, and she sniffles. "Thank you. I never tried to explain it before, but that's perfect. I just don't know why you'd want to get involved with me when I'm literally in the middle of this mess."

"Because I chose a family once too, and now I'm choosing another." I reach over, taking her hand, and her soft smile eggs me on. "When I left, I was young and thought I knew everything. I mostly needed to get away, not because my family was awful but because they thought they knew me when I didn't even know myself. I had to pass through the crucible of the Navy to find out what is really important, though."

Flashes flick through my mind like an old-school movie projector. Men and women I got to know almost as well as myself, each of us searching for something. A purpose, a meaning, a mission.

Charlotte touches my hand. "I've seen videos. Tough isn't a strong enough word to describe it."

I shrug. Even those who make it through have their moment in the dark. Mine just happened to actually be at night.

The sound of the bell rings out in the middle of the night. It's the third day of Hell Week and it's too dark to see who's next to you, so I don't know who just gave up. All I know is . . . it's not me.

I want to, though. Whether it's the surf breaking, or the swims, or everything else they've thrown at me, I've taken it.

But this . . . this is so much. I huddle with my boat crew, our wet bodies pressed together in a futile attempt to stay warm and fight off the hypothermia, but all I can think is . . . whose bell was that?

"Focus," my closest buddy named Wisenbury says to our boat crew. "Stay steady, one evolution at a time. Right now, our only goal is staying alive till sunrise. Anything after that, we'll worry about then. Don't quit, don't ring the bell."

He's right, and I find the strength to shiver a little more.

Don't quit.

"You're right," I admit, coming back to the present. "It was harder than tough, but there isn't really a word for it. I learned about who I am, and that was enough. I was happy. At first."

"At first?" Charlotte asks, and I nod. "What happened?"

"Reality happened," I explain simply. "During training, it's all artificial to some degree. I mean, they're never going to intentionally let someone die. Their goal is to push your boundaries further than you think you can go to show you what you're capable of. And that's dangerous, but there's always this sort of safety net that you knew was there. No one on that beach with you actually wanted to kill you."

Charlotte's eyes meet mine, horrible realization dawning. "But on missions, they really did want to kill you."

"The first time I truly felt how real it was, I busted through a door," I reply softly.

"The door went, and a bullet cracked off the frame six inches from my head. I turned to see the gunman, and I . . . shot. Just like I'd been trained to do. In my head, I was glad I was alive, but at the same time, I realized that the gunman who tried to kill me couldn't have been a day over sixteen. Not even a man himself."

The pause stretches out as I get lost in the memories, but Charlotte lets me be, not pressuring me to continue unless I want to. When I look up, she's chewing a bit of spaghetti slowly.

171

"I shot a kid. Yeah, he had an AK, and all that *him or me* justification can run through my head on a loop, but . . . it stayed with me a long time. I've seen and done some awful things in the name of my country. It's left . . . scars." I swallow thickly, forcing down the memories that threaten to overwhelm me.

"We all have them," Charlotte says. "You've seen every inch of me and know that my greatest damage isn't visible to the naked eye. It's here," she says, touching her heart, "and here." She touches her temple.

I know exactly what she means. I do have some physical scars, lines where cuts didn't heal cleanly, nicks from the occasional piece of barbed wire, and even a gnarly one on the back of my left hamstring from an IED.

Luckily, I wasn't any closer than I was, and even luckier, it hasn't impeded me in any way. But the deepest, angriest red scars are internal, the ones that pull and pucker, turning me into the man I am now, no longer the ready-to-tackle-the-world dumbass I'd been but something sharper, more careful, more intention-filled.

"I don't think I can go back," I whisper, looking down at my hands. I'm used to seeing them chipped, a line of black under the nails, ragged tears along the cuticles, but now they're clean, trimmed, and soft. The confession pains me. It's something I hadn't fully given form to in my mind, but now that I'm home, it's not only my parents' desire for me to stay that's keeping me here. It's not only the sexy, sweet redhead in front of me either.

It's me. When I was in the thick of things, training day in and day out, with missions sweeping me around the globe at the drop of a dime, I could stay in character. But now, it's like those sharp edges have washed away. I'm still hard, but I've lost the drive. I don't have anything to prove to anyone by trying to be a wetsuit cowboy out to save the world. Maybe I can stay right here and save Charlotte's world, and that can be enough.

"Then don't. Stay here," Charlotte says just as softly. Neither of us says that I could stay for us, but we're both thinking it. I know

I'm choosing to focus on her, the curve of her smile from across the table, the flipped-up red hair at the end of her braid, and the way she makes me feel like I'm enough just the way I am.

"I want to stay here with you. See where this goes. I'm not going anywhere, Char." It's a declaration, not of love, not yet, but of intention, that she's not scaring me off with her busy life, her crazy family, or her baggage. I hope she feels the same way about me.

She reverts to humor, awkwardly telling me, "Well, you're not moving in, if that's what you're after. I'm not really the married, two-point-five kids kinda gal."

I let it fall flat, not letting her escape the deeper truths we've been exposing. "Do you really believe you'll never find that?" I ask with a cocked eyebrow, probing the wound, not to inflict pain but so I can heal it appropriately.

Her shrug is answer enough, her doubt and cynicism revealed in its power. "Guys say they want the whole fairy tale and get you to believe you want the same things, but when push comes to shove, it's all a pretty lie. A carrot on a string to tease you along."

I get up, pulling her to the couch to sit beside me. I leave the dishes on the table for later, though it pains my habitual tendencies, but this is more important. I wrap an arm around her shoulders, and she lays her cheek on my chest as she curls her legs beneath her. "Tell me who hurt you, Char. Tell me everything."

She doesn't speak for a long time, but the words come.

"Daniel. He was my college sweetheart. We met soon after I started college and were joined at the hip almost from day one. We had all the wedding plans for after graduation, but he wanted to save up for a ring. We had an apartment together, and we both got jobs at Blackwell. It was perfect."

A tear lands wet and hot on my shirt, her pain hurting me more than a knife would. "Until he started spending late nights with his boss—his older, beautiful female boss. They were doing more than working, obviously."

"Bastard," I whisper, and Charlotte nods, probably thinking quite a few other names for him.

"After that, I tried online dating, mostly. Met a few frogs, but I was doing okay. Until I met Ryan. He was a little older than me and divorced. He said he wanted the whole fairy tale, and I bought it hook, line, and sinker. Right up until his wife walked in on us in bed, their baby girl on her hip. They weren't divorced after all. I'd been the other woman and hadn't even known it."

She closes her eyes, like she's waiting for my judgement, my sneered blame that she wrecked that guy's happy home. But that's not true at all. She was an innocent victim of both those guys, of her Dad's crappy choices, of Blackwell's plotting. Like a precious stone, she's been sliced away, shaped and filed into the woman she is now, with jagged edges and flaws deep inside.

But beautiful, not despite that but because of it.

She won't take her fairy tale for granted when she gets it. She'll grab it with both hands and never let go, thanking the heavens every day for it. But not until she believes she deserves it, until she trusts her prince won't go anywhere.

I tilt her chin up with the soft touch of my fingers and look into her eyes. "I don't like carrots, Charlotte. Dangling or otherwise. And I don't believe in pretty lies, but I do believe in happily ever afters."

I lean in and kiss her, letting her taste the truth, hoping she can feel the honesty in my soul.

Forgetting the plates still on the table, I scoop her up and carry her in my arms. In her bedroom, I set her down before slowly, methodically undressing her and then myself. Carefully, I unplait her hair, letting it fall wild and free around her shoulders.

Charlotte looks up at me through her lashes, more vulnerable than she's ever been. Not because she's nude, but because we're both naked, having revealed more of ourselves tonight than I think we have in a long time. Maybe ever.

Pulling the blankets back, I tell her, "Climb in." She does as I say, lying on her back like she's ready for me to cover her with my body. I want that too, but not the way she thinks.

As much as I love being inside her physically, right now, we're so emotionally inside each other that I need to just hold her. I lie down beside her, rearranging her so that she's curled up, the little spoon to my big spoon. I pet her hair, twirling the ends around my finger. "Get some sleep. I'll be right here."

I think she's going to argue, her sass coming out when I least expect it, but tonight, she gives in, sighing as she settles. Within moments, she's fast asleep, worn out not only from her baker's hours but from the energy it took to give so much to me at once.

It's a long time before I fall asleep too, cocooning Charlotte in my arms, keeping her safe from any threats, inside or out.

CHAPTER 17

CHARLOTTE

I don't remember falling asleep. We were snuggled up and my mind was racing, fears and worries washing over me, drowning me. But Lance was holding me close, giving me time, giving me space, giving me oxygen to be okay.

But I must have fallen asleep because I'm waking up, still surrounded by his arms, his warmth permeating me where our skin touches.

He touches me everywhere, not just where my back is pressed to his chest or where my ass cradles his cock, and not only where even our feet our tangle together. He touches me inside my soul.

It's terrifying, it's exhilarating, it's everything I've always wanted but been too afraid to wish for. The little seed of hope is the scariest thing I've ever felt, because I've felt it before and had it ripped away, ugly strands of my innocence left in its wake.

I need to stop this or slow this down. Put us back where we were somehow, before I slice myself open and give him my heart. Because he's going to leave. It's what men do. They lure me in, make me think I can have it all, be it all, do it all, and then they leave. I'm left to pick up the pieces of my shattered soul, again and again, ever since I was a little girl.

I can't do it again. I can already feel that if Lance leaves, the shattering will be epic, a disaster I don't know if I can recover from.

Reset. I need a reset.

I must move, or somehow twitch, because Lance pulls me in closer, his arms caging me against him. As he rearranges, his hips press forward, drawing my mind and focus to where we are only inches apart.

That's what I need to pull us back to before, thrashing and pounding and exuberant in the physicality of fucking. No drama, no baggage, no gamble that he might destroy me.

I wiggle again, this time purposefully, grinding my ass back to tease him. Slowly, Lance wakes up, a moan already on his lips. "Good morning to you too," he says, gravel in his tone.

"I need you. I need to feel . . . everything . . . nothing," I say, likely revealing too much.

Lance's hand grips my hip, stilling me, but he thrusts against me, his cock sliding through my ass cheeks. "I've got you."

He slips an arm underneath me, holding my chest in place. He kicks the blanket off, his other hand pulling my thigh up and back over his, opening me to the cool air of the room. It feels cleansing, purifying, vulnerable to be held in place, though the physical exposure is so much less than the emotional.

His cock nudges at my entrance like he's testing my wetness, but I'm drenched for him, needing this. "Please . . ." I beg, my head falling back to his shoulder. "Hard."

He nuzzles my neck, inhaling me, and I grip his hair, holding him to me too. With a fierce thrust, he enters me to the hilt, impaling me on his cock. I jerk at the intrusion, the feeling a perfect blend of pleasure and pain, much like Lance's presence in my life, but when he starts to stroke into me, pleasure takes over.

He's rough in the dark, both of us only going by feel, the sound of slapping skin filling the room. I can't hold back the moans, the symphony pouring from my mouth as he plays my body like an instrument he already knows too well.

His hand moves from my thigh to my clit, teasing it in slow circles, soft in comparison with the hard way he's fucking me. "I know what you're doing, Charlotte. But don't be scared. I can handle your demons. Can you handle mine?"

I don't answer, afraid the answer is no . . . more afraid the answer is yes. He smacks at my pussy, a sharp sting that puts me on the edge, crying out as I teeter, ready to fall into my orgasm. Ready to fall into him.

He pops me once more, punishing my lack of faith, my unwillingness to jump, and I spasm. I can't hold back the tidal wave washing over and through me any longer. "Yes. Yes . . . yes!" I cry. We both know I'm not simply calling out my pleasure but answering his question.

I tried to fight, tried to deny, tried to protect myself. But it didn't work. In one orgasm, he's decimated my defenses and we both know it. I may never get a happily ever after, if such a thing truly exists. But I'm fully on this ride with Lance until it goes off the tracks, which I know it inevitably will.

But I'll take as much of him as I can get. Soak it up to get me through the days after he's gone because even if he doesn't go back to the SEALs, he'll leave me eventually. They always do.

For now, though, I feel him bucking deep into me, bottoming out like he can imprint himself on my most private of places and make me believe. As he comes, his hot cum splashing inside me, I almost do.

Afterward, Lance stays inside me, his long fingers tracing along my skin like he's leap-frogging from one freckle to the next in the dark. It feels right, like we could stay here like this forever, no ghosts of the past, no shimmery future, this moment enough to live in.

But sleep overtakes us, and once again, I relax into him and let the dreams wash me under.

My alarm is an annoying chirp that's loud enough to wake the dead. It has to be to rouse me from the peace of the early morning hours to begin baking, but this morning, it's even worse. I feel like I've been running all night, mind churning from dream to nightmare and back again.

Lance reaches over, swatting at the alarm, and blessed silence returns. But he doesn't let me fall back asleep. He kicks the covers off us, the shocking cold making me cry out. My eyes only open to slits, but I look back and see him smiling. He's one of those chipper morning people, which usually I don't mind since he makes coffee first thing, but this morning, I could really use a few more minutes of shut eye.

I relax back into the soft mattress, mumbling, "Five minutes." Or at least I think I say that.

Lance is having none of that. He spanks my bare ass, the pop loud but not as loud as my cry of surprise. "What the hell?" Yeah, as much of a morning person as he may be, I'm most definitely not.

"Rise and shine, porcupine. We've got work to do, muffins to muff, cupcakes to cup, and pies to . . . pie? I don't know. I was on a roll, so work with me," he says, laughing.

It doesn't feel weird or heavy. In fact, it's like he's doing his best to make things between us seem just the way they were before, but I can see the darkness in his blue eyes, the way he's watching me carefully, even though I've only got one eye fully opened now.

"Coffeeeee," I say, sounding like a zombie hunting for brains.

"On it," he snaps, salute and all, before disappearing out of the bedroom. I can hear him in the kitchen, the beep as the coffee maker starts, then the water turning on as he cleans up the plates from last night.

He's nervous too. That's his tell. Or maybe he's just being a neat freak. Hard to know for sure, but I should get out there and help him.

I roll over, stretching long and lean on the bed, and stand, reaching for the ceiling once again to get all the kinks out of my muscles. I don't bother making my bed—not my tendency, unlike some people—instead, grabbing Lance's T-shirt from the floor and pulling it over my head.

When I pop through, he's standing in front of me, blessedly bitter nectar of the gods in hand. "Thank you," I say, taking it. It's so dark I can feel my body getting energized just from the smell.

"Hop in the shower. I'll make you breakfast," he offers, taking my half-empty cup from me. "Promise, it'll help."

I smile. "I'm headed downstairs to make breakfast for half of Roseboro. I can grab a muffin hot out of the oven."

His single lifted brow dares me to argue with him. "You need protein for the long day, and I saw eggs and bacon in your fridge. Now, get." He swats at my ass again, and I squeal, running for the bathroom like he's chasing me.

I want him to chase me, I think.

God, I'm wishy-washy as fuck. From my middle of the night freakout to wanting him by the light of day.

I suds up my hair and body, noting that I'm deliciously sore from the rough, pounding way Lance took me in the middle of the night. After a quick rinse, I dry off, braiding my hair out of the way and foregoing makeup. It doesn't do me any good in the hot kitchen, mostly melting right off.

I yank on jeans and a *Cake Culture* shirt, the smell of bacon teasing at me enough to make me hurry. In the kitchen, I see Lance standing at my stove, naked save for the apron he's tossed on. His bare ass looks downright edible peeking out the back.

181

I slide up behind him, standing on my tiptoes to peek over his shoulder. "Something looks delicious," I purr.

"SEALs can cook, you know. You don't have to sound so surprised."

I grin, smacking his ass the way he did mine before getting in a pinch. "Wasn't talking about the bacon."

He kisses me, quick and casual, before telling me to sit down. I sit at the now clean table, and he sets down two plates of eggs and perfectly crisped bacon.

As he sits, he says, "Wanted to talk to you about something."

Shit. That didn't take long for the shoe to drop. Some fucking Cinderella I am, shattering glass slippers everywhere I go.

The bacon that was delicious a second ago now tastes like ash as I swallow, forcing it down. "Okay," I say, resigned.

"Thomas's challenge, the Hope Initiative. Are you doing anything yet? I thought we could do something together if not."

Errrk! My brain gets whiplash as his words sink in. "Wait. What?"

He picks up his own fork. "The Hope Initiative. Wanna do it together?"

I can feel my eyes widen, my heart grow, and my stomach flip-flop. "You want to do a project together?"

When he nods, I almost don't believe it. Is he for real? Like for-real, for-real? I keep feeling like I'm getting punked, but maybe that's my own cynical self-sabotage? That starts a whole hamster-wheel of thoughts running through my mind, so I stop them with a single word. "Yes."

With one question, my fears are pushed away and we end up discussing ideas to make a difference in Roseboro at four thirty in the morning, over breakfast in my apartment. It feels . . . amazing. As long as I keep the door shut on the little demon in my head that whispers *it won't last*.

"So, Trixie suggested we do a subsidized preschool at a nursing home, bridge the generations-type thing. Or scholarships for those who need them for a brighter future." I can't help the grin that crosses my face at her *Scholarships for Strippers* idea.

"You think she'll be okay working with me too?" Lance asks, and I can tell he doesn't want to step on anyone's toes by jumping in on this.

"Might cost you a couple of stories about sweaty soldiers playing volleyball in the sand, complete with descriptions of the guys' bodies, but you can handle that, right?"

"Oh, yeah," he says, a devilish smile on his face, and I wonder how he's going to torture Trixie with the tales. "But seriously, the bridging the gap type deal is a good idea. We could call it 'Generations of Hope' or something like that. There was something similar for our K-9 dogs when they'd retire or get injured. Usually, they'd go to their handlers, but for the dogs who needed to be adopted, they'd pair them up with a vet, usually someone with PTSD. The K-9 acts as a type of emotional support for them because they've both been through the same things. It's a perfect match for them both. The generations thing sounds like that, helping them get through similar things or address universal issues."

"Wow, I didn't know anything like that even existed," I say, sad at the need for something like that but thankful it exists.

Lance shakes his head, shrugging. "It doesn't in Roseboro. But we don't have to do that specifically. We should all get together— you, me, and Trixie—and figure something out."

Plan made, he takes my empty plate to the sink, rinsing it before putting it into the dishwasher. "Have I told you how sexy you are when you clean things?" I say, a sultry tease woven in the question.

He flexes his arm and winks at me. "Yep, I figured that's why you were letting me wash your cookie sheets every night. Wait, no . . . suds your pan." He smirks like his pun is creatively hilarious.

I can't help but laugh. He's trying so hard sometimes. "Stick with the food puns. They're tastier."

"You've got me there." He looks down, noting that he's still naked except for my apron. He pulls the white fabric over his head, hanging it on the hook and damn-near strutting back to the bedroom, dick swinging like a fucking god. Or a Fucking God. Honestly, he's both.

Which both scares me to death and thrills me beyond measure.

It's okay, Char. You've got this.

CHAPTER 18

LANCE

*I*n Charlotte's bedroom, I get dressed, grinning that my T-shirt is back on the floor where she dropped it. I leave it there, grabbing a fresh one out of my duffel that's sitting in the chair in the corner. I'm far from moving in, but after the crazy dinner, it'd seemed prudent to mostly stay out of my house and be backup for Charlotte. I travel ultra-light so it didn't seem like a big step.

But after last night, it does. I want to put my socks and underwear in her drawers. Literally, that's not even a pun. I want to wake her grumpy ass up with coffee every morning and cuddle her to sleep each night. I want to fuck her until she realizes she's mine. I want to prove to her that a man stays.

That I'll stay.

We head downstairs, and just I reach for the doorknob, it opens to reveal Trixie. "Well, good morning, you two. Hope you had a *good, long, hard* night." She drawls out every syllable, making it sound as dirty as possible.

I don't have to look behind me to know that Charlotte is blushing hard. "It was great. Uh, thanks again for taking over closing duties so I could . . . uh . . ." Charlotte trails off, and I grin,

LAUREN LANDISH

knowing she just unintentionally lobbed that softball in the air for Trixie.

Trixie's glee is obvious. "So you could open? Your legs!" She laughs like it's the height of humor, and I can't help but laugh too.

It takes Charlotte a beat to give in, but she laughs too.

I press a kiss to her cheek and toss her a rescue line. "You made a delicious dinner, thank you. But now I need to go run five or twenty miles or so to burn it off, so I'll see you later. After that, I'm going to reach out to Thomas and see if I can help at all with security."

She shakes her head, her braid bouncing from shoulder to shoulder. "No, he's got it covered. You don't have to—"

I give her a firm look, inviting no argument. On this I won't budge, not on her safety. Everything else, I can take at her pace, even when it's two steps forward and one back.

But this is life or death, possibly, and I won't take no as an answer. "You said Izzy has Gabe because of who he is?" I ask, and she nods, eyes flicking to Trixie. I guess Trixie doesn't know that part of the story. "Well, you have me, and I've got some skills of my own. I just want to help, be in the loop. I think I know the guy Thomas has coordinating things. I'll just have a friendly conversation with him."

She bites her lip, still not sure, but nods.

Trixie is done being patient, though, and shoves at me, pushing me toward the back door. "Yeah, yeah . . . smoochey, smoochey. I'll see you later and all that jizz. Get it? Jizz, not jazz because well, you know. That's why you need to go. We've got girl talk to do, dicks to dissect, orgasms to evaluate, and such. So buh-bye."

I laugh, grabbing at the door frame and hollering back, "Hey, are you really going to tell her about my meat? The bacon, I mean." I toss her a big wink, which she swats out of the air with a laugh.

186

I don't care in the least if she's in there spilling the dirty details of every last bit of what we do. Especially to Trixie, who I'm pretty sure is on my side and will tell Charlotte to hang on tight to me with everything she's got. Good thing that only makes it easier for me to hold on to her too.

Getting in my car, I pull a card out of my wallet.

"Hello," the voice answers flatly. "Who's this?"

"Hey, Jon, it's Lance Jacobs. Could I take you to lunch today?"

AFTER CHARLOTTE'S STORY, IT SEEMS IRONICALLY APPROPRIATE THAT we meet at the Gravy Train, the diner that seems to be the lynchpin of not only the three girls' friendship but the scene of so much of the skull fuckery that's led to all this.

The coffee's good, the company not so much so. Gabe Jackson, the wolf in sheep's clothing, stares at me openly from across the room. He probably thinks his look is neutral, but I can read the hostility and distrust plain as day. I've handled guys like this before, though, and I know that what most people would see as friendliness he sees as weakness.

But I can't 'swell up' on him either, as he'd see that as a threat. So instead, I give him a nod. He's part of Charlotte's chosen family. I must pass his muster, as he slides his eyes back to Izzy, who's running her ass off.

I've only met her once when she came into the bakery, but she feels familiar because of the way Charlotte talks about her and the numerous pictures in Charlotte's apartment.

I finish my first cup just as Jonathan Goldstone walks in, looking for all the world like a Secret Service agent in his black suit, white shirt, and shined black shoes. I can even see the slight print of his piece under his jacket, and the sight reassures me.

"Lance, good to see you again," Jonathan says, shaking my hand as he slides into a booth. Izzy comes over, already carrying a cup of coffee, which she sets it down in front of him. "Thanks . . . tell Henry no usual today. Maybe tomorrow?"

Izzy nods and leaves, and I'd bet my left nut she's already texting Charlotte and Mia to make sure they know about this meeting. I give Jonathan a raised eyebrow. "You've become a regular here? You have my interest piqued."

"Good food, conveniently located . . . and the coffee's not too bad," Jonathan says, but I can read something behind his eyes. He's always been one to play things close to the chest, and I realize that he chose this location for our meet because Gabe would serve as his backup. Smart guy, one I can respect. "What can I do for you?"

"I'm sure you're well aware that I'm seeing Charlotte?"

Jon's smile is placating, neither confirming nor denying.

"She told me everything," I continue, moving this conversation ahead a few hops and skips. "I assume you're the coordinator on all of this."

His posture changes, from his relaxed meeting-a-friend laidback style to something more serious. He leans forward, hands stacked on top of one another on the table, letting me see that he's not making a move. Yet.

"Depends. Define *everything*."

"She told me about the saboteur. And Gabe." My eyes flick to the side, seeing that Gabe is taking a keen interest in our conversation.

"Stop. Don't say another word. Let's go outside," Jon says, already getting up. He tosses a five on the table and heads for the door. Gabe starts to get up too, but Jon gives him the smallest headshake, confirming what I already knew.

Jon's here at Thomas's behest, coordinating the security and likely doing more. I know he's a skilled man, perhaps better-equipped mentally than I am for this job. Para Rescue is about saving lives, not taking them, even if he's skilled tactically as well. He's got cojones that would help him stand strong against the likes of someone like Blackwell, especially for family.

Outside, he doesn't head to a car, instead motioning for me to follow him. We walk side by side down the sidewalk, and he talks without looking at me. "Bad history with mics. But directional mics on a moving target with ambient traffic noise involved are pure shit eighty percent of the time, so we walk. And fill me in on what you think *everything* means."

I sigh, giving him the basic rundown of what Charlotte told me last night, finishing with, "You're on this, right? You're going after Blackwell? I'm in."

Jon shakes his head, seeming almost amused at my go-getter attitude, but I can sense the anger underneath. "Figured you would, but it's not that easy. We've already looked at it from every angle. This isn't a door kicker op. A ghost couldn't get into Blackwell Tower right now, not even an angel, fallen or otherwise." He looks back at the diner, but I don't get the joke he seems to be in on.

"So we sit on our hands?"

Jon shrugs. "Thomas is taking a different tack, more strategic long-game. He's cutting away Blackwell's supports, one by one, until he's ready to fall. In the meantime, we secure the perimeter."

He doesn't sound happy about that. We're men of action. But if the higher-ups say hold, then we hold, and I guess in this instance, Thomas Goldstone is the highest-ranking officer on this op.

"Okay, then loop me in the security detail. Gabe is watching Izzy. I can help watch Charlotte." It's not what I'd hoped for, but it's something, at least. As much as I don't want to go back to war, for Charlotte, I'll go to battle right here on my home ground.

Jon wavers for a solid minute, eyeing me up and down like he can measure my intention, value, and more if he only looks hard enough. I must pass his inspection because he finally says, "Unofficially. In uniform, you outranked me, but this is my team. Still, another pair of eyes and set of hands couldn't hurt. I'll introduce you around, keep you informed, but that's it. You're backup, not the primary. You armed?"

I shake my head. "Recommend a local store?"

"I'll cover you," he says. We've made a lap around the block, returning to the Gravy Train parking lot. He heads to his SUV and opens the back door, flipping the seat to reveal a hidden compartment below. He reaches in and hands me a beauty of a Sig, just like the ones I'm used to. "Too big for my carry rig, but it's a good gun. Don't fuck it up."

I nod, sliding it in my waistband and pulling my shirt over it. It's too big to really hide this way, but I only need to get to my car across the lot.

"Let's go meet the team," Jon says, and I nod, glad to be able to help.

CHAPTER 19

CHARLOTTE

*T*he end of the week comes, including another successful custom cake creation, this one for a birthday party. It's perfect, nothing big and fancy like the wedding cake but a small, double-layer round with a rainbow of flowers laid out to look like a mane, flowing from a golden unicorn horn. I'd even played with edible glitter and candy sequins to make it more 'extra'.

Throughout the busy week, Lance is still here. He's spent every day working on his laptop, leaving to make appearances at the office, or to get what he calls PT in, but coming back to help me in the kitchen or feed me takeout for dinner.

It's nice to have someone to lean on, and I'm trusting more and more that he's got my back.

He's a genuine American hero who wants to make me his number one. I might be his toughest mission to date, but I'm trying to have a little faith.

"I know that look," Trixie says, jostling me from my reverie as she takes the tray of Ooey-Gooey Buttery Goodness Bars from my hand. "The *'I'm in love but don't want to admit it because I'm a scaredy-cat that's scared'* look." She fakes a cat hiss, grinning. "All

Trixie smirks, one brow lifting in a twist and the other lowering over her eye. She looks like a girly version of The Rock with his famous expression. She's not remotely convinced but offers me a lifeline. "Fine, if you're thinking about the event, then tell me all about it. Give me the latest update."

Trixie had been thrilled to go in with Lance and me on the Generations of Hope idea. Over several days, we spent every spare moment trying to figure out how to make the biggest impact and finally landed on a big festival-type event for the kickoff with smaller get-togethers on a regular basis after that. We're hoping to win Thomas's funding to keep them going.

But first, we have to make the kickoff a huge hit to showcase the idea. So Lance has been steering the ship, making every wish we come up with actually come true.

"Well," I tell Trixie, going through my mental checklist, "he's scouted several locations, and I think he's actually going to get Main Street to let us use the park in front of the community center. We'll be able to use the basketball courts for a charity game, set up tents with the various activities, and he got a burger place to sponsor the food. It's actually happening, Trix! We're going to bring everyone together, from the youngest to the oldest, and Roseboro will be better for it."

She nods but frowns. "Hey, I thought we were doing the food?"

I shake my head, transferring mini-tartlets to the bakery case. "We're doing mini-cupcake samples and sponsoring the Bake-a-Thon tent, where grandmas like my Grandma Winnie can teach the next generation how to bake. But we'll also have a grill for burgers that the grandpas are going to man."

She smiles. "We are doing it, aren't we? I talked to Terry

192

Maxwell, the computer fixer guy, about having a booth too. He said he'd facilitate a social media workshop for the older set, get the tech-savvy kids to help out. He said he'll have everybody, young and old, safely on Instagram before the end of the event."

"And I talked to Mrs. Petrie, Izzy's neighbor, about doing an arm-knitting demonstration," I conclude. "She makes these monstrous blankets out of fluffy yarn. I think the kids will love them. Hell, I love them so much I'm hoping I have time to get to her booth to learn myself."

We stand back, looking at the case filled with the first round of today's goodies. "Ready for the before-church crowd?" Trixie asks, and I see the first car pull up outside.

I nod, and Steven flips the lock and turns on the buzzing neon sign.

Trixie is helping the first customer when I feel my phone buzz in my pocket. I look down, seeing it's Mia. "Hey, Trix, I'll be a second," I say, waving my phone at her.

I can't be gone long. The rush is going to start any minute, but I always take time to answer Mia if I can. Besides being my bestie, she'd be the one to notify me if there was something to worry about with the whole Blackwell situation.

"Hey, girl," I answer as I swoosh through the double doors to the kitchen.

"What's shaking, bacon?" she says, my food puns rubbing off on everyone.

"Busy, busy, just starting the Sunday rush. You awake already or still awake?" Either option is equally likely. Mia is a total video game nerd and will start a game at ten p.m. to play for 'just a minute', and boom, here comes the sun. She's tricked me into that more than once, but not since I opened the bakery and had to start getting up around the time she goes to bed after a gaming session.

"Still awake, actually, though not from gaming. A little birdie told me to do a full background check on your boy, which of course means I need to know what the fuck's up with you and GI Joe!"

My jaw drops, even though somehow, I'm not surprised. "You did not do a background check on my boyfriend."

The word rolls off my tongue before I can stop it, but it feels good. It feels true, and I like that. A lot.

I can hear her eye roll. "Of course I did. I checked Gabe out too, though his file is unsurprisingly thin. Your man's, though? Thick, like thiiiick. I know it all, family, military, et-cetera, et-cetera. But what I don't know is, how're you doing and what're you doing with him?"

I fidget, drawing invisible shapes on the clean stainless-steel prep table. "I'm good, I'm . . . uh, I'm *seeing* him?"

Mia isn't one for pussyfooting around, and she slips into her Russian accent, which makes everything sound like a threat. "In Mother Russia, man is seen or not seen. No questions. So which?"

"Seeing," I admit. "I'm still not sure what he's doing with me when he could have someone easier, more beautiful, less *me*, but he's still here so I'm trying to believe him when he says he's not going anywhere."

"Wow," Mia says breathlessly. "It's about fucking time. You are the shit, girl, and we've been telling you for years that you deserve the very best and to stop settling for assholes. It's not that all guys are shit—helloooo, Tommy?"

I can't decide if she's merely talking about how awesome her guy is or if he just walked through the room, but the result's the same either way. He's one of the good ones. A moment later, she continues. "You've had your pick of the assholes, or let them pick you. I don't know which is worse. Sounds like you got a good one this time, though."

"He is, isn't he?" I know I sound like a lovesick teenager, but honestly, I feel a little spun out like I did the first time the boy I was crushing on looked my way. And that was in third grade. Her words start to sink in and I can't help myself. "What do you know about him?"

He's already told me so much, but I want more. I want it all. Like maybe if I truly understand everything about him, I can somehow figure out how to make him stay. I know it's a weakness, but my experiences weigh on me, making me feel like not enough no matter how many times my friends tell me I am.

"Well, Jonathan knows him well enough to vouch for him. Jon's the guy who controls your security and is helping me snoopity-doo-dah into Blackwell. I hear the guys on the ground respect Lance, but *you'd* know that better than *me*," she accuses.

"We went out to meet the SUV guys. I'd only ever met Steven, but Lance introduced me to Brian-slash-Larry and Paul-slash-Curly too," I say, confirming her accusation and reminding myself to use their real names, not the *Three Stooges* ones Trixie prefers. "Jon got Lance a gun, which made me nervous at first, but he showed me how he takes it apart, cleans it, and stores it safely. I don't want to ever touch it, but it helped me feel comfortable that he was confident with it. Silly, I know, considering he's a SEAL."

"Look," Mia says quietly, "he's clean as a whistle on paper. The timing just makes me nervous. Are you sure he's not some Blackwell sleeper agent? I mean, Blackwell's got more tentacles than a giant squid, ones we never even considered." For all my trust issues, Mia has some of her own. I know she feels guilty she didn't catch on to the saboteur's deception at Goldstone sooner.

"I trust him, Mia, and that speaks volumes," I reassure her. "Not just in my brain, but in my gut too. I know my picker's been a bit broken in the past, but I really think I'm doing the right thing this time."

Funny how trying to convince Mia helps me convince myself.

Not that I need convincing, exactly. I do trust Lance, can feel it in my bones that he's good for me, but my pesky demons keep trying to steal my happiness. But I won't let them. I refuse to lose something this good because of my cynicism and lack of faith.

"Okay, if you're with him, I'm in. I'll let Tommy know the family grew by two feet. What size shoe does he wear, anyway?" Mia says casually. Too casually.

"Big enough for me to feel it the morning after," I reply to the question she's really asking. I don't know where the stereotype came from that only guys engage in locker room talk because Mia, Izzy, and I share way too much. I know everything from how dominant Thomas can be to how sweet Gabe often is, which seems counter-intuitive if you knew the men, but I guess you never know what goes on behind closed doors. Unless you spill *all* like we do.

"Gotta go, honey. Trixie is going to kill me if I leave her out there alone for the rush much longer," I tell her honestly. She says something about our usual lunch date, the ones I've been missing out on in favor of doing custom orders, and I agree noncommittally.

As soon as I hang up, Trixie pokes her head through the doors, her eyes wide. I get a good look at her eyes and see the horror there. Something's wrong.

"Oh, my God, Char, you have to come!"

CHAPTER 20

*O*ut front, Steven is on his feet, his phone pressed to his ear.

"What's wrong?" I ask, customers looking around in confusion. From behind me, I hear Lance barreling down the stairs, so he must be who Steven is calling in as backup. But from what?

I make my way toward the counter and see a small man in a brown three-piece suit who somehow reminds me of wheat bread. He adjusts his glasses down his nose, somehow managing to look down at me though we're basically the same height.

"Are you Charlotte Dunn, proprietor of this establishment?" he sneers, running a finger along the glass case, leaving a smudgy fingerprint.

"Yes, can I help you?" I reply, even if I'm pissed about that fingerprint.

His eyes are sharp, his smirk arrogant as he speaks slowly and clearly so that everyone in the room can hear him. "I'm Barrett Williams, Roseboro Health Department. I'm here to investigate some rather troubling complaints." He glances at the clipboard in his hand. "Red hair in several cupcakes, unclean surfaces in the kitchen, and most disturbing of all, a nasty roach infestation."

He leans in as he says the last part, like he intends to keep it between us, but everyone in the room has gone silent and hears every bit, judging by the gasps of disgust that resonate through the crowd.

My head is already shaking, refuting his words. "That's patently untrue. We're exceptionally clean here and follow every rule regarding health and food safety. You're welcome to do an inspection now, if you'd like," I say, pushing the double doors to the kitchen open.

There's nothing to see but a standard working kitchen. Food storage containers on a baking rack by the wall, several prep tables in the middle with treats in various stages of preparation, a sink full of this morning's dishes waiting to be scrubbed and run through the washer, which is steaming with its current load.

But Mr. Williams doesn't frame it like that. He looks disgusted. "Are those pies uncovered? A fly or a roach could crawl right up onto them. And is that butter at room temperature? That can lead to foodborne illness if not refrigerated properly."

I can see my customers shuffling uncomfortably, several with their phones out, either typing away or discretely filming.

"The pies are cooling as per protocol. And butter has to reach room temperature to make frosting. There must be some misunderstanding. We're compliant with all the guidelines." He's hearing none of my explanations, though, and I hear the jingle of the bell as people make an escape for the door empty-handed.

My mouth opens and closes, no sound coming out. This is ridiculous, unfounded complaints and accusations that aren't even in the food handling safety guidebook.

"I'm afraid we'll have to close for the day for the inspection. I certainly wouldn't want to eat anything from here until this *misunderstanding* has been cleared up." He sneers, like my label is obviously untrue.

Trixie and Lance help escort customers out, promising them that everything is fine and that we'll be cleared of any concerns and reopen with an A-plus rating as soon as possible. Murmurs of 'Well, I still won't be back' and 'Roaches? Ew!' sound as loud as a death knell for my fledgling bakery.

I turn back to Mr. Williams, wanting to wipe the congenial smile off his face with my fist. But I force myself to stand tall, escorting him into the kitchen for a thorough inspection.

An hour later, he's been through my dish machine with a cotton swab to look for mold, he's knelt down in my freezer to look beneath the storage racks for any evidence of infestation, and he's bagged several different foods as 'samples' for lab inspection. From what I can tell, he's found nothing. My kitchen is virtually brand-new and we take great care of it.

Lance has been typing away on his phone, but I've been too busy worrying to give it much thought until there's a knock at the back door. "Finally," he sighs. "This isn't my kind of fight."

He opens the door, and Thomas steps through with a severe-looking woman in a black suit and sensible heels.

I can feel Mr. Williams shrink next to me, the snarky bite he's had dulled just by this woman's presence. Her words neuter him even more. "Anita Culpepper, Ms. Dunn. I'm the Health Commissioner for Roseboro. I oversee all public health inspectors, including Mr. Williams here. Mr. Goldstone asked that I be present for the investigation. May I see the complaint?"

Mr. Williams flips to a page at the back of his clipboard, handing it over to his boss, who reads it aloud. "First complaint, two weeks ago . . . *several red hairs found in red velvet cupcakes.* Second complaint, one week ago . . . *door to kitchen opened and 'it looked grody back there.'* Third complaint, yesterday . . . *disgusting place, roaches everywhere, even upstairs where the owner lives.* That one has a vomiting emoji added." She flips the paper over and scans it again before looking around the kitchen.

"Have you found any evidence of health code violations?" she asks Mr. Williams.

"I sliced into a few cupcakes but didn't see any hairs," he starts, but I interrupt, anger boiling over.

"Four dozen cupcakes! He destroyed forty-eight cupcakes to crumbs looking for something that's not there."

He has the decency to look chagrined, at least. "Freezer and dish machine are clean. I was just about to look behind the equipment for evidence of roaches and mice."

Ms. Culpepper's jaw is set in stone as she grits her teeth. "By all means, do so." We all watch closely as he goes over to the stove-top, turning on his penlight and looking at the burners. He kneels down and looks underneath, then behind. "Anything?"

He gets up, shaking his head.

"So what you're telling me is that you bust in here, loudly proclaiming to all of my customers that I have a filthy business, making sure to enunciate for every camera as you made claims that you can't remotely substantiate. Is that what you're telling me, Mr. Williams?" I stare him down, thankful for my business classes. The lessons are still in the filing cabinet of my brain, and I pull them out, ready to rage now. "That sounds like defamation, malicious intent to destroy my business, and a gross disregard for standard protocol."

Ms. Culpepper takes over before Williams can dig his own grave with his own mouth. "Miss Dunn, you have the apologies of the Health Department. It does appear that everything is in proper order here. Your A-plus rating of a month ago stands unchanged, and I will be sure to review investigative protocol with Mr. Williams."

She turns to go but pauses, looking back. "In my experience, when a new business opens up, people are harsh, sometimes needlessly so, going so far as to file unwarranted complaints. Perhaps there's another baker who is jealous of your new and successful venture? I hate to suggest that, but it wouldn't be the first time I've seen something like that. Just be certain to uphold your own high standards, and everything will come out okay in the wash."

Her hand on the doorknob, Lance calls out. "Wait, Ms. Culpepper. Would you possibly help alleviate some citizen concerns about the food of *Cake Culture*?"

Her eyes narrow, the ironclad persona once again coming out. "I do not accept bribes, if that's what you're suggesting. Nor make recommendations. I merely verify that rules are followed."

"No, nothing like that," he quickly reassures her. "It's just that, given how clean the kitchen is and the fact that there are zero concerns with any violations, would you consider eating a cupcake of your choosing on the way to your car? It'd go a long way in making it seem like everything is okay here if you're willing to eat one out of the very kitchen you're inspecting, know what I mean?"

She tilts her head, almost as if she's reading bylaws in her mind. "That is acceptable under the guidelines." A grin breaks out across her face, making her look ten years younger. "Can I have a Sinful Secrets? I've been dying to try one."

I start to box up a Sinful Secrets, but she holds up a hand. "No sense in boxing it. The point is to eat it." She takes a dainty bite, moaning in delight. "Oh my gawd, it's as good as I thought it'd be. I'll be back. You just gained a customer."

And with that, she and Mr. Williams walk out. Her, cupcake in hand and a smile on her face. Him, sad and droopy, and likely a bit scared at facing her wrath at the office.

I look around the room at my people. Trixie looks worried, nibbling on her lip like its candy. Lance looks pissed but under control, while Thomas looks resigned.

"I'm sorry, Charlotte," Thomas says. "I've dealt with this before. False complaints are one of Blackwell's tools." His brows knit together, and he looks around. "Though I'm not sure I see the play here."

"I don't think it's him this time," I respond. "Did you hear Ms. Culpepper? Jealous rivals?"

"But there's not really another bakery that we're competing against. It's just grocery stores, for the most part, that make cakes around here," Trixie protests. "Though I guess their bakers might be out of work if you go huge?"

"Not a bakery rival, a family one," I explain. "I think Sabrina did this because I took Lance away from her in the twisted fairytale in her mind. She's trying to get back at me by taking away something important to me."

It makes sense. I haven't heard from Priscilla or Sabrina since the third run of bitchy texts they sent me. And this is just nasty enough, juvenile enough, that it fits Sabrina's style perfectly. She's not the type to come at me directly. Having someone else do her dirty work is right up her alley.

"Oh, shit," Trixie whispers, covering her mouth with her hands.

Lance seems unsure but says, "It's worth a conversation. Do you want me to go with you?"

I shake my head, wishing he could but knowing differently. "Thank you, but no, I need to do this alone."

CHAPTER 21

CHARLOTTE

*T*he house looks like it did last time I visited, but it feels different. The anger and disgust I've been getting from Priscilla and Sabrina feel tacky, like their oily aggression is reaching out to me, pulling me into their games.

It took me so long to escape, right up until I graduated high school, then I ran like hellhounds were on my heels. Ever since, I've visited infrequently, and usually by force.

Today, I come freely, no longer the scared little girl they can keep under their thumbs. Today, I'm ready to war. Don't mess with my baby, my bakery, or I'll go full Mama Bear on your ass.

I knock on the front door, my heart already racing in anticipation. But it's not Sabrina's smug face when the door opens. It's Dad. Probably a good thing, because there's a fair-to-good chance I would've punched Sabrina on sight. I guess that's still to be found out.

Dad looks exhausted, his face drawn and his shoulders slumped and withered. It's like he's aged ten years in only a few weeks. "Dad? You okay?"

His huff of laughter is humorless as he waves me in. "Of course, but it's been a rather taxing time."

He walks off, not waiting for me to apologize or explain, though I don't truly feel the need to do either. I follow him into the kitchen, closing the door behind me. Dad grabs a glass from the cabinet and then his own personal disgusting poison, V8 juice, from the fridge. He pours carefully, talking to the glass. "I've been chastised rather fully over that dinner, and after. I hope it was worth it?"

I nod, biting my lip and feeling like a little girl who's disappointed her daddy once again. "I am sorry it all went down like that, but I'm not sorry I didn't let Priscilla and Sabrina steamroll over me again like they always do. I'm not sorry that Lance stood up for himself and for me."

He sighs, turning to lean against the counter and give me a hard look. "Am I to take it that you and Mr. Jacobs are still seeing each other? That this is something more serious, and you weren't stealing your sister's man just because you could?" I can hear the tagline Priscilla and Sabrina have been selling in his words.

"Is that what you think?" He doesn't answer but tilts his head questioningly. "I met Lance at the gala. After that, he started coming by the bakery every day. He'd do his work, and he'd help me. We spent quite a bit of time together, then the dinner came. Priscilla and Sabrina obviously had all these plans, but by then, Lance and I were . . . something." I don't know how to describe us now. I certainly don't have a label for what we were then.

"So he stood up for you when he felt you were being insulted," Dad summarizes. "And now?"

I move closer to him, standing right in front of him so he hears me loud and clear. "I'm following my heart, which is hard and scary, but he's being patient with me."

Dad looks at me carefully, and I feel like he's weighing our future. If he can't see that I've done nothing wrong here, I don't know that I'll ever forgive him. It's not about Lance, or not just about him, but about how my Dad perceives me. Growing up with Sabrina was hard on me, and he didn't get that, but this is far beyond any petty insults and stunts we pulled as kids.

This is my heart. This is my life.

I freeze, realizing that I'm thinking about both Lance and the bakery.

Finally, after an eternity, Dad nods. "My little girl is seeing an American hero, one who will stand up for her, protect her, and care for her. I guess I can't be angry at that, now can I?"

He smiles, and I can't help but hug him. He hugs me back, patting me softly. It's on the tip of my tongue to tell him about what Sabrina's done, but I don't want to ruin the moment, the progress we just made. So I keep my mouth shut to him, but I won't to Sabrina, who deserves my full wrath.

"Is Sabrina here? I'd like to talk to her," I say carefully.

Dad seems to think I'm here for amends with my stepsister as well because his smile grows. "She's upstairs. Go on up."

Upstairs, I pause outside her door, taking a steadying breath. "I'm an adult, not a kid she can walk all over. I can be mature about this," I remind myself as I knock.

"Come in," I hear through the door. I open it slowly, seeing her Princess Barbie room, white and pink with frou-frou ruffles. It feels like a Southern Belle child's room, circa 1950.

Sabrina is lying on the bed on her stomach, scrolling on a tablet. If I had to guess, I'd say she's online shopping.

"What the hell are you doing here?" she bites out, flipping over to glare at me.

I grit my teeth, forcing my voice to not quaver. Not with fear, but with fury. "I had a rather surprising visit at the bakery today. I thought you'd be interested in it," I say, baiting her to see if she'll reveal anything.

LAUREN LANDISH

"Why would I give a fuck about anything at your little sweat-shop?" she says with an eye roll.

"Because it seems someone made some rather specific complaints to the Health Department, completely unfounded ones designed to hurt my business. Would you know anything about that?"

Her smile is pure malevolence, her glee palpable. "You think I made complaints to get back at you for Lance?" Her laughter is sharp, bitter, but she shakes her head. "Hell, I wish I'd thought of that. Pretty fucking genius, if you ask me."

I can't hold my anger back anymore. "Is this a joke to you? This is my livelihood. I've got every cent tied up in that bakery, not to mention my blood, sweat, and tears. It's off limits from whatever family shitshow we have going. Be mad at me about Lance, bitch and whine to your mom about it like you always do, but leave my bakery alone."

"Or what?" she says, smirking. "Did you think I'd just sit back and be happy you got some grade-A dick? Lance is a fucking catch, *my* catch, and you stole him. As far as I'm concerned, this is Karma coming back to bite you in the ass like you deserve."

"He was never going to be interested in you. Ironic that you talk about Karma, but this is what happens when you're a shallow, vindictive, entitled brat."

I take a breath. God, that feels good to say. Ugly words, but a long time coming. The vitriol continues to pour out from my soul, repressed so many times that the dam has given way. "Good guys see that coming a mile away, and the number-one bro rule is 'Don't stick your dick in crazy.' Making false complaints just shows how far gone you are. And a little FYI, those complaints aren't anonymous, not really. Thomas Gold-stone is on the paperwork as an investor in *Cake Culture*. You think he won't get that info?"

It's a huge bluff, an idea that just occurred to me, but she doesn't know that. "Fine," she finally admits, intimidated. "I didn't do it. But I'd shake the hand of whoever did, that's for damn sure."

"Whatever." I'm losing steam, not because I'm reverting to my teen self but because I'm never going to trust her, to be honest. I've been burned too many times by her. She could tell me the sky is blue, and I'd go check for myself before believing her.

"Really. I didn't do it. I wish I had," she says, and that at least sounds like the truth.

But if not her, then who?

She sees the track my mind is already racing down. "And Mom didn't either. She can barely even text, says it's bougie, so filling out an online form is beyond her. I have to do her online shopping or she has the maid do it." She points her thumb at the tablet she set aside when I came in. "Trust me, if I had done it or if she had, I'd be dancing around, yelling for you to *suck it, bitch.* But *we didn't.*"

She makes a point. She would be gloating over her victory if she'd done this. And she's not.

"Fuck. I'm sorry, I guess. I just figured . . ." The apology is bitter on my tongue.

She rolls her eyes. "You figured that if something bad was happening to you, it had to be the evil stepsister's fault?" Sabrina shoots back bitterly. I glare at her, not disagreeing with her assessment. "Newsflash, you're not exactly the sister I wished for either," she says snidely. "Man-stealing bitch."

"I think we're just going to have to agree to disagree there. He was never yours. But he most definitely is mine." I turn, opening the door to escape, then closing it behind me.

I hear a loud thump, a pillow hitting the door, probably, and then a strangled cry. "Ugh!"

Yeah, you're not my idea of a dream sister either, girl.

CHAPTER 22

LANCE

*C*harlotte's visit home makes me consider a bit of a trip down memory lane. While her relationship with her sister has always been shitty, my relationship with Cody was once so much better.

I've got to figure out what the hell is going on with him, so I head home too, figuring I can refresh the gear in my duffel bag, grab a workout, and see if Cody's around for a chat, brother to brother. Hell, maybe I can get Dad involved too, and we can really lay all this shit out and get ourselves straightened out.

I don't even have a chance to knock on the front door before Hamilton's opening it, looking professional, as always. "Mister Lance."

"Hamilton, good to see you. Anybody home?" I ask, coming into the foyer.

He dips his chin, his eyes neutral. "Indeed. Mister Jacobs is in his study. Mister Cody is in his room. Can I get them for you? Or perhaps you're trying to avoid them?"

He has a glint his eye, and I'd bet he doesn't miss a thing that happens around here. I grin before telling him, "Nah, I got this." I lick my lips, putting my thumb and index finger in my mouth and letting out a piercing whistle that echoes through the house. "I doubt you use that one?"

"Indeed, sir." Still, Hamilton looks slightly amused as doors suddenly slam and heads pop out. Dad, Cody, and Mariella stick their heads into the foyer, but Mariella quickly disappears again.

"What the hell's going on?" Dad asks.

"Wanted to talk to you two, if you can spare a minute," I say, already walking toward the great room.

I can hear Cody grumble, "Oh, of course we can . . . for you." But he follows.

We sit down, and Hamilton offers everyone a drink, but I decline for us all, giving Cody a look that dares him to disagree. He sighs and waves his hand at Hamilton, telling him it's fine.

Once Hamilton excuses himself, I look from my Dad to my brother. "I've been going over files, reports, projections, spread-sheets, and more until I'm damn near blind. I wanted to tell you what I've found."

Dad leans back, listening. Cody's eyes glaze over, already done with the conversation.

"Admittedly, I'm coming in at a disadvantage. I'm a SEAL, and my MBA isn't from a fancy school like Yale. But I didn't need that to get a fair assessment of the current standings. What I've found is that the company is doing well, exceedingly well." Dad's brows shoot up, and even Cody looks slightly more interested.

"Compared to?" Dad asks.

"Compared to the rest of the bio-tech industry."

Using visual aides from my computer, I explain the points where the company is doing well, above expectations in most areas. "The only area I see that needs true improvement is employee retention, which in my experience is based on morale. The company can use some more *esprit de corps*."

Dad remains unconvinced. "What about the prototype project for spinal cages with brain-computer interfaces? It was an utter failure, to the tune of *millions*."

Cody tenses, jaw so tight I'm surprised his teeth aren't breaking from the sheer force. Dad looks at him accusingly, and I start to get a clearer picture of what's going on here. Dad is a brilliant man but can't see the forest for the trees because he's stuck, running the same loop in his mind about who and what we are—Cody, me, even the company.

"Dad, one of your biggest failures is the coffee on the first floor," I shoot back, a side flank attack to wake him up. "I've had better on a hospital ship in the North Atlantic, and it's the first impression you make. You never could make a decent cup of coffee, so why are you even trying? Make tea or smoothies or something else because you're a shitty coffee maker."

It's a nonsense approach, but I need something to shock him out of his rutted path. Dad's face immediately pinches, and I know I've made an impression. "What the hell are you talking about? Coffee? Who cares about that? I don't even make the coffee! If it's shitty, talk to whoever makes it."

He looks at me like I've lost every marble out of my skull, and I deliver my point. "Exactly. You don't make it, just like Cody didn't make the spinal cages. But yet, you're blaming him for the whole project just because he managed it. You know what I saw when I took a close look at that venture?"

Dad huffs. "Is this the part where you gang up on the old man?"

"You asked me to do this," I growl. "Do you want to hear it or not?" I take his silence as answer enough. "I saw a project that was earmarked as a long-shot from the get-go, but one with the potential for a huge payoff. And *you* were the one who signed off on it. No one else. So, project underway, budget is within parameters, initial reports promising but very early. Then, the expo comes up and it was decided that the cages should be paraded out as the wave of the future, one that Jacobs Bio-Tech is designing themselves. Who decided to show the cages at the expo?"

Cody looks at Dad, who begrudgingly admits, "Me. They were promising at the time."

"I know, but your hurry to showcase led to overtime hours, rush orders on materials, and other costly expenditures," I point out. "None of which would have been a problem except the tech didn't work. It's still in R&D but looking less promising than some other projects, so their budget's been slashed."

Dad growls, looking at Cody. "That's right. It didn't work."

I growl right back, frustrated that he's not seeing the big picture here. "Cody, what settings do you use for the microscopic lens to see as you work?"

Cody smirks, already seeing where I'm going. "Not a fucking clue, since *I don't use them*. I'm a paper pusher." Then he looks Dad dead in the eye, years of resentment in his words. "Not a barista."

Every bit of Dad's air escapes as he plops back in the chair, his hands going to his salt and pepper hair to pull at the strands as his volume gets louder and louder. "But this isn't coffee, it was a multimillion-dollar project! And all that money was lost on your watch."

"You'll never get it, will you? I'm not a fuck-up!" Cody says, standing up. "I'm the one who's done everything you've ever wanted—stay here and work the family business. Hell, if you'd asked me to marry the damn blonde and start popping out grandbabies, I would've hopped to it. But I'll never be *him*. And that means no matter what I do, it'll never be good enough."

He stomps out of the room, and from far away, I hear a door slam and music start blaring.

Dad shakes his head, exhaustion and frustration washing through him. "Do you see what I'm dealing with? He's immature, always folds under pressure. This is why I need you here, Lance. It's too much for me. I'm not old, still got some years in this ticker," he says, patting his chest. "But I thought I'd be able to slow down by now. I promised your mother I'd take her to Europe for her birthday, but I can't even see leaving for a week, much less the month-long trip she wants to take."

I lean forward in my chair, looking Dad in the eye. What I'm about to say is one of the hardest things I've ever had to say, and I've informed wives that their husbands are never coming home.

I steel myself, thankful for my years of training to face the hard shit head-on.

"Dad, Cody's not the problem. *You* are."

That gets his attention.

"I don't know what happened between you two after I was gone, but he's a good worker. His projects are managed well, on time and under budget, and his staff loves him. You, on the other hand, are this tornado that blows through the office, blowing his projects up and then blaming him. I don't know if it's stress or just something you've got personally with Cody, but it's clear. *You're* the problem, not him."

I wait, expecting the explosion of justifications, explanations, and arguments. But he sags, broken, his eyes unseeing as he stares at the floor. I wish he was yelling instead of *this*. He's always been larger than life to me, a role model I hoped to live up to, but now he looks small, uncertain, and it kills me.

Still looking down, he says quietly, "Did I ever tell you how I took the company from pharmaceuticals to bio-tech?"

I shake my head, not seeing the connection.

"I'd been working at Jacobs Pharma for decades under your grandpa, and it was getting to be a tough market to capitalize on. Fewer and fewer projects were panning out, and the amount of work to get that one-percent edge over the competition was ridiculous. So I proposed that we expand at least, diversify a bit so we had a more stable revenue stream." He huffs, his eyes glassy as he remembers. "We argued so loudly and so often the walls of the old headquarters would shake and people would scatter if we were in the same room together. Dad wouldn't hear of it. He was convinced I was throwing away two generations of hard work to chase some crazy dream. He just wanted to make another cholesterol med, a sure thing."

"Build a better mousetrap?" I say, and he nods.

"And so we held steady until he retired and I took over the reins. I made the transition slowly at first, but when the name changed, he was furious. Accused me of ruining his legacy, of being a young upstart who didn't know my ass from my elbow, and vowing that I'd see the day he was right and I was out on the streets." He's quiet for a moment, and I try to think back to the grandpa who died when I was just a boy. I have impressions of peppermint and pipe smoke, but not much else.

"He died before he saw the success I'd made of what he started. Never saw the dream come true. He died thinking I was a fuckup, and he knew best," he says sadly.

"But you did know what you were doing and have done a damn fine job of turning Jacobs into the primary bio-tech company on the West Coast, and it's positioned well to be a global force against the big dogs of the industry. You did that."

He looks up at me, pride shining in his eyes, but I have to finish the thought. "But you didn't do it alone. Let go, Dad. You're holding on too tightly, to the company, to Cody, to me. And it's killing you and killing everyone around you. You've earned some time to relax. Take that trip with Mom, and trust that the people you trained will take care of Jacobs Bio-Tech."

"I don't want to become obsolete," he confesses. "Hell, maybe now I know how your grandpa felt. I thought your coming home would help. Though I'm not sure if I thought it'd give me more time because you'd have to be trained or less time because you've always been your own man. Maybe a bit of both?"

"You don't need me, Dad. You never have, and I'm not sure I'll ever come onboard at Jacobs. Cody's your guy. He knows that company inside and out. He's young, and you're stressing him out to his limits, but he's a believer in bio-tech and that'll make all the difference. I'm not saying you just toss him the ropes, but you need to step back, let him shine on his own. You might be surprised what he'll show you if you let him engage and show you his skills. He's got plenty."

He looks down the hallway where Cody disappeared, pensive and thoughtful. "I really fucked up with him, huh?"

I nod, agreeing with him. "You really did. But he wants to please you, so I think you can make it up to him. Admitting you're wrong will go a long way, and better behavior going forward will go even further."

Dad turns back to me, smiling for the first time in over an hour. "I raised two strong-willed, intelligent, good men. You two are my greatest accomplishment."

I lift a brow, grinning wide. "Pretty sure you had help there too, Old Man. Mom was the one who patched us up when we did stupid shit. You were the one who yelled at us for doing it."

"Both equally important parts of parenting," he jokes before narrowing his eyes. "You know, I think your mother is having a bit of a crisis herself. My guess is that's what the matchmaking was all about. I'm having growing pains about stepping back from the company, and she's having the same thoughts, that her family doesn't need her anymore. A grandbaby seemed like the perfect solution to her, I think. Don't be too mad at her, okay?"

"I'm not. She's backed off after the dinner," I admit. "Or I guess juked and is now throwing her eggs in Charlotte's basket for a grandkid. Wait, that sounds . . . wrong."

Dad laughs. "I know what you mean. Just promise me that you

won't let Mom influence you in this. You've always gone your own way, and I've always been proud of you for doing it. I am proud of you, Lance."

My eyes burn. The words feel good down to my soul. I think every child has a desire to make their parents proud, and though I've never acted with that goal in mind, it feels good to know that I've done something good.

"Thanks, Dad."

He gets up, and I swear his eyes are a bit teary too. "If you'll excuse me, I think I have another difficult conversation I need to have, some crow to eat, if you will."

I smile, glad that he's going to make amends. "If you'd like, I happen to know a great baker who could probably put those blackbirds into a rather delicious pie. Might make it easier to get down?"

He shakes his head, laughing lightly as he heads down the hall, shoulders wide and proud.

CHAPTER 23

LANCE

"All set?" I ask Brian, standing behind the ribbon.

He holds up a finger, using his other hand to press a button on his headset. Moments later, he gives me a thumbs-up to let me know security has done their full sweep and we're clear to proceed.

I take Charlotte's hand on my left, Trixie's on my right as we step onto the small stage just off Main Street. Charlotte steps forward, happiness shooting off her like fireworks as the assembled crowd claps.

"Thank you so much for coming. Today, we begin a new chapter in the story of Roseboro. Once upon a time, families spent hours together. I remember my Grandma Winnie teaching me so much. How to bake, how to garden, how to sew—though that lesson didn't go so well." She pauses as everyone laughs.

"But over the years, our culture has succumbed to the dreaded 'busy' bug, and the divide between generations grew. There aren't Sunday dinners where everyone gathers around the table together, or daily phone calls to catch up. In my Grandma Winnie's honor, I'd like to see this change."

She looks back at me and Trixie, smiling. "*We'd* like to see this

217

change. So welcome to the first ever Generations of Hope event. We've been fortunate to partner with people of every age, businesses of every industry, and hopefully, your hearts today. Meet, talk, share, impart knowledge, and let us bridge the gap and create a new generation of hope."

Trixie and I step forward, giant scissors in our hands, and Charlotte holds the ribbon as we cut, the three of us kicking it off together, making the idea we sprouted over work in the bakery come to life before our very eyes.

The crowd cheers as the ribbon drops, the mob surging forward. It's a good mix of seniors and kids, and everything in between, which I'm glad to see. That's the vital key to making this a success.

"We did it," I say proudly. "Mission accomplished."

Trixie rolls her eyes, punching me in the shoulder lightly. "Military talk, really?" She moves her hand, mimicking a talking mouth. "Roger wilco, hooah, hooah, sir!"

Charlotte, though, has stars in her eyes. Admittedly, they probably have more to do with the smiling faces all around us, but I'll take some credit for her smile when she curls into my side, wrapping an arm around my waist. "Hush, I like it when he talks all military."

Oh? I could think of some orders I'd like to give her.

But now's not the time, even though Trixie says, "And that's my cue to leave you two alone. Don't do anything to scar the little kiddies or cause one of the old farts to have a heart attack." She winks as she walks off, laughing.

Charlotte and I walk around, checking in with the various booths and getting to see our handiwork firsthand.

In the first tent, Jeanine Matherson, a retired fine arts teacher from Upstate who retired to Roseboro, is leading a beginner class on pencil drawing. She's got a group of mixed students, some young and some old, but all concentrating on the line technique she's demonstrating. The next tent has a tiny, grey-haired woman with thick ropes of yarn looped over her arms as she coaches her students through some tricky method of over-under.

"I'll be back for your second lesson, Mrs. Petrie," Charlotte calls out, and the woman smiles and nods. Turning, she giggles. "And there's the competition."

I look over to see a white-haired woman with a gleaming smile handing out cookies, waving when Charlotte waves. "Who's she?"

"Joan Harris, the police chief's wife. I don't think there's been a single school bake sale, charity event, or church bazaar in town that she isn't there with her cookies."

"Oh?" I ask, amused. "How are they?"

She sighs, but not unkindly. "They're delicious, and gorgeously decorated by hand. Each and every one of them piped to perfection. Diabetics are warned to stay ten feet away from her at all times. That's why I stick to every other treat and let her have the corner on the decorated cookie market."

We watch the storytelling area for a while, where kids are sitting enraptured as older citizens read them stories. A few of them seem to be telling stories of their own, sharing their wisdom with the next generation.

The picture of the day has to be a little girl, probably only three or four years old, fast asleep in the arms of a grey-haired man in a wheelchair. She'd asked if she could sit in his lap, declared him her new grandpa, skin color differences notwithstanding, then promptly passed out from all the excitement.

It's enough to make a hardened soldier like me get a bit choked up.

We walk on, and I find Cody at a booth showcasing the Jacobs Bio-Tech arm prosthesis. It's a current offering from our product catalog, though it's always being updated as new technologies become realities. But the kids and adults gathered around him don't seem to think it's outdated. Based on his current discussion of whether the 'robot arm' or Iron-Man would win an arm-wrestling competition, he seems to be doing quite well, actually. My favorite is the young man who's explaining to a grandma who Iron-Man is, using the image on his shirt as a show-and-tell.

I offer a wave, which he answers with a bro chin lift and a smile. Then his eyes turn to Charlotte, and he calls out, "Thanks again for inviting Jacobs Bio-Tech, Charlotte. Your Generations of Hope event seems to be a raging success!" The crowd around him turns to look at Charlotte, who's blushing at the attention as they all thank her, saying how much fun they're having and asking when the next one will be.

Eventually, we make our way down the rest of the row. "Your brother is pretty slick with the name dropping," Charlotte says, "and the gaggle of people mobbing him."

Pride bubbles up, not that I had anything to do with Cody's prowess as a representative of the company or the family, but just that he's my brother and is doing so well.

"You want to head to the grills and grab a bite to eat before your cake decorating demo this afternoon?" I ask Charlotte, who's looking around with a beaming smile on her face.

She agrees, but before we take a step to follow the delicious aroma wafting through the area, a deep voice sounds from behind us. "Charlotte."

She whirls as I automatically reach for my Sig, which is stored in a fanny pack, much to my displeasure. Unfortunately, it'd been the best family-friendly way to carry. Instead of a threat, though, I find Thomas and Mia approaching.

Charlotte lets out an ear-splitting 'eeeee' and grabs Mia in a big hug, the two of them going total girl-giddy.

Thomas eyes me up and down. "Things look wonderful, Charlotte. And you're enjoying yourself, Lance?"

"Always. It's better to build than destroy," I reply honestly. We didn't get too much of a chance to talk during the whole Health Inspector drama, but that's okay. I've gotten my measure of the man, and he's good.

"You know, Lance, you're quite the subject of conversation," Thomas says with a chuckle, glancing at Mia. "These two seem to be unable to stop gossiping about you."

"Hopefully, good things," I hedge, and Thomas grins, not really divulging any more.

Mia shoves at my shoulder, grinning. "All good, trust me. You were the topic of a whole dinner a couple of weeks ago. Jonathan vouched for you. That's the only reason we didn't sic Gabe on you. Well, that and Charlotte says you're quite—"

"Sweet!" Charlotte interjects, splotches darkening her cheeks as she gives Mia a look that communicates 'shut up' loud and clear.

I laugh at the obvious compliments she's been divulging, throwing my arm around Charlotte's shoulder and kissing her on the temple. "As long as it's good, I guess I'm okay with that."

Mia smirks, nudging Charlotte with her elbow. "Humble, too? Looks like you've got a keeper, girl. Lucky bitch."

I look to Charlotte, half expecting her to have questions, doubts, and nerves rising in the depths of her eyes. But what I find takes my breath away.

I can see the trust she's placing in me, the hope that I won't betray her the way others have. It feels like the most important responsibility I've ever taken on, one I won't fail to live up to. Especially not when I know what it's costing her to have faith in a future with me.

"I think I'm the lucky one as she's adding me into her busy

schedule," I say, letting Charlotte off the hook. "We were heading over to grab a burger. Want one too?"

Mia links her arm through Charlotte's, pulling her away from me. "Absolutely! You think you're getting away from me that easily?"

Thomas and I meet gazes, both of us happy to trail along after our women as they chatter away.

Once we all have burgers in hand and Charlotte has thanked the guy manning the grill for his sponsorship of the event, we find a tall table to perch at. Mia steps away for a moment to grab us all cold bottles of water, returning quickly, and we dig in.

Conversation is light, and Charlotte relaxes without teasing digs for gossip from Mia.

Our burgers disappear bite by bite, and the girls start rambling about a video game I've never heard of before, something called TERA.

"They do this often?"

Thomas grins, shrugging like this is a normal occurrence. "Give Mia two months, and she'll have you playing too."

I look around and see a surprising sight heading this way.

"Dad! Mom!" I call, giving them a welcoming hug. "Good to see you here."

Mom is smiling at Charlotte like she hung the moon and stars, or like she might be the key to keeping her baby boy here in Rose-boro. Dad, however, is focused on Thomas.

"Great to see you again, Thomas."

"You too, Bishop. Couldn't miss an event like this."

"All for a great cause. Lance and Charlotte did a wonderful job with this," Dad says, beaming, "launching from idea to reality so quickly. It'd be an amazing asset to continue the get-togethers throughout the year, help the connections grow for all the citizens of Roseboro for generations to come."

"No need for the hard sell, Dad," I warn with a chuckle. "Whoever Thomas chooses at the winner for his Hope Initiative will be deserving. And the real winners are the people of Roseboro, no matter what."

Thomas inclines his head. "Didn't I see your other son here too?"

"Yes, Cody has really gotten on fire with this. He's demo'ing our prosthetic arm. He's quite the showman, but he knows that product inside and out, manages that project team in fact," Dad brags.

It's been a little over a week since our sit-down chat. I don't know what Dad said to Cody or what Cody said to Dad, but their relationship has been improving. It's still not perfect, but I think Dad finally sees that his fear of the future was the real problem all along, not Cody's work, which Dad admits is significantly better than he'd let on.

The best side effect of Dad's epiphany is that Cody and I are no longer getting pressured to perform, at work or with the whole wife-kids-picket fence combo platter.

Thomas and Dad begin discussing how a Jacobs prosthesis project might help with patients at Goldstone Health, and Charlotte leans over to me.

"I need to head over to the community center kitchen for the decorating demo. You coming with me?"

I nod, whispering so I don't interrupt Dad and Thomas. "Of course. You're my number-one priority. I'm on your six all day."

Heat fills her eyes, and I know she reads my double meaning. "Excuse us. We've got to be in the kitchen in fifteen. Thanks so much for coming, though."

Dad and Thomas nod, going back to talking immediately. Meanwhile, Mia is watching us with a knowing look.

Before we're three steps away, Charlotte pulls on my hand to stop me. She lifts up to her toes and presses her lips to mine. She tastes salty and sweet, my favorite combination.

When she pulls away, I lick my lips, getting one last taste of her. "What was that for?"

Pulling me down, she whispers into my ear, her breath hot and her tone suddenly sultry. "One, for helping me pull this off. Two, for that military talk. You know what that does to me."

My lips quirk as I fight the smile that wants to stretch my face so desperately. "Oh, you like that? Well, I'll be on your six all night, making sure every bit of intel is drawn from your body. Three, four, five times, if I have to. I won't stop until my mission is complete."

It's the weirdest dirty talk I think I've ever said, but if she knew radio code, I'd fill her ear with word salad. Whatever this woman needs from me is what I'm damn well going to give her.

She laughs, pushing back a little. "On second thought, I think my baking puns are better."

I growl, pulling her in tight. "You think your dirty talk is better than mine?" I feel her head nod against my shoulder. "Red, all damn day, I've been walking around being polite and well-mannered for your event. But what I really want is to take you home, yank those jeans off your ass, leave on that Generations of Hope T-shirt that fits you so damn well, then fuck you until your screams bounce off the walls. I want you coming on my hand, my tongue, and then, if you're real nice, I'll stretch that pussy with my thick cock until you come on me again. Then I'll flip you over, wrap that braid around my fist to force you to arch for me, and I'll fuck that bubble ass of yours until I fill you up with so much cum you can't even hold it. But I'll help you slip your panties back on, pat that pussy, and hold you all night while you sleep in the mess we made."

She shudders in my arms, and I wonder if she just had an orgasm from my filthy words. And when she pulls back, I can see that she's damn close, ripe for the picking.

Her eyes are blue flames, fire I want to burn me, mark me as hers. Her chest rises and falls as she pants, her puffy lips open and waiting for mine.

My cock surges between us, thick and hard and wanting to mark her too. Inside and out, cover her with cum so she always knows that she's mine and I'm not going anywhere.

The lust is palpable, electricity sparking on our skin, but there's a deeper layer to it, a foundation we've built brick by brick, sometimes slowly and other times, faster. All at whatever pace Charlotte needs.

But I can see it now. She's with me, no longer dancing around the fire but engulfed in it with me.

She bites her lip, taking a jagged breath. "You fight dirty. Because all I want to do is run straight for home, or hell, the nearest deserted corner, and do just that. Fuck yes, to all of that. But I can't. I have to—"

"Not fighting. *Promising.* That's my mission tonight," I say with a soft vow in my voice. "But right now, you need to go decorate some cupcakes, so let's go." I run a finger down the bridge of her upturned nose, an oddly intimate gesture, then *boop* her at the tip. "Let's go, Sweet Scarlet. There are cupcakes that need frosting."

I pull her hand, directing her to the community center kitchen, but I hear her growl behind me, "Yeah, there is. *My cupcake.*"

CHAPTER 24

BLACKWELL

$\mathcal{I}$ peer through the telescope, watching the street below from my living room window, sneering as the happy rabble leave the community center. Of course, the ginger honeypot will be there for hours, breaking down equipment and finishing up the event.

I'm sure she feels it was a success, and from a standpoint of charitable goodwill, it probably was. Too bad charity is a misplaced effort, a pathetic attempt to level the playing field when, by life's very nature, there are leaders, followers, those who achieve, and those who are sacrificed.

The greater good for the many? No.

The greatest good for *me*. Earned through strategy and manipulation. And it will be mine.

I'm growing impatient, ready to move past the small annoyances to the large-scale plays that will truly get me to the top of the mountain. King of the hill? I'll be King of the entire Pacific Seaboard, no matter what it takes or who I have to step on to get there.

Speaking of destroying the weak and useless, I decide to reach out to a resource, one well-placed and with the potential to be exceedingly useful. For a time. They are all only useful for a time, then they are parceled out the same fate as so many others before them.

The fate I will receive too, for none of us escape the Reaper forever. But I will go out on my own terms, cheating him with a golden crown proclaiming that I created this town, and it will forever be mine.

"Hello?" the voice answers.

"Are you alone?" I ask, wanting to be sure I maintain the utmost secrecy for the next phase of my master plan.

There's some muted conversation in the background, then my pawn speaks again. "My apologies, sir. I'm alone now."

"Any suspicions?"

My pawn laughs lightly. "No. Not at all. Can I help with something?"

Though they are obviously eager to get off the phone, I'm more than eager to move pawns where I wish them. "Today's charity event disturbs me. Everyone mingling with smiles on their faces and Goldstone's 'hope' in their hearts. Useless drivel."

Though I can't see my operative, I can hear the shrug. "It doesn't make a difference if people have hope. You'll do what you want and they'll be left in your wake, but you'll still be in control." Such resignation is in contrast to my pawn's previous commitment to my goal, but as long as orders are carried out, I can tolerate some flagging spirits.

"I see," I muse. "You'd do well to remember that as well. When the dust settles, I will be in control. Of Roseboro, and of you."

The threat need not be more explicit, though I let my mind wander for a moment at the joyous beauty an extra death would bring. Shock and surprise for some, and glorious victory for me.

"Of course, sir."

The speedy acquiescence pleases me. Most of my minions think themselves strong. And perhaps to the average person, they are. Most of them are self-starters, overachievers who have reached and tried to grasp the proverbial brass ring. But like a Shakespearean hero, they all have that tragic, fatal flaw. Hubris, insecurity, lust for power, it doesn't matter. I take it, I mold it, and when they think they are free, I show them the full extent of their self-made prison. Only then are they ready to be the weapon I desire, to strike down my enemies like an arrow loosed from a bow.

Even if Golden Boy knows I am coming, it is the unseen dart that strikes deepest.

"I will have use for you soon. Be aware, be cooperative, and you will reap what you sow." I toss out the promise that has always yielded results, with of course, the irony unnoticed. The wishes aren't outlandish, merely a life that they've been denied. But I can easily repair that discrepancy. That is assured. "And maintain secrecy. No one need know of your motivations. Yet."

"Yes, sir. I understand."

I hang up and sit back, considering the fortitude I require of my operative. Each one has been a wealth of information, insights I wouldn't have received otherwise, and have successfully completed backhanded actions at my command. But this pawn is dangerous, moldable by me, yes, but also able to be influenced by those around them. I will have to remind them that my orders are paramount, even more than friends, family, or conscience.

I might need to advance my timeline, not dilly-dally and allow questions to take root. I am ready to proceed and will do so as soon as possible.

One other area of my schedule to address. I make another call.

"Yes, sir," he answers, all business.

"The preparations, are they complete?" I say, not letting my urgency color my words but instead feigning mere interest in his progress.

"Nearly, sir. We were delayed ever so slightly because we do have to actually do the upgrades Mr. Goldstone requested to his systems or our presence would be noticed. But I'll do my final assessment to sign off on the completed work and will make the special adjustments you requested."

"Excellent. And when it's completed—"

"You will be in total control." I do not appreciate that he interrupted me in the least, but his promise of control is an exhilarating one. Another step in the direction I will take Roseboro.

I smirk at his choice of words. "Aren't I always?"

He chuckles, agreeing, and hangs up with a promise to notify me when the job is complete.

My mood lifts from the dark pall today's events brought over me. Because it's true. I am always in control, and this time, there's nothing Golden Boy can do to stop me.

I will take it all. His money, his friends . . . but most importantly, his life.

And Roseboro will once again be mine alone.

I take a piece of stationary from my top drawer, heavyweight linen beneath my black ink pen. It is an old tradition of sorts. A declaration of war, an opportunity for surrender. But there will be no mercy given by my hand.

Not now. Not ever.

My hand flows surely across the page.

Thomas,

I will admit to you a failing. A breach of the confidence I bore for so many years, heedless of the future and certain of my standing as the rightful creator of this fine town of Roseboro. For it is my town, my creation.

But much like the intrusion of the Black Plague in 1348, you came to

Roseboro. I am a bit of a history buff, you see, and much like the Italians attempted to forestall the spread of the destruction, I did the same.

Small movements to slow your progress, underhanded deals to stop you at every opportunity. For your attempts to become the King of the Rose-Covered Throne were unwelcome, most of all by me.

But the time for sacrificial pawns has passed. Checkmate.

My pen starts to flow faster and faster, and before I know it, I'm smiling with mirthless glee at a future he doesn't even see coming for him, faster than a speeding bullet and more dangerous than he could imagine.

This rough draft might not be perfect, but it will be. Just in time for his ultimate destruction.

CHAPTER 25

"*We* did it!" Charlotte exclaims.

Coming up to the roof of the *Cake Culture* building was a stroke of inspiration, and now I'm glad I agreed to her idea to grab the fire escape ladder and head up here.

Laid back on a blanket on the roof above her apartment, the night sky glittering above us, she's stunning. Her red hair is fanned out over my arm, her head cradled on my chest as she curls up next to me.

"*You* did it," I correct her, grinning to myself in the dark. Trixie and I certainly helped, but Charlotte was the driving force behind the whole event. She's already got ideas for the next one. It'll be smaller, for sure, not a kickoff event like today's, but still just as impactful for the generations of people who have already committed to coming.

She snuggles in closer, sighing happily. "Thank you, for today and for . . . everything."

I press a kiss to her forehead, inhaling her scent. "Anything for you."

I mean it. She's set my world off its axis. She is why fate brought

233

me here. I'm sure of it. I was put in this place for her. And she, for me.

She says she doesn't believe in happily ever afters, but I do. I believe enough for the both of us. And something tells me she's starting to believe too.

"Did you see that?" she whispers, tension shooting through her body.

"What?" I say, moving to get up and defend her if necessary. We're safe here on the roof. The fire escape ladder is one of those hyper-secure ones that you can't reach from the ground level. But her alarm puts me on alert.

She pulls me back to her, laughing softly. "Down, boy, I meant the shooting star. No need to go Battle-Bot on me."

I relax back into the blanket beneath us, rolling her to her back and looming over her, keeping her caged in the frame of my arms. "A shooting star, you say? Did you make a wish?"

She bites her lip, driving me mad before confessing, "Well, I remembered some rather filthy things you said to me earlier. What if I wished for those to come true?"

"Then I'd be happy to make that wish come true."

I press my lips to hers, not sweetly, not this time, but rough and forceful, all the need we built up from our little touches and looks over the course of today driving me hard. I take her mouth, owning her as we share breaths, promising more. More pleasure, more time, more us.

She writhes beneath me, moaning as she returns the passion in my kiss in equal measure. Moving lower, I kiss along her neck, tasting her salty sweetness, savoring the air of vanilla that permeates her. She turns her head, giving me access and begging for more.

I nip and suck at the satiny skin, whispering in her ear. "Tell me what you want."

"Everything," she repeats, her earlier word having a new meaning in the heat of the moment. "Fuck me."

"As you wish," I tell her, committed to making her every dream come true.

I trace my hand along her side, following the curve and brushing along the side of her breast. Her back arches, and I shove her shirt up, revealing her lacy bra. "Shit, you've had this on all day? These candy-pink nipples barely covered by lace? If I'd known that, I would've pushed you into the first deserted alleyway I could find and fucked you right there."

She grins, like she thinks I'm exaggerating. I'm not.

I nuzzle her cleavage, feeling her softness against the scruff of my cheeks, and reach behind her to unhook her bra. She reaches for the hem of her shirt to pull it off, but I stop her. "Nuh-uh, I told you I was going to fuck you in this T-shirt and I'm going to." I pull the loosened bra down as she watches, letting her tits rest on the shelf it creates before I trace her pinkness, biting her playfully, just the way she likes.

I unbutton her jeans, and she lifts her hips to help me, kicking her shoes off with a toe. Grabbing her waistband, I pull at her jeans as I lift up, turning them inside-out as they come off, leaving her bottom half-bare, save for her panties. I rip them off too, revealing her slick and needy pussy.

"Fuck, Char." My voice is a deep rumble against her hip as I tease a finger along her wetness, tracing her lips. "On my hand first," I tell her, slipping a finger inside her.

She whimpers as I curl my finger, petting the front wall of her pussy. The wet sounds of my pumping finger send electric tingles through my spine as I speed up, holding her down with my free hand until she's on the edge.

With a final stroke, she spasms, her scream rising in her throat. I swallow her cry in a kiss, and her hips rise, bridging up to my hand. I plunge into her as deeply as I can, stroking her inside as she falls apart for me.

"I've got you. Let it go, Charlotte."

Her honey coats my fingers, thick and sticky. Needing a taste, I kiss my way down even as my finger keeps stroking her. She's still coming when I flick my tongue over her clit. She bucks, her hands going to my hair.

"I can't, too much," she protests, though her hands are pulling me to her, not pushing me away.

"On my hand, on my tongue, and on my cock," I remind her. "You can go again, I know you can."

I hold still, letting her have control for a moment. She lifts and lowers her hips, running her clit over my flattened tongue. My tongue dips inside her every chance she gives me, lapping up her sweetness and swallowing her down.

"That's it . . . use me, fuck my mouth." She tries to keep going but she's getting so close already, the edge rising up to meet her. Her movements stutter, losing their rhythm, and I take over.

I suck her clit into my mouth, fluttering my tongue across the hardened nub. Her back bows and then reverses, curving her hips and shoulders together as a guttural grunt, primal in its depths, erupts from her. It's music to my ears, a buffet for my tongue as she comes again.

I've waited for her my entire life, the one I never even knew I was looking for as I escaped to save the world. But she's here now, with me in this moment, and I need her.

I rip my shirt over my head and unbutton my jeans, shoving them and my boxers down my hips but not able to wait long enough to take them off entirely. Charlotte looks down my body, drinking me in with her eyes. I rub my hand across my chest, over the ridges of my abs, and down to take my throbbing cock in hand. I stroke for her, enjoying the way her eyes widen and her lips open like she wants to suck me.

"You want it?" She bites her lip, nodding. "Where?"

I had a plan, a promise I'd made to her, but the way her tongue peeks out to wet her lips taunts me, teasing me to diverge from the path. She drives me mad with the desire to claim every sweet inch of her, inside and out.

"My mouth," she whispers, breathless but sure.

She sits up, flipping her knees beneath her and sitting back on her heels. She leans forward, licking my crown, making a slow circle to taste the precum that's leaking freely for her. My knees spread, dipping into her mouth deeper, and she takes me inch by inch into her mouth and throat.

I weave my fingers into her hair, cupping her head to guide her as I begin to fuck her mouth. She moans, the vibration zinging all the way to my balls, which are already tightening up, ready to come for her. The *gluck* sound as my cock leaves her throat is sexy and thrilling, and she swallows reflexively. I give her a moment to breathe before sliding back into the wet heaven of her mouth. Her cheeks hollow, her tongue curling to tease my shaft, and suddenly, I'm right on the edge.

I pull back, leaving her mouth gaping open, a line of spit from her lips to my cock. "Not yet, not in your mouth this time."

She nods and lies back on the blanket, knowing what I want. Her eyes sparkle in the moonlight, full of lust, full of *more*, speaking to my heart.

But I don't say the words, not yet. Though I feel them, deeply and acutely, I don't want to scare her. Not now, when we've come so far.

She surprises me when she flips over, giving me her back. At first, I think she's overwhelmed with the emotion of the moment and hiding once again. But she looks over her shoulder, braid

LAUREN LANDISH

swishing along her freckled skin, and she arches, presenting herself to me.

"You did promise me something naughty." Her hips sway seductively, reminding me of what I vowed earlier today. I'd been teasing in a way, testing her limits, but now . . .

My God. She's committing to me fully, trusting me to stay with her, to give her exactly what I promised. And I'm a man of my word.

I fall over her, catching myself on one hand and wrapping her messy braid around my fist to keep her eyes on me, not letting her escape this moment. The moment she is mine, I've already been hers.

Dipping my fingers into her wet honey again, I coat them before reaching up to massage her asshole, watching her eyes. She moans thickly as I press in, pushing back as my finger penetrates her.

I take my time opening her up, preparing her for me. When she's ready, I line my cock up with her ass, watching the spit-covered head nudge against her. "Ready?"

"Please," she begs. "I'm so ready."

I thrust into her slowly, relishing her body stretching around my thick cock. I can feel the quivers of her body, the tight ring of her ass squeezing me and not letting me go, as if there's anywhere else I'd rather be than inside her. Body, mind, and soul.

When she pushes back again, I pound into her just like I promised, feeling her orgasm rising quickly. "Come for me, Red. I need to feel you come on my cock."

She's riding the edge, a hairsbreadth away from falling but clinging on. "What do you need?" I ask, and she whimpers.

And I know. She's ready. Fuck knows, I'm ready.

I pull her hair harder, turning her head to look at me, not letting her doubts color the moment. I need her to hear me, see me, trust my truth.

"I love you, Charlotte. With all my heart. I love you."

She cries out to the dark night, the words releasing not only her orgasm but the restraints she's placed on her own heart too. And as she shudders beneath me, I hear the words fall from her mouth too.

"I love you too."

It releases me, and I claim her final secret . . . her heart. Finally mine.

It's hours later, or maybe minutes, when I slip out of her. I turn her to her back, lying beside her and tracing the curve of her collarbone. Everything has changed tonight, here on this roof.

"Did you mean it?" she asks, but the teasing tone says she already knows the answer.

I tickle her, making her squirm and laugh. "I think I made good on my word," I say, touching my thumb to my fingers as I tick off, "on my hand, on my tongue, and on my cock."

She rolls her eyes, and I give her what she wants. "Yes, I meant it. I've felt it for a while, but didn't want to scare you. Are you scared?"

She dips her chin, closing her eyes for a second, but she's smiling so I don't get too nervous until the moment stretches. My heart stops beating until she opens her eyes once again, her blues meeting mine.

"Surprisingly, I'm not. I feel bubbly, warm inside. Like bread dough is rising inside me and I'm so full of carb-y happiness I want to explode like the Pillsbury Dough Boy."

I can't help but laugh. She's funny and sexy and perfect just as she is. "I don't think I've ever heard of love being compared to bread, but somehow, it seems fitting for you."

Eventually, I do pick her up and carry her back downstairs to bed. I don't put her messy panties on her, though, instead curling up behind her, both of us naked, to fall asleep.

I'M AWAKENED BY THE SOUND OF A BUZZING CELL PHONE, AND I look over to see it's Jonathan. It's the middle of the night, hours before Charlotte's alarm will go off to start her morning baking.

I extract myself from Charlotte's side and quietly head to the living room so I don't wake her. "Hello?"

"Am I interrupting?" he asks, a chuckle in his voice. "Heard there were some fireworks over the bakery tonight."

"Shut up, asshole," I joke back. "I'm sure you're not calling in the middle of the night to give me shit. What's wrong?"

"Just an update, like you asked. We've got some reliable intel that Blackwell's got local law enforcement in his pocket, all the way to the top. You got a problem, call me or state police. Got it?"

"I understand. Keep me informed."

I hang up, sensing Charlotte behind me. "Who was that?"

"Jonathan. He just wanted to give me an update. Nothing actionable, but he knows I'm here to help keep you safe," I promise.

Charlotte wraps her arms around me, burying her head in my chest. "Thank you. You're one of about a half-dozen people I trust right now, so thank you for watching my back."

I kiss her forehead, picking her up in my arms and carrying her back to bed. "I've got you, Charlotte. I'll keep you safe, body and heart."

She relaxes into my arms, falling asleep quickly with the reassurances. But as I lie awake for hours, I find my mind analyzing every angle Blackwell could be coming at her and at Thomas from. I'd been worried about the event today, enough to work with Jonathan on adding extra security, but it'd gone off without a hitch.

So if not something big like that, what's he planning? Because a man like Blackwell is always planning something. And we need to figure out what it is before anyone else gets hurt.

CHAPTER 26

*T*he bakery is hopping busy, a line out the door once again. The Health Department issue fizzled quickly, and the Generations of Hope event had an added benefit of making my bakery *the* place to go for all your baked good needs. Old and young, and every age in between, have been clamoring for *Cake Culture* for the last week.

Trixie and I have been baking our asses off, and Lance has been helping even more than usual. With his dad and Cody patching things up, he hasn't been as needed at the office, nor at his secondary office at the table in the corner. I'm glad because I wouldn't have been able to get through these last few days without his support. He's my number-one dishwasher.

Right now, he's in the back, though, doing his other specialty, making buttercream. It's the tenth batch of the day, a creamy lemon sorbet frosting for the 'Sock It To Yo Mama Sucker Punch' cupcakes that are cooling on a rack.

As I serve up box after box, I smile and thank each customer from the bottom of my heart. They're the ones letting me do exactly what I've always dreamed of doing, and I appreciate their business.

A blonde woman in a fitted dress that highlights all of her assets steps up to the case next. She looks like she's ready to go on a date, hair and makeup perfect and high heels shaping her calf muscles. If I weren't so damn busy, I'd feel like a frumpy-frump next to her, but luckily, I'm way too busy to care about my barely-there face or pulled-up hair. *Function over frivolity* has become my motto.

"How may I help you?" I ask, already grabbing a box.

She looks at the case but seems to be uncertain, her eyes darting to the tables throughout the space. Twirling a lock of stick-straight hair around her finger, she says quietly, "Uhm, there's usually a guy here. He helps sometimes, but mostly, he sits over there." She tilts her head like she doesn't want to get busted pointing. "I think he's like the owner or manager or something. Is he here?"

Trixie hip-checks me, a beaming smile on her face. "Oh, you mean Commander Cookie? He is here, but unfortunately, he's elbows-deep in frosting at the moment. I'm sure Sweet Scarlet here can get you a delicious treat, though, and if you sit down, maybe he'll come out to deliver some hot, fresh cookies right out of the oven."

It's on the tip of my tongue to tell the woman that his name is Lance and he's mine, mine, mine, but Trixie's wink makes me back off. Staking my territory is a bit of a new instinct to me, but I don't know if I've ever been this far gone over someone, so maybe it's normal?

The woman nods in thanks to Trixie and asks me for a 'Shangri-Vanil-La' cupcake. Once she's served, she makes her way to an open table, barely pecking at the cupcake and obviously wasting time as she waits for Lance to make an appearance.

"What the hell?" I ask Trixie, about ready to resort to the 'licked it, he's mine' defense. Or is that an offensive move? Sports have never been my strong suit, so I don't know the first thing about offensive or defensive. Hell, I'll go for both, just to be sure.

Trixie rolls her eyes but smiles. "In case you didn't know, while the cakes and cookies and pies are popular, we're also famous for serving up a fair bit of eye candy to go with it. And despite our obvious assets, it's not us."

She pouts, but it's fake as can be, and I can sense her desire to flip her hair around, but the messy bun at the back of her head doesn't lend itself too much drama. She looks towards the double doors that hide Lance from the front of the shop.

"Ain't nothing sexier than a hot man who can cook, bonus points that he can string more than three words together."

She gestures to the line of women who are focused on the case and menus on the wall until . . .

Lance comes out from the back. "Got the next batch of zucchini bread in the oven. What's next, Boss?"

His eyes are on me, but I can see every head in the place swivel in his direction. Jealousy squirts into my bloodstream, hot and sour, and heat rises in my cheeks.

Trixie whispers from right next to my ear, chuckling. "He's only got eyes for you, Char. Don't worry your pretty little head about that boy. Hook, line, and sinker, he's done for."

It's not her words that soothe the beast in my belly but Lance's smile as he comes over. "How's it going? Need anything?"

My body, semi-functional brain included, wants to say that I need to take him upstairs and claim him. Ride him like I did before, blow him like I did before, remind him that he's mine and everyone else can step the fuck off. But he doesn't need the reminder. His eyes tell me that he knows exactly what's going through my head.

He stands next to me, possessively throwing his arm over my shoulder and rubbing lightly at the skin below the short sleeve of my T-shirt. Leaning down, he whispers in my ear, "Whatever you're thinking, I fucking *love* that idea. Let's serve all these people as fast as we can, then you can slowly and with lots of adjectives tell me exactly what you have in mind."

His cocky smirk is full of heat, but I don't mind because it's warranted. He's mine, I'm his, and every woman in here is wishing he was whispering sweet nothings and dirty somethings in their ears. But he belongs to one person. Me.

"All right, Commander Cookie," I say, lifting my brows. "Let's get these people fed. Everyone's starving today."

There's a murmur through the crowd, and I think I hear someone murmur, 'hungry for him,' but Lance ignores it and gets to work. He's friendly and charming but professional, and slowly but surely, the line shrinks.

There's only a few more people waiting when the one person I don't want to see comes strolling in the door. Actually, scratch that, one of the two people I don't want to see.

"Charlotte, can we talk, please?" Sabrina says haughtily.

Gesturing to the line, I tell her, "Kinda busy here. Can it wait?"

Or just never happen, I think, wishing she'd just leave.

I'm still not 100% sure she didn't send in those anonymous complaints, even though she denied it. I'm also not 100% sure she did it. Which leaves me in a state of limbo. I don't like her, that's a ship that sailed long ago, but there's a difference to who we were as kids and who we are now, as adults. Or at least, there should be. Lance taught me that with Cody, their relationship evolving and improving now that they're talking more.

"You think I'd be here if it wasn't important?" Sabrina hisses, her eyes narrowing. I don't answer for a moment, trying to see what her play is here. Because there's always a play with her.

"Fine, let's step to the back so we don't air our family laundry in front of everyone. Can you guys watch the front?" I ask Trixie and Lance. When they nod, I lead Sabrina to the kitchen.

"Okay, what's up?" I ask, not wanting any small talk. Whatever she's here for, she can speak and get the fuck out. Especially since I'm betting it's more whining about Lance.

I cross my arms, leaning back against the table, but she paces a bit, looking at the kitchen. "This looks great," she says, and it's all I can do to bite back the remark about her saying the opposite on her complaint form to the Health Department.

When I don't thank her, she sighs and says, "I'm worried about Dad."

"What's wrong with him?" I say, instantly scared to death that Priscilla has finally done something that will drive him into an early grave.

Sabrina shakes her head, holding up a hand. "Not like that. He's not dying or anything. Or at least, no more than the rest of us, but he's just . . . stressed. More than usual, and it's wearing on him. I can tell by the worry on his face, and he's not eating enough. I think *we* wear on him. Not that I think we're ever gonna be besties, but a little less 'at each other's throat' would probably help."

It's a ridiculous request, one I have serious doubts I could honor even if I wanted to. But he's my dad, and he's forgiven me for so much over the years, only asking for one thing . . . that I be kind to his family.

They're not mine, but as much as I chose Mia and Izzy and the whole gang and would defend and support them no matter what, Dad's chosen Priscilla and Sabrina to be a part of his family. And I can respect that, or at least I should.

The door creaks open, and Trixie's head pops in, blonde permed hair springing from her bun. "Sorry to interrupt, but we need you for a minute."

I nod to Trixie before turning back to Sabrina. "Can you wait one second? Let me deal with this and I'll be right back." I run out front, dealing with a customer who wants to order a custom cake.

It takes a little longer than I'd expected, and after a few minutes, Sabrina comes out of the kitchen. She waves as she walks by, calling out, "Check in on Dad. He'd like to hear from you."

It irks me that she's telling me what to do once again, but she's only suggesting that I get closer to him, like maybe she knows he needs me. That's oddly *kind* of her, which is not a descriptor I'd typically ever use for Sabrina.

When Sabrina's gone, I go back to helping the lady who's ordering a tiered quinceañera cake with various edible pearls, sequins, and icing designs. It's going to be another major show-case for my decorating skills, and I'm excited about it, ready to tackle more large-scale orders.

While the line is manageable, Trixie sneaks off to the back to take the zucchini bread out of the oven, toss a batch of muffins in, and grab a tray of cookies. It feels like we successfully made it through another rush.

"What'd Sabrina want?" Trixie asks cautiously. "World War III beginning today?"

I shake my head, still not completely believing Sabrina. "Surprisingly, no. She was telling me that she's worried about Dad and thought I should give him a call. She even said maybe we could lighten up on each other for his sake."

Even as I repeat her missive, I can't believe she would be so mature, not after our last near-knockdown-drag-out fight over the health inspector.

"Hmm, that is surprising—" Trixie says.

But she's interrupted by a loud BOOM.

My eyes meet Trixie's, whose are wide with alarm. Lance jumps into action, moving straight for the double doors to the kitchen.

But when he opens them, the wafting air from the back fills the front room, smoky and hot.

"Oh, shit, the kitchen's on fire," Trixie blurts out.

They say there are two types of people in crisis situations, fighters and flighters. I'm here to say that there's a third type, freezers. Because I'm frozen in place, disbelieving my eyes.

Through the open doors, a haze of white billows near the ceiling, and flames jump from the oven. Lance grabs the fire extinguisher, quickly pulling the pin and aiming at the base of the fire as he sweeps the white foam through the chaos.

Finally, the alarm goes off, a shrill beeping tone that repeats annoyingly, then the sprinklers rain down cold water on everything. It's the signal for people to go from 'Oh, my God' to 'get me out of here', and there's a mad dash for the front door.

Steven pulls on my arm with a firm grip. "Miss Dunn!"

"Everyone out," I call out, finally coming out of my shock. It feels like an eternity has gone by, but it's only been an instant. Just an instant, but my dream is going up in smoke, in flames that are reaching the ceiling now despite Lance's efforts. "Come on, Lance. We have to go."

He tries to shake me off, his eyes gritted against the heat and smoke. "I can save it. I can—"

"Save you, save us. That's all I need. Let's get out of here," I say, pleading with him. He lowers the near-empty extinguisher, realizing I'm right.

The three of us are the last ones out, me, Lance, and Steven busting out the door as the fire trucks are pulling up. Firefighters pull hoses, aiming for the bakery, and with a whoosh of water, they begin fighting the fire.

It's terrifying and heartbreaking, but at the same time, I feel an overwhelming sense of relief that we're all okay.

"What happened?" I ask, not expecting an explanation but needing to give voice to the question running on repeat in my head.

Lance shakes his head, looking at the flames. "I don't know. The oven was completely engulfed."

Trixie's mouth drops open in horror. "Oh, my God, I was right there by it. I took out the bread and put muffins in. If it'd exploded a minute sooner, I would've been standing right there." She's shaking, and I gather her into my arms, patting her hair that's gone wet and frizzy from the sprinkler water. "How did this happen?"

Ice chills my veins. This isn't an accident. I haven't even fully absorbed what's happened, but I know this isn't an accident. This is Blackwell. It has to be.

"Blackwell."

The word galvanizes Lance and Steven, the latter grabbing his phone from his pocket, pressing one button. He starts talking to whoever he quick-dialed.

Lance puts a hand on my shoulder, careful to not disturb Trixie, who's crying silently, tears running down her cheeks to puddle on my shirt. "We don't know it's him. It might've just been an accident."

"We just had a clean inspection and everything was in tip-top order," I hiss incredulously. "This wasn't an accident."

My vehemence catches the attention of a police officer standing nearby. He must've responded to the 9-1-1 call for the fire.

"You said this wasn't an accident, ma'am?" he asks. "I'm Officer Vaughn. And who are you?"

I stand straighter but still keep Trixie and Lance at my sides for support. "I'm Charlotte Dunn. This is my bakery. *Was* my bakery."

He nods sympathetically, flipping open a notebook and taking out a pen. But my announcement has also caught the attention of several customers too. Most of them lean in, as hungry for gossip as they had been for cake. One guy, in particular, comes stomping over.

"This is your bakery? We could've all been killed! What the hell kind of business are you running here?" He's yelling, angry, and aggressively gesturing with his arms, but for the life of me, I can't remember ever seeing him before.

"Sir, I'm sorry for any inconvenience, of course. Right now, we're just glad that everyone's okay." I try to be reasonable, digging deep and finding a degree of customer service, even though what I really want to do is curse the sky for this disaster.

But the man is having none of it. He gets right up in my space, his long finger pointing in my face threateningly. "You're lucky, bitch, you know that? I should sue you for almost killing us all."

Lance tries to intervene, wanting to calm the situation. "Sir, we're all upset, but this is not the appropriate way to treat someone who just lost their business."

The man turns his beady eyes to Lance, and you can almost see his excitement at a new target. He moves his hand from my face, using both to push at Lance's shoulders as he sneers. "You gonna defend your bitch here now?"

Lance is static, not stepping back at all. "Chill out, man!"

The angry customer rears back, telegraphing a punch so big that even I can see it coming. One tight fist heading straight for Lance's jaw. Trixie and I yell out, but Lance steps in, letting the haymaker go over his head and back before lifting the man into the air. When he's up, Lance twists, his hand planted in the man's chest as he does a WWF-like suplex and slams him to the concrete hard and so fast that I don't even have time to call out. He points to the man, his eyes burning in anger.

"Stay down. Last warning."

The guy looks to Officer Vaughn, who's been standing there,

uselessly watching the whole showdown. "You saw that! I want to press charges!"

"Go ahead," Lance growls. "You press charges, and so will I. You laid hands on me first. And my lawyers are a lot better than yours."

Another officer helps the guy to his feet, escorting him off to the side, probably to ask the guy questions about what happened. I look around, watching in horror as I realize people are filming, typing on their phones. Great, just what I need . . . more bad press.

But bad press won't matter, though, because the bakery is demolished.

Officer Vaughn clears his throat, getting my attention. "Ma'am? Can you tell me who has access to your ovens?"

I answer reflexively, picturing my pristine kitchen. "We all do. Me, Trixie, she's my assistant manager, Lance, he's my boyfriend who helps out, and Steven, who's . . . a friend." I don't say that Steven is our guard because I know that'll only lead to questions I think are best answered by Thomas, or at least if I have to answer them, I want to make sure I'm saying what Thomas wants me to since that part of the party is all his.

He scribbles something down. "Anyone else? Maintenance workers, customers, family, friends?"

"Sabrina, my stepsister," I whisper, my stomach dropping. "She came to see me out of the blue today, we talked in the kitchen, and I left her alone to deal with a customer. But I don't think she would know how to tamper with anything." I'm arguing with myself even as the suggestion that she could be responsible gets written down too.

"I think we're going to need you four to come down to the station to answer some more questions," the officer says.

But Lance balks. "Take Charlotte and Trixie, and Steven too. I have some things I need to attend to, but I'll be along as quick as I can to answer any questions." It seems reasonable, but something in his eyes tells me he's not spilling his guts, not fully. I wonder if he's going to go after Sabrina or to talk to Thomas about the possibility of this being a Blackwell act.

Vaughn's demeanor flips like somebody pulled his switch. "Mr. Jacobs, I said you're all going down to the station for questioning. You, especially," he says, lifting his chin toward the assaulting guy who's loudly proclaiming that Lance started it. "Let's not have an incident."

He grabs at Lance, who steps back, calm and controlled. "On what grounds are you detaining me?" His voice is loud, drawing attention as questioning eyes look our way.

Vaughn comes at him again and they tussle, arms flailing. I can tell Lance is trying to not hurt the cop and is just defending himself.

Still, Trixie gets into the mix, throwing catfight-worthy scrabbling arms and flailing hands as she yells like a banshee, "Leave him alone! We have rights!"

Somehow, I end up trying to separate all three of them. "Stop it, all of you. Stop!"

I see a phone fall from Lance's pocket. I drop down to pick it up, thinking I'll hold it for him until after this weird attack by the police. But it's not his usual phone, the one that sits on my nightstand every evening as we drift off to sleep in each other's arms.

Why would he have two phones?

My gut drops like I'm on a roller coaster as one answer bubbles up. *It's a hoe phone.* Been there, done that, burned that bridge to the ground with kerosene and matches.

Wait, that's not funny, given the current situation.

But my heart cracks at the thought.

The screen lights up as I turn it over and the last message displays.

Blackwell—Mission is a Go. Execute.

Bile rises in my stomach at the jargon and the name attached to the message. I look up to Lance, my heart painfully shattering in my chest. It's not another woman. It's another man. The worst man in all of Roseboro, telling Lance to do what?

Did Lance blow up my bakery?

Hot tears flow as he calls out my name, but I shake my head. The officer grimaces and hauls Lance away, shoving him into a waiting police car.

I fall to my knees, right there on the street in front of my dream. Both of them . . . the bakery and Lance.

I thought I was finally going to get everything, that maybe happily ever afters could be true and happen to me. But I know better. It'll always be the happily *never* after for me.

CHAPTER 27

CHARLOTTE

*T*rixie helps me up, shooing me off to the sidewalk to sit on a bench. "Oh, my God, I can't . . . I thought Sabrina . . . I never thought Lance would . . . Blackwell—"

I can't string a coherent sentence together, but Trixie gets the gist. She saw the same thing I did.

Lance had a phone with a message from Blackwell. All signs point to his being a sleeper agent, just like Mia said.

But how? He couldn't have been faking everything all along, could he?

The charming smiles. The panty-melting kisses. The dick me downs. My heart cries out. Not just the sex, but the emotions are what I really can't believe he faked. He made me believe again, made me hope. And I thought he was right there with me.

He said he loved me. I said I loved him.

I meant it, I really did. But for him, was it all just a ploy? A way to get close to me, a way to hurt Thomas?

I don't want to believe it. But the phone holds the proof. I look at it again, though tears cloud my vision, and Trixie looks over my shoulder.

There's no passcode, so it's easy enough to look through the data. There are pictures of the kitchen, of Steven, of me. It's almost like he was building a file on the bakery for Blackwell.

But it's the messages that hurt the most.

Concerns about your cover?

No sir.

Then weeks later . . .

Expect a visit.

That had been the day before Barrett Williams had shown up for his health inspection with the phony complaints. Apparently, that was Blackwell too. Sabrina really is in the clear. It seems I'm a worse judge of character than I thought. I suspected her both times, but it was the one person I never considered who was betraying me the worst.

And today's message . . .

Mission is a Go. Execute.

The betrayal burns me to the core, and the tears that have been pouring slowly refresh their hot trails down my cheeks. Trixie holds me, taking the phone and putting it in her apron pocket.

"Honey, I get that Lance has done something really awful, but I don't get *why*. Why is Steven pacing around on the phone like someone tried to kill the president? What the hell does Blackwell have to do with the bakery? This is all just . . . *what?*"

She looks to me, fear lining her face as her brows pinch together.

"It's a long story," I say, drained after all this.

She shrugs, looking across the street where the firefighters are doing all they can do. "Hell, the bakery just burned down. We've got time. Tell me what the fuck's going on."

But I can't. It's not my story to tell, and the last time I told someone, he ended up being Blackwell's agent.

The phone buzzes, and both of us jolt.

Trixie pulls it out, holding it so we can both see the screen.

Blackwell—Move to final phase.

Our eyes meet, horror dawning. Burning the bakery wasn't the end of whatever plan Blackwell has.

"Should we give this to the police?" she asks, looking at the cops and then the phone. She's acting like the phone is a snake, about to bite her.

I shake my head, knowing the truth. "No, I need to give it to Thomas."

She tenses as an SUV peels into the lot across the street, drawing everyone's attention and putting us all on alert. But it's just Jonathan, who looks at me with haunted eyes. "I'm sorry, Charlotte. Are you all right?"

"It was Lance all along," I say sadly.

"Start at the beginning," he says crisply, all business.

I give him the basics that we've put together and hand over the phone. He listens carefully, asking questions about what I saw today, but shakes his head when I say it had to be Lance and that the police took him in for questioning. "It doesn't make any sense. I know Lance Jacobs and this isn't his style. Did the police see the phone?"

"No, it fell out of his pocket when he was scuffling with the police officer who was trying to arrest him," I reply, shaking my head. "I thought it was just his phone, so I held onto it, for safe-keeping, you know? Then I realized I'd never seen it before and read the messages on it."

"So they took him in with no evidence? But left you here?" he clarifies, looking at the phone in his hand, and I nod.

"The last message said, *final phase.* What do you think that means?" My voice is shaking, but I can't help it. Today has just been too much.

He looks grim, slipping the phone in his pocket. "I don't know yet. Stay here, stay with Steven, and Brian is on his way to be backup. Don't talk to anyone." He runs back to his SUV, catching Steven's eye and pointing at us, assigning responsibility.

Trixie leans in to me, whispering, "Who the hell are you? A secret princess or something?"

My mouth opens and closes, wanting to tell her everything, but no sound comes out.

She sighs, looking worried. "Fine, I get it. But whatever the fuck is going on, I don't think that guy is right."

I look to her and she explains. "You said you needed to get the phone to Thomas. It doesn't take a genius to know that this has something to do with your friends. Whatever is going on, you need to get to safety. And it sure ain't sitting on a sidewalk bench in the open, across the street from the bakery that just got burned down. You need to get together, circle the wagons, and have each other's back to stay safe." Trixie points at Steven, who's still talking in his earpiece. "Don't keep him here, Char. Go be safe."

I can hear the fear in her voice, the concern that something else is coming and we're out here like sitting ducks. I look around, seeing the crowds gawking and pointing, the building, and finally, the stress on Steven's face.

She's right. I need to go, get to Thomas and Mia's so we can all be together and be as safe as possible. Blackwell can't take us all out, not with full security.

"You're right, Trix. Safety in numbers, that's what they say. Come with me," I suggest.

She shakes her head, sadness in her eyes. "Honey, you can't even tell me what's going on because I'm outside the circle. I get it."

I take her hands, desperate. "You're important to me, Trixie. I don't want anything to happen to you."

She smiles, but I can tell it's forced, given the situation. "I know. You're important to me too, and that's why I don't want anything to happen to you, so go. But I don't want anything to happen to me either, and you've got some shit coming, I think. I'm just going to head home and chill. But I'm still on the clock." The tease is bitter. I know she's hurting and is scared for me.

I hug her tight, her arms wrapping around me too.

"Love you," I tell her honestly.

"Love you too. Now go give Blackwell hell, rip his nuts off, though still not for a 'Nutz for Nutz' cupcake. Ew," she says, her nose crinkling. "Still the grossest thing you've ever thought of."

"Thank you, though you're a crazy bitch, you know that?"

She grins, and it seems the slightest bit more real this time, until she looks across the street and the smile fades. "This is our bakery, damn it," she spits out. "Nobody gets to take it."

CHAPTER 28

LANCE

*T*he interrogation room is freezing cold, likely to make suspects talk. Same reasoning behind the uncomfortable chair, the plain table in front of me, and the cuffs locking me in place.

My internal clock says I've been here for less than an hour, but staring at my own reflection and wondering who's on the other side of the one-way mirror is making time stand still.

What the hell happened at the bakery?

One second, we were all thankful to have gotten out, blessedly breathing fresh air and watching as the bakery burned. I'd been so glad no one was hurt because it'd been a full house in there. The next minute, some guy is throwing punches and a cop's going Full Metal Jacket, trying to bring me in without reason.

Resisting arrest probably wasn't my best move, but something felt off and I was worried about leaving Charlotte.

Charlotte. Her face when she saw the phone.

She was arguing for me, standing up for her man like the badass I know she can be, but something on that screen broke her. Her face had gone pale, well, paler than her usual, and her eyes were shocked and angry.

I don't know what she could've seen. Or where that phone came from. Was it hers? If so, I'd never seen it before, but maybe she has a backup from Thomas?

My mind is swirling, questions layering on top of one another as I try to dissect and consider each one carefully and methodically. I'm still trying to figure it out when the door opens.

An older man, grey-haired with a paunch belly, comes in, shutting the door behind him. He sits down across from me, a gentle smile on his face that makes the thick mustache over his top lip wiggle at the ends. "I'm Frank Harris. Wanted to ask you a few questions."

"Lance Jacobs. I have a few questions of my own too," I reply, keeping myself steady. If he thinks his little act so far has me intimidated, he's got another thing coming.

Jonathan warned me about the police, and I'm not going to play this like some greenback. I've handled interrogations myself, and this Harris guy won't be resorting to waterboarding to get his answers, which bodes well for me. I'm leaving this room with more information than I give, that's for damn sure.

"Hmmm . . . your information says Navy. Do we need to call the Pentagon?"

He shrugs like it doesn't matter, but he's just trying to get under my skin and we both know it.

"Currently on terminal leave, but I can give you my old CO's name, sir. Should I call you 'sir'? I'm afraid I didn't catch your role here at the Roseboro Police Department." I look around the interrogation room like I'm evaluating it for a Yelp review.

His mustache twitches, then he inclines his head. "Chief Harris, at your service."

What the fuck is the Chief of Police doing interrogating me? First off, there's no reason for them to hold me, but his presence hints at something much larger. Chiefs don't get involved for a swing at a cop, even in Mayberry.

Needing more information, I hedge my bets. "Nice to meet you, Chief Harris. Though I do wish it were under better circumstances."

He shrugs, opening a file on the table between us and pretending to read it. I can tell he's faking. His eyes aren't focused. So, this is a show, but for what? Or maybe more importantly, who?

"Says here you were behaving suspiciously at the fire over at *Cake Culture* today. That true?" he says casually.

"No." It's the only answer I need to give because it's the truth.

He grunts. "Why don't you tell me about today." It's an order, not a question.

"It was a busy day at the bakery, so we were all out front, serving customers, when there was a loud boom in the kitchen. We went to the back, I tried to put it out with the fire extinguisher, but it got too big, too fast. We had to get out. Outside, a guy got physical and I defended myself. An officer was asking the same questions you are now. Then he said we needed to come in to the station—"

"And that was Officer Vaughn?" he interrupts to clarify.

I nod. "Yeah, Officer Vaughn wanted us to come in. I told him to bring everyone else down and I'd be here shortly. He didn't like that, became aggressive, and next thing I know, I'm here and everyone else was dismissed without further question. Are they okay?" There's something going on here, but I need to at least know if everyone else is fine after the fire.

"As far as I know," he says, a gleam in his eye. "Though I haven't seen Miss Dunn yet."

He's trying to make me worry about Charlotte, but why? Is it a tactic to get me to talk, hoping to get back to her? Not going to happen. I don't trust this guy. He may be the boss around here, but he reads slimy to me.

"So, you didn't want to come with Vaughn. Where were you planning to go?" Harris asks slyly.

Thank God for my training. There's a time to be emotionless, and a time to lose it . . . coolly. This is one of those times, and I spit out, "To my parent's, to a friend's, to take a shit . . . it doesn't matter. He had no right to detain me, and you have no right to hold me."

Harris's good-old-boy act disappears. "I may not be able to charge you with burning that bakery down just yet, boy. But I've got a guy out there talking about pressing charges for you doing some body slam move, a serious accusation with your being a trained killer and all. And an officer with a helluva shiner, so yes, assaulting a police officer is the charge right now. See what your CO thinks about that."

If it was just the bakery misunderstanding, I'd get up and waltz out of here. But the officer assault is a serious accusation, one I'm not sure isn't true. I don't remember hitting Vaughn when we tussled, but I wouldn't swear to that in a court of law.

"In that case . . . lawyer."

Chief Harris turns a mottled shade of red and knocks on the mirror two times. An answering single knock must communicate something to him, or at least he acts like it does. "Your family has been notified and my guess is they'll have your lawyer running up here to save your entitled ass any minute now."

I dip my chin, not speaking.

"Got a little story to tell you. Now, you don't talk." He points a thick finger at me in warning. "Just wait on that lawyer, but you can listen, right?"

He waits for me to answer, but I just glare at him.

After a moment, he continues.

"Once upon a time, there was a guy called Prince Charming, and you'd think he'd be the hero of the story, but no. Instead, he went into the kitchen of the local bake shop and waited until he was alone. Now, everyone thought he was just baking some cupcakes or something, but he wasn't. No, our not-hero was tinkering with the ovens, opening the gas intake too much until BOOM!"

I grit my teeth, needing to refute these accusations, but I know he's baiting me. So as hard as it is, I just keep my mouth shut.

He smirks, like he knows exactly what he's doing to me. "This Prince tries to make his getaway. But he gets caught and his web of deceit is discovered by everyone. He's arrested, goes to trial, and ends up spending the next twenty years of his life in prison."

He eyes me, gauging my reaction to his story and the threatening ending. But I give him nothing.

He tries a few more times, saying variations of the same accusations to see if I'll flinch, but I'm stone-cold against his onslaught.

In my mind, I'm still trying to piece things together. I don't believe for a minute that the oven blowing up was an accident, and the obvious person to do something like that is Blackwell.

But what does he stand to gain from destroying a bakery? From hurting Charlotte?

From what Jonathan has told me, Blackwell is escalating, getting grander and more complex in his elaborate plans. And this seems small, comparatively, even though it's everything to Charlotte. And she's everything to me.

Unless . . .

It's not about the bakery or Charlotte. It's a power move, a play that directs the next few steps. But how is he funneling this to get at Thomas, because he's most definitely the end game?

Harris is getting frustrated with his lack of progress and my lack of attention. "Are you listening to me?" he barks.

I refocus my eyes on him, cold and collected to his mad fury. "Law-yer."

He growls, pushing the table toward me as he lumbers up. He grabs my upper arm, strongly *encouraging* me to stand. "You want to be that way, fine. But we need the room. Guess you'll have to wait down in holding for your fancy lawyer to get here."

It sounds like a threat if ever I've heard one. He uncuffs me from the table but makes sure to sneakily press each bracelet a notch tighter around my wrist. The delight in his eyes at the small shock of pain is more worrisome than the discomfort.

Downstairs, he leads me through a checkpoint, where the officer on duty acts like the president is coming through. I'm betting the chief doesn't come down here too often, especially not hauling a prisoner. It's another odd puzzle piece in this picture.

Why in the world is someone like Harris the one investigating me and the fire, and not a run-of-the-mill detective? It must be because he wants this case for some reason.

The bars slide open in front of me and Harris shoves me. He's obviously hoping I'll lose my footing and go sprawling across the filthy concrete floor, but I do a good job of maintaining my balance. It's a small win given today's catastrophes, but hopefully the start of a good roll.

The door slides closed, and Harris sneers from the relative safety on the other side. "I'll be sure to let you know when that lawyer gets here." His tone tells me that he'll have me waiting long after the family attorney arrives.

Once he's gone, I turn around, looking at the handful of other guys in the holding cell with me. There's a drunk and disheveled guy curled up in the corner, snoring lightly. A tall, bald guy with tattoos on both forearms who looks menacing, but I'm betting it's his version of resting bitch face. And lastly, a middle-aged guy in khakis and a polo, with gold-rimmed glasses. He looks like someone who'd love to discuss the merits of quantum physics.

I lift my chin, greeting each of them silently, then move toward an empty section of bench to claim it for myself. My mind is still working, churning over everything we know and trying to piece together the rest of the puzzle.

I've got my head hanging down, my elbows resting on my spread knees when I hear a quick shuffle of feet. I look up to see the physics guy making a run at me, murder in his eyes.

I stand up fast, chin tight and ready for his assault. Not going to happen, but I'm surprised he's more than I thought. "Sit down," I growl.

Physics guy freezes a foot from me and veers off to sit down on the bench next to me like that was his goal all along. Creepy and strange.

Baldie lifts his eyebrows at the scene, then nods his head at the bench next to him. I take the invitation, moving to sit down. "I'm Dave, in for drunk and disorderly," he says with a shrug. "I'm a happy drunk, what can I say?"

"And him?" I ask, looking to Physics Guy.

Baldie twists his lips, scowling. "Don't know, but I can sense that little fucker's wrong in the head."

I concur, but thankfully, the buzz of the gate down the hall opening stops further conversation.

A familiar face soon appears in the bars. "Holy shit, I'm glad to see you, man!"

Jonathan smiles, but it's grim. "Let's just get you out of here. We've got a lot to talk about."

Paperwork to get released takes twice as long as it did coming in when they were ripping my watch off and damn near drooling to get their hands on my wallet. I don't know how much cash I had in it, but I'm betting it's a little lighter now.

Finally, we get to Jonathan's SUV and he pulls out of the lot, looking in the rearview mirror more times than safe driving requires. But he must see there's no one tailing us, and my side-view mirror tells me the same.

"Thanks, man. I feel like there's so much we need to talk about," I say as he pulls out of downtown.

His jaw is set, teeth clenched. "Not yet."

After a long stretch of silent minutes, he pulls into a treed driveway on a rural country road outside Roseboro. He reaches into his pocket and pulls out his jammer. He flips it on and sets it on the dashboard.

Then he pulls his gun on me.

CHAPTER 29

CHARLOTTE

*S*teven hands me another tissue from the console, which I take thankfully. "Sorry I'm such a mess," I say between sobs.

I'd cried through telling Trixie what I could, but sitting still in this quiet car is too much, and the sobs have been racking my body for the last fifteen minutes as we get closer to the Goldstone building. Poor Steven seems at a loss and just keeps handing me tissues. Guess they didn't teach him about this in badass school, whichever one he went to.

We pull into the garage, and I swear his shoulders lower a solid two inches from his ears. But he clears his throat and says professionally, "Miss Dunn, let me help you upstairs."

I let him open the door after scanning the parking lot, then lead me to Thomas's private elevator. After a whoosh that makes my belly climb into my throat, the doors open to reveal Mia.

Her eyes are red and puffy too as she launches herself at me. "Oh, my God, Char," she says, gathering me in her arms. I let her hug me, soothe me, and eventually, my arms come up to circle her too. She's mumbling into my shoulder, "Could've lost . . . what the fuck . . . so glad you're . . ."

I nod, hugging her back. "I know, but I'm okay. Well, physically, anyway. My heart hurts."

I rub at my chest, and Mia's eyes shoot to Steven. "Why didn't you take her to the hospital if she's injured?" she demands.

He shakes his head almost imperceptibly as I place a staying hand on Mia's arm because she looks like she's about to launch herself at Steven too, and not in such a caring way. "Not from the fire. Lance."

"Lance?" she asks, confusion pulling her eyebrows so tightly together they look like caterpillars about to battle above her nose. "What about him?"

She looks between me and Steven, who's staring into space like he wishes he could be anywhere but here in this moment. Mia's fire is growing by the millisecond, her face already a deeper shade of pink than her current hair. "What? Somebody better start speaking or I'm gonna track him down and introduce him to Thunder and Lightning." She holds up one fist, then the other. "And then a friend I like to Hail, because it'll drop you to your knees." She kicks her leg up in a hi-yah motion.

Even through the tears, she breaks me into a laugh. A snotty, ugly one, but a laugh, nevertheless. "Can we sit down?"

"Oh, yeah, of course." Mia leads me to the couch, and Steven stays at his post by the elevator, pulling his phone back out to text. I wonder if he's texting Jonathan and if he knows anything about what's happening to Lance down at the police station.

We sit down, and I curl my feet up underneath me, needing to be small and less of a target because it feels like the universe is taking pot shots at my life today. Mia waits exactly two heartbeats before saying, "Speak, *Tovarich*. Tell me what the fuck is going on."

I don't know where to start. It feels like I've lived a lifetime in just a few hours. "You know about the fire?"

270

"Yeah, something about an oven, but everyone got out, right?"

"Yeah, so we got out ,and I'm watching my baby burn when this cop comes over and starts asking questions. He's all 'who has access' and I tell him just me, Trixie, and Lance, but then I remember that Sabrina came by today and I left her back there for a second while I stepped to the front." My eyes are unseeing, cloudy behind unshed tears as I remember, but I blink them back.

I've cried enough. I need to be strong. I've been through bad shit and come out the other side, stronger for it. This is worse than anything else, for sure, but I'll be invincible, savage and cold as ice after this. *And alone again,* a small voice whispers.

"Sabrina?" Mia growls. "That bitch!"

I shake my head before she can get too far. "I thought the same thing, and thought it might be Blackwell too. Just grasping for straws, you know? But then the cop wanted us to go to the station to make statements and Lance lost it. At first, he said he'd meet us there, but then when the cop tried to force him to go, Lance fought him. That's when the phone fell out of his pocket."

I swallow thickly, wringing my hands. The hands that held the proof of his betrayal.

"What phone?" Mia asks quietly. I think she can tell this is the crux of the issue, the reason for the tears. Even more so than the bakery. I can rebuild that, but my heart? It's shattered beyond repair this time.

I meet her eyes, wishing she could erase the memory, that I could go back a couple of hours and never have seen that screen. "Lance had a second phone, and his last text message came up on the screen when I grabbed it. It was from . . . Blackwell." The tears won't be held back, but I don't give into them fully. I let them trail hotly down my puffy cheeks but keep my head held high, refusing to break.

Mia jumps from the couch, pissed. "Blackwell? Lance is . . . he's working for . . ." She turns down the hallway, bellowing, "Tommy!!"

He comes running, phone held to his ear. His eyes search the room wildly, looking for a threat, but when he sees only Mia and me, he tells whoever's on the phone, "Hold up."

He looks at Mia, and he says, "What's wrong?"

"Did you know about Lance? That he's working for Blackwell?" she demands, a hand on her hip. If you didn't know her, it wouldn't seem all that scary. I mean, she's a small, nerdy woman with streaked hair who's currently wearing ripped jeans and a K-pop T-shirt.

But you'd be wrong. Mia's the second-scariest person I know. Second only to Gabe, but he's a different kind of scary.

Thomas cringes, nodding. "Yes, we're working on it."

Mia sputters, and I think she was hoping Thomas would tell her it was all a big misunderstanding. "But he . . ." She turns back to me, sadness in her eyes. "I thought he was going to crack that cynical heart of yours and be your happily ever after."

"Me too, honey. Me too," I agree hollowly.

I shake it off, remembering why I came here in the first place. "He's got a head start. None of us saw this coming, least of all me. So we need to circle the wagons," I tell Thomas, using Trixie's phrasing that rings true. "You've got to get Izzy and Gabe here. Whatever Blackwell's planning, he can't get us all at once, not if we're here, surrounded by security."

He nods, taking his phone back out. He presses a couple of numbers and has a quick conversation with Gabe. When he hangs up, he tells us, "They're already on their way. Steven reported to the crew that you were coming here, and Gabe said he couldn't hold Izzy back from getting to your side. They'll be here any minute."

The tiniest smile tries to break free at the idea that Gabe couldn't hold Izzy back. She's strong, but he's . . . Gabe. Which is actually why he couldn't stop her, because as scary of a guy as he is, and as deadly of a hitman as he used to be, Izzy's got him wrapped around her little finger.

The elevator whirs, and Steve lifts his gun, pressing the button on the headset at his ear.

There's a tense moment where I irrationally fear Blackwell himself is going to walk off the elevator. But when the door opens, Gabe and Izzy walk into the apartment.

Izzy rushes me, much like Mia did, wrapping me up for a hug. "Motherfucker, I'm going to slice his balls off and serve them as the Blue Plate Special." Izzy's language has taken a turn for the worse, or at least the more creative, since she started seeing Gabe. It's oddly funny because I rarely hear him curse, but Izzy says he curses like a sailor.

A sailor . . . *my* sailor.

Lance.

Fuck, is everything going to bring me back to thoughts of him? I sigh, telling Izzy, "Thanks, honey, but don't blow the Gravy Train's health inspection over me. Those people are hardasses."

It's the barest hint of humor but the first sign that I'm going to be okay. Eventually. After I kill Lance, slowly and painfully. I chance a glance at Gabe, wondering how much it'd cost me to hire him, but he winks like he already knows what I'm thinking and I'm betting his family discount is pretty steep.

Gabe breaks into my murderous thoughts. "What do we know? What's the plan?"

I appreciate the move to action, because I can't say stagnant in my pity party of heartbreak or I'll drown. I need to do something about this attack on my bakery and my heart. Action, that's what I need. Retaliation.

I sit back down on the couch, Mia on one side and Izzy on the other, while Thomas and Gabe face each other. I feel like I've got my people around me, but my stupid broken heart still feels like there's someone missing.

"Jonathan and Mia have been digging, and we've made some moves. Business moves to hurt Blackwell, but obviously, they're not enough," Thomas says.

"And we've found sketchy stuff, loads of it, actually," Mia adds. "But no smoking gun, and we don't know where enough of the bodies are buried, literally or figuratively."

"We need more time," Thomas growls. "We need solid proof or making an accusation like this could backfire majorly. He's got major clout in Roseboro, damn near built the city. We can't let anyone he's got in his pocket sweep this under the rug. We need undeniable evidence that he's doing all of this."

Thomas looks to Gabe, but Izzy gets up and stands in front of him. "No, we've talked about this. I get that the most damning evidence we have of Blackwell's wrongdoing is that he hired Gabe to kill me, but if we go to the police with that, they'll arrest Gabe, especially if they do any looking into his past. So no, there's got to be another way. He's a maniacal mastermind. He's got to have left a trail. We just have to find it." She looks off into space like she's searching too, but she's coming up empty-handed, like we all are.

"There is another option to get information," Gabe says carefully. He looks at me, apology in his eyes. "We have another of Black-well's pawns. We could ask him questions."

I flinch, electricity shooting through me. "Bring Lance here? Why? He's already in jail."

Thomas clears his throat. "Jonathan bailed him out fifteen minutes ago."

I look at Thomas incredulously, bile in my gut threatening to come up. "What? Why would he do that?"

Thomas looks at Gabe, who says gently, "Because it's our best option. I'll take care of it."

I know he's not just talking about walking Lance back down to the police station to turn him back in. And as much as Lance has hurt me, I don't want the ending Gabe would give him. He might deserve it, but I'm not the sort of person who could do that someone, nor let Gabe do it in my stead. As much as my superficial knee-jerk reaction is *kill the bastard*, my true nature isn't so sadistic. I won't become that for Lance's betrayal, not for anything.

I don't begrudge Gabe for what he's done, but I won't bear the same weighty responsibility he does for that drastic of an action. I don't want him to kill Lance. So why bother asking the questions he won't answer when the threat isn't real?

"It's not like he's going to spill his guts and tell us everything. He's obviously a great liar, had me completely fooled and believing in fairy tales," I say, and everyone in this room knows how unlikely that is, and by extension, what a good liar that means Lance must be. "We need to just go after Blackwell head-on."

Thomas and Gabe meet eyes over my head, and I've never felt so inconsequential. I'm just a cog in the wheel, but Thomas owns the wheel and Gabe is the one turning it. I pull my legs up to my chest, placing my head on my knees and sighing as I close my eyes.

I'd thought my life now was different. I'd finally stepped out of my stepmother's control, Dad's passive awareness, and all the heartbreaking drama there. I was in control, free to make my own way, my own choices. But it was an illusion.

My bakery, the one I'd poured every bit of my blood, sweat, and tears into? Partially Thomas's. My friends have men of their own now. My life, the one I thought I was master of my own destiny for? It's just a linchpin in someone else's game.

I'm just a pawn, always have been. And apparently, always will be.

"Fine, whatever you want to do," I say, the words echoing in the cavern between my chest and my thighs.

I just don't want to hurt anymore.

CHAPTER 30

LANCE

*H*is gun's a Glock 29, small enough to fit comfortably between us in the small space of the SUV's cab. The doors are locked, and I'm betting Jonathan has the child safety engaged so that I can't open the door next to me without his unlocking it from his side.

"Explain," he says evenly. He's stone-cold in this minute, not the friend I shared a battlefield with but the cold-eyed warrior I remember. He may or may not like what he has to do right now, but he'll do it either way.

I hold my hands out, though he knows I'm unarmed since he watched them check the returned inventory they handed me at the jail. Wallet, set of keys, and a small pocket knife. No gun.

"There was a fire, everyone got out, asshole cop power-tripped about us going down for questions and arrested me. Got the full-court parade of interrogations, complete with the damn Chief of Police, then you showed up." I narrow my eyes, looking at him carefully. "But you already know that. What's going on?"

I'm hoping he'll tell me what's brought this on because I'm clueless.

Something Charlotte said echoes in my mind. Blackwell has people all over the city, and she doesn't trust anyone. *Oh, fuck.*

"Are you working for Blackwell? Are you spying on Thomas for him?" I growl.

It'd make perfect sense, Infiltration 101, get close to your target. Jonathan's insinuating himself as the head of Thomas's security team would be perfect, getting him into all sorts of top-secret places and able to direct every move Thomas makes, for good and bad.

I'm already looking for an opening to take Jonathan out, grab the gun, and remove the threat to Charlotte and her friends, when he scoffs.

"Me? Nice try, but you're the operative for Blackwell. What does he know? What's he planning?" Jonathan says quietly, ice in his voice.

I read his face, looking for any sign of dishonesty but finding none. "Wait, you're not on Blackwell's payroll?" He shakes his head slightly, but his eyes and the gun stay locked on me. "I'm not either. Charlotte said Blackwell was a sick fucker, with resources all over the city. But I'm not one. I swear it. On Stockton's grave."

James Stockton. He wasn't the first death letter I'd had to write, nor was he the last, but it was the hardest. And Jonathan knows that because he was there for the worst of it.

We're most of the way through the dusty field, just after 2200 local. Ahead, less than a hundred meters now, is our target when the AK opens up and we grab dirt.

"Move, move, move," I yell to my men. We're a small group tonight, just one platoon of sixteen, but we're good. My guys do as trained, alternatingly laying down covering fire and hauling ass for the single shack on the property.

Inside, the family of caretakers, employees of the area warlord, shrink back in fear, but they each hold weapons. A father, a mother, and a ten-year-old boy. Thankfully, they're more scared of us than their warlord.

Stockton, our interpreter, tells them we aren't there for them and even gets them to lower their guns, which we promptly secure. We stay still and quiet for two hours as a patrol sweeps the fields outside.

We're ready to kill every one of those patrolling men, which in the civilian world sounds horrifying, but there in the quiet of the night, I'm ready to do whatever I have to for my men.

Eventually, the guards retreat, and I silently celebrate that our cover held. I call for pickup, and we prep to leave as the tut-tut-tut of the chopper blades gets closer in the distance.

Stockton speaks to the father, something I can't understand but sounds kind, like he's thanking the man for our safety. Stockton even smiles, a flash of white teeth in the dark shack.

Suddenly, the man lashes out with a knife. I return fire automatically, killing the father instantly as the mother and child cry out, yelling in a language I don't understand.

He'd been sitting on it the whole time, and he gets Stockton across the calf, taking him down. We'd all been so close to surviving this unexpected meeting, but the father forces my hand.

We leave the shack, one dead, two grieving, but all of my men alive. They're my responsibility, and I'm not going to fail them.

We haul ass for the Blackhawk that's just setting down. I help Stockton, who's limping badly and not able to put much pressure on his left leg. We make it aboard, and one of the guys who's already loaded helps me pull Stockton inside.

He's half in-half out when the ratta-tat-tat of automatic gunfire loudly sounds out, even though we're right under the helicopter's rotating blades.

I shove Stockton in, climbing in behind him. We both take hits, I can tell by the way his body jerks in my arms and the fire that shoots through my leg. But the chopper takes off, getting us out of there.

"Are you hit?" someone asks, and I nod because my mouth is so dry, I can't speak. But I'm okay. It's not serious, even though it hurts like a motherfucker. "Stockton?"

No answer.

I roll over, where the medic's working, but I can tell already that it's not good.

Five seconds. If we'd been five seconds faster . . .

I'd had to tell his wife, as she held the tiny baby Stockton had kissed goodbye less than a week before, that he hadn't made it. I'd been the man right next to her husband as he kept us all safe in that shack and paid for his kindness with his life. She hadn't said it, but I know she'd wished it'd been me.

An inch or two to the right and it would've been.

I tell Jonathan, back in the cab of his SUV at gunpoint, "You were on pickup that night, Jon. Your boys were our backup, so you know. I swear on Stockton's grave, it's not me."

Jonathan lowers the gun, sighing. "Fuck. I had to be sure. It'd be so much easier if it was. One and done."

I know just how close Jonathan was to shooting me, can hear the desperation in his voice. "We need to back up. Our intel is wrong. It's not you, and it's not me."

He nods, putting the Glock away. "Then who?"

I look out the window, replaying the day. "Charlotte was sure it was Sabrina, and she was in the kitchen alone for a few minutes this afternoon. She came by unexpectedly, which could track that it's her. I could even see her being so mad at Charlotte that she could be turned to Blackwell's side, not because she cares about Thomas but just to get back at Charlotte."

Jonathan shakes his head, drumming his fingers on the steering wheel. "But what about the phone?"

"What phone?" I ask. "Charlotte picked up a phone when the police were hauling me away, but I'd never seen it before."

Jonathan opens his center console, pulling out a phone. "This phone. Check the text messages."

I do as he says, and fury rushes through my body, my blood catching fire in my veins. "What the fuck?"

"I know. Charlotte thinks it's yours," he says hollowly.

"No, she knows I wouldn't do something like this, wouldn't betray her. I love her," I protest. But I can see her, the color draining out of her face and the look of hurt in her eyes.

I hadn't understood then, but I do now.

She *would* believe I'd do something like this. Not because she doesn't trust me, but because she doesn't trust anyone and is always waiting for the other shoe to drop. And this? This is like a size-thirteen combat boot dropping on her life. *She'd believe,* I think sadly.

Her scars run too deep. I've been healing them, but not fast enough, not enough for her to know without a doubt that this is a lie.

"I'll make her understand," I vow to Jonathan. "I'll prove to her that it's not me. I love her, and she does this dance. Two steps forward, one step back. This is a giant one back, but I got her to trust me once. I'll get her to do it again."

"That's sweet and all, but not really the issue at hand. Whose phone is this?" Jonathan says. "We were sure it was yours."

I play back that moment.

Vaughn could've dropped the phone in the scuffle. His vehemence that he take me in could be a play from Blackwell to separate us. Even Chief Harris's involvement could track with that. Dirty cops on Blackwell's payroll makes sense, and Jonathan knows the cops are in Blackwell's pocket.

But Vaughn didn't have access to the ovens in the kitchen. He might be dirty, but he's not the guy for this.

I flip to the camera folder on the phone, scrolling.

Steven? Maybe it's not Jonathan who's the plant in Thomas's crew but the guard closest to Charlotte. He'd been there today and has been in the kitchen dozens of times.

But a picture on the phone stops me. It's a picture of Steven. If he's the plant, he couldn't take a picture of himself. He's too far away. I study the picture, horror dawning as I realize who.

Only one person has gotten Steven to smile and flash a peace sign.

"Oh, fuck. I know who it is," I say, still not believing my eyes even though the proof is right in front of me.

"Who?" Jonathan says.

"It's Trixie. She was always taking pictures of Steven. I thought she had a crush on him. And she's got full access. To everything. She was there, fighting Vaughn when he tried to take me in. Maybe the phone fell out of her pocket or she dropped it into mine?"

Jonathan's eyes narrow, and I can see his mind flipping through files in his mental filing cabinet. "Trixie Reynolds, Oklahoma. Business degree, assistant manager at *Cake Culture*. . ." He goes on, repeating things I already know about Trixie, but he's missing the vital piece and so am I.

How in the fuck does she know Blackwell, and more importantly, why would she betray Charlotte?

CHAPTER 31

CHARLOTTE

J'm still trying to breathe, Thomas and Gabe and Mia discussing angles and options like I'm not even here. At least Izzy is rubbing my back in soothing circles and cooing in my ear that everything's going to be okay.

I want to tell her that it'll never be okay again, but that would be rude. She's been through *way* worse things than I ever have, and she came out the other side, strong and fierce. She also got her man by walking through the fires of hell with him.

So, while I'm devastated, I try to believe her, have a little faith that I'm going to recover from this, rebuild my bakery. After that, I'll probably become a spinster because I'm sure as fuck never letting a man inside my heart again.

Steven steps into the room, addressing Thomas. "Excuse me, they've arrived."

I look at Thomas, shaken anew. "They? Is Lance here? Now?" At his grim nod, I shake my head. "I can't do this. I'm going to just go to the guest room."

Izzy's hand is tight on my shoulder, and she sits me back down. "The hell you are. You're going to sit right here, glare holes in him, and show him that he didn't fucking break you. You're better than this, stronger than him. He knows it hurts, and that's why you're going to stand up to the pain, rise from it like a goddamn phoenix, and tell him to go fuck himself and his back-alley betrayal."

Mia cups my face in her hands, her eyes gleaming. "We've got you, *Tovarich*. Let's give him hell."

The contrast in their support helps me in ways I wouldn't have expected. I look at Steven and nod.

Just in time, because the elevator dings.

Jonathan and Lance walk off the elevator, purpose in their stride and looking like the warriors they both are.

Lance beelines for me, but I flinch back into the couch. "No," I say, but my voice is weak. I swallow, wanting to be as strong as Mia and Izzy think I am. "No."

Lance stops, his eyes hurt but searching mine. "Charlotte, I didn't do what you think I did. The phone isn't mine."

My chin stays high, but the tears silently streak down my cheeks. "I get it, really, I do. What better way to get an in with the last mark in Thomas's circle than to play on my loneliness, give me all the things I thought I'd never get, that I never deserved? I made it easy, didn't I? Fell right into your trap and believed you, even though I knew better."

I stuff the hurt down, knowing I'll have to deal with it later, and letting the softness he's brought out in me come through for only a moment. "I loved you. When you look back on what you've done here, remember what you threw away. It might have been an act to you, but it wasn't to me. I truly, honestly loved you."

I get up, having said what I need to say and shown that my back-bone, while bent, is not broken by his deception. But he follows me toward the hallway. He grabs my arm, turning me and pressing me up against the wall, caging me in with his arms.

Mia and Izzy cry out, but in my peripheral vision, I see Jonathan hold up a staying hand and shake his head at Gabe, who's pulled his gun.

"Look at me, Charlotte," Lance commands.

I can't help it, I do. That stupid seed of hope that he planted wants to have faith, even as my brain knows the real truth of what he's done. The disconnect is a painful wrenching of my soul from my body.

His blue eyes are fierce, his jaw clenched. I get a glimpse of what he must look like as a SEAL ready for battle. But this is one he can't win, one I've already lost.

"Love," he says gruffly. Confusion mars my face, and he continues. "Not past tense, not *loved*. Love. You love me. And I love you. It wouldn't hurt so damn much if you didn't."

I shake my head, not wanting the words to water that fucking seed, not wanting to feel like I'm home inside the circle of his arms.

"You said what you wanted to say, and now it's my turn," he challenges. "I'm not working for Blackwell. That phone wasn't mine. Yes, I'm here for you, because you are the most gorgeous woman I've ever met, inside and out. I see your damage, just like we talked about." He slowly, torturously moves his hand to brush my hair from my face, pressing the softest of kisses to my temple and tracing a finger down my neck to rest his hand over my heart. "You're dancing away from me again. This time, it'd be warranted, but I didn't do this."

Jonathan starts to speak. "We've analyzed the phone—"

"No, she needs to believe me," Lance growls over his shoulder. "Not a report, not someone else. Me." He cups my face in his hands, fingers woven into my hair and holding me in place with his eyes. "You know me, know that I love you. Trust that, Charlotte. Trust me. I. Love. You."

I want to believe so badly, but it feels like another trap. I'm going to fall back into his arms, only for him to drop me later. I always end up on the floor, broken and forgotten.

But as I search his eyes, beseeching me to believe, I reconsider.

What if he's telling the truth, that the phone isn't his? Blackwell could've done something sneaky to make me think it was Lance all along. That'd definitely be in his wheelhouse. Do I really believe Lance would betray me this way?

I want to say yes. I always believe people will disappoint me, and all signs point to that being the case once again. But in my gut, I know the answer's no. He wouldn't. I have to believe that he wouldn't.

That seed of hope again blooms into a dandelion in my soul. Because I do believe him. For the first time since I was a little girl, I do trust—him, his denial of wrongdoing, and . . . his love.

I sob one time, collapsing onto his chest. "Oh, my God. I'm so sorry, Lance. I thought—"

He shushes me, pulling me into him, holding me until I lift my head and brushing my lips with a feather-soft kiss. "There you are, Red. I love you."

I answer him, but the 'I love you too' is mumbled against his lips as he kisses me again. It feels like a fresh seal on what we are, what we have. What I almost threw away because my cynicism misled me.

I vow to not let that happen again and to have a little faith in myself, the people around me, and the world at large. Yes, there are douchebags, but there are also Prince Charmings. And maybe even a happily ever after or two. *Or three*, I think as I smile against Lance's lips.

A throat clearing interrupts us, and Lance pulls back, but his eyes stay on mine. They shine with joy and happiness that I put there, and I know mine shine back just as brightly. The storm may be raging outside our little circle, but at least I know Lance is by my side through it all. Not sheltering me—I don't need that—but supporting me and letting me support him in return.

He slips an arm around my shoulder, holding me tightly against his body, and we turn back to the room. Mia and Izzy are the ones with tears now, though mine are all dried up. Thomas, Gabe, and Jonathan look a bit touched too but are covering it with an armor of 'time to work' stoicism.

"Now can I say what we've found out about the phone?" Jonathan asks, grimacing slightly.

Lance waves permissively, and everyone looks at Jonathan, who's pulling the phone out of his back pocket.

"I haven't had enough time to have the data fully analyzed, sorry. But Lance could tell. He knows . . ." Jonathan lets the sentence trail off, looking to Lance to see if he wants to be the one to spill.

"Out with it already! Who burned down my bakery?" I shout, pissed. Okay, so whatever Blackwell is doing to Thomas is probably more important in the big scheme of things, but *Cake Culture* is my dream. And someone destroyed it.

Lance places his hands on my shoulders, forcing me to look at him. "I'm so sorry, Charlotte, but it's . . . Trixie."

I laugh, an unladylike bark of disbelief. "No, it's not. Trixie's almost as committed to the bakery as I am."

But if it's not Lance, who? Sabrina was there, so she'd been a consideration, but she wasn't the one with the phone. That scuffle involved the police officer, Lance, me, and . . . Trixie.

I don't want to jump to conclusions, not again, but it has to be.

"It was the pictures, not the text messages."

Jonathan shows me the phone, and the photo folder has all those shots, and I recognize the one that damns her. Steven, with a peace sign.

"I was there. I remember that one," I say, my shoulders shrugging in confusion. "But why?"

"There's no telling what Blackwell's angle with her is. But we'll figure it out," Thomas promises. "We were ready to ask Lance some hard questions, but it sounds like those need to be directed elsewhere."

A phone rings, and Thomas holds up a finger, moving to answer it while Gabe, Lance, and Jonathan discuss ways to ask Trixie some questions.

Thomas nods and sets the phone down. "Steven, my assistant and a courier are on their way up." Steven nods and a moment later, the elevator opens.

Steven does a quick frisk of the assistant and the blue-uniformed courier, who seems surprised by the security. "Just need a signature, man. Order says it has to be Thomas Goldstone himself."

Steven nods his approval of the guests, and Thomas walks over to sign the digital clipboard. The courier reaches into his bag and pulls out a black envelope, handing it over. "Thanks, here ya go."

"Kerry, go home," Thomas says afterward. "It's late."

"Everyone else is already gone home for the day, hours ago," she replies with a smile. "That's why this is the best time to get everything done without interruptions, especially by my boss." Her smirk tells me they have a teasing, comfortable relationship. "But I'm on my way out now too."

She pats her oversized purse and waves 'bye to Mia.

"Careful, this feels like retribution by Blackwell," Gabe says after she leaves. "I might've sent him a little present once that required his signature. It was . . . unpleasant, to say the least."

Thomas nods and opens the envelope carefully, holding it far from his face like there might be poisonous powder in it. He slides the enclosed paper out, unfolding it and reading it, his eyes scanning left and right.

"What's it say?" Jonathan asks.

Thomas's face pales all at once, and he looks up. His eyes are bright with fear, his mouth hanging open in disbelief.

Hoarsely, he barks, "Everyone, OUT! Now!"

He makes a dash for the elevator, shoving Mia as he goes, and everyone follows his lead. Lance grabs my hand and drags me toward the elevator while Izzy and Gabe haul ass. Jonathan and Steven take up the rear, visually sweeping the room to make sure we're clear.

"What's going on? Tommy?" Mia demands fearfully.

Thomas ignores her, pressing a complicated order of buttons on the elevator panel. "Crouch down and hold onto the rails. We're going down fast."

We do as he says, understanding that we need to follow orders more than ask questions right now. Thomas finishes his button pushing by slamming a fist on the fire alarm, and the whole building erupts in a loud siren.

The elevator doesn't so much as lower as it falls all at once, and my stomach threatens to come up at the sudden drop. Only a second later, it seems, the elevator doors open to a concrete corridor.

"Run . . . Run . . . RUN!" Thomas yells.

I don't know what's happening, but I run as if my life depends on it.

CHAPTER 32

BLACKWELL

*T*he suit is perfect, far better than the one I wore to the office today. An occasion such as this requires the best finery I can afford, and I can afford the best. The custom-tailored handmade suit is a favorite of mine, though only for auspicious events.

A hefty glass of my finest tequila completes the accoutrements, and I sit in my favorite leather chair by the floor-to-ceiling wall of windows, overlooking the city. The first sip is rich with agave notes and the alcohol, a favorable combination along my taste buds, but the intensity builds, becoming darker, deeper as the oak shows its smokiness. The second sip amplifies the flavors even more.

It is a worthy drink, as worthy as my suit to be a hallmark of this moment in my mind when I remember the importance of this day.

I look over the city, watching the ants scatter this way and that. Leaving work and heading home, to what? A second job that pays nothing, cooking for unappreciative partners, or cleaning a worthless shack? Such futile endeavors.

I look through the telescope toward the Goldstone Building, which glints obnoxiously. Run, little ants. You leave every day thinking tomorrow will be another day in the wheel, never reaching new heights because the running is all for naught.

But not this time.

Tomorrow will be a new day, a gift for each and every one of the peons below me in the city.

I don't show them mercy because they are important but merely because a god's power comes from his worshippers. And they will all be mine.

I will not become irrelevant like some pagan deity who's had his day and is no longer remembered, his legacy dying out when his most devout believers pass on.

No, the people of Roseboro will understand that I built this city. They will appreciate that I continue to bring abundance to our borders, making each and every one of them thrive, and they will revere the hallowed ground that I tread.

They will be my congregation, recognizing the true greatness I deign to share with them. This city will be my legacy, and my flock will see that my immortalization knows no bounds.

As soon as I defeat those who dare to oppose me.

Him.

The Golden Boy.

The only one to ever stand up to me, both in action and in achievements. But my greatest success will be in taking him down.

Quite literally, I think with mirth.

I listen in to the bug I had placed in his penthouse apartment, amused. Thomas is a fan of bugs. Used one to catch my saboteur, in fact. The irony seems poetic.

He thinks his security is top-notch, and I'll admit that his investigative cousin did a thorough job of vetting each and every member of his team before allowing them to upgrade their system. But not thorough enough to thwart me.

I listen to him opening the envelope, another instance of poetic justice that I hope Gabriel Jackson will note. Ah, he does.

Glee burgeons forth in my soul, righteous joy that I've not known in years.

Finally, Thomas Goldstone will know my wrath.

I hear Thomas's exclamation, instructing everyone to get out. But it's far too late for that. He should've never come to Roseboro in the first place. The day he stepped foot into my city is the day his fate was written.

I have controlled his destiny all along, letting him grow in my fertile soil for this moment where I smash him beneath my shoe like the weed he has become.

A text comes through my phone . . .

10 . . .

I continue the countdown myself, eyes locked on the monstrosity across the city.

5 . . .

I stand, leaning forward toward the glass, wanting to be as close as possible to the hell I bring to Goldstone's existence.

3 . . . 2 . . . 1.

There's a rumble, audible even from here. A growing, deep guttural boom that demands everyone's attention. Down at the street level, ants freeze, cars slow as confusion percolates their dulled minds. But they'll know soon enough.

A deep boom rends the air, then another.

I watch, childlike glee filling me as the Goldstone building implodes in a dramatic chain-reaction series of explosions, just like Thomas Goldstone's empire. Glass shatters upward, floor by floor as each level collapses, and his monument falls from the sky, rushing toward the ground, a cloud of dust billowing out from ground zero.

Chaos reigns.

It's a symphony composed by my own hand. A beautiful destruction, a swarth of dark now visible where gold once stood. Not a new beginning, for I've never stopped my direction of Roseboro, but perhaps a fresh claiming.

A consecration of the land, that this city is mine. Always and forever.

My lips quirk, my teeth reflecting in the glass before me. I've done it, reduced the competing king's castle to crumbs while mine stands tall, resolute, eternal. A laugh erupts, fogging the glass, and my hands move of their own volition, applauding the show I orchestrated.

My phone buzzes on the floor where I dropped it in my excitement. I bend to pick it up and see one last text.

Mission complete.

Indeed.

Bravo.

CHAPTER 33

CHARLOTTE

*T*hick dust fills the air as we follow Thomas, though we're at least a few blocks away from where the Gold-stone building stood.

Holy fuck! The building is demolished.

We were *this close* to being inside when it gave way but sprinted down the hidden corridor Thomas led us through, and moments later, the world shook around us. It was like an earthquake, but so much worse. Seconds later, the rush of dust and smoke billowed up behind us, and we were all running as hard as we could. Only when our lungs could do no more did we slow down, but still, we walk.

It's unimaginable, unfathomable. An entire building in ruins.

There's no doubt that it's Blackwell's doing. The pure, absolute madness leaves no question.

But at least we're all alive.

We emerge into the night, sweet air filling my lungs for the first time in what feels like forever. Jonathan pulls keys from his pocket, and a huge Suburban beeps. We automatically aim for it and pile in. Steven takes the wheel, pulling out carefully. It feels like he should be peeling out of the lot, getting us clear of the

LAUREN LANDISH

danger zone, but he can't. There are too many onlookers, and debris clogs the street.

Steven carefully makes his way clear and gets us on the move away from downtown.

"Escape Plan Omega," Jonathan says when we're clear of downtown. Steven nods once and accelerates slightly.

The vehicle is silent as we drive. I think no one knows what to say. I certainly don't. I knew that Blackwell was sick, devious, and cruel, but this is on a completely different level.

This is more than murder. This was wholescale, indiscriminate slaughter.

Lance leans over, putting a hand on my thigh. "Are you okay?" he murmurs in my ear. "Any injuries, anything?"

I shake my head, biting my lip as I meet his eyes questioningly. "I'm clear too. Everyone clear?" he asks the rest of the car.

A hum of 'Okay' and 'Just shocked' sounds out, and while it's hard to believe considering the devastation, we're all uninjured, just dirty and dusty.

The Suburban returns to silence, and Lance takes my hand, like I'm precious and he almost lost me. The truth is, I almost lost him because of my own insecurities and lack of trust. But this second chance is all I need to do better and have a little faith. In him, in myself, in us. And it was almost taken away by Blackwell's devastating action.

Lance presses his lips to the top of my head, rubbing his lips across my filthy red curls, and I sigh, closing my eyes. "I love you, Lance."

"Thank you," he whispers, shuddering as his body starts to purge itself of the emotions inside. "I know how much it cost you to say that. I won't betray that, I promise. I love you too."

Well outside the city, in the woods surrounding Roseboro, Steven pulls into a hole in the trees lining the roadside. I would've driven past and never even seen the opening. He stops, tapping a quick code on a camouflaged keypad, and a near-invisible, green-painted gate slides open in front of us.

Steven continues driving down what's basically a grass path until he pulls up in front of a cabin. Well, it's built with logs, so I guess that makes it a cabin, but it's huge, like a mountain version of a mansion.

Izzy asks the question we're all thinking. "Where are we?"

"A cabin I bought through a line of shell companies," Thomas explains. "It can't be traced to me. It's stocked, secured, and prepped."

"It's basically our *shit hits the fan* property," Mia says. "Just in case."

I think it's safe to say the shit hit so hard, the fan was reduced to bits and baubles. *Just like Thomas's building*, I think sadly.

But we're together. We're safe. We'll survive.

Inside, the cabin is breathtaking, hand-carved creatures shaped into the wood beams and warm, cozy looking furniture dominating the large space. I'd love to come back some time when I can truly appreciate it, but right now, it doesn't seem appropriate to ask about Thomas's decorator.

Not that I have anything to decorate since the bakery is gone. But I'll rebuild, a better 2.0 version of *Cake Culture,* I vow. I only hope Thomas can do the same.

"Okay, here's the game plan," Jonathan says, his voice making me jump in the quiet. He's been on the phone most of the way here, texting away and even having a couple of quick, hushed conversations before we'd plunge back to silence. But he knows things, has been working his network, apparently, because he says, "The assumption is that we are all dead."

My jaw drops open, and Izzy cries out, "What?"

"Emergency personnel are onsite. Looks like the building was already mostly empty, and the fire alarm made everyone else evacuate. But being on the top floor, no one thinks the elevator would've been working, much less get us downstairs in time. Your assistant told the police who was in your apartment when she came up, so the assumption is that everyone is dead. The only good thing is that she didn't see me."

He pauses, pulling up early media reports on the collapse. After a moment, the video shifts, and there we all are . . .

Thomas Goldstone, CEO. Mia Karakova, fiancée. Gabriel Jackson. Isabella Turner. Charlotte Dunn. Lt. Comm. Lance Jacobs. Steven Wilson.

"Good," Thomas says, handing the phone back to Jonathan.

"Why is that a *good* thing?" Mia asks, confused. "And no offense, but I'm more than just your fiancée, for damn sure."

"I know. We'll make sure they fix it for the real obituary." Then he looks to Jonathan. "So, what's your read, Jon?"

Jonathan looks around our assembled group, stroking his chin. "I don't know yet, but at least we've got something held to our chest."

Thomas and Jonathan talk through options and scenarios. Honestly, it mostly goes over my head, and since it's beyond my involvement, I just try to stay supportive. Especially of Mia, who looks to be near losing it as Thomas talks about next steps.

"Wait, the first step is making sure we tell our *families* that we're not dead!" she protests. "Papa's going to be heartbroken!"

"We can't," Jonathan says, and in the corner of my eye, I see Gabe and Lance nod. "Your safety really depends on Blackwell thinking you're dead. And Vladimir Karakov acting like anything other than his daughter being dead would cause suspicion."

"I think Vladimir can be told," Thomas says quietly. "But the folks at the Gravy Train, our colleagues, others . . . they have to be kept in the dark. Charlotte, your family—"

"Priscilla and Sabrina aren't losing any sleep," I assure him. "And Dad . . . it's better if they don't know."

"Lance?"

He frowns. "My family's assumed I've been dead before. They'll understand why . . . later."

Eventually, it's decided that Jonathan will go back and speak as a representative for the company and for the Goldstone family.

"Next, we need to find Trixie," Jonathan says, setting off a new discussion.

I try to dissuade them from that, but in the end, I get outvoted. She's our closest link to whatever Blackwell is planning.

"We have to think strategically," Gabe says, his voice low and rumbling. "Blackwell thinks he has us in checkmate. But he doesn't. We have the advantage. Once Thomas comes back to life, though, that advantage disappears. We need to make our plays before that happens."

"And Trixie could be the key to that," I reply sadly. I look around, seeing the faces of my family.

Plan agreed upon, or mostly, at least, we break. Jonathan heads back to Roseboro to start his end and get a handle on the press while Steven sets up watch on the bank of security camera feeds.

Slowly, we all drift into separate bedrooms in the cabin-slash-mansion.

The guest room Lance and I walk into is stunning, or it would be any other day. There's a dark wooden king-sized bed, covered with white cotton linens, and a bank of windows that look out to the treetops. Through an attached door, I find a well-equipped bathroom decked out in white and grey marble and bright lights that blind me.

I blink, and Lance comes up behind me, adjusting the lights with the dimmer switch I hadn't noticed. "Let's take a shower, wash this grime off." I turn to look at him and realize he's still filthy, remnants of the fire, of jail for him, and the building collapse. I must be too, and all I want is to wash it away, start fresh and clean, hopeful and loving.

"That sounds good."

The shower is hot and steamy, but there's no romance to getting undressed. We both just want to be out of these clothes.

Naked, he opens the shower door, letting me step in first. He follows and watches as I let the hot water sluice over my skin, wetting my hair to run in fiery waves down my back. We switch places, and I watch as he does the same, running his rough hands over his chest and abs.

"Lance," I say, but when he opens his eyes and pins me in place with his gaze, I don't know what to say. "I'm sorry," falls off my tongue, but it doesn't seem like enough, not remotely so.

"I know. It's okay," he says gently, cupping my face. "I get it that it was a shock, and everything pointed to me, and it was all too easy for you to think I was just like everyone else who'd let you down. But I'll keep proving to you that I'm not them. I'm here and not going anywhere."

I lean into him, and he wraps his arms around me. "You're amazing, you know that? You could have anyone. Why me, when I'm so difficult?"

I feel his smile against my hair, and his hands pull me tighter. "I've told you, I like you just as you are. Sassy, fiery spitfire and scared, untrusting heart. It makes you real, makes you mine, and I'll keep proving that to you, show you that you're safe with me."

I snuggle in, warm in the water and his embrace. "I am safe with you—heart, body, and soul. I just . . . *forgot* for a minute?" I say, letting a bit of levity into my tone.

"I won't let you forget again," he rumbles, his voice full of lush, dark promise. "I'll make sure you know, without a doubt, inside and out, that you're mine. Always."

His hands rub up and down my back, and instead of the comfort he offered earlier, this is an offer to make me forget.

Forget the war raging at our door. Forget the way I almost destroyed us as surely as Blackwell destroyed Thomas's building.

"I need you," I whisper. "I need to apologize . . ." I don't finish the sentence but slip from his arms, sliding down his body and lowering to my knees before him.

"Char, you don't have anything to apologize for, and you damn sure don't have to do it on your knees, ever," he says gruffly, but his cock is thickening before my very eyes, bobbing toward me greedily.

"I know. I want this." He's right, and I'm not blowing him as some sort of twisted apology but because I need to feel him, love him, worship him. The way he does me. I want his light to suffuse me, fill in every dark corner of pain I hide, and show him that I am worthy of his love. Because finally, I believe that I am. He's taught me that, and I will forever be appreciative of his patience with my 'fraidy-cat heart.

I lick a long line from just above his balls to his crown and press a soft kiss to the velvety skin there. After a swirl of my tongue around the ridge, I take him into my mouth fully, getting deeper, inch by inch, as I bob up and down on him. He looms over me, blocking the water with his broad back as he watches his cock disappear into my mouth.

His thumb swipes along my brow, catching the few water droplets that threaten to run into my eyes, then his hands weave into my wet tresses. He guides me, feeding me his cock and dipping into my throat as he groans and grunts. "Fuck, Red. Take me."

And I do. I take him gladly, letting him have control. Of my mouth, of my heart, of my everything. It's all his.

He holds me still, thrusting into my mouth so fast I can barely keep my lips closed around him, slurpy, wet sucking sounds echoing against the tile surrounding us. I spread my knees, letting my hands dip down to cup my pussy.

As he fucks my mouth, I slip my slick fingers over my clit, matching his pace. I moan at the dual pleasures, and he freezes deep in my throat. "Do that again," he snarls.

I moan, vibrating my throat along his head, and I can taste the precum that's leaking from his tip, the first tease of the treat I want. He picks up the pace again, long thrusts but occasionally holding me to him, my nose buried in the short scruff of hair at the base of his cock, not letting me breathe.

My fingers speed up too, keeping tempo with him, and we're both getting close.

Without the walls of civility, he fucks my mouth raw and rough. This is punishment for not trusting, absolution and forgiveness wrapped up in one. This is fear that we almost died but celebration that we'll live to see another day. This is a promise for the future, that whatever comes, we'll handle it together.

I cry out around him, ready to fall but wanting to take him with me. He yanks himself free of my mouth, his voice rasping in control. "No, not yet."

I whine, need fiery in my veins and the edge so tantalizingly close, promising release and relief. He grabs under my arms, pulling me up, and takes my honey-coated fingers into his mouth, savoring my flavor.

"Bed. I want you in the bed."

CHAPTER 34

LANCE

$\mathcal{I}$t's too much, or I thought it would be too much for her, but Charlotte virtually runs for the bed. She's tougher than she knows, maybe stronger than I give her credit for, and I think she's pretty fucking badass. There's a core of steel surrounding the fluffy softness of her soul.

But as roughly as I fucked her mouth, she took it. Gladly, gratefully, and so fucking sexy she almost sent me over before I was ready. It's my turn to show her what she does to me.

Charlotte lies down on the white comforter, opening her arms and legs to me, offering to cradle me. But I grab her ankle, pulling her to the edge. "Turn over," I order.

She does as I command, and I shove her knees up underneath her. She's quite literally face down, ass up, presenting herself to me. It's a vulnerable position but one of the lesser ways she's finally opened up to me, though her slick pussy is wide open, her asshole right there, begging me.

I bend down, licking from her clit to her ass, and she writhes wantonly against me. Her sweet taste makes me hungry for more, makes me want to bury my mouth against her until I can't breathe, and I can hold my breath for a long fucking time.

But we both need more right now. I stand back up, gripping her hips so hard my fingertips leave dimples in her skin and she'll probably have bruises tomorrow, but I don't care.

Actually, that's not true. I do care, but I *want* the marks on her skin, need them in a way I never have before. I want to leave indelible, permanent marks on both of our bodies, declarations to the world that she is mine, and I'm hers, and neither of us is going anywhere without the other.

Neither of us needing or wanting gentleness, I slam into her balls-deep in one powerful thrust. I bottom out hard, and she cries out but bucks back into me, ready for more. "Touch yourself," I tell her, my breath harsh as I force the words out.

She wiggles, her right shoulder dropping beneath her, and I feel her fingers brush over the base of my cock where I disappear inside her. I feel her pussy lips kissing my cock, moving as she roughly rubs herself. Not tame circles, not this time. She's thrashing her fingers across her clit, chasing her orgasm, and I oblige, slamming into her over and over.

I want to be deeper in her than anyone has ever been before, in her tight pussy, in her even tighter heart.

I need her eyes, to see her fall over the edge with me. I pull out, manhandling her to flip her over. I watch her eyes trace down my chest, my abs, and her tongue peeks out like she wants to eat me up like one of her cupcakes.

I feel the same way about her.

I pull her legs up over my shoulders, not just her ankles, but to the bend of her knees, and her toes link behind my head. Her hips are up off the bed, totally in my control. When I push back into her, my head falls to the side, resting on her calf.

The hypnotic bounce of her tits drives on my every thrust, and Charlotte's hands flail, like she needs something to hold on to or I'll bounce her away. But I've got her, hips cradled in my hands as I push into her, so rough I fear I might split her in two, but her moans of ecstasy tell me she's loving every brutal bit of our lovemaking.

Because that's what this is. I am fucking her like a damn beast, but there's too much emotion underneath the lust for it to be anything but love.

Her hands finally find a home, one on her tits, teasing and pinching her nipple, and the other at her clit, where she resumes her rough swipes.

Her eyes meet mine, blue to blue, both of us gone for the other. A chance meeting, an unexpected connection, and both of our lives will never be the same. No matter who tries to tear us apart, she will always be . . .

"Mine," I growl at her through gritted teeth. I don't know if I'm telling her or asking her. Not that I'd let her say no, but I need to remind her about who we are and who we are to each other.

But she agrees, mewling out, "Yours. And you're mine." She says it with certainty, finally.

The relief of knowing she trusts in me fully, all doubts obliterated, is freeing, and I fall. My cock spasms before I can hold back, and I grunt, "Come . . . Charlotte." It's half command and half a cry of her name as the wave overtakes me, jets of my hot cum filling her.

I feel her walls clench, milking me as her legs quiver, her thighs shaking against my chest. I hold her tight, staying deep but giving her short strokes as she cries out her orgasm. A combination of her honey and my cum gushes around me, her pussy too full of cock to hold any more.

I hold her there, impaled on me as our breathing returns to normal. I nibble at her calf, then soothe the soft bite with a kiss. Charlotte stretches out, her legs going straight and tight on my shoulders "Mmm, fuck, that was . . . " She searches for a word.

"Life-affirming," I offer, knowing that after a life and death situation, people will often need something to ground themselves to the reality of still being alive.

She blinks slowly, then nods, eyes on mine. "Life, and love. I love you, Lance."

I lean forward, testing her flexibility, bending her damn near in half to lower my lips to just an inch above hers. "I love you too, Charlotte."

The world may fall to ruins, but as long as I've got her in my arms, I won't give a shit. It's the first time I don't feel the need to rush out and save the world, do my part and make a difference. Instead, I'm locked in place with her, literally and figuratively. As long I can save her, it's all I need.

As much as she has trust issues, I finally feel like I'm enough just as I am. Charlotte doesn't care what my last name is, where I live, or what I can provide for her financially. She only cares about my heart. And I've already given it to her fully.

THE BLACK CADILLAC CUTS THROUGH THE LATE NIGHT, HEADING back to Roseboro. I'm driving, and Gabe sits in the passenger seat, both of us in head-to-toe black.

I don't know the man well, more innuendo and underhanded remarks from Charlotte, but I know he's shutting down. Whatever façade of congenial warmth he wears to blend in with the masses is gone, and he's gone cold, matter-of-fact, and methodical.

I do the same, a mission mentality taking over my mind, but it's harder than it used to be. Before, I was easily able to set aside the part of me that my team called 'Stateside', the kinder halves of our natures that rejected the horror of battle. I could easily divide myself and become who I needed to be. Not this time.

This time, I have something to actually go home to . . . and that worries me.

The SEALs taught me control, care, and caution, and that busting down the front door isn't always the best course of engagement. Missions are not made-for-television action scenes where the good guys always win and plot armor is stronger than Kevlar.

Real men, good men, have died in front of me, and bad guys have won. But with Charlotte counting on me, I find the shields, lock down my defenses, and prepare myself for what we're about to do.

The little house is on the far side of town, the street silent, and in a stroke of luck, the single lamppost light is burned out. Under the cover of darkness, I coast the quiet car to the curb.

"Set?" I ask Gabe, pulling out my Sig.

He repeats, taking out his own piece. "Set."

Silently, we exit the car and make our way to the back of the house. The back door is an easier entry point, with less visibility in case any nosy neighbors decide to check out the sliver of moon in the sky tonight.

Three seconds, through the door and carefully into the house. We're not expecting a fight, but recent evidence points to the fact that maybe our expectations are not exactly accurate.

I point to the hallway, and Gabe nods, moving the other way. I head to the single bedroom to search. A quick check of the bed, closet, and bathroom yields no results.

I hear a quiet lip pop, Gabe's signal, and head back to the front of the house.

He's waiting for me in the living room. "Couch, passed out drunk, I think," he whispers softly.

He goes around one end and I mirror him on the other. Gabe makes a quick move, pulling the target's wrists together and above her head, holding them tightly as he wraps a zip tie around them.

"Wha—what's going on?" she slurs, her voice like sandpaper on her unused and alcohol-dehydrated throat. Before she can react, I have another zip tie around her ankles, not as secure, but enough for our purposes.

Slowly, her eyes creak open, unfocused and twitchy behind half-closed lids. But when I step to Gabe's side and she sees me, her eyes go wide, adrenaline shooting through her blood, waking her up and sobering her a little.

The fear on her face mixed with shame is the confirmation I need. I'd known the truth, trusted my gut, but her reaction at seeing me alive? She might as well spill her guts to us right here and now.

But that's not enough. We have questions, lots of them. And she's going to answer each and every one.

"I thought you were dead," she says, still confused at my presence.

"Death by building collapse instead of death by chocolate this time?" I say, though the slight food pun is dry, bitter with disdain.

"I didn't know, I swear I didn't know." Her head shakes back and forth wildly, begging us to believe her. "Why do you think I'm drowning myself in so much wine I'm damn near pickled from the inside out? I didn't know!"

Gabe is done with her excuses. He pulls a black bandana out from his back pocket and forces it over her mouth. She fights him, thrashing and grabbing at his arms with her bound hands. But in seconds, she sags, the ether knocking her out.

"Let's go," Gabe says. He picks her up, tossing the limp body over his shoulder, and I lead the way out.

At the car, he slides her into the backseat and climbs in next to her. I try to tell him that I'll get back there and he can drive. Even though she's done awful things, I feel nervous leaving her at Gabe's mercy.

"She got you too," Gabe says, looking at me with empty eyes. "Not just Charlotte. She betrayed you, right under your damn nose."

"And you think I'll want revenge."

"No," Gabe explains. "But I'm not risking it when so much is riding on this. Get in the driver's seat."

He's right. He may be a stone-cold scary fucker, and as dangerous as that is, I'm the real danger. Not because I'm bigger or badder than him but because I'm personally invested, and we can't afford any mistakes.

Gabe's a damn pro, for sure, and my respect for the man goes up a few notches. He's still a wolf, but not a lone one, it seems. He's found his pack, and at least he tries . . . not to hide, but to fit in.

And he's right. This isn't a team. This isn't a squad or a platoon. Nobody's here because they're getting a paycheck. This is more. This is a family. Not one by birth, but by choice, just like I told Charlotte. I'm part of them too, now. It feels like home.

Back at the cabin, we quickly get our prisoner down to the basement wine cellar. It was deemed the most secure space, no windows, below-ground, with a single entry/exit point.

Thomas stands off to the side, needing answers but not suited for the type of work that will be carried out here tonight. I could do it, have done multiple interrogations in my time, but Gabe's right. I'm too close because this is personal.

So I stand back, letting Gabe take the lead.

He looks from Thomas to me, his voice hard but also somehow vulnerable. "Whatever happens here tonight stays in this room. I don't want Izzy to see me this way . . . not anymore."

Thomas steps forward, putting a hand on Gabe's shoulder and telling him fiercely, "Izzy knows exactly *who* and *what* you are, better than anyone. She's not upstairs because she can't watch you. She's upstairs because she understands that you don't want her here. So, thank you. For letting us see the side of you she already knows and accepts."

Gabe nods and looks at me. I nod in agreement, letting him know that I'm no threat, in this room or out of it.

He takes a deep breath, and I can see the light dim in his eyes. The humanity fades, and the disconnect between what he's about to do and who he is snaps into place.

I understand. He's a warrior, maybe not the same kind I was, but a warrior, nevertheless.

He shakes the woman in front of him, hard enough to jostle but not hurting her . . . yet. "Wake up, Trixie."

The interrogation begins.

CHAPTER 35

CHARLOTTE

I can't sit here by the fireplace. Not when I have a good idea of what Gabe, Lance, and Thomas are doing to Trixie downstairs.

I'd seen her when they brought her in, limp and haggard-looking. At first, I thought that'd been Lance and Gabe's doing, but as they passed me, I could smell the liquor on her and realized she was in rough shape before they ever got there.

Lance had offered me a single nod, a sign that everything was going to be okay, then they'd disappeared, leaving us to sit around the fireplace.

I pace, wishing I could go outside and get some fresh air but knowing Steven won't allow us out of the triple-locked doors.

"Sit down, woman," Mia chastises. "You're making me antsy with all your pacing."

I shake my hands out. "Sorry. I just can't believe Trixie did this. I mean, she was close. Not like you two, but . . . like a sister in some ways. She's been there since before I even opened. I just don't know what to think."

"They'll find out everything she knows," Izzy says, trying to be reassuring and failing.

"You mean Gabe will." It's judgmental, ugly, and mean. He's doing what he's doing for us, but I don't know how anyone could be comfortable with Gabe's methods.

Izzy shrugs, accepting. "Yeah, he will. He'll do whatever it takes, and I don't think less of him for it. He takes that stain on his soul because he knows he can bear the weight on his shoulders better than you can. And it's heavy, have no doubt."

I don't know what Izzy has been through. She kept a lot of what happened to her close to her vest, but I know hurt when I see it. And I don't want to be the one who does that to my friend.

"I'm sorry, Iz. This is all just so far beyond my outer limits, you know? I don't think less of Gabe, or you. It's just . . . I never thought it'd go this far."

She gets up, coming over to hug me. "I know. Not exactly the story I wrote for myself, either, but it's mine. He's mine, and I'll do anything for him. And he'll do literally anything for me."

Mia interrupts our moment of friendship to say, "Speaking of our guys, that was some upper-tier Jedi shit that Lance pulled on you back at the apartment before things went to hell."

She gets up, miming waving a lightsaber around in a figure-eight pattern. "Trust yourself, trust me," she says in a high Yoda voice, "and you went all 'Yes, Master' for him."

She starts humming like Yoda, and I laugh at her antics. "I did not go 'Yes, Master' for him. I just . . . realized he was right."

I blush, the splotches hot on my cheeks as I remember that I basically did submit to him last night. But I chose it, and that's between Lance and me, not the girls. Not that I won't overshare with them again in the future, but last night was . . . special, and ours.

But they know me too well, can read the freckles on my face like tea leaves. "Ooh, she might not have been submissive to him then, but she sure has been since," Mia says sagely. "No shame, girl. I like a bossy man."

Lord, does she ever. Again, we overshare on the regular. Fifty shades of Goldstone is pretty much *de rigeur*.

"Seems like you might get that happily ever after you thought was never coming after all?" Izzy says, nudging me. "Gonna make a new cupcake for that?"

I bite my lip, ducking my chin because I was thinking the same thing this morning. Finally. And it feels good and right, warm and beautiful. Like as crazy as it may be, Lance was made just for me, a perfect fit.

An intense energy fills the room, and we all turn to see Lance standing in the doorway. He looks hard, the line of his jaw sharper somehow, the faint lines around his eyes from too much time squinting in the sun deeper than usual. "Char, she's asking to talk to you," he says neutrally. "Your call."

I stand up, not sure I want to do this but my feet already deciding. "I need to know why. I'll talk to her for that, at least. Did Gabe get what you need?"

Lance looks at Izzy, sharing in what I swear looks like respect to her. "He did. He's a good man, and Trixie sang like a bird with very little encouragement. But he'll need you tonight. I think this was *different* for him."

Izzy nods, thanking Lance for the warning.

Lance takes my hand as we walk down the short flight of steps to the wine cellar. I gasp when I see Trixie tied to a chair, her hair a blonde mess of curls, and makeup running down her face in rivers. There's no blood, at least, and she looks unhurt.

"Charlotte, Oh, my God . . . Charlotte. I'm so sorry I didn't know about the building, I swear it. I'm so glad you're okay. I'm . . . sorry." The words spill out of her mouth, each one chasing the previous in a long run-on torrent of emotion.

"Why?" I whisper, forcing my back to remain straight, my eyes dry. She was my friend, and those emotions don't die overnight. "That's all I need to know . . . why?"

Trixie swallows, looking down. "I'm so sorry. When this whole mess started, I didn't know you. On paper, you were just some rich bitch with a life of ease. From the outside, it looked like you grew up in a wealthy family, a dad and mom, and even a sister. It seemed like you were just doing the crazy dream thing with the bakery, like you didn't have any real worries, just got everything handed to you on a silver platter. I was jealous because I'm . . . me." She says it like it's a death sentence, sadness pouring from her.

"And you kept going even after knowing the truth?" I ask, pissed. She knows all about my life. I shared so much with her during those long hours before we even opened. And even more later, as we got closer. There's only one real question left, then. "Was any of it real?"

Fresh tears shine in the corners of her eyes, and she nods. "Remember what I told you about my life back home? It was all true. And I told myself when I left that hellhole that I was never going back. No matter what. I had nothing after the internship, so when Blackwell made me the offer, I had to take it. I didn't know you, and I was desperate."

I take a deep breath, understanding, in a way.

"And then I met you," she says. "You were nothing like what I thought you'd be. Your life wasn't any better than mine. Just different. You still had worries, and shitty parents, and had to work hard. It was just different than my life. But it was too late. I was stuck."

"Stuck how?"

"If I told you the truth, you would've fired me on the spot. And without a job, I would've had to . . . I don't know, probably dance like the girls back home. I would've ended up just like what I'd run from. And it would've been worse than before. Poor and hungry isn't so bad when it's all you know, but once you've had a taste of a good life, with friends and something to care about, I couldn't—" She shakes her head vehemently, and in a way, I can almost see her point, although it hurts to think that.

I want to frame her as a villainous mastermind in my head, paint her with one stroke of personality, or maybe a personality disorder, that she could do something so conniving behind my back while simultaneously acting as my friend. But people aren't that way, not me, and not her.

"I couldn't go back, no matter what. So I thought if I kept my mouth shut, I could mitigate the damage as much as possible. It was the best I could do in a really shitty situation. So I made false claims to the Health Department, knowing that if they showed up, they wouldn't find anything. And I let a guy in the back door to tweak the ovens. I thought he was making them run hot to just burn the cookies, not the whole store!"

"That was the guy who ended up attacking you," she tells Lance. "I think they just wanted an excuse for the cops to arrest you."

Turning back to me, she says, "I didn't mean for you to find the phone. I'm sorry for making you doubt him. And I swear, I didn't know about the bomb or whatever it was Blackwell did."

"But you were complicit in all of it," Lance growls. "You followed his orders, sent him intel, let Charlotte think I had betrayed her, and guided her to Thomas's."

Trixie sags. I really just want to ask why again, but I think it's one of those questions that'll never have a clear answer. "It didn't have to be like this, Trixie."

Gabe stands up, his eyes dark. "I think you should go upstairs, Charlotte."

I look at Trixie once more. "I loved you like a sister," I tell her honestly. "Truly, in my heart."

She cries out again, "I'm sorry, Charlotte."

But then her eyes flick to Gabe, fresh fear bubbling up as she struggles against her restraints. I go back up the stairs, her apology echoing in my ears until I close the wine cellar door.

I force my feet back to the living room, where Mia and Izzy are waiting for me, each on one end of the couch. I sit between them, and they wrap their arms around me. The Three Musketeers, always. No matter what.

CHAPTER 36

BLACKWELL

*C*haos still reigns at the site where the Goldstone building stood. The golden building, which served as a landmark for Roseboro, unexpectedly collapsed last night shortly after the majority of the workforce thankfully left for the day. Investigations are still ongoing, but early reports are that there were at least seven deaths, including entrepreneur Thomas Goldstone.

The screen on my television switches from the microphone-holding newscaster over to a panoramic shot of the destruction. The voiceover continues the update.

I'm here with Chief of Police, Frank Harris, who is coordinating the investigation. Chief Harris, do you have any evidence of what caused the building's collapse?

Frank fills the screen, looking right at home in the media spotlight. He's an excellent upstart, one who has served me well over the years.

Nothing concrete yet, he says with an aw-shucks shrug. *Right now, we just count it a miracle that the building was mostly empty. Most of the employees had already left for the day. We'll conduct a full investigation, dig through the rubble, look for any workmanship flaws, and determine whether there were structural issues with the tower.*

He's planting the idea that this was a symptom of Goldstone's lack of attention to detail, that he would let his very namesake building be built poorly. The implication that his empire is also built on quicksand is an easy jump.

Could there be something more sinister at work here? Is there evidence that this could be a terrorist act?

The newscaster is a persistent pipsqueak, I'll give him that. If he were on my payroll, that'd be a boon, but he's not. I find it annoying and troublesome. The last thing I need is the word 'terrorism' being linked to this.

Frank laughs congenially, looking at the newscaster like he's a young kid who's a bit big for his britches.

Son, there's no evidence of that, so don't go scaring the good people of Roseboro with your inciteful speech. We live in a good, safe city. We'll find out what happened to this building and you'll be the first to know. Good day.

Frank walks away, pointing and talking to small groups of officers who are pretty fruitlessly poking through the twisted mess. It gives the effect that he's the boss, the leader in charge, and knows what he's talking about.

Well done, Frank.

My phone buzzes at my side, a message from the chief himself.

Did what I could.

The newscaster presses the button at his ear then speaks into the microphone once again. *I'm getting word that Jonathan Goldstone, a relative and friend of the late Thomas Goldstone, will be holding a press conference very soon. We'll send you over to that, live at the courthouse. This is Trevor Olliphant, Channel 5 News.*

Interesting. Jonathan Goldstone.

Former military-cum-private investigator, and cousin of the

Golden Boy. I wonder what he's going to do and watch as he takes the steps of the Roseboro courthouse, looking like a rough man who's tried to slick himself up.

He's playing the part of businessman, but his worldliness is readily apparent. Oh, you can hide it from the sheep, Jonathan Goldstone, but I can see you. I can see it in your eyes.

I sense a potential enemy. Not on my level. You are swimming in unfamiliar waters. But you are more than one of the sheep.

He takes the microphone.

Roseboro mourns the loss of a great man, a man who only wanted to make this city the best it could be. Not only through his business and charity ventures, but by encouraging each and every citizen to be kind, compassionate, and to care for his fellow man.

We are all responsible for continuing that legacy.

I will be serving as the Interim President of Goldstone Inc, and I vow to continue on as Thomas would. Because Goldstone did not end yesterday with the collapse of a building. It lives on inside each of us.

As for last night's tragedy, I have seen that investigations are being specifically targeted in a singular direction. He pauses, and Frank's vehemence that had seemed so perfect a moment ago now seems like a smoking gun of his erroneous ways.

There are those who will try to misdirect you. But this was an act of terrorism, a violent and aggressive move by a coward who is more willing to destroy Roseboro than to share the city we all call home.

This man has stones, bordering dangerously close to calling me out by name. Looking directly into the camera, his eyes narrow and his jaw clenches.

The truth will come out. Justice will be served. Goldstone will go on, as will Roseboro. In Thomas Goldstone's honor—be good, do good, and leave a legacy of hope for a brighter tomorrow.

Jonathan Goldstone walks away from the makeshift podium, lights flashing and reporters calling out to him.

My response? I laugh. I laugh at his foolish wish for justice and truth, as if this is some comic book from my youth. Yes, I read them as a guilty pleasure, snuck from the library and enjoyed as banal, nutrition-devoid entertainment. But I would quickly and rightfully return to my studies, my music, my work.

Because that is where the true value lies.

Jonathan Goldstone forgets this, or perhaps never learned it, likely a young, silver-spooned boy, much like Thomas. The latest version, I think, but so much weaker than the original, who at least had innovation and charisma on his side.

The good times roll as the news continues on with their morning reports. It seems that Goldstone stock has plummeted to nearly worthless this morning, as there's simply not much of a business remaining. Regional managers and entities are frozen, chickens with their head cut off.

I have done it, I sank his golden warship, and the city is none the wiser of the monster in their midst.

The only one who knew was Thomas himself, and he took that knowledge to the grave. I do wish I'd been able to hear his fatalistic thoughts as he realized exactly what I had done right under his nose.

I wish I knew what his last thoughts were as he ran for his life.

My phone buzzes again. This time, an incoming call.

"Hello."

"What the fuck, man? I didn't know you were going to do something like that! I *liked* Charlotte. She was good to me. You never said this was going to happen!"

Trixie Reynolds. Her twang comes out when she's angry, like pencils being jammed into my eardrums, highlighting her lack of education in proper enunciation. And people do not speak to me this way. Ever.

"Watch your tongue, Miss. Reynolds. I take it you were unhappy with yesterday's events?"

I'm baiting her, more curious than anything. She's been useful along the way as a low-level resource, stirring up trouble without causing dissention in the ranks of Goldstone's friendly fools.

"Unhappy? Yeah, you could say that," she snarls. "I want to meet, finish our business, and get the hell outta dodge."

I grin, pursing my lips. She is a ballsy one. Though stupid courage has next to nothing to do with intelligence. Because if she were smart, she'd already be on her way out of the city, running like a scared country mouse. That she delays to get payment she feels entitled to is laughable. Survival of the fittest, I'd say, and she's showing her lack of longevity. "I thought your desire was to take over the bakery yourself?"

It is something she mentioned in passing after having been placed in position, and it'd seemed a rather easy payout at the time, less liquid funds and more endorsement of her wares as she began a new business. And potentially another ally in reserve, should her usefulness be needed.

"Nope," she says, popping the *P*. "Those days are past. I want out. Cash money and I'm gone. You and Roseboro will just be a cloud of dust in my rearview mirror."

"Very well," I say, sounding amenable. "I will send a car to pick you up. Be ready in ten minutes."

Ordering a car for her is a simple matter of texting my driver. I don't bother going to my safe to pull out money to pay her off. She won't be leaving with cash in hand. Nor her life. She has run her course of usefulness and dares to have such a demanding demeanor with me, so a loose end is all she's become. How efficient of her to expedite her own demise.

I consider whether I should offer a choice, a game of sorts, as I did with my previous resource when he became a liability. But where that one had held some element of amusement for me, a man who truly believed himself at rock-bottom being forced to dig even deeper for his own grave, Trixie Reynolds doesn't intrigue me the same. She's merely . . . forgettable.

So her death need not be orchestrated and engineered. A quick shot should suffice.

Minutes later, my private elevator dings, announcing the arrival of my guest.

"Come in, dear," I say, guiding her to a chair in front of my desk. She is hesitant, perhaps scenting that this meeting is not as wise as she thought, but she does sit. Her back is straight, both feet on the floor like she could run at any moment. But we know she's not going anywhere.

She thinks she's waiting for the money.

I know she's waiting for a bullet.

I move to the bar, pouring a healthy dose of tequila into a tumbler as her eyes follow me closely. I take a sip, not offering her one. It matters not. The move was merely calculated to place me between her and the door, which she foolishly allowed.

"Well?" she asks, her fear making her bark like a scared puppy.

"Miss Reynolds, have you said anything to the investigating teams looking into the bakery or the Goldstone building?" It is a test of sorts. Frank would've told me if she'd spoken out of turn, but she doesn't know that.

She shakes her head, unruly waves brushing her shoulders. "No, the police asked some questions at the bakery and took Lance away for it. I comforted Charlotte and laid the breadcrumb trail for her to gather her troops. I didn't know what you were planning in getting them all together."

The accusation is meant to be biting, but it's merely a nip on my rough armor. I sip my tequila, saying sagely, "You know what you are meant to know."

"No one said anything to me about the building," she sneers. "Though that Jonathan guy from the news called me to give me condolences on losing Charlotte. Well, he asked if I thought the two incidents were connected, but I told him I'm just a cake maker. I didn't know anything about Charlotte's friends. He seemed to believe that."

Ah, now that is interesting. Perhaps young Goldstone is adept enough to put pieces together, although the two incidents on the same day would be obvious to even the stupidest of people. And Frank says that Jonathan Goldstone isn't dumb, just unaware of how this city works.

"It seems you've done well enough at covering your tracks," I falsely compliment her. "And now you want to simply skip town and start fresh somewhere else?"

She stands, jumpy as the conversation lengthens more than she wanted. "Look, just pay me what you owe me and you'll never see me again."

She holds her hands out, palms facing me as if I need to calm down.

But I am calm, for this is nothing other than business. And I am utterly in control of my destiny where my business is concerned.

I pick up the gun from beneath the bar towel, pointing it at her. "Indeed, I will never see you again, Miss Reynolds. But I'm afraid it won't be because you've left town. At least, not the way you expected."

Her eyes widen, looking comically large with the massive amounts of eyeliner and mascara she has on. Young women these days don't seem to understand that men prefer to see them, not some cartoonishly fake version created with layers of spackle and paint. Her pink lips round into an O, which would be prettier if it weren't covered in sticky gloss. I will need to be careful that her body doesn't leave any trace evidence.

"Blackwell . . . wait . . . let's talk about this, please," she begs, her twang coming on stronger as she pleads for her life.

But the decision has been made.

My will, be done.

CHAPTER 37

LANCE

*J*onathan drives, following the SUV that picked up Trixie, staying far enough back to not be busted as a tail. I'm in the passenger seat, having worked with him before, while Gabe and Thomas are in the back.

We correctly assumed Blackwell would bring Trixie to him, but we'd hoped it'd be somewhere more public and less secure. The Blackwell Tower isn't an ideal location, but it'll have to work.

Thankfully, Gabe did quite a bit of legwork on the strengths and weaknesses of Blackwell's fortress when he fought his way out from underneath the man. And while it'd been a fool's mission then, with only one man, our current team is much more experienced and better armed.

Two Special Operations vets, a freshly-retired hitman, and a billionaire.

It'll have to be enough.

Dressed in head-to-toe black, we stick to the shadows, smoothly closing on the tower.

The guys follow my lead, not because this is my show but because I have the most experience leading a team, and though this ragtag assembly isn't composed of the operators I'm used to, what they lack in finesse, they have in heart.

We approach a side door, guarded by a single man. If this were a military op, we'd take him out. A silenced *pffft* in the night air, and that'd be it.

But we'd prefer to not leave a trail of bodies behind. It'd be too messy and lead to too many questions. Plus, while the men we'll encounter tonight are employed by Blackwell, that doesn't necessarily make them evil themselves. We won't punish them for the actions of the man who signs their paychecks.

I hold up a fist and everyone freezes behind me. I scan, looking for cameras, and when I see the dark orb above the doorway, I watch with bated breath. After what seems like an eternity but is probably only seconds, Jonathan places a hand on my shoulder signaling that we're good. His guy did his job, hacking into Blackwell's computerized security system. We should be clear of alarms and all cameras should be disabled for the next ten minutes.

Ten minutes. Watch a clock and the time will drag, infinitely slow and seeming like plenty of time to do just about anything. The reality is, ten minutes is a tight timeline for what we need to accomplish tonight. But the system hack couldn't be any longer, so that's the time we get.

I close the distance with a sprint, using the darkness and the guard's attention to take him low, my shoulder hitting him in the stomach just as I wrap my arms around his legs and lift him. A quick twist, and I dump him to the pavement, his head bouncing off the ground harder than probably necessary, but he's a big motherfucker and he'll be okay other than a bad headache when he wakes up.

Inside, we progress to the stairwell. The elevator would be faster, but it's a blind point we can't risk. Not when everything is on the line. But each floor is a new threat, that we might be seen, that we might be confronted, that we might have to fight our way to the top floor.

The possibility becomes all too real when a door opens just as we start past the fifteenth floor. A tall, broad guard calls out, "Hey!"

Jonathan reacts quickly, his right leg lashing back in a powerful thrust-kick to the man's stomach. The guard is thrown to the wall behind him, the back of his bald head bouncing off the drywall before he sags to the ground.

We're all surprised, but Jonathan puffs up, sarcastically bragging, "I've got some moves too. Not just a supervisor sitting on his laurels."

The smallest of grins quirks my lips behind my mask, and judging by the crinkles around Thomas and Gabe's eyes, they're doing the same small, hopeful smile. It feels righteous, like we have fate's guiding hand endorsing our mission. Two guards, two down.

We don't see another guard the rest of the way up the stairs, but we pause outside the top floor, knowing it's Blackwell's domain and will therefore be guarded by his best man. Gabe has been here before, met with Blackwell himself in his office, so he takes the lead.

He confided on the way here that his natural instinct is to snap the neck of the guard that'll be stationed outside Blackwell's office. Force of habit, he'd said darkly. But he promised to try and restrain himself, to go along with our *less is more* approach, and I hope he can.

He opens the door, shoving his way inside as quickly and quietly as a ghostly breath. I'm glad I've never been on Gabe's bad side. His choke hold is silent but very effective, and he drags the guard into the stairwell. We close and lock the door behind us as we enter Blackwell's private office area, ensuring the guard won't interrupt, even if he does regain consciousness while we're working.

LAUREN LANDISH

But I can see the adrenaline burning through Gabe, the fire in his eyes. Time for being nice is over. He's out for blood now.

Thankfully, so are we.

We don't go in slowly this time, not wanting to give Blackwell time to arm himself or run. Instead, we burst through the door in a crashing singular movement, guns out, Jonathan and me sweeping the front while Thomas and Gabe cover us.

"What the—"

Blackwell's cursing exclamation of surprise is short-lived. He's standing at a wet bar near the door, blocking Trixie in. But as we enter, he snatches her, grabbing her forearm and twisting her around to act as a shield.

She doesn't cover his entire width, but it's enough. He already has a gun pointed at Trixie's head. He must have already had it pulled and I wonder if we just saved her life from this crazy monster.

"Let her go, Blackwell," I command, lifting the MP5 Jonathan lent each of us. Hopefully, the threat of facing four men with guns will convince him to give up.

He licks his lips like he's eager to put us in our place. "I don't think so. You boys have made a grave mistake tonight."

Thomas pulls his balaclava off his head, raw anger in his eyes as he glares at Blackwell. "You're the one who fucked up."

Blackwell's jaw drops in surprise, his hands going slack on Trixie for a split second. But when she tries to move, his grip retightens as his mouth clicks closed.

Through gritted teeth, he protests the truth before him. "NO! You're dead! The building collapsed with you inside," Blackwell rasps. "There's no way you could've gotten out."

"Ever heard of an escape plan?" Thomas taunts. He pats his chest. "Feels pretty alive to me. Want to check for yourself?"

Ironically, Blackwell does actually take a step forward, keeping Trixie in front of him, and we all prep for battle. But it's not to test whether Thomas is a ghost. It's to threaten him. "How dare you? You should've stayed dead. Never should've trusted someone else to do what I should have done myself."

"Just can't get good help these days, can you?" Thomas needles. He's using his weapon, not the gun but his mouth, pushing Blackwell's buttons. It's smart. It might make Blackwell sloppy and give us an opening to make a move.

"You think you're so brilliant, coming into *my* city, with your insufferable talk of hope and community," Blackwell sneers, while out of the corner of my eye, I see Gabe sliding to the side for a shot. "You make ridiculous business decisions, have the gall to buy my own companies, and go against me on contracts. You're an entitled brat whose only value is in your death. The absence of you from my city will be nothing but a small footnote in Roseboro's history."

"Your city? This city belongs to the people, the ones who get up at the crack of dawn to work their asses off for it," Thomas argues. "The ones who work late into the night to keep us all safe, the ones who work hard, day in and day out. Roseboro is everyone's city."

Blackwell scoffs. "Their city? It's MINE. I own it, from the riverfront to downtown and beyond. It's all mine—the land, the people, the government, all of it. I am Roseboro."

"All I see is a pathetic old man with delusions of grandeur," I growl, pulling Blackwell's eyes to me as Gabe takes another side step.

His eyes go wild, spittle gathering at the corners of his mouth. "They will all bow down to me. *You* will all bow down to me. I have earned it! I have worked tirelessly to reach this point, and I will not have you destroying my grand vision for this city."

"You blew up my building," Thomas charges, tiring of the

madman's grandiose rants. Gabe takes another step but doesn't raise his gun . . . not yet.

Blackwell's answering grin is full of malevolence, no sign of remorse for his actions. "I did. Right under your nose, stupid boy. Demolished your building and your entire empire. It will all be mine for pennies on the dollar, every last bit. I will wipe away any legacy you thought to leave, remake it in my own image, and you'll have nothing, even in your death."

His speech is odd, like he's forgotten that Thomas is standing right in front of him, alive and well. He's stuck in a rut of his own making, looping his own maniacal plans for the future.

But his plan becomes clear as he turns his gun on Thomas, Trixie still a shield held in front of him. "Now, you'll stay dead."

Trixie has been silent, frozen in fear in the middle of a circle of men out for blood tonight. But she shows her guts, taking the opening when Blackwell points the gun at Thomas.

She twists, shoving Blackwell away, but before Gabe can take the shot, Thomas rushes into the grappling pair. Trixie's caught, her shirt snared in Blackwell's left hand, and the three of them go dancing across the office, fighting for the gun.

"Thomas, get down!" Jonathan yells as he and I lift our guns, but before he can, Blackwell's gun goes off, freezing everyone.

The split second stretches out, ending when Trixie's mouth opens in a round O of surprise. Her hands go to her belly, a red bloom of blood growing quickly against her pink shirt.

"No!" I call as her legs give out and she collapses to the floor, but no one can catch her or even watch because Thomas is still wrestling with Blackwell for control of the gun. With a hard yank, he steps back, gun in hand, pointing it at Blackwell.

Impotent fury washes over Blackwell's face for a moment before he laughs, a bark of amusement contradictory to being held at gunpoint.

He holds his hands wide, challenging, "Go ahead, *boy*. I dare you."

Thomas holds the gun steady, his eyes narrowed. Jonathan drops to his knees, doing what he can to help Trixie. Gabe moves to Thomas' left shoulder and I take a step closer but keep half-focused on the door.

"Let me," Gabe says, lifting his MP5. "This isn't your—"

"No." Thomas shakes his head, his eyes haunted by what he's seen. "I have to. This has to be me." His voice is hollow, but resolute.

"You won't do it. You don't have the balls," Blackwell taunts. "And even if you did, this city will still be *mine*. Built by my designing hand, my legacy in every corner. You'll never be half the man I am. Even now, you hesitate, letting your friend here die. *So weak.*"

Blackwell looks down to Trixie, who's in Jonathan's arms, but we're not carrying first-aid kits, so there's not much he can do besides hold pressure on her wound. "So pathetic, but a reasonable resource loss so that my plan can succeed."

Trixie looks up with a bloody smile. "Pathetic? Who do you think told them where you'd be tonight?"

Blackwell lunges for her, angry that she might've gotten one over on him, furious that she might've been our pawn instead of his tonight.

A second shot rings out, and Blackwell's head jerks. His eyes look shocked as he crumples to the floor, and Thomas lowers the gun. "My job. My burden."

Shock is setting in quickly, his first kill, especially at close quarters, already hitting him hard. We understand, having all been there once ourselves. Gabe comes up, taking the gun from Thomas's hands.

"It's okay, man. I've got this."

331

Gabe examines Blackwell's still body, making minor adjustments to his placement then setting the fired gun down. "It'll look like he did it himself."

"You sure? We can't risk being wrong here."

"I'm sure," he tells me. "No fingerprints since we have on gloves, Blackwell has residue on his hands from shooting Trixie, and the placement will look like he fell after a self-inflicted shot. I'm sure." The look in his eyes tells me this isn't his first rodeo at staging either, and I have to trust his skills. We're in this together.

Trixie makes a gurgling noise, Jonathan squeezing her hand desperately.

"Trix—"

Her brows are pulled down, her eyes half-closed in pain. I don't know what to say. I can't reassure her that she's going to be okay, because she's clearly not. But she sacrificed herself to try and help us, by coming here at our behest tonight and in fighting for the gun, even if she was unsuccessful.

She tries to smile, her lips trembling at the corners. "Tell Char I'm sorry. Tell her to believe. Take care of her, Commander Coo—"

She doesn't finish the silly nickname she bestowed upon me, a last breath pushing past her lips without sound. She relaxes in Jonathan's arms, no longer in pain, no longer trying to escape her meager beginnings and become something else. She dies as a friend, a member of our family.

Her eyes stare blankly, and though we know we shouldn't touch her, Jon closes them for her.

I look up, realizing Gabe is at Blackwell's desk, his laptop open. "I kept the note simple, just *I'm sorry*, even though I don't think that asshole was sorry for a single thing he did in his life."

"Sounds right for the scene we're setting, at least," Jonathan says, getting up. He's going to take it hard later. He's a born lifesaver, and while he's lost them before . . . it's always hard. I know he remembers each and every one of the souls he's escorted to the Reaper's door.

We gather at the door, the four of us partners in this, and look around one last time. "We clear?"

"Yeah," Gabe says. Thomas finally nods, and I remind myself to check in with him later too. He'll need to purge himself.

I lead us back out the door, down the stairs, and finally, into the dark night.

Mission accomplished. Another hollow victory.

CHAPTER 38

CHARLOTTE

*T*he cabin is silent, all of us too choked to speak but sitting side by side on the couch, hands wrapped around each other. Three mugs of coffee sit on the table in front of us, long ago gone cold.

"They've got to be okay," Mia says. It's a variant on the one thing we can find to say, begging, pleading, hopeful affirmations that tonight will go as planned. That our men will come back to us.

That we'll all have our happily ever afters. Even me.

Doubt tries to creep in, that anything good will surely be ripped from me, but I squash it down and choose to have faith this time. Lance is surrounded by good men, and they are all uniquely gifted for this work, as ugly as it may be.

Steven calls out from his station in front of the monitors, "They're back."

I'm surprised he can see at all. He's been on duty for hours straight, only catching a catnap when Jonathan traded watch with him. We don't trust anyone else with the situation so tenuous, so Steven has been the only guard.

Thomas had this cabin set up as a safe space, so there's basically an armory, a full security system, and it's completely enclosed with razor-wire fencing.

None of that matters now, because they're back.

We all hop up and run for the door to the garage but stop short when Steven reminds us, "Stay inside."

"Are they okay?"

He shrugs, not helping any. But a moment later, the garage door opens, and they're back. All four of them.

"What happened? Are you okay?" we ask simultaneously.

I'm not sure if they guide us or we pull them, but we all end up in the living room. Thomas pulls Mia into his lap in a chair, Gabe sits on the floor at Izzy's feet, and Lance wraps his arm around me on the couch, pressing us together from knee to shoulder. Jonathan stands, arms at his side and eyes scanning our group.

"Are you sure about this?" he asks Thomas.

Thomas looks slightly shaken, honestly, like still waters on top of churning rapids, and my gut clenches as I wonder what happened.

"I am. We're in this together, and I'm not going to keep tonight from Mia, so I wouldn't expect Gabe or Lance to keep it either. Besides, we all need to have our stories straight."

His words send a chill through me. What would they need to keep secret? What story?

Slowly, they begin to tell us about what their night entailed. The tension builds as they tell us about getting to the top floor of Blackwell tower, but my mouth drops open when Lance gently tells me about Trixie.

"I'm sorry, Char. She was trying to get free, trying to help us. I know you're hurt at her betrayal, but in the end, she sacrificed herself for us. She said to tell you she was sorry and to believe in yourself." The words choke in his throat, matching the tears that catch in mine.

Lance rubs soothing circles on my back as I bury my face in his chest. "She . . . she's gone? I didn't get a chance to tell her . . ."

"She knew."

I hiccup, remembering all the good times. She did awful things, ones I don't know if I could've ever forgiven her for. But I would've liked to have had the chance. At least for us to try. We'll never have that chance. Now I'll . . .

Never hear another outrageous baking pun as she waits for me to laugh at her silliness.

Never pull an all-nighter, high on sugar and karaoke-style singing of old Britney Spears tunes.

Never work by her side, a common dream of success and friendship fueling us.

She's dead.

She gave up her dream of something greater, giving everything she had, even her life. For me, for us.

No matter what she'd done before, in the end, she was my friend. Trixie was in my life for a short period of time, but she burrowed into my soul.

I will always remember her that way. Not confessing her coerced sins, but bubbly and vivacious, singing and dancing, and so full of life that she brightened my world with her very presence.

Mia quietly asks, "Then what happened?"

I can't hear, can't really focus on the rest of their report, too lost in my own emotional tidal wave.

But Thomas keeps talking. "I struggled with Blackwell for the gun and got it. He taunted me, but when he went for Trixie, I had to." His eyes lock on Mia, hard as marbles. "I killed him."

His words jolt all of us. I pick my head up from Lance's chest, but he squeezes my shoulder. I need to control myself.

I see Gabe doing the same to Izzy's calf, where he's got himself wrapped around her leg.

But Thomas, the one who made the confession, is waiting for Mia's judgement.

Her eyes are wide, full of fear, her mouth hanging open. "You killed him?" she asks, looking for confirmation. When Thomas nods, she gathers him into her arms, not condemning him but comforting him. "Are you okay? Oh, my God, are you okay?"

He mumbles something I can't hear, and Mia turns to Jonathan. "You fixed this, right? No one is taking Thomas from me. *No one*, you understand me?"

Her voice is icy, stone-cold threatening. Though Thomas is the one confessing to murder, Mia is the one to fear and we all know it. She loves big and hard and would do anything for any of us. Most of all, Thomas.

"It'll look like a murder-suicide," Gabe interjects. "Not sure how they're going to spin that with the unconscious guards, but there's nothing to point at any of us. We do need to figure out our re-entry to Roseboro, back from the dead. And what you want to share about Blackwell."

The last part is directed to Thomas, but he's had enough for now. "Let's talk in the morning. It's late," Mia says, reading Thomas' mind.

She looks out the window, where the night sky is already lightening from purple to blue. "Or early, I guess. Let's all crash for a few hours and reconvene to discuss what's next."

We make our way to our bedroom, the same as before, but everything is different now.

Before, we'd been scared, running for our lives and unsure if we were going to make it after the building collapsed behind us and we'd escaped by a narrow margin. Now, the threat has been eliminated, and the responsibility of that is heavy on each of us.

Especially Thomas.

But there is also hope, that damned seed burgeoning forth to bask in the sunshine of our safety. No sword dangling over our heads, a sense of freedom replacing it.

"Is he going to be okay?" I ask Lance, and though I don't name him, he knows I'm talking about Thomas.

Lance pulls my sweatshirt over my head, then moves to undo my braid. Though I hadn't been baking today, it'd seemed familiar and comfortable, giving my hands something to do.

"I think so," he says as he spreads my curls around my shoulders. "He did the right thing. But your first is difficult."

He blinks, then corrects himself. "They're all difficult, but he's not trained. Blackwell forced his hand, made Thomas pull that trigger, sure as if he'd done it himself. He knew Thomas wouldn't let him make a move toward Trixie."

I'm quiet, letting that sink in as I pull Lance's shirt over his head. "Thomas is a good man. He did what he had to for all of us."

Lance gives me a small smile, but it's sad. "I know. We all know. He's going to feel that stain is on his soul for the rest of his days."

"Mia will love him, no matter what."

"Which is why I know he'll be okay," he says, smiling gently.

I return the smile, reassured. "If he gives himself too much of a hard time, Mia will rip him a new one and probably order him to 'let it go'. She'd probably even sing it Elsa-style." The joke falls flat, but it's the truth. Mia won't let Thomas beat himself up over this. She'll help him however he needs.

"I need to hold you," Lance says, changing the subject but

somehow just as on point. He needs me the way Thomas will need Mia tonight. Likely the way Gabe will need Izzy too.

In the back of my head, I hope Jonathan has someone too, but I've never seen him with anyone, so I don't know.

I let that thought go, focusing on Lance and being what he needs tonight.

I push my jeans off, taking my panties with them as Lance shoves his black cargo pants and boots off. When we're both nude, I pull the covers back.

"Lie down," I say, not allowing any argument.

Lance reclines, his back stiff and straight, and holds out one arm, inviting me to him. Instead of curling up at his side, letting him be my protecting cocoon, I lie on top of him, my knees at either side of his hips, my arms wrapped around his torso, and my cheek laid against his chest. Tonight, I will ground him, keep him here and now, with me, and be his guardian, his shelter from the world.

Incrementally, he relaxes into me, accepting my comfort.

"I love you," I tell him, wanting him to know that no matter what happened tonight, that will never change. He could've gone into Blackwell's tower with guns blazing, shooting his way to the top floor, and killing Blackwell himself in cold blood, and I would still love him. Because I know that he's a good man, *my* good man, and if he did something like that, it would be for honorable reasons.

Because he's an honorable man. One who was patient with me when I ran scared. One who stays. One who loves me.

"I love you too, Charlotte," he says, and I believe him.

Minutes pass, and slowly, heat builds between us as the stress of the night fades into the rising sun's rays. I lift my hips, and he easily slips inside me. We stay like that for a while before I arch my back, beginning to move. I fuck him this time, and he lets me. I choose him, knowing who he is and what he's done.

And when he comes with my name on his lips, I fall apart for him too, his name on my lips, because we know who we are to each other. Everything.

CHAPTER 39

LANCE

*T*he mass of reporters swirls and mobs on the courthouse steps, surrounding Jonathan like sharks around bait. I, for one, am glad to remain in the shadows for this one.

Thomas and Mia stand next to me, ready to make their dramatic return to the living, while Gabe is likely hiding in plain sight somewhere. Izzy and Charlotte are at Izzy's house with Steven.

Gabe has a top-notch security system in place, more befitting Fort Knox than a private residence, so it'd seem like a safe place for them to stay while we break the news to the world that we're all alive.

Jonathan holds up a hand, stopping the barrage of questions being shouted at him. "Yes, we do have a statement about the news of Custis Blackwell's death this morning. If you'll please indulge me a moment."

The reporters closest to him stop barking questions and lean in closer, trying to get their microphones as in his face as possible even though he's speaking into one at the podium.

He looks back, and that's Thomas's cue. He takes Mia's hand,

and together, they step out from behind the column and begin to walk down the steps toward the podium.

It takes all of two seconds for someone to shout out, "Thomas Goldstone! Mia Goldstone!"

Thomas smiles congenially, but I know he's still feeling the effects of last night. It's not just playing down to fit into the 'sad news' of Blackwell's death. At least, that's the way the media has been reporting it today.

"Hello, everyone. Yes, I am Thomas Goldstone, and I am very much alive. As is my fiancée, Mia Karakova." He emphasizes her last name, politely correcting the reporter who prematurely gave her his last name. "As are my friends, Gabe Jackson, Isabella Turner, Charlotte Dunn, Lance Jacobs, and Steven Wilson."

There are murmurs all across the crowd, and Thomas waits a moment for them to die down before continuing. "The strikes against Roseboro over the last few days have done more than sadden me. There are no words to describe the pain and horror inflicted on our city. But as is so often the case, there is a lot going on behind the scenes. In the interest of transparency, I would like to pull back the curtain, if you will, for the only way forward is with the truth. It's not comfortable, not pretty and poetic, but it is the truth."

I worry about just how much truth Thomas is going to spill but hold my tongue, knowing that Jonathan and he practiced this speech multiple times today in preparation for this press conference.

"When I came to Roseboro, I found an established and thriving city. At the time, that was under the leadership of one man, Custis Blackwell. He turned a small town into a booming metropolis, but he was not alone. The citizens of Roseboro worked along with him. Unfortunately, Blackwell didn't do this for the good of us all, but for one purpose only. Absolute power."

Speaking ill of the dead apparently is like catnip for the reporters because they're hanging on Thomas's every word.

"I was unaware of his ambitions and set out to make Roseboro my home as well. And I built an empire of my own, with the blood, sweat, and tears of those in the Goldstone family. By that, I don't mean those who bear my last name but every single Goldstone employee. We created that building, that community, together. And I aimed to spread positivity and kindness within its walls and out to Roseboro at large. And we've succeeded. We succeeded so well that Custis Blackwell felt threatened by our community, our caring for one another, as if by my very presence, his importance was diminished."

It's a serious accusation, but just the tip of the iceberg Thomas is about to reveal.

"In the last few months, I discovered a saboteur inside my company. I recently discovered that man was working on Mr. Blackwell's orders. More recently, one of my smaller investments, *Cake Culture*, which is run by a close personal friend, Charlotte Dunn, was targeted by arson. Her employee, Miss Trixie Reynolds, confessed to us that she was also working for Mr. Blackwell." He pauses, swallowing thickly. "And then, our headquarters . . . my home . . ."

The crowd is deadly silent, not a whisper of a question, not a pen scratching on paper. But they are hungry, ravenous for the dirty gossip.

"I was indeed in my apartment with my friends, as my assistant told police. She came up to have me sign for a letter from Custis Blackwell himself. The words will stay with me always. He felt I was usurping a role that was rightly his. In his god-complex-addled mind, there simply was not a place for the two of us in Roseboro. So he was taking out the competition by any means he felt necessary. The destruction of Goldstone Tower was for two purposes—to kill me and everyone I care about and to erase my name from Roseboro forever. It was by the narrowest of margins that we escaped the collapse."

Thomas looks over at Mia, knowing that this is where things get sketchy. "We went into hiding for our safety while we investigated what happened."

I hope Thomas is up to the task because his every word is going to be reported, replayed on every channel at six, ten, and again in the morning. Probably for days to come. The truth must be very carefully shaded.

But I shouldn't doubt him. He may not be a SEAL, but he didn't build his empire easily, and he's commanding with his version of the truth, no matter how directed it may be.

"My security has been working day and night, quite literally, to ensure our safety. And only after Mr. Blackwell's reported suicide and the tragic and unfortunate murder of Miss Reynolds did we feel a return to Roseboro was prudent. As for the future, I feel certain that Mr. Blackwell's involvement in the terroristic destruction of Goldstone Tower will be revealed by the authorities."

Thomas looks over at Chief Harris, who looks red-faced and uncomfortable, but he stops fidgeting with his mustache long enough to nod in agreement.

"These events have shown me that Mr. Blackwell had *friends* in many places inside Roseboro." He pauses, scanning the audience pointedly. "I would like to believe that without his malevolent influence, these *friends*, whomever they may be, will feel the freedom of a fresh start in this changing time. May we all pull together, reconnect with one another, and rebuild Roseboro. Not in the image of a self-appointed, self-aggrandizing king, but because of every one of us. We are Roseboro!"

There's a half-beat of silence, then the audience applauds. Even the reporters are touched by Thomas's rallying cry. He's a hell of a slick speaker, taking them on a journey through shock, awe, horror, disbelief, and finally, leaving them with a hopeful call to action. I just hope it works.

Thomas steps back from the podium, not taking questions. But a booming voice follows us inside the courthouse. Thomas stops, and we turn to see Chief Harris barreling over.

"Mr. Goldstone, those were some serious allegations you just made. I hope you can back them up," he says, blustering.

I step in front of Thomas, holding out a hand. "Chief Harris. Good to see you again. I was meaning to contact you after our previous discussion. Before she died, Trixie told us that she'd let a man in to tinker with the ovens under Blackwell's order. It was the same man who assaulted me. I'm confident he was employed by Blackwell. I'm sure there's a way to find the connection. *There always is.*"

It's a pointed dig, a strong suspicion I already had when such a high-ranking official showed interest in such a low-level charge as a lame assault. But he takes my meaning just as intended.

"Are you trying to pussyfoot around saying something, boy?" Harris's face is getting redder, his chest puffing up.

Thomas steps forward. "I think what Lance is saying is that Blackwell had lots of friends in this town. I'm sure they'll all be found with our own investigation and the federal investigation into his business practices. But like I said out there, what I'd like to hope is that those who were caught in Blackwell's web, whether through their own choice or by manipulation and force, can feel free now that he's dead. And we can all work together, doing what's right and doing what's right for Roseboro."

Harris narrows his eyes, searching Thomas's face for something, or maybe searching his shriveled heart for an ounce of integrity. But he offers a hand, and as he and Thomas shake, Harris says, "This is a good city, and I'll do *whatever it takes* to keep it that way. Always have, always will, so you just let me know if there's

LAUREN LANDISH

anything that needs addressing." He dips his chin and saunters away.

He's obviously been on Blackwell's payroll for who knows how long, but maybe he has some twisted sense of trying to do the right thing too. It's obvious that Blackwell preyed on people's weaknesses. It seems Harris's weakness is that while he's a big shot with the police, he wants to play with the big dogs of the city. He's willing to do their bidding, for Blackwell, and now, for Thomas.

"I'd be careful with that one. Fresh start or no, I think he plays to the highest bidder," I warn Thomas, and he nods.

Once we're alone, I call home. Not telling my family that I'm alive has been hell on me, and I know it's been even worse for them.

"Lance? Is it really you?" It's Dad, and I can hear the hesitant hope in his voice, the tears making his voice rough.

"Yeah, Dad. It's me. I'm alive. I'm okay." It's a relief to tell him, and his yell thanking God is a boon to my spirit.

"Miranda! Cody! He's alive!" There's a rustle, then the sound changes as Dad puts me on speakerphone.

"Lance?!?" Mom cries.

"Hi, Mom. Hey, Cody. It's so good to hear your voices. So much has happened."

For now, I don't tell them any more than what Thomas said in the press conference, but I think they're glad to hear it from me. Within minutes, we all feel better, reconnected.

"Okay, I've gotta go, but I'll be home as soon as I can. Probably" —I look to Jonathan, who mouths the answer I'm looking for— "tomorrow."

"Okay, tomorrow then. And bring Charlotte," Mom gushes. "I'll make dinner, I'll make . . . a roast."

She says it like a slab of beef is the cure to all the world's problems. "Mom, you don't cook. Maybe just have Chef make something so we don't die of food poisoning?"

Cody snorts at my dark humor. "Good one, Bro."

But Mom harrumphs. "Lance Jacobs, if I want to make a gosh-darned roast to celebrate my son being alive, then I will certainly do so."

I let her indignant and humorous anger wash over me. It feels good. It feels like home. "All right, Mom. Cook away. We'll see you tomorrow night. And guys?"

"Yes?" Dad says.

"I love you all," I say, realizing how much they need to hear that from me and how much I need to tell them.

CHAPTER 40

CHARLOTTE

*D*inner with the Jacobses was the only thing that made me able to make this call. That, and Lance by my side in our hotel suite. I sit cross-legged on the bed, nestled between his thighs.

Lance's parents had exuberantly offered to let me stay at their house, either in a bedroom of my own or with Lance, since my apartment was pretty obliterated by the fire too, but that felt too awkward.

Not staying with him—that's a given and not weird at all. But I think my ideas about parents are pretty fucked up from my own experiences, so staying with the Jacobses seemed wrong in an after-school special sort of way.

Maybe I can learn to accept their style of love the same way I did Lance's, though? It'll just take some time.

Time I don't have as the phone rings.

"Hello?" my dad says. He sounds fragile, older than he is. I remember Sabrina's visit to the bakery before everything went to shit. If she wasn't there to sabotage me, maybe she really was concerned about Dad.

I'm sure the stress of the last few days hasn't helped any issues he's been having.

"Hi, Daddy," I say, the endearment slipping out.

"Charlotte?" he says. "Honey, is that you?" The tears in his voice hit me viscerally, the little girl in my center whispering, *He really loves me,* and sealing over a gaping wound I didn't know was still there.

"Yeah, Dad. It's me. I'm okay. Are you okay?"

He laughs, the sound taking me back to the days when he was happier, less encumbered by the drama the women in his life stir up. Me included.

"Yes. In fact, I'm better than okay. I'm great now that I know you're okay."

We talk for a little while, but before we hang up, I ask Dad to tell Priscilla and Sabrina hello from me. It's a small gesture, but we've got to start somewhere.

Lance runs his finger over my arm, tracing freckles from my shoulder down to my hand. "Well?"

"I think that went really well, actually," I reply, letting loose a pent-up breath. "Shockingly so. Maybe there's hope for us yet."

"And us?" he asks, a cocky grin charging the air between us.

I play along, asking coyly, "What about us?"

He tackles me, laying me back on the bed and tickling me. I thrash beneath him, laughing loudly and feeling so very alive. He pins me with his hands and his blue fire gaze. "Is there hope for us?"

I shake my head, grinning. "None whatsoever." I draw the moment out, but the light in his eyes doesn't waver in the least. "I've completely and utterly fallen for you, and I don't think I'll ever recover. You're stuck with me, Commander Cookie, because believe it or not, I love you."

"Ha-ha, funny girl. Guess what, my Charlotte, my Sweet Scarlet?" His voice drops down, darker and lower. "My Red, I do believe you. I believe enough for the both of us because I love you too."

He presses his lips to mine, soft but sure, like he's sealing our words so I can never take them back. Not that I ever would. He's made a believer out of me. He's my happily ever after.

He pulls back, smiling. "So, there is one thing I need to tell you."

Before, my heart would've jumped into my throat, my mind racing with awful possibilities as fear shot through my veins. But none of that happens. Not now, not with Lance. I just look at him questioningly, trusting that if it's good news, we'll celebrate together. And if it's bad, we'll face it together.

"I've decided to find a new job."

"I've decided to officially retire. I'm not going back to the Teams."

His voice is steady, but I swallow, not because I'm scared for me, but because that's a major life change for Lance. "Are you sure? You don't have to give up something you love, not for your family, and not for me. I will be here for you, a home base for you to return to. And I'll send you sexy pictures of cupcakes, the baked kind, not my . . . you know. I love you, and that won't change, even if you're half a world away doing the thing you love."

He smiles, "I am doing the thing I love." It's half-dirty, but I can tell he means it to be sweet when he continues, "Staying right here with you." He smacks another kiss to my lips, squashing any further discussion of his military career.

"So you're going to work for Jacobs Bio-Tech?"

He shakes his head. "No . . . that's Cody's baby. I was going to tell you. Jonathan sat down with all of us guys. Now that Thomas doesn't need a private investigator, Jonathan is ready to

LAUREN LANDISH

move on. It was always a short-term contract for him. So Thomas needs a Head of Security. I told him I'd only take it if he promised me I never had to protect him from Mia."

I laugh because that's warranted. She might be little and look like your average anime convention attendee, but she would cut a bitch first and ask questions later.

"So you're going to work for Thomas? What about the bakery?" I give him a wink "We made a good team."

"That we did. What's your plan?"

"I've already proven once that I can do it. I'll do it again. Your new boss and I are going to renovate the previous location because it's perfect, other than the fire and water damage. Should be a fast turn-around. The construction crew said I could be opening the doors again in three-ish months."

I pause, biting my lip. "Do you think it'd be weird if I made a flavor in honor of Trixie? It seems weird to do this without her, even after everything."

Lance brushes the hair from my face and says, "I think Trixie would've liked that. What are you going to call it?"

He looks hesitant, like the only flavor worthy of a wild personality like Trixie's would be something outrageous. 'Better Than Sex Cream Pie', or 'Pop That Virgin Cherry Pie', or something Britney Spears-themed, like 'I Know That You're Toxic', a chocolate cupcake with green icing and a gummy snake on it. She'd actually suggested that one once.

"I want to call it Trix—Not for Kids. Like Rice Krispies treats, but made with Trix cereal. And it has to have a white drizzle of glaze on top, of course."

He laughs, getting the reference. "Obviously. I think she would be honored to still be welcome as a part of your bakery."

There are still so many questions. Investigations. A huge building that blew up. Thomas's new headquarters . . . but we'll get there.

Thomas will get his business situation straightened out, with Mia at his side to crunch the numbers. They'll get married soon.

Lance is staying here and has a job. I'm going to reopen the bakery and get my happily ever after.

Izzy is done with school now, ready to tackle the world as a freelance graphic designer. And Gabe . . .

"Hey, with us all being safe from Blackwell now, what's Gabe going to do? Do you think he could work with you as security at Goldstone?" Gabe doesn't need me to solve his career situation, but I can't help but want to fix that final piece of the puzzle.

Lance shakes his head. "Nah, he knows that his background wouldn't hold up to corporate scrutiny. So he's going to do contract work with Jonathan."

My face must show my shock because Lance quickly explains. "Not *that* kind of contracts. Jonathan has lots of different types of gigs—security, investigations—but one of his most lucrative contracts is gap discovery."

"What's that? Tell me faster that Gabe is not going back to being a hitman," I beg.

"He'll be a hitman for a *good* cause, without the death and dismemberment at the end. High-profile people hire Jonathan to find gaps in their security—online, residential, their protective detail. So when it's needed, Gabe will make an 'attempt' on someone's life to see where he can get in, where the breeches in coverage are so they can be corrected. The best part is, a lot of it is in the research, so he can do it from home. And when he has to go out on assignment, it'll be a short trip, usually. With Izzy being freelance, she can probably even go with him sometimes."

I let that sink in, confused but relieved. "So basically, a hitman stopper? If that's even a word."

Lance shrugs. "I'm sure there's a fancy name for it like Security Loss Specialist, but basically, yeah."

"Okay," I say as the last puzzle piece clicks into place in my mind. "So we're all good, then."

Lance nibbles on my neck, and I instinctively tilt away, giving him greater access.

He whispers into my ear, "I've heard I'm not just good, but *great*. Might even make you walk funny tomorrow from having that pussy pounded."

God, I don't know why his cocky arrogance gets me. Well, his silly jokes get me too. So does his sweet and gentle, and his rough and hard.

I can feel his cock already growing between us, hard against my belly. But the thing I feel the most is his heart, beating in time to mine.

Still, I can't let him off the hook that easily or he'll get too big-headed. *Ha!* I laugh but keep the pun to myself as I challenge, "I hear you talking, but I'm not feeling you backing those words up yet. Just a whole lotta chatter without much substance, like a sugar-free cupcake. *Wah-wah*," I say, mimicking a game show losing sound.

"Sugar-free? That's blasphemy! Oh, you're gonna feel it, Red. Challenge accepted," Lance says, and he sounds like he means it to be a warning, but all I hear is a promise.

A promise for forever.

A promise for happily ever after.

CHAPTER 41

LANCE

I take that challenge and dive in with every intention of owning Charlotte, body, mind, and soul, wearing her out as I fuck her all night, and I'll eventually put a ring on her finger.

After dinner with my parents, Mom slipped me her original wedding set, the one my Dad bought her when they were young and poor. It's not fancy or flashy, but it's sentimental. A sign that I believe we can have just as many happy years as my parents have had together.

We're not ready yet, but soon. Last night, I dreamed of a little redhaired girl who looks just like her beautiful momma and holds my heart just as tightly.

But for now, that dream disappears on a wisp of hope for the future, and I take in the beauty laid out before me in the present. "You feel that?" I growl, grinding my hips against her and using her belly to rub my cock.

She gasps and nods but says nothing, a sure sign she wants me to say more. For all her sass and fire, she loves it when I talk dirty, tell her what I'm going to do, then follow through on every filthy promise. She likes the build-up the anticipation gives her.

I've taken it as a personal mission to make her come with my words alone, and one day, I'll complete that mission.

"I'm going to strip you down bare, spread that pretty pink pussy wide open, and fuck you with my tongue so I can taste your sweetness right from the source," I whisper in the meantime.

"I'm going to suck your clit and slide my fingers inside because I want to feel you clamp down on them when you come for the first time. But they'll be a poor substitute for my cock because I'm going to slam into you balls-fucking-deep and fuck you hard . . . deep . . . and rough. You wanna walk funny tomorrow? I'm going to have you bowlegged, with my marks all over your fair skin. Everyone will know that you got fucked all night, will know that you're mine."

"*Fuck*," she moans, loving it. "God, Lance . . . please."

And I know she's mine, totally gone for me. Just like I'm hers.

I make good on my promise, pulling her shirt over her head and using the moment she arches to flick her bra undone. Before she settles back topless, I'm pulling her jeans and panties down in one yank.

Fully nude, I sit her up on the edge of the bed, kneeling between her bent knees, memorizing the feast laid out before me.

I don't delay, plunging right in to lick her with the flat of my tongue, and she shudders beneath me, her hips chasing my tongue. I wrap my arms around her thighs, using my thumbs to spread her slick pussy lips. "Mmm, look at that pussy, already pulsing like it's greedy for my cock. Is that what you want? My cock or my tongue?"

She's too incoherent with lust to do more than moan, so I follow my original plan and lick, suck, and tease along her folds. I dip my tongue inside her, loving the way she tenses even against that small invasion. So hungry, both of us.

I replace my tongue with two fingers, curling them up to caress the front wall of her pussy as I circle her clit lazily. Her cries get louder, begging for more, and I can feel the spasms starting deep inside her, still irregular but growing stronger.

I place a hand above her bare mound, holding her in place, and fuck her as hard and fast as I can, my fingers slamming into her. It looks violent, her cries tortured until . . .

"Oh, my God, Lance!" she cries out, flying into an abyss, my hand the only thing tethering her to this place, still thrusting in and out, forcing more pleasure upon her.

My fingers drip with the evidence of how hard she came, her sweet girl cum coating my fingers. I give her a moment's reprieve, sampling her honey from my own skin and groaning at the sweet taste.

Unable to hold back, I reach behind my head and rip my shirt over my head, tossing it without regard for where it'll land. I unbutton my jeans, shoving them and my underwear down and off.

"You ready, Red?" I ask, notching my cock at her entrance.

"So ready," she replies.

It's heaven. Zero barriers between us, both finally naked, nothing hidden between us. Physically, mentally, or emotionally.

Though Charlotte is stunning, her red hair wild from her head thrashing, the blue of her eyes almost gone from the wide darkness of her pupils, her true beauty is inside her.

Her bravery.

That even when she'd been hurt, disappointed, and betrayed time after time, she courageously got back up and tried again.

I will never let her down. I will earn the faith she has in me every day for the rest of my life.

I shove into her, stretching her pussy around my thick cock even after that hard orgasm. But her cry is one of pleasure, tinged in the pain that only makes it feel better, that teetering edge she loves so much.

I don't give her time to adjust. She doesn't want it, not really. I just start fucking her, bottoming out with each stroke and battering her thighs with my hips. I grip her legs, pulling her to me as I thrust into her, making her take more, take all of me.

Her tits bounce, garnering my attention, and I lean forward to take one into my mouth. I bite and suck, pulling hard enough to raise a bruising mark on her fair skin. The pink connects the brown freckles, making them seem to encircle my mark.

"Do it again," Charlotte orders, her hand cupping her other breast for a matching mark. I oblige, tracing along her fair skin, drawing lines with my tongue to memorize each tiny spot. Until I find one that makes her squirm.

There. I kiss the freckle first, swirling my tongue in a porn-inspired pirate's version of 'X marks the spot' and when she arches, I latch on, nibbling at the skin before sucking hard.

I draw deeply as I mark her, plunging into her pussy as I roughly guide her hips. I can feel her velvet walls grasping me, and I pull off her breast long enough to tell her, "Come, Charlotte."

Her hands grasp for me, one at my shoulder and one on my head, pulling me back to her chest for more. She explodes, her whole body shaking as she cries out my name. She squeezes me so tight, milking the cum from my balls, that I go with her, losing suction on her skin as I grunt out my pleasure through gritted teeth.

We've had sex, we've made love, and we've fucked. This is all of those mixed up together. A foundation of love and trust, with sparkly layers of fun and a future. We're writing our own future, our own fairy tale.

Forever after.

EPILOGUE

CHARLOTTE

I point a blue-tipped finger, annoyed. "Touch your face again and I will tie your hands at your side."

I intend for it to sound threatening, but Mia smirks. "You'd probably need to get Tommy for that. He's the only one who can tie me up where I can't get out."

Izzy squeals, shaking her head. "T-M-I, girl. I do not need to know your kinky shit. Save it for the honeymoon." But I can see her thinking. Something tells me that Izzy is going to be asking Gabe to try a little rope play tonight too, in their own way.

"Focus," I say, placing a hand on each of Mia's shoulders. "Hair, check. Makeup, check, if you'd only leave it alone. Dress, check. Potty break?"

She shakes her head, grinning. "No, I'm good. I'm ready. Are you? Got a little extra weight on that bouquet-carrying hand now. Wouldn't want it to be too much for your weak little arms."

Her tease breaks the nerves we're all feeling. Not about the wedding. Mia is more than certain about marrying Thomas. But none of us are particularly 'spotlight' people, and there are going to be lots of spotlights on us today.

Mia and Thomas elected for a small, private wedding. Just family and about fifty of their closest friends and business associates. It's safer than inviting the whole town of Roseboro. But the pictures are going to be the first story on the ten o'clock news and the front-page spread in the paper in the morning.

It's taken a few months, but the timing couldn't be better. The investigations are complete, and all of Blackwell's dirty laundry is out in public.

Well, most of it. Thomas is holding a few secrets close to his vest to call in markers if he has to. He's used a few already, filing suit against Blackwell's estate and getting liens against the Corporation. The Blackwell Building has been renamed the Roseboro Tower, and houses Goldstone Incorporated. Thomas even brought several of Blackwell's companies and subsidiaries under the Goldstone umbrella. He's slowly but surely taking over the Blackwell mantle and reshaping it into something brighter and better. A new start for the city.

What better time for a wedding?

I strike a pose, making sure my new diamond engagement ring is prominently displayed. "How's this?"

Lance proposed six months to the day after our initial meeting at the gala. Crazy fast, supposedly, but he jokes that he knew right away but waited *forever* for me to decide that he'd do for a husband.

I appreciate that he makes it seem like I'm the reasonable one when the truth is, he was healing me, wound by wound, scar by scar.

Mia and Izzy clap, chiming in unison, "Perfect!"

"All right, today's my day. Charlotte, you're up any time now. Izzy, what's it gonna take to make this a done deal with Gabe?" Mia asks, sounding more like a car salesman than a computer genius.

Izzy blushes. "It's not like that, guys. Gabe can't have paperwork floating around with his name on it, especially not with my name too. It's like the number-one way to wave a flag and highlight your weakness. We won't risk it."

"Well, that man is weak for you. Weak in the knees!" I tease.

Mia raises her brows. "He'd damn well better be on his knees for you, girl." We all laugh, already knowing that Gabe going down on Izzy is a regular thing. Again, we overshare. "But what about something unofficial, just private with the two of you or our little group? That way, there's no paperwork. That'd be okay, right?"

Izzy bites her tongue like she's forcing down words. But she loses the battle, her hands covering her face—ugh, her makeup! —as she looks down at her lap. She mumbles something I can't decipher.

Mia looks at me, eyes questioning whether I got that, but when I shake my head, she says, "Louder for the people in the back, Iz."

Izzy looks up, apology in her eyes. "We already did. A month ago, when we went to Mexico for that assignment."

"WHAT?" we both yell.

There's a knock at the door, and Steven calls out, "Ladies?"

"We're fine," Mia calls back. Then to Izzy, "Explain."

"I'm so sorry. I wanted to tell you, but this is your day, Mia," Izzy begs. "I didn't want to take all the attention by getting married first. I mean, you started this . . . us."

Mia scoffs. "Girl, I don't care. I just want you to be happy. Congratulations!"

I repeat the sentiment and Izzy smiles a little wider. "I love you two."

"We love you too."

Mia grabs her hand, lifting an eyebrow. "Uhm, I think he forgot a step though. Where's the bling-bling?"

Izzy flinches and Mia rushes to backpedal. "It's okay if he's saving up or something. The vow is in your heart, not a shiny stone."

Izzy shakes her head. "It's not that. I told him to wait until after, so I know what size my fingers are going to be."

"After what?" I ask hesitantly.

"The baby," Izzy says, her hands going to her still-flat belly.

"WHAT?!" we yell again, and this time, Steven knocks, always the worried security expert. We ignore him to focus on Izzy.

"I'm only two months along, but that was why we wanted to rush the wedding a bit. Not that it'll matter since there's no paperwork, but I want the whole picturesque family. Mom, Dad, baby, picket fence."

It's bittersweet. Izzy's struggled her whole life to feel at home, like she belongs, and I'm so happy for her to finally have the family she's always wanted. With Gabe, her Prince Charming.

"Honey," I say, gathering her in a hug. Mia piles on top, and we're all hugging each other, tears running down our faces as we snottily proclaim to be the best aunties this baby has ever known.

Even though we're not being loud, there's another knock. "Thought you might need a ten-minute warning. Last chance for makeup fixes, bathroom breaks, or to make a run for it, Miss Karakova."

Steven's funny, in a dry humor sort of way. But I also think he'd take Mia right out of here if she asked him to. He might be employed by Thomas, but all the guys on the security team have a soft spot for the crazy, geeky video gamer who captured their boss's heart.

Thomas used to be a bit of a beast, but Mia domesticated that right out of him. Or gave him a better outlet for his monstrous urges. I laugh at my own dirty joke, thinking Mia would approve.

We touch up our makeup and hug one more time. "Ready?" I ask Mia.

She smiles, nodding. "I'm getting married, guys. Let's go!"

And with that, she hitches up her dress and heads for the door, ready to tackle the world. Or forever.

Mia pauses outside the closed doors, taking her dad's arm. Vladdy's in tears, whispering in her ear, probably threatening to kill Thomas if he ever mistreats his princess. Mia definitely gets her scariness from her dad, who's a total teddy bear.

Unless you piss him off, or so I've heard. I wouldn't know, because he's always a sweetheart to me.

The doors open, and Izzy walks in first, slow and steady. She looks beautiful, glowy, and happy. Gabe stands at Thomas's side, looking ready to run down the aisle, snatch Izzy up, and steal away with her.

Then it's my turn. As I walk, I glance over at Lance, who's next to Gabe, thinking that the next time I do this, it will be to become his wife. Where once, that would've terrified me, it now sounds exciting.

I can't wait.

Looking in his eyes, I know he feels the same way. Maybe we could sneak off with the officiant during the reception and do it quickie-style like Izzy did?

We won't, of course. Lance wants to give me the whole princess fairytale wedding, his romantic streak unending. I can dig that. It doesn't have to be big and fancy, but something our friends and family can come to.

I want them to see me choosing love, choosing Lance, choosing faith.

The music changes, and Mia begins her trek down the aisle. She's gorgeous. Her hair is blonde and pink, curled up in an elaborate updo with a funky bow, and her dress is pink, of course. But it's the softest, palest shade of blush that just looks warm and ethereal against her skin.

The ceremony is beautiful, with vows of love and promises of all-night game play on video game release days. Gotta love Mia. She thinks ahead and gets that stuff in writing. No take-backsies.

Before I know it, the ceremony is over and Lance is escorting me out behind the bride and groom.

In the hallway outside, we look at each other. The six of us, all from different backgrounds, shaped by different experiences, with different hopes and dreams. But all here together.

Our family, not by birth but by choice.

And forever begins for Mia and Thomas.

It's already begun for Izzy and Gabe and their new addition.

And soon, it'll be my turn with Lance.

Our version of happily ever after.

Thank you for reading! Did you enjoy this series and would like to see more? While this concludes the original 3-book series I had planned, if readers would like to see more fairy tale themed books, I would love to add more! I have written a scene that follows the end of Happily Never After. This book would be a forbidden Hansel and Gretel themed story with Custis Blackwell's children, Ace and Alyssa. Alyssa Blackwell would be the heroine, with Jonathan Goldstone her man. Will their families accept their relationship? **Read the opening scene here!**

ABOUT THE AUTHOR

Dirty Fairy Tales:
Beauty and the Billionaire | | Not So Prince Charming | |
Happily Never After

Get Dirty:
Dirty Talk | | Dirty Laundry | | Dirty Deeds | | Dirty Secrets

Bennett Boys Ranch:
Buck Wild | | Riding Hard

Irresistible Bachelors:
Anaconda | | Mr. Fiance | | Heartstopper
Stud Muffin | | Mr. Fixit | | Matchmaker
Motorhead | | Baby Daddy | | Untamed

Connect with Lauren Landish
www.laurenlandish.com
admin@laurenlandish.com
www.facebook.com / lauren.landish

If you enjoyed this book, stay in contact! You can join my mailing
list here. You'll never miss a new release and you'll even get 2
FREE ebooks!

Made in the USA
Coppell, TX
11 May 2020